# big girl blitz

also by

DANIELLE ALLEN

*Curvy Girl Summer*

*Plus Size Player*

# big girl blitz

DANIELLE ALLEN

BRAMBLE

TOR PUBLISHING GROUP

NEW YORK

This is a work of fiction. All of the names, characters, organizations, places, and events portrayed in this work are either products of the author's imagination or used fictitiously.

BIG GIRL BLITZ



A Bramble Book
Published by Tom Doherty Associates / Tor Publishing Group
120 Broadway
New York, NY 10271

www.torpublishinggroup.com

Bramble™ is a trademark of Macmillan Publishing Group, LLC.

*EU Representative:* Macmillan Publishers Ireland Ltd, 1st Floor, The Liffey Trust Centre, 117–126 Sheriff Street Upper, Dublin 1, D01 YC43

The Library of Congress Cataloging-in-Publication Data is available upon request.

ISBN 978-1-250-33116-8 (trade paperback)
ISBN 978-1-250-33117-5 (ebook)



First Edition: 2026

Printed in the United States of America

10 9 8 7 6 5 4 3

To my best friends . . .

my Aaliyah, my Nina, my Jazmyn:

Thank you.

This is for you.

# big girl blitz

# 1

"Dates are just romantic interviews, and I don't have the emotional bandwidth," I explained to my best friends on a three-way call.

"What's your plan to get back out there?" Aaliyah James questioned. "I don't think you're taking things seriously."

"What?" I squawked. "What do you mean?"

"She means you need to stop automatically telling men you're not interested and to leave you alone," Nina Ford chimed in. "Whole time, you haven't had sex with someone new in ten years!"

"Has it been that long?" Aaliyah gasped.

I groaned. "Don't remind me."

"I'm going to remind you until you fix it," Nina joked. "I'm surprised you're not hopping on the first big dick you see."

"Because I'm feeling like I just might," Aaliyah muttered.

We all laughed.

"I need a connection," I reminded them. "I can't just fuck a stranger."

"Ah. Makes sense that you want to line up a boyfriend for summer," Aaliyah mused.

My eyebrows shot up. "I did *not* say that."

"You said you were gonna finally take your coochie out the plastic and use it," Nina teased, causing me to chuckle. "I'll keep my eye out for candidates so you can build your roster."

"I never said I was building a roster either! All I said was that it would be nice to have sex again . . . someone I can call on whenever I need it."

"I thought you were against a friend-with-benefits situation," Aaliyah pointed out.

"Mainly because once I start talking football with men, they friendzone me." Letting out a light laugh, I shook my head. "At this point in my life, a friend with benefits would be ideal. I don't need the feelings. I just need the benefits."

"So, you fucking friends now?" Nina quipped, ignoring the main point of what I'd said.

"You could also fuck your boyfriend or your husband-to-be," Aaliyah offered.

I rolled my eyes. "Been there, done that, not interested in doing it again."

"Not everybody is looking to settle down, Aaliyah," Nina remarked. "Some of us like the streets."

I laughed. "Speak for yourself!"

"I am," Nina deadpanned.

For almost two of the five hours it took to get to Chance, Virginia, the three of us chatted on the phone, expediting my commute. Located on the border between Virginia and North Carolina, my hometown was a sore spot for me. And the closer I got to the exit, the more my energy shifted. When I shared that with my best friends, Nina read us some of the vile comments on her most recent social media post.

"Nobody hates fat women more than men we never said we wanted and women we never viewed as competition," I pointed out.

"That's a fact." Aaliyah laughed. "We don't even be checking for them, and they be coming for us!"

"But as soon as I say, 'His bulge is all balls, no meat,' or 'She's not pretty; she's just thin,' I'm doing too much," Nina responded. "Whole time, I'm not doing enough."

We cracked up.

"I don't know how you do it, Nina." Aaliyah sighed. "You are strong, girl."

"Yeah," I agreed. "Subjecting yourself to public scrutiny is brave."

"I'm not worried about that bullshit," Nina said dismissively. "My reason for sharing is to make a point . . . People are going to say wild shit unprovoked. Don't let anybody, especially not the random townspeople of Chance, get under your skin, Jazz. They don't matter. And if they don't matter, they don't get to have any kind of power over you."

I let out a deep breath and nodded even though they couldn't see me. "You're right. I've just always hated being here. You know that uncomfortable feeling of walking into a room and realizing everyone was just talking about you? That's how it feels here." My stomach roiled as I took the exit to Chance. "If it weren't for my aunt . . ." I stopped talking abruptly as an incoming call beeped in. "Hey, I need to take this."

I yelled my goodbye into the speaker before clicking over to answer the other line. "Hello?"

"Ms. Payne?" The soft, compassionate tone of my aunt's nurse of three years instantly put me on high alert.

After taking a deep breath, I responded, "Yes? It's me."

"It's Monica," she introduced herself, even though I knew her voice and I had her number saved. She was a tall, wiry woman with a very distinct tone of voice.

"Hey, Monica," I replied nervously. "Is everything okay?"

"Addison is resting right now. Can we talk?" she requested gently.

I gripped the steering wheel tightly. "Is everything okay with Aunt Addy?"

"Where are you?" Her voice was even, compassionate, and extremely different from the upbeat, chipper tone she'd had when I'd spoken to her last week.

"I'm about fifteen minutes away from the house."

"I need you to meet me at the address that I just texted you instead."

I swallowed hard. "Monica, what's going on?"

"Your aunt is a fighter," she answered. "We've had to discontinue hospice services three times because she's bounced back. She is a strong woman."

She paused, and I felt my heart in my throat during that silence.

"But . . ." she started again, "her circumstances have changed."

When Aunt Addy had told me she'd gone to the hospital a few days ago, I figured it was related to her heart issues. We didn't talk long, but I noticed her words were slurred and assumed it was the medication. I asked her if she needed me to come a few days earlier, and she said no. Because of her battle with congestive heart failure for the last several years, everything about her hospital visit had felt routine. She'd get checked out, maybe have an overnight stay, but it was never for very long. So hearing Nurse Monica sound so pessimistic freaked me out.

I stopped at a red light. "How have things changed?" I asked, putting the address she'd given me into the GPS.

"She had a right-side stroke a few days ago. Those who have congestive heart failure are two to three times more likely to have one," she explained.

"I don't understand. She was doing all the things on her list. She was taking her meds, getting exercise, eating well." I shook my head in confusion. "I thought things were going well."

"She *was* doing well. But remember, heart failure means her heart isn't pumping as it should . . ."

As she used medical jargon to explain what was going on, I stepped on the gas.

"She's going to need more intensive care," Monica continued. "Her medical team just moved her to Stark Recovery Rehabilitation Center for at least the next couple of weeks. *At least.* The first three months are the most important for stroke recovery. She agreed to two weeks. She's just getting settled in now before dinner."

My eyes watered as I nodded. "Okay."

"Stark Recovery is strict, but it's the best in the state. There are no overnight visitors, no outside food, no outside medical teams—"

"So you can't be there?" I interrupted.

"I can but as a friend and a source of support. And she's going to need a lot of support. I know she doesn't like for people to see her when she's going through it, but if you're able to get her to agree to have visitors while she's here, I believe it would help."

Holding back tears, I made a left turn. "I can do that."

"If anyone can convince her, you can. How long are you in town for?"

"A week," I answered softly. "But if she'll be in there for two, I'll make arrangements for two weeks."

"She's been looking forward to your visit since spring break."

I swiped at the tear that rolled down my cheek. "I've been looking forward to it, too."

We said goodbye, and I took a breath.

I wasn't fond of my hometown; in fact, I hated it. But I loved my annual weeklong visits with my aunt. We had always been close, but once I'd left Chance, our bond had become even tighter. She was the only reason I returned. Over the years, I always worried about Aunt Addy's health, but it had been a while since I'd been truly scared.

Trying my hardest to hold it together, I rolled my shoulders back and entered the rehab center praying. I went to the room number that Monica had texted me, and I froze. As I peeked through the cracked door to see my aunt, something inside me broke.

*No, no, no, no, no, no, no, no, no.*

Addison Payne was my role model. She was my real-life inspiration. She was the person who helped me see that there was a world outside of Chance. She was the person who allowed me to be my full self. She was the person I went to for advice. She was my first best friend. As much as I loved my parents, my aunt was my everything. So nothing could've prepared me to see her like that.

Looking small in that hospital bed, she had tubes and wires coming from under her gown. She was too young to have endured so much. Squeezing my eyes shut, I reminded myself of the words she'd instilled in me since she got sick three years ago.

*We have faith in God's plan, and we don't let fear control us*, she would say.

She had overcome everything that had hit her in her lifetime, so I was going to have faith that she'd come out of this, too. I took a deep breath and plastered a smile on my face.

"This is niiiiiiiiiiiiiiiiiiiiiiiice," I remarked as I walked into the spacious hospital-style room. The bay window with the view of the courtyard caught my eye immediately. "I see they put you in a suite!"

Aunt Addison sucked her teeth, amused. "Jazmyn, stop."

My jaw dropped, feigning shock. "What?"

"The view and the TV don't change where I'm at."

The slight slur in her words pained me.

My smile faltered as I made my way to her bedside. "But it helps."

She laughed lightly. "Yeah, it helps. But I'd rather be home." Sighing, she reached out for me with her right arm. As soon as her bony fingers gripped my hand, she continued. "I'm happy to see you."

"I'm happy to see you, too." I choked back the emotion welling up inside me. "You know I can't start my summer without seeing my aunt Addy."

She shifted in the bed a little. "I ain't much to see right now." Her eyes darted to the back of the room. "Monica let me come out the house in a bonnet, no earrings or lipstick."

"Well, it was a bit of a medical emergency," Monica replied with a grin. She walked to the foot of the bed. "And with all the tests that they had to run on you this week, you didn't need any of that stuff."

Aunt Addy pursed her lips. "There is never a good enough reason to leave the house without earrings and lipstick."

She put her hand on her hip. "A stroke is a good reason, Addison."

My aunt gave her an aggrieved look. "You would really deny me my dignity?"

Her longtime nurse choked back a laugh. "Because I didn't put your earrings in?"

My aunt's lips pulled downward. "So that's a yes."

"You two are funny," I commented, before they could continue their normal back-and-forth. "What can I bring you to make your room feel more like home?"

"Discharge paperwork."

I laughed. "I'm serious!"

"Flowers," she answered quickly. "The pictures from my mantel and my bust . . ." She continued her list, and I took notes on my phone.

I nodded when I thought she was done. "I can do that. I'll get everything you need to fix this place up. And I'll pack a bag of clothes—"

"Don't forget my bras," she interrupted. "Monica has me out in public with my titties loose."

I burst out laughing.

The three of us talked until someone brought in a dinner tray of what appeared to be Salisbury steak, mashed potatoes, and peas. About an hour later, her medication was dispensed, and Monica said good night. Thirty minutes after that, Aunt Addy started to drift off.

"Are you comfortable?" I asked her as I watched her face twitch reflexively.

"It's not my bed, but it's fine," she murmured.

"You won't have to be here long," I told her.

Her eyes remained closed. "I sure won't. Two weeks max."

"I'm going to head out and let you get some rest. I'll be back in the morning with your stuff."

Her eyes opened fractionally. "Okay, and we need to talk about how you're living."

I leaned over the bed and hugged her carefully. "Sounds good." My voice broke as I pulled away. "Love you."

"Love you, too."

I watched her for a moment, and my eyes filled with tears. Blinking them away, I turned and rushed out the door. I drove to her house in silence, my stomach in knots. I couldn't stop thinking about how all the plans my aunt and I had made were changed in an instant.

I'd seen her unwell before, but I'd never seen her like *that*. She'd been on hospice three times, but she'd never *looked* sick. I knew she was going to die one day—everyone dies eventually—but it was the first time it seemed like that day could come soon.

I was not ready to lose her.

I pulled into her driveway, dropped my head to the steering wheel, and took a deep breath. When I felt ready, I wiped the tears from my cheeks, grabbed my bag, and went inside the four-bedroom rancher.

I set my suitcase down in the room Aunt Addy had deemed as mine. Passing the guest bedroom and the reading room, I paused in the doorway of Aunt Addy's room.

*She's in rehab. She'll be back soon*, I reminded myself as I started to pack a bag for her. *She'll be fine.*

I grabbed everything she needed, including several pairs of earrings and her favorite lipsticks, then rushed to the nearest store that sold boxes, and arranged the plants, the flowers, and the bust in one box. As I stacked photos in the second box, I dropped one on the floor.

"Shit," I cursed, praying the glass didn't break as I bent to pick it up. "Phew."

Breathing a sigh of relief when I turned it over, I realized it was the picture of me at my eighth-grade graduation. My aunt was holding two of my awards, and I was holding the other two.

*As a fat girl, you have to be nearly perfect in every other aspect of your life so the only thing they can say about you is that you're fat.*

My parents drilled those words into my head to combat the teasing I faced from the popular girls in school. Reflecting on the adage that had kept me in a chokehold since I was thirteen years old, I blinked back tears. I spent more than half my life holding on to those words.

*If it weren't for Aunt Addy . . .*

I shook off the thought and stacked the rest of the photos into the box. When I noticed the photo that was on top of the stack, I froze. It was of me and Aunt Addy on my Hamilton University graduation day. She looked so proud. The longer I stared at the image, the harder it became to keep my emotions in check.

"I need to get out of here," I said aloud, hopping to my feet.

I grabbed my handbag and my keys as I rushed from the house.

Chance didn't really have nightlife, but I knew there were two bars on either side of town that stayed open until two o'clock in the morning. One was the closest thing to a club in Chance. And the other was a sports bar. Being that it was mid-June, I was sure the sports bar would be full of basketball fans watching the playoffs. Eating greasy bar food and getting sucked into the hype of a game would be the perfect way to quiet the thoughts flooding my mind.

I checked my reflection in the rearview mirror and saw my glassy, red-rimmed eyes, my downturned full lips, and my flushed caramel complexion. I pulled down my ponytail and let my brown with honey-blonde highlighted locs fall over my shoulders. Hoping to hide behind my hair, I climbed out the car, straightened my gray T-shirt, and tugged at my skintight black yoga pants.

Even though I was extremely casual, I thought I looked good enough for the bar. I had second thoughts when I walked through the door and the first few women I saw had on heels, short skirts, and revealing dresses. I was underdressed by comparison, but the way I was feeling on the inside, I didn't have the energy to care. I just needed a distraction.

"Table for one, please," I told the hostess who'd greeted me as I approached.

She frowned as she looked around. "I'm sorry. I think there's space at the bar, but there are no available tables right this moment." She glanced at her book and then at the television screen. "If you give it fifteen more minutes, the game will be over, and a lot of these people will clear out."

"I'll grab a seat at the bar," I told her, eyeing an empty stool on the end.

I made a beeline to the spot and narrowly avoided getting elbowed in the face when a blocked shot caused the room to erupt.

"Sorry," a man apologized quickly, before high-fiving a bunch of people around him and then sitting back down.

I climbed onto the stool and directed my attention to the large screen in front of me. Players hustled across the court, scrambling for the ball, and everyone around me was riveted. I took that opportunity to grab the bartender's attention.

"Hey! Welcome to Stadium," she greeted me with a bright smile. Even though her eyes looked tired, she seemed upbeat. "I'm Trina, and I'll be taking care of you tonight. Our late-night menu is right here. Is there anything I can get for you now, or do you need me to circle back in a few?"

"Hi, I am going to order food. But for right now, I'll just take a Blue Motorcycle," I told her, handing her a twenty-dollar bill.

She winked. "Thank you."

The basketball game ended just as I placed my order for a bacon cheeseburger with seasoned fries. The chaos resulting from the come-from-behind win caused most of the patrons to leap to their feet. Some people left, but most of the others were standing, yelling, and causing a commotion. The cloud of gambling failures and financial loss hung in the air, and the place was in disarray. It was so wild to witness the collective shock followed by the immediate stampede around the bar.

Looking around, I sipped my strong drink with my eyes wide. The remaining members of the crowd were rowdy, angrily recapping the end of the game. There was so much going on, I didn't know if there was going to be a fight or a mass exodus.

I'd wanted a distraction, and I got it.

My attention bounced from the people in the bar to the large television in front of me. Someone changed the channel from the basketball game highlights to a football game from the previous season. A large portion of the crowd cleared out after that. But it was still noisy enough for me to not be alone with my thoughts. I knew the outcome of the game already, but I was still interested in how everything played out on the field.

"Here's your food," Trina announced.

I gawked at my dish. "Oh wow. Thank you."

Pulling my hand sanitizer out of my bag, I cleaned my hands and then took a big bite of my burger.

"Mmm," I intoned as the burst of flavors exploded in my mouth.

"That looks good," commented a man who sat in the recently vacated seat next to me.

My first inclination was to put my guard up and tell him I had a man and that I wasn't interested in making small talk. But the conversation with my girls popped in my head, and I chose a different route.

I just nodded politely.

I heard him, but I didn't truly acknowledge him. I hated talking to strangers while I was eating—especially in Chance. And since he wasn't really talking to me, he was talking about my food to himself, I didn't engage. I just stared at the large television in front of me and continued to chew my burger.

Seconds later, he lifted a large hand to flag down the bartender, and his cologne hit me, stealing my attention. I closed my eyes for a moment and inhaled the bergamot-and-cedarwood scent. It was intoxicating.

He didn't just smell good. He smelled luxurious, expensive.

I glanced over at him as I swallowed.

When the male bartender started walking our way, he tugged down on his dark blue fitted cap. I couldn't get a good look at his face, but he smelled like he looked good.

I shifted my eyes so he wouldn't catch me staring. Popping a fry into my mouth, I turned my attention back to the game.

The bartender took the man's order as I minded my business.

"Wasps or Monarchs?" the man asked.

I looked over at him to see if he was talking to me, and he was watching the instant replay.

"Wasps or Monarchs?" he repeated.

"Monarchs," I answered, staring at his profile.

"That's my team."

When he turned his head toward me, his dark brown eyes bored into mine. The intensity caught me off guard.

"Nice," I breathed.

# 2

“Here you are,” Trina said, causing us to tear our eyes from each other. She set his brown liquor down on a white napkin. “And your food should be out shortly.”

I continued eating but focused my attention on the game. Several hard-hitting plays resulted in a third-down interception. The first time the quarterback for the Wasps dropped back with the ball, the Monarchs sacked him. It would’ve resulted in a thirteen-yard loss, but a late yellow flag came out.

“What?!” I exclaimed, almost choking on my fry.

“Bullshit,” he reacted at the same time.

The man and I looked at each other.

“That was . . .” I was distracted when he lifted the lid of his hat.

I could see his face clearly. He was strikingly handsome with his flawless mahogany complexion, impeccably manicured beard, and full, thick lips. His thick eyebrows framed beautiful brown eyes. It was almost jarring how attractive he was.

I cleared my throat. “That was *not* roughing the passer,” I continued. “That was a bullshit call.”

He let out a short chuckle and shook his head.

I glanced at the TV screen again before giving him a look. “What’s so funny? It *is* a bullshit call!”

A small smile pulled at his lips before he flashed the brightest, whitest teeth. “You said it like *I* made the call. Like, damn, I agree with you! You don’t have to yell at me!”

His smile was infectious, so I felt myself grinning as I rolled my eyes. “I didn’t yell at you.”

“You know the outcome of this game, right? I don’t want you to be surprised and act like them.” He gestured with his head to the few rowdy basketball fans who were across the bar, still reeling from the earlier loss. “They might put you out next.”

My jaw dropped when I saw a security guard ushering a group of people out the front door. "It's never that serious."

"They must've had money on the game because ain't no way they're acting like that for no reason."

"I thought the same thing! The stench of lost wages was in the air."

A deep, rumbling laugh erupted from him. It was the kind of laugh that spread warmth to everyone in its radius. It warmed me in areas where I hadn't felt heat in a long time.

"I'm Lamar," he introduced himself. "Lamar Anderson."

"Jazmyn Payne—friends call me *Jazz*."

Before he had a chance to say anything else, Trina slid his food in front of him.

"Thank you," he told her. "This looks good."

"It is good," I replied.

Lamar picked up his burger and took a huge bite. Nodding, he confirmed my words with a series of appreciative grunts. After he swallowed that bite, he looked at me and pointed to his plate. "This shit right here!"

"Okay!"

"I was going to get wings. If I didn't come sit next to you and see what you had, I would've missed out."

"I guess it was meant to be."

He licked his lips. "I agree with that."

Heat crept up my neck and spread across my cheeks. I tore my eyes away from him and tuned in to the game. The Wasps' star running back dashed across the screen.

"That was a hell of a run," I pointed out as I munched on a fry.

"It was. But Channing slipped on the grass, and that's how he got open," Lamar responded. "The Wasps' offense isn't as good as everyone gives them credit for."

"Yeah, but if we're honest, Channing has been losing a step for a while now. And he got progressively worse as the season went on. The Monarchs' defense is good, but Channing has been playing a little off."

He looked impressed. "You noticed that, too?"

I nodded. "Yeah, it's obvious only if you're paying attention. Watch his feet. His footwork has changed. You need defensive tackles who are big *and* athletic, who can open field tackle *and* rush the quarterback, who can observe *and* communicate. Watch him the next time he's out there. Something is wrong. He's getting off the line funny. I'm telling you."

He assessed me with a healthy dose of amusement, amazement, and suspicion.

Unprovoked, I continued: "I learned early on that defense wins games, so I pay attention to the defensive players."

"Most people pay more attention to offense," he pointed out.

I smirked. "Most people don't know any better."

"I like the way you think." He grinned. "If you were Coach, what play would you call to get at the Wasps?"

"I love a good blitz. It's organized disruption. It takes timing, execution, and adaptability. And when done right, it can be a game changer," I rambled. "It's the ultimate 'go big or go home' play."

"A blitz, huh?" There was a playfulness and familiarity to his tone. "And what about for offense?"

"It depends on how the defense is set up. I mean, I love to see a quarterback with a strong arm slinging it."

"A gunslinger."

I nodded. "A gunslinger. What about you?"

"I've thought about this a lot," he answered, pointing to how the teams were lined up. "A hybrid three-four defense would've made the most sense. Look at how the Wasps . . ."

He was knowledgeable, and even though I was listening, I found myself becoming distracted. The tone of his voice was sexy. But as he continued to talk, his voice became huskier.

"I can see that," I commented once he finished speaking. "I don't agree, but I can see how you'd come to that conclusion."

"You don't agree?"

I shook my head. "Maybe if we had the Channing of two years ago. But with the 'star' defensive player playing like he's hurt, there's no way your defensive scheme would work."

He let out a light chuckle. "I've had people talk football with me my whole life, but there's something about the passion in you . . . the way you light up as you talk."

My lips twisted ruefully. "I've been told I can be a bit much during football season."

"I don't see how you could ever be too much." With his eyes trained on me, he took a gulp of his drink. "So, when did you get into football?"

Ignoring the heat creeping up my neck and flushing my face, I answered, "I grew up on it. My dad and my aunt were big fans—still are."

"They taught you the love of the game?"

"They introduced me to the game, and I fell in love with it all on my own." I pointed a fry at him. "What about you?"

"Football is life. I've played since I was five years old. My mom said it was initially to channel my energy into something productive, and then they noticed I was nice with it, so . . . I've been in love with the game since the beginning."

"Your first love."

He smiled softly. "You could say that."

"So, you played in high school, college, all that?"

He nodded. "All that."

"Offense or defense?"

"What do you think?"

I looked him up and down, appreciating the opportunity to truly gawk at him.

He was wearing a dark gray jogging suit in a lightweight material. The logo looked familiar—like one of those brands that sold one-hundred-dollar T-shirts. But by the way the material stretched across his body, it was clear that he was solidly built and muscular. His broad shoulders and perfect posture led me to believe that even though he was big, he was agile.

I was only five feet five inches, and my feet dangled on the final rung of the stool I was sitting on. His feet were comfortably planted against the floor, so I guessed he was over six feet. I took account of the size of his hands and the way the burger almost looked small in comparison. My eyes traveled back up his face, and I realized how long I'd lingered, taking him in.

"Defense," I said definitively.

He turned his body toward me, leaning his elbow against the bar. "And why do you think that?"

"Your size mainly," I told him. "You're probably six-three—"

"I'm six-five," he interjected.

"Close enough," I teased. "But the biggest giveaway for me was when you tried to wave down the bartender. With your broad shoulders and long arms, your wingspan has got to be incredible."

"Wingspan?" He nodded. "Okay, I'm impressed. So, instead of playing with dolls, you were in front of the TV watching the game."

"Me *and my dolls* were watching the game. They were also fans."

"You're funny." He snickered before he took another bite of his burger.

We ate and watched the game together, making comments about the plays as the seconds ticked down in the quarter.

He made me laugh.

He made me think.

He made me forget.

"Can we get another round?" Lamar asked the bartender.

We talked about players, stats, coaches, and games. We made jokes and laughed heartily. We had something to say about every commercial that came on, every commentator's commentary, and every referee's call. We were on our second round of our respective drinks, and it felt like time was just flying by. It wasn't until the bartender cleared our plates that I realized that we'd gone from strangers to friends within two and a half quarters.

"Hm," I mused under my breath as I looked at a man with a bouquet of roses. The mirror caught his image behind us, so I didn't even have to turn around to be nosy.

Following my eyes, Lamar asked, "You like that?"

"Flowers are nice, but . . ." I shrugged and returned my attention to the TV screen. "Those are gas station 'forgive me' flowers."

Lamar craned his neck to get a better look. "How do you know?"

"Look at the way she's pushing him away from her. She's not feeling it. Look at the way her friends are side-eyeing him. He did something, and he's trying to get back in her good graces."

"Yoooooooo! I didn't even notice the way her friends are looking at him." He shifted his attention to the play on the screen. "He's fucked."

I snickered, nodding in agreement. "What would you do?"

"For the woman I love?"

"Yeah."

"Well, let's set the record straight: I wouldn't do anything that would necessitate me bringing gas station flowers to the bar at midnight."

With my eyes glued to the game, I felt my lips tug upward slightly. *Good answer.*

"You don't believe in grand gestures?" I asked sarcastically.

He let out a light chuckle. "I mean, yeah, if the situation calls for it. But I'm more low-key with it. I move in silence."

"Closed mouths don't get fed."

"True. But if I'm doing my job, a closed mouth won't stop me from feeding her."

I glanced over at him and found him staring at me.

My heart slammed into my chest.

He licked his lips. "Making sure she's good, taking care of her, keeping her happy, safe, and wanting for nothing." His eyes dropped to my mouth. "I take my time, but I'm thorough. You feel me?"

My pulse quickened. Swallowing hard, I nodded. "Yeah, I feel you."

"You like grand gestures?" He jerked his thumb over his shoulder.

I looked at the man groveling across the bar and shook my head. "I like what's real," I answered, getting back to the game. "I don't like a lot of attention, so doing all that would be"—I hesitated before settling on a word—"embarrassing."

"Like that call?"

I smiled, pleased at how he'd read my mind. "How are the refs not seeing anything the Wasps are doing but flagging the Monarchs for everything?" I complained.

"And they're giving my boy a fifteen-yard penalty for the same shit the Wasps did and weren't penalized for," he added.

"You and I both know that Tim Bradley is the league's golden boy." I rolled my eyes. "That's the only quarterback who can literally cheat and everyone turns a blind eye."

He chuckled under his breath. "That's the truth."

"I can't wait until the truth comes out about him."

"Believe me, the league knows. There's just too much money wrapped up in him to do anything about it."

I tapped my nail against the bar. "And that's the problem. It's all about the money."

"It's a business. They run it like a business, and the players are pawns. That's why players need to invest in themselves and not *just* be pawns for the system."

I wasn't sure if it was the passion in his words or the way in which he was articulating his point, but I was *very* attracted to him in that moment.

"I feel the exact same way. I always wondered if there's something in place for them."

"There is, but . . ."

His hesitation intrigued me. I tilted my head to the side. "But what?"

"I've been working on something that'll help bridge the gap. I have the business plan, but I don't know . . ."

The tinge of uncertainty was endearing.

"You should do it," I told him, resisting the urge to pat his back or squeeze his hand. For some reason, I felt compelled to comfort him with physical touch. Instead, I clasped my hands in my lap. "You really should."

"You think so?"

I nodded. "Something that helps players empower themselves sounds necessary and important. Honestly, I'd need to know more about it to say for sure, but I feel the passion when you speak."

"I wouldn't mind telling you more." He lifted his glass to his lips with his eyes trained on me. "Maybe you could look it over."

Staring into the depth of his brown eyes, I murmured, "I could do that."

Neither of us said anything as we held each other's gaze.

He took another sip before placing the glass back down. "You're cool as fuck, you know that?"

I bit down on my bottom lip and nodded. "Yeah."

He smirked. "I don't usually—"

Before he could finish his sentence, two attractive women in low-cut tops ran up on the other side of him.

"Hey, excuse me," one interrupted with drunken giggles and flirtatious vibes.

"Hi!" the other one chirped, grabbing his shoulder.

He glanced over his shoulder at them.

"Are you Lamar Anderson?" the shorter of the two wondered. She tucked her ash-blonde wig behind her ear and smiled up at him.

He shook his head. "No, I'm not," he responded, turning back to me. He wasn't rude, but it was clear that he wasn't interested in entertaining them.

"Are you sure? You didn't play football for Spring Hill High School?" the taller one asked.

With a tight smile, he turned toward them. "I think you have the wrong guy."

"No, I'm sure of it . . ." The taller one leaned forward.

The shorter one, the one closest to me, looked over his shoulder at me and then did a double take. "Jummy?"

The childhood moniker that had haunted me from eighth grade until senior year knocked the wind out of me. I stared at the shorter woman as she tossed the ash-blonde hair over her shoulders. She didn't look familiar to me at all.

"Oh my God, Olivia, it's Jummy," she said in a singsong tone.

*Olivia!*

My eyes darted to the taller one and then narrowed as her features came into focus.

*I know that's not who I think it is.*

"Morgan, I don't know who Jummy is," Olivia said, even though I saw the flicker of recognition in her eyes. She shifted her attention to Lamar and put her hand on his shoulder. "I'm more interested in getting to know him."

The shorter one, Morgan, continued. "She went to high school . . ."

As she talked, I decided to excuse myself to the restroom. I needed to compose myself. I slipped off the barstool and immediately caught Lamar's attention.

His head snapped my way, and he reached out for me. His hand wrapped around my wrist, and his touch sent a jolt of electricity through me.

I gasped at the unexpected sensation.

"My bad," he apologized in a rush, removing his hand from me. "You're, uh, you're not leaving, are you?"

I could still feel his touch and the way he'd engulfed my wrist. "Just going to the restroom," I told him. "I'll be right back."

He nodded. "Okay, cool."

I glanced beyond him, and the two women were glaring at me.

I started to turn, and I caught his eyes sweeping over my body. My face flushed, and I made a beeline to the bathroom. As soon as I got in there, I grabbed the porcelain sink and hung my head. My heart was racing, my mind was spinning, and my blood was boiling.

Morgan looked completely different, but I remembered her name. I remembered how she'd always followed Olivia's lead. She was Olivia's right-hand woman. And from the looks of things, nothing had changed. She was a follower. She was part of the problem, but she didn't do anything without Olivia's say so.

Olivia Chapman had been the quintessential mean girl—a pretty, popular cheerleader who most girls wanted to be and most boys wanted to be with. But she wasn't a good person. She perfected nice nasty. She did her dirt in such an underhanded way that only those affected by her saw her for who she really was. She had teachers, parents, and her minions fooled. But anyone who'd had the bad fortune of getting in her way saw her for the conniving, heartless bitch that she really was.

I squeezed my eyes shut and then let out an exasperated breath. "What the hell?"

I'd spent the last twelve years recovering from their bullying. Rebuilding and rebranding myself, I broke out of my shell and became the woman I'd always wanted to be. Therapy helped me achieve a sense of peace that I could hold on to through the emotional turbulence of the last few years. Yet seeing Olivia and Morgan and hearing them call me *Jummy* had almost taken me back to a dark place—a place that made me want to fight. I hadn't seen them since high school graduation, and I wasn't surprised that they hadn't changed. But I *was* surprised by the visceral reaction I had.

Lifting my head, I stared at myself in the mirror. My almond-shaped light-brown eyes were framed by naturally long lashes. My caramel skin was flawless thanks to a host of skin-care products and removing stress from my life. Even without lipstick or gloss, my bow-shaped lips had a natural tint and shine. I hadn't seen my beauty back then, but I saw it now.

"Fuck them."

Taking a step back, I turned to view myself from the back. The yoga pants fit perfectly and accentuated my bubble butt. The way my clothes clung to my thick, pear-shaped body was the saving grace to my otherwise-bland attire. I wasn't dolled up like Olivia or Morgan, but I looked good, and as a grown-ass woman who was very secure in myself—inside and out—I wasn't going to let them disrupt my night.

Pulling out my cell phone, I sent a text to my best friends in our group chat.

> **Jazmyn Payne**: Why is the one person I hoped to never see again at this bar?

My phone rang almost immediately.

"Hey, Aaliyah," I answered.

"Who?" she screeched, forgoing a greeting.

"Do you remember that bitch who bullied me in school?" I replied.

"The one you beat up?"

I nodded, even though she couldn't see me. "Yeah. I mean, I wouldn't say I beat her up. I knocked some sense into her."

"You knocked her ass out, so you beat her up." I tried to interject, but she continued. "Anyway, what is she doing at the bar? Better yet, what are *you* doing at a bar?"

I started pacing from one side of the bathroom to the other. "I needed to get out and clear my head." I rushed past that to get to my point. "So, I'm talking to this man—"

"Oh really? And you didn't tell him you were unavailable?"

I rolled my eyes. "Stop. I'm at a sports bar talking to this man about football," I clarified. "And Olivia and one of her minions come up to him and start flirting—while we're mid conversation!"

"Rude!"

"Right?"

"So, are you interested in him?"

Heat crept up my neck. "It's not like that. We just . . . clicked. We're talking football, so inevitably that means I'm friend zoned." I sighed loudly. "Regardless of that, I refuse to let Olivia get her gnarled hooks into him because . . ."

*Olivia always got what she wanted*, I continued my sentence silently.

"Because what?" Aaliyah asked.

"Because she's not a good person, and he is."

The surety with which I said that gave me pause because I'd just met the man. But the statement rang true in my gut, and it had taken me a long time to trust my gut again.

"If he's as cool as you think he is, he'll see through it. And if not, it doesn't matter because you're not interested in him." She paused for a second. "Or are you?"

"It's giving friend vibes. But you are missing the point! These two walked up and called me *Jummy*. After all these years! It took everything in me not to flip."

"What is Jummy?"

"It's their clever play on *jumbo*. This boy Olivia liked in eighth grade chose me to be his partner in science class, and she decided to make my life miserable from that point forward by calling me Jumbo Jazmyn. She shortened it to Jummy so the adults wouldn't know what she meant."

"I'm so sorry, Jazz."

"It's fine now. But just hearing that bullshit name sent me to a place where I was seeing red. If they had said it one more time, I might've hit them. So I just walked away."

"You did the right thing," Aaliyah encouraged. "So, what's your plan now?"

"I'm going to take his attention back." I walked out the door and made my way to the bar.

"Good! Don't let them mess up your night."

"Exactly," I told her as I took my seat next to Lamar. "There's five minutes left in the game, so I'll call you tomorrow."

"Okay, but listen . . . this is a meet-cute—"

"Good night, Aaliyah," I interrupted, snickering as I ended the call.

# 3

I slipped my phone into my bag and then made a show of looking around. "Your friends are gone?"

He let out a short, dry chuckle. "My friends?" He twisted his face as if he were offended. "Don't put them on me."

I smirked. "My apologies. The way they were in your personal space, I thought you knew them. I thought they were your type of people."

"Nah, I'm selective about who I let in my personal space and who I consider my type of people. And they weren't it." He lifted his glass to his lips as he stared at me. "You're my type of people though."

Grinning, I turned my attention back to the game.

"You're my kind of people, too." I bumped his shoulder with mine. "Now, what did I miss?"

"The only thing you missed was a drive that resulted in nothing, a three and out for the Monarchs, and it's about to be a three and out for the Wasps," he told me.

I pointed at the TV. "Watch Channing's feet and tell me he isn't losing a step."

"This was from back in October though."

"Yeah, but it was the same all season with no improvement. I'm telling you—something is up."

I felt him staring at me before the game went on commercial break. When I turned to face him, his piercing stare grabbed me. I felt him assessing me, trying to read my thoughts.

He tilted his head to the side. "You know your stuff . . ."

"I do."

"Confident. I like that."

I rolled my eyes before turning back to the game.

A minute or so passed before a time-out was called. The camera zoomed in on two young kids screaming with excitement.

"Do you remember the first professional game you went to?" I asked.

"I do. My dad took me for my tenth birthday." He hesitated for a moment. "My dad was born in Baltimore, so I grew up a Monarchs fan. We were in the nosebleeds, the Monarchs lost the game, and I dropped my hot dog, but none of that mattered." There was a nostalgic smile that pulled at his lips, and his eyes shined. "That was a great day."

I studied his face, enjoying the underlying emotions that played across it. "It sounds like it."

He blinked rapidly as if clearing the memory. "I don't usually vibe with random strangers like this."

"Me neither." I smiled. "Feels like we already knew each other. Like we were already friends."

"Can I get either of you a refill?" Trina asked, startling me.

Either I was too wrapped up in the conversation, or she was tiptoeing.

I broke eye contact with Lamar, and my head whipped toward her. "Um, I'll take a water please."

"I'm good for right now," he answered, before turning his focus back to me.

My heart was thumping in my chest as I shifted my attention to the television. Even though I was following the play on the screen, I could still feel his eyes on me.

"I like watching you watch the game."

I turned to look at him, my eyebrow quirked. "Why?"

"Your facial expressions." With a light chuckle, he stroked his beard. "Your eyes. The way you lock in. You really didn't see this game?"

"I have an expressive face. And no, I didn't. I know the Monarchs won this matchup, but I was busy and missed this game during the season."

"Outside of church, what's more important on a Sunday than football?"

"This was a Monday-night game, and I had parent-teacher conferences and got home extremely late."

A smirk twisted his lips. "Which are you? Parent or teacher?"

"Teacher."

"Nice. I wouldn't have guessed education."

"Why not? 'Education is the passport to the future, for tomorrow belongs to those who prepare for it today.'" I licked my lips. "That's a quote from—"

"Malcolm X," he finished for me.

My heart thumped.

An electric charge surged between us, and I felt it on a cellular level.

*Whoa.*

Swallowing hard, I tore my eyes from his. "It's, um . . . it's something that I say at the beginning and end of every school year to every class."

"They're lucky to have you. How do you like it?" he questioned.

"I enjoy it. It feels like it gets harder every year, but I like a challenge. I was ready for this break though."

"You have the whole summer off. What are you going to do with it?"

"I'm here for a week. And then . . . maybe the aquarium or a concert or a date with a book. I don't know . . ." I swallowed hard, ready to change the subject. "What about you? I know you're not in Chance for vacation—there's three things to do here. So I'm assuming you're from here."

"I grew up on the border of Chance and Spring Hill. I went to school in Spring Hill. And you're right, ain't shit to do here. I've been here for a week, helping my mom with some stuff around her house. I leave on Sunday for a work trip. I come back on Saturday to finish up at Mom's house, and then I'm heading back up to Maryland."

I almost choked on my water. "I live in Maryland, too!"

He tipped his hat up like he was trying to get a better look at me. "Are you serious?"

"I'm so serious! I live in Richland."

"I'm right outside of Baltimore." His eyebrows shot up. "We're about an hour away from each other. That's wild."

"This is why we get along so well!"

He bobbed his head knowingly. "I knew I fucked with you."

I giggled. "So, what do you do right outside of Baltimore?"

Shifting his eyes back to the TV, he picked up his glass with melted ice and the remaining rum and tossed it back. "I work with professional football players, helping them with their game."

"I can totally see you doing that. It fits you."

"I get to do what I love."

"I love that for you. That's how it should be. I mean, I love being a teacher. I do. But sometimes . . ." I made a face. "It's a lot."

He nodded in agreement. "I get it. Kids are a lot."

"Are you a parent?"

"No. Hell no. I'm trying to wait until I'm married before I get into all that. I have a niece and nephew though. What about you? You got kids? A boyfriend? Husband?"

"No kids. And I'm . . . single."

He narrowed his eyes and looked at me suspiciously. "You hesitated a little bit before you said single."

I grinned. "No, I'm single for real." Because of his expression, I laughed out loud. "I'm serious! After what I've been through, I've been good off relationships and marriage. I've been single for more than two years now."

A slow smile spread across his lips. "Good to know."

"Why?" I murmured cautiously.

"Because I like you, and while we're in the same place, I'd like to see you again." He gave me a look. "It makes it a lot less complicated if you're single."

Nerves and anxiety twisted my gut at his words. "Valid. Are you single?"

"Yes." He pointed at me. "You see how I didn't hesitate?"

I laughed.

He opened his mouth to say something, and then he stopped abruptly and pointed at the TV. "Watch this."

I turned my head just in time to see the Wasps squander an eighty-one-yard drive, taking eight minutes off the clock.

"Woooooooow." My mouth was agape.

"Yeah." He shook his head. "Tipped into an interception."

"All they had to do was keep running. The run game was working. Wow."

"That's what happens when you try to do too much."

Watching the aftermath of the play, I was in disbelief. "Time is so valuable," I commented.

"You mean in the game?" he guessed.

"In general," I replied, watching the replay. "Doesn't matter if it's football, relationships, life. Time is a valuable asset to have, a valuable gift to give, a valuable resource to mine . . ." I lost my train of thought when I looked at him. "What?"

"I'm just listening to you," he replied softly.

He wasn't *just* listening to me though.

My stomach fluttered.

"Don't miss the best part," he said in a low tone.

I tore my eyes from his and witnessed the Monarchs kick the game-winning sixty-one-yard field goal with one second left on the clock.

"And it's good!" I cheered, lifting my arms to mimic the refs.

He clapped loudly, and then we both laughed again.

"Tonight was exactly what I needed," I admitted.

"Was something wrong?" he wondered.

Our friendship was in its infancy, and I didn't want to lie to him. But having someone to joke with and be in the moment with was the perfect remedy for how I was feeling. I saw the sincerety in his expression and the kindness in his eyes and it made me *want* to tell him. But if I opened up about Aunt Addy, I was going to start crying.

*And I am not about to break down crying in front of this man.*

"Just some family stuff," I answered vaguely.

"Is that why you're in town? Visiting family?"

I swallowed around the lump in my throat. "Yeah. I come back one week a year, right after school lets out for the summer."

"I'm surprised we've never crossed paths before."

"When I'm here, I don't be outside."

I could see the wheels turning behind his eyes. With a contemplative look, he took me in. "Why's that?"

"Chance never felt like home to me. Now, in Richland, I've found where I belong." Before I could say too much, I turned the conversation on him. "Spring Hill is just as small as Chance. How was your experience?"

"Spring Hill was cool. It's home, and my immediate family is there. But I always knew I wanted more than what Spring Hill could offer, so I was ready to leave after high school."

"I'm glad you made it out and you're doing what you love."

"I'm glad you made it out and you found where you belong."

We exchanged soft smiles.

"Can I get you two anything else?" Trina asked. "We're still going to be open for another hour, so there's no rush. Take your time."

"I'll take my bill, please," I answered.

"It's already been taken care of." With a pointed look at Lamar, she smiled and walked away.

Surprised, I turned to him. "You didn't have to do that. But thank you."

"I wanted to. I like you, and the least I could do is cover your meal."

"I appreciate that."

"I'd appreciate seeing you again."

I bit down on my bottom lip as if I were considering the request. "I think we could make that happen."

"I'm glad to hear that." He pulled his phone out. "What's your number?"

I rattled off the digits, and he saved me in his contacts.

"This has already been the longest amount of time I've been in the area since I graduated—and I'm still here until Sunday," he admitted. "Since you're here too, I'd love to link up." He lowered his voice and leaned close. "I just met you, and you're probably my favorite person in Chance."

"I'm going to take the compliment, but the competition isn't stiff."

"Damn." He snickered. When his amusement subsided, he asked, "What's better for you? Saturday night or Sunday afternoon?"

Not knowing what my aunt's schedule was going to be, I decided to play it safe. "Sunday."

He nodded. "My mom has me taking her to this plant nursery

in Richmond to pick up some materials for her yard. When we get back, I'm going to hit you up with the move for Sunday. That's cool?"

I smiled. "That's cool." I shifted on the stool, glancing away from him briefly. "Are you waking up early for the gardening expedition?"

"Not particularly." He stared at me, searching my eyes. "You're not ready to go home yet?"

Holding his gaze, I wordlessly shook my head.

His voice lowered. "Then I have time."

Thankful he didn't ask me why and appreciative that he didn't need a reason to stay, a small smile tugged at my lips. "Good. That'll give me a chance to get a good read on you."

"We've been talking for the last couple of hours, and you don't think you have a good read on me?"

"I thought I did, but then I saw you bobbing your head to this"—I gestured to the speaker in the ceiling—"and so now I'm not so sure."

He burst out laughing. "Okay, that's what we're doing?" Turning his body to completely face me, he gave me a look. "Because if you think I didn't notice you doing your little"—he wiggled his shoulders, mimicking me—"dancey dance, I did."

"Don't do me like that!" I playfully pushed his shoulder. "All I'm saying is that I won't know for sure what your vibe is until I know your musical tastes."

"Okay," he said, rubbing his hands together. "Top five albums, in no particular order . . ."

We talked until the bar manager announced it was closing time.

And it was the most at peace I'd felt in a long time.

Between the dissolution of my marriage and my aunt's health battles, the last few years had been rough. I loved my friends and family, and I was thankful for their love and support. But it had been a long time since I'd had someone look at me without a hint of worry or sadness in their eyes. Even if they didn't say it, I heard the concern in their voices. And because of life's circumstances, meeting and connecting with new people just felt like more work than it was worth.

But tonight wasn't like that.

There was no pressure with Lamar. We clicked organically and we talked easily. He didn't know about my baggage. He didn't know about my past. He didn't know about the heaviness of Aunt Addy's condition. He just got to know me.

And I liked that.

"After you," he said as I hopped off the barstool.

In the mirror behind the bar, I watched his eyes sweep down my body, and my stomach, heart, and pussy fluttered. It had been a long time since someone invoked that reaction, and I didn't know what to do about it.

"When did you get into town?" he asked, rising to his feet.

My eyes widened. He was as tall as he'd said he was. But with his broad shoulders and thick yet muscular build, his large frame loomed over me.

I looked up at him. *Well, damn.*

He put his hand on the small of my back, and my stomach flipped. It was the combination of his touch, his cologne, his build, and the way he was looking at me that did it for me.

I didn't know if he felt that spark between us or if it was all in my head, but our connection was real. And even though I was attracted to him physically, it was his presence that attracted me most.

Lightly clearing my throat, I remembered I was supposed to be answering his question. "I made the five-hour drive this morning and got here this afternoon."

"Wow, and you still came out this late?"

"Yeah. It's been . . . a day." I smiled up at him. "But talking to you tonight ended things on a high note."

He grinned. "Same here. I almost didn't come out. I was working in my mom's yard all day. It was hot and I was tired. But I had a taste for some wings . . ."

"And didn't even get your wings."

His eyes darted to my lips. "What I got was better."

I folded my arms over my chest, covering my hardened nipples and forcing my feet forward. He kept his hand on my back and escorted me through the exit.

He cleared his throat. "There's this expensive reservation-only restaurant downtown that makes the best wings," he continued.

"I don't believe a place like that could have the *best* wings."

"They do, and they're on the menu only as appetizers. But if you're ever up my way, I'll have to take you to get some. Best wings of your life."

"Ain't no way."

"Let me take you to get some."

I smirked. "You want to take me to get fancy wings to prove me right?"

"I want to take you to Ember and Flame to prove *me* right." His tongue ran from one corner of his mouth to the other. "Where did you park?"

My stomach flipped.

I pointed my key fob toward my silver sedan and unlocked it. "I'm right there. Where are you?"

"I'm right beside you." With a chuckle, he pointed to the black SUV with heavy tint on the windows that was parked in the adjacent spot. "Looks like I've been right beside you all night."

"I guess it was meant to be," I joked, looking up at him.

He licked his lips again. "I agree with that."

"Jazmyn Payne?!" a woman's voice called out as we walked across the parking lot.

"The girl from high school?" a man wondered loudly with a gruff voice.

I hated being recognized in Chance.

Discreetly, I looked in the direction of the voice and saw a woman with a blonde Afro and bright red lipstick pointing at me. A man wearing a hoodie in the summertime stood next to her.

I looked back up at Lamar, who was watching me intently.

"Yes! Look! That's her!" the woman said.

Ignoring them, I continued putting one foot in front of the other. Lamar's hand remained on my back. I wanted to start talking so I could drown them out, but words wouldn't form.

"I thought Olivia and Morgan were lying." The man laughed. "That *is* her. I thought she died. I swear to God, I thought she did."

"She disappeared, and she wasn't at the reunion," she said. "Jazmyn! She got a man in her face, and she thinks she's too good to speak."

"I heard she got married before she died," he commented. "I'd go over there and say something, but he's big as hell."

"You think she's giving him her tax money, and that's why he's with her?" the woman speculated loudly.

They both snickered.

Lamar's hand remained on me as we approached my car. It wasn't lost on me that he wasn't saying anything. He was hearing the exact same thing I was hearing.

We stopped at my car, and I looked up at him and immediately looked away, mortified.

*How do I explain that I'm a social pariah in this town?*

Lamar leaned down, and for a split second, I thought he was going to kiss me. I froze, unsure of what to do.

"Let me get this for you," he said as he reached for the handle and opened my door.

"Oh." *Embarrassing.* "Thank you."

I took a step and then glanced back at him before getting in.

His eyes darted from my body to my face.

"It has been an unexpected pleasure meeting you," I admitted softly.

"Believe me, the pleasure is all mine."

He took a step back as I started the engine. He closed my door, and I rolled down my window.

"I'm going to hit you up with the plans tomorrow," he stated, pulling out his phone. His fingers flew across the screen. "But text me when you get home."

My phone vibrated with his text.

"I will—"

"Was her ass that fat in school?" the man asked at the same time I was speaking. "I might've risked the backlash for—"

"Yo, you good?" Lamar asked, turning toward the man and woman diagonal from us.

My eyes widened. The bass in Lamar's voice and the way he shifted gears had caught me by surprise.

"I ain't mean no disrespect," the man stated, lifting his hands in surrender. "Me and Jummy go way back."

Lamar took a few steps toward them. "I don't know a Jummy, but I do know if you talk about her"—he pointed at me—"ass again, I'm going to put my size-fifteen foot in yours."

I didn't immediately react because I was shocked and mesmerized.

And turned the fuck on.

"You ready to risk it all for that tax-refund money, huh?" the man clowned, making the woman laugh. With each step Lamar took, he stepped back. "I'm playing! I'm playing! I'm playing!"

"Hey, it's not worth it," I called out. When he kept walking in their direction, I raised my voice. "Lamar! Please."

He stopped walking, but he continued staring their way. "The fuck is wrong with y'all?"

"We're just playing. She knows we're just playing," the woman said with a drunken laugh. "It's just a little harmless fun." She looked at me. "Jum—Jazmyn, we're just playing."

He stared them down for what felt like a solid minute.

"Keep her name out your mouth," Lamar warned, before coming back to my window. "I'm sorry about that."

"No, I . . ." I reached for his hand, and when I had it, I squeezed. "Thank you."

"That was some bullshit."

I nodded in agreement. *Another great example of why I hate it here.*

A spark ignited between us suddenly, and I realized I was still holding his hand.

I quickly let it go. "Sorry," I mumbled.

"You don't have anything to apologize for."

Thinking about the things being said by people I didn't even remember, I felt the weight of being in Chance on my shoulders. "I should get going," I whispered.

"See you Sunday?"

My lips curled into a smile, and I confirmed, "See you Sunday."

I pulled out of the parking spot. As I looked back at him in the rearview mirror, my stomach fluttered again. *He defended me.*

It was equal parts sexy, sweet, and surprising.

I spent most of my life in Chance ignoring the bullshit, but sometimes, if necessary, I'd confront them and defend myself. But I'd never had someone defend me before. I'd never had someone be willing to fight for me before.

Certainly not in Chance.

Checking my mirrors before I turned, I caught a glimpse of myself. Surprisingly, I looked a little better than I had when I'd arrived. And I felt a little better, too.

# 4

Aunt Addy's first cardiac event had been so intense that she'd been put on life support. Less than a year later, her heart issues resulted in a critical hospital stint followed by hospice care. And earlier this year, she got sick, and the doctors couldn't explain it. They said there was nothing else they could do for her.

She'd graduated from hospice services after two months.

She wasn't just a survivor. She was a fighter.

It was clear each cardiac event had taken a physical toll on her. She'd be slightly slower and weaker. But her mind was still sharp. She'd kept her same attitude, her same quirky responses, and she'd be back home within a couple days of recovery. But watching her go through her morning and afternoon therapies, I knew this time was different. The stroke hadn't just impacted her speech; it had impacted her mobility.

"I'm proud of you for not hitting them," Aunt Addy responded to the end of my story. "But you should've. Clearly, they forgot what those fists of yours can do."

Snickering, I nodded. "Clearly!"

She sighed loudly as she gazed up at me. "You deserved better than what this town gave you."

"I wish Mom and Dad saw the world like you. Maybe I could've gone to school in another town or even a boarding school."

"The accelerated program at Chance is still one of the best on the East Coast."

"And they weren't going to prioritize my social life over my education."

"Your parents love you very much, and they did the best they could."

"I know. But . . ." I exhaled. "They weren't going to do anything that made them look like bad parents."

She smirked, knowing what I'd said was true. "They were wrong, but they had good intentions."

"Their good intentions paved the way for me to live the perfect little life." My sardonic tone and eye roll communicated my true feelings.

She gave me the same sympathetic look she always did. "Your dad always felt like he had to prove people wrong. He has always been a 'never let them see you sweat' kind of guy—even when he was young. So the way he handled your issues at school was more about him and less about you. You know I tried to talk to him, but . . ." She made a face. "There's no reasoning with people who have to be right all the time."

"And not to mention that Mom and Dad are both perfectionists. They have a hard time straying from their idea of how life should be lived."

"How could I forget?" She rolled her eyes. "Sweetheart, before they had you, they practiced on me. They're only ten years older, but you would've thought they were my parents. So I know all too well how overbearing they can be. How they push for perfection in every facet of life." She frowned. "But I used to remind them that they weren't my parents. You didn't have that luxury."

Sitting back in the tan recliner, I looked up at the square-paneled ceiling. "No, I did not."

We were both quiet.

"But you're grown now," she reminded me gently. "Perfectionism is a flawed way to move through an imperfect world. And I believe everything you've been through was for a reason. Who you were has made you who you are and has prepared you for who you're about to be. Honor all the versions of yourself, and go after what you want."

"I'm still figuring out what I want now after . . . everything."

"Are you figuring out what you want, or do you know what you want and you're afraid to stand in it?"

The question rocked me.

I stared at her with my mouth slightly agape.

"Mm-hmm," she intoned. "Now stop being scary. What's your type now?"

"My type? Of man?"

She nodded.

"After that shitshow of a marriage, I would say my type is a good man who is compatible with me," I answered.

She snickered. "That's not very specific. You have to be specific when you're asking God for what you want."

"Who said I was asking God for a man?"

She looked at me like I'd lost my mind. "Who else would you ask? Because that last one you had was not of God."

"Oh, I know," I scoffed. "He was a weapon formed against me."

She laughed.

I smiled as I watched her. For a moment, it was almost like we were sitting in her living room or on her screened-in back porch, laughing, talking, and exchanging stories.

"You seem like you're feeling better today," I remarked, when the amusement had subsided.

"I feel okay." She glanced at her left side and forced a smile. "I'm optimistic. A couple weeks inpatient, and then I can make arrangements for outpatient."

"Good." I reached over and squeezed her forearm gently. "You'll be home before you know it."

"I just hate that this happened during your visit."

"Don't worry about that. The whole point of my trip is to spend time with you."

She frowned. "But not cooped up here. Your vacation doesn't need to be in this place the whole time."

"Aunt Addy, I'm here for you. What else would I do? They tore down my only other safe space in town, so it's your house or wherever you are. That's it."

"They were supposed to rebuild that gazebo by this summer, but funding delays . . ." She rolled her eyes. "Anyway, I want you to practice being intentionally happy."

"What?"

"Happy on purpose," she explained. "Intentional happiness forces you to create a happy life for yourself wherever you are, whatever the circumstance, whenever there's air in your lungs. You make a point to be happy, to create happiness, to feel happiness. Do you hear me?"

I nodded. "Intentional happiness."

"And I can think of something"—she smirked—"or someone who can spark it off."

I could tell by her tone what she was insinuating, so I rolled my eyes. "Aunt Addy, please."

"All I'm saying is that you seem fond of that man from the bar. You said you two talked all night."

"We did. He seems cool. But . . . I don't know." I lifted my shoulders. "I'll wait and see if he calls me."

"Of course he will. That's why those billy goat bullies were being rude." She gave me a knowing look. "They were trying to impress that man, and he was already impressed by you."

I lifted my shoulders. "All I know is that they were gone by the time I got back to my seat."

"Because he sent them on their way."

"I don't know what happened."

"Well, he didn't ask for their number; he asked for yours."

"As friends, yeah. He said he was going to text me today, but . . ."

It was close to noon, and he'd been radio silent since we'd said good night via text.

"But what?" she inquired.

"If he reaches out, I don't know if I'm going to meet up with him."

"Why not?"

"I don't want to leave you here without me tomorrow."

"It's been a long time since you liked someone. So, friend or otherwise, I'm proud of you for getting out there again."

"Thanks. It wasn't that big of a deal. We just . . . clicked."

She had a serious expression on her face. "You don't dismiss the instant connections you have with people. Every connection means something."

"Yeah," I agreed softly.

"I met Rose, and it was an instant connection. We've been best friends ever since."

"That's true."

Her cell phone rang loudly from under the thin comforter that was spread over her body. When she pulled it out and saw who it was, she smiled.

I excused myself to find the cafeteria or at least a vending machine. I was gone for about fifteen minutes, and when I returned, she was still on the phone. As I searched my bag for my book, I realized who was on the other end of the line.

"And I don't plan on being here that long," Aunt Addy told my father, glaring at me. "I don't know what Jazmyn told you, but I do not need you running up here. Don't get on no plane, Richard! You stay right there. You said you were coming back at the end of August, so I will see you at the end of August." She shook her head. "No, no, no. I have your daughter here. Rose is coming tomorrow. Monica is coming back on Monday. I'm fine—stop worrying!"

She talked to my father for another twenty minutes. When she was done, I put my book down and looked at her.

"What did you tell your father?" she asked without any intention of letting me answer. "Because he's talking about flying here from Florida. I don't want him and your mother coming down here, fussing over me. I hope you didn't tell anyone else I'm here, because I'm going home soon, and no one needs to see me like this. I've had this same bonnet on for days. My locs can't breathe!"

I laughed as I stood. "I'm on it."

I pushed the button to lift the back of the bed to sit her up more. Then I got her toiletry bag and grabbed the jojoba oil and a moisturizer. Placing a pillow behind her back, I removed her bonnet and oiled her scalp. She continued fussing about the number of people who had reached out asking how she was doing. From her tone, it was clear that even though she was complaining, she appreciated how much she was loved.

Addison Payne enjoyed being the center of attention. She relished her social community. She was popular and eccentric and uniquely herself. So I knew that she wasn't fussing because people cared about her. She was fussing because of her situation.

As a fifty-four-year-old woman from a small town who'd gotten out and come back, she was the it girl. She made things happen. She had a bunch of different hobbies, activities, and friends. She was so involved and invested in the community, and she meant so much to so many people. It was unimaginable that she would be able to be in a local rehab center without someone finding out. But I knew she hated for anyone to see her down.

"... and that's why I told Rose not to tell anyone," she concluded. "Oh! And her son who got divorced a few years ago is engaged again."

I completed her hair and then rubbed the excess on my hands into my scalp. "That's cool."

"What do you think about that?"

"About a man I've never met being engaged to someone else I've never met?"

She laughed. "About getting remarried."

"Good for him." I stopped on my way to the sink and gave her a look. "That's . . . nice?"

She waited until I was done washing my hands to continue whatever point she was trying to make. "That *is* nice."

I made a face. "Well, I've been there, done that."

"Yes, you have," she relented. "But don't let one man ruin it for all men."

"You are the one who told me to not make men my focus!"

"I told you not to make *that man* your focus! I didn't tell you to give up men altogether."

I laughed. "Fair."

"And I told you that when you left that bastard, and you were separated. You were beginning your healing journey. I told you to focus on you." She waited for me to remove the pillow from behind her back before she continued. "And you did. You picked up the pieces. I'm very proud of you."

"Thank you."

"But what are you doing *now*?"

*Working*, I thought as I sat in the chair next to her bed.

"And don't say *working*," she added.

"They added eight kids to my class size and—"

She lifted her right hand to point at me. "That's an excuse, not an answer."

Her signature call-out caused me to purse my lips. She wasn't wrong, but it *was* a busy school year.

"What do you do *for you*?" she asked.

"I'm here. I'm spending time with my favorite person in the world."

"For a week!" Her brows furrowed. "What are you doing with the rest of your summer?"

Seeing my sweet talk didn't work, I sighed. "I don't know yet. The only thing I had on my calendar was to spend this week with you."

"A few weeks ago, I told you to come up with a plan to make this summer better than last summer. Did you?"

I frowned dramatically. "Not yet."

She stared at me for a long moment, and I saw a lot of emotion behind her eyes. The longer she held my gaze, the more it triggered my own emotions. Inexplicably, my chin quivered.

"Jazmyn, I want you to listen to me," my aunt said in a soft yet stern tone. "You have everything you need within you to thrive. You've existed for long enough. Now it's time for you to live. You need to ignite that fire within you."

It wasn't just what she said. It was the way she said it and the emotion behind her words. All I could do was nod. If I opened my mouth right then, I would've started crying.

"Get a piece of paper and a pen, please," she instructed.

I got up and walked to the counter where her flowers and photos lined the space. When I'd set up her stuff that morning, I noticed a pen and pad in the corner. I returned with it, and I plopped down in the chair.

I cleared my throat. "You want me to write something?" I guessed.

"Yes, I want you to make a list for me. This is ten things *I* want to do this summer to shake things up."

I wrote the title on the top of the page and then looked up at her. "What do you want to do?"

She started listing things without hesitation. "I want to get my locs dyed a fun color, like blue or purple. I want a tattoo. I want to go to a festival—there's a jazz festival coming up, and I missed it the last two times they've had it. I need a photoshoot and a spa day. I want to start a book club and have a picnic. I want to throw a party. I want to go to a Monarchs game, but I'll settle for an outdoor movie. Oh! And do you remember what I told you back in April?"

Looking up from the paper, I frowned. "About how you wanted us to get yoni steams?"

"Yes!" Her eyes widened. "Rose and I found a spa that does them, and the three of us were supposed to do that this week!"

With a skeptical look, I cocked my head to the side. "We were?"

"Yes. I was going to surprise you."

"I don't think extra-hot steam on my vagina is the kind of surprise I want, Aunt Addy."

She snickered. "You need to shake things up. That's what I want as my tenth thing on the list: yoni steam."

I wrote it down and then looked back up at her. "This is *your* summer list."

"And now it's time for you to make yours. Turn the page, and let's make your list."

I would've tried to deflect, but she'd told me to put a list together in May, and I honestly forgot. Even at the time, I didn't know what I wanted to do. I'd spent the last couple of summers on my healing journey. It was hard for me to even think about planning a summer of fun. But I turned the page anyway.

"I'll . . ." I lifted my shoulders and my eyes bounced around the room. "I don't know."

"Remember the first year I lived in California and you came to visit for a few weeks?" she asked.

*How could I forget?*

It was the summer before seventh grade, and it ended up being one of the best summers ever. "Of course I remember."

"Do you remember putting together that list of things you wanted to do before we came back to Chance?"

"Oh yeah." I smiled.

The last thing on my list was to record a music video to my favorite singer at the time, Vanessa Coffee.

"You wore one of those gem stickers on your belly like a belly ring, and you'd wear a pink wig," my aunt reminded me. "You said when you got older, you were going to dye your hair and get your belly pierced like Vanessa Coffee."

Vanessa Coffee had released a hit album that summer, and then she disappeared from the spotlight. She hadn't crossed my mind in years, but her flashy outfits, bright pink hair, and body jewelry were essential parts of her lore.

My brows furrowed. "But what does that have to do with anything now?"

"Those should be on your list," my aunt insisted. "Dye your hair. Get your belly pierced."

"What?" I balked.

"It's something you wanted to do—"

"When I was twelve!" I interrupted with a laugh.

"You also said you wanted to be a teacher when you were twelve, and look at you now."

My lips snapped together because I didn't have a retort. *She got me there.*

"Do you even know *why* you stopped wanting that?"

I hesitated, suddenly remembering.

"Exactly," she interjected. "So we're adding it to the list!"

"Fine." I shook my head and added it.

She stared at me. "What else?"

We sat in silence for at least a minute. "Um . . . stay up all night and watch the sunrise?"

"We can do better than that," she encouraged. "This needs to be a list of things that will shake things up in your life. Like I told you last month, these lists are to remind us of who we were and who we've become."

I was checking the time on my phone when a text popped across the screen.

> **Lamar Anderson:** Since you're not feeling Chance, I'm taking you to Spring Hill tomorrow. Let me know if eleven is good for you.

I stared at the message for a moment.

We'd briefly texted last night. I told him I'd made it home, and he confirmed that he had as well. We said good night and that we'd speak on the next day, ahead of our Sunday plans. I'd gone to bed with a smile on my face. But staring at his message, I didn't know what to say.

*What was I thinking? I can't leave my aunt and go off with some man I just met. I should tell him no.*

"Stop, Jazmyn."

My aunt's exasperated tone forced my eyes from my phone. When I met her gaze, she was studying me.

"Stop," she repeated.

Shifting uncomfortably, I tucked my phone between my thighs. "Stop what?"

"Stop overthinking."

My eyes widened slightly. The way she always seemed to read my mind was uncanny.

"Explore a new city," I blurted.

"That's a good one. A little safe, but good. Give it here." She outstretched her right hand until I situated the notepad on her thigh and put the pen in her right hand. "I'll make your list."

"Aunt Addy," I protested with a laugh.

"Throw out some suggestions, and I'll add the suitable ones."

Shaking my head in amusement, I did as I was told.

After her rejecting my ideas and throwing out some outlandish ones of her own, my resulting list was a perfect blend of semi-attainable goals and absolutely wild aunt-inspired shenanigans.

"There's no way I'm going to be able to do everything this summer," I argued, after she added the seventh item on the list.

*She can't be serious!*

Aunt Addy stared at the flowers that lined the back of the room with a contemplative look on her face. "Fine. You have until the end of the year—eleven fifty-nine P.M. on New Year's Eve."

My jaw dropped. "You're serious?!"

"I am." Looking down at what she'd written, she nodded. "One, explore a new city because you need to stop and smell the roses. Two and three, get a belly ring and dye your hair for the twelve-year-old you because you wanted to and got scared. Four, get a tattoo for the pain thirty-year-old you has experienced and overcome. Five, go to a Monarchs game because you love it and haven't been in years. Six, finally write your book because it's your dream. Seven, learn how to swim because you've put that off long enough as well." She stared at me. "What's eight?"

"Vegetarian diet for a month," I answered.

She frowned. "Why? You love burgers."

"I wanted to put something on there that seemed hard but doable," I explained. "I think it'll be hard to be a vegetarian for a month, but I'm interested in doing it."

She nodded. "I like that. And speaking of something hard but doable, I'm going to add that you pay off your student loans."

"Pay off my student loans?" I balked, my eyes bulging out of my skull. "Is this a summer list or a bucket list?"

She let out a strained laugh as her lashes fluttered shut. "You need something hard but seemingly impossible because you have faith. And you have until the end of the year. That's nine."

"I don't think I'm going to be able to—"

"Faith," she interrupted.

"But—"

"Would you really deny me this?"

"Fine, that's nine." I sighed loudly.

She smirked and then cleared her throat lightly. "And we both know what your last one needs to be."

"What's that?"

"Getting back on the horse."

"What horse?"

"A man. A date. Dating."

"What?!" My voice squeaked as I reacted.

"A man. A date," she repeated, opening her eyes and giving me a look. "Several dates. And you can start with that man from last night. What's his name?"

The corners of my lips quirked upward as I said it. "Lamar."

"Did you pack date attire?" she asked.

Feeling heat creep up my neck, I shook my head. "It's not like that. I can wear my regular clothes."

"You can borrow something from my closet if need be."

Even though she was twenty-four years my senior, she was stylish, and her closet was flush with things I'd wear. But because she was a size eight and I was a size sixteen, her clothes would not fit me.

"It's not necessary because it's not a date," I assured her, shifting uncomfortably. "He just offered to show me around Spring Hill in exchange for me looking over some paperwork for him." I shrugged. "And I don't even know if I'm going to go."

"Oh, you are absolutely going."

"I don't want to leave you—"

"Rose will be here."

"I don't think—"

"You've been divorced for two years, single for almost three," she interrupted. "It's time."

"I told you I'm not interested in relationships and marriage anymore."

It was her turn to balk, making almost the exact same facial expression as I had moments ago. "Who said anything about getting married?!" She shook her head wearily. "You need to . . . have some fun with a man."

I rubbed her left hand as it rested, slightly elevated, on a pillow. "Aunt Addy, I don't think I have it in me after everything that happened with Tyson."

She quietly assessed me.

A minute or so passed before she finally spoke again. "Sweetheart, Tyson wasted your twenties. You want to let him waste your thirties, too?"

*Damn.*

# 5

The thing about Addison Payne was that she was always going to give me something to think about. Her words forced the unanswered text to the forefront of my mind.

I cleared my throat and forced myself to look at my aunt. "So, um, if I *did* go hang out with Lamar, what time is Rose coming tomorrow?"

"She said she'll be here when the doors open. So, while I catch up with her, you're going to go on your date. And when it's over, you'll come here and tell me about it." Her lopsided smile grew, and her eyes twinkled. "If it goes *really* well, you'll come here on Monday and tell me about it."

My head fell back, and I let out a laugh. "Auntie! It's not like that!"

"While I'm laid up in this room for the next couple of weeks, you would deny me the opportunity to live vicariously through you?"

I shook my head, slumping back into the chair. "You can't use your condition like that."

"What's the saying? Use what you got to get what you want."

I rolled my eyes. "You must be stopped."

She looked like she was about to say something when an extremely buff physical therapist came in to take her to her session. While she was gone, I pulled out my phone and responded to Lamar's text.

**Jazmyn Payne:** Eleven sounds good. See you tomorrow.

Between physical therapy, occupational therapy, and psychotherapy, Aunt Addison returned four hours later exhausted, borderline defeated. My heart hurt watching her get settled back in bed. She was out of it for the rest of the afternoon. I rubbed her hand and watched TV with her until she nodded off soon after dinner.

"I'll see you tomorrow, Aunt Addy," I murmured as I gave her a hug.

"Date," she mumbled, turning her head toward me.

Sadness swept over me when I left the rehab facility. I thought about her the entire ride back to her house. And as I closed my eyes and prepared to sleep, hot tears slipped from between my lids and slid down the sides of my face.

For years, I'd kicked off my summer by spending time with my favorite aunt. But being in the stillness of her house while she wasn't there felt empty—and not just because the house was. My aunt had such a big presence. Before her therapies, it had almost felt like she was getting back to herself when we were compiling our lists. But afterward, she was a shadow of herself. And as I'd watched her lying in that bed, unable to walk, unable to move her left side, unable to enunciate when she spoke, unable to hide her frustration, my heart had hurt for her.

And it still hurt for her.

I didn't remember falling asleep, but when the phone rang loudly, I startled awake.

"Hello?" I answered, almost frantic when I saw my aunt's cell phone number. My heart thumped in my chest. "Aunt Addy?"

"Did you check my closet?"

I sat up abruptly. "For what? What do you need?"

"Not for me. For *you*. You need something to wear today. Something nice."

My mouth hung open for a second as my brain caught up with what she was saying. "What?"

"You can't wear jeans and a T-shirt on your first date in years."

"I don't have *just* T-shirts. I have some nice shirts in there, too."

"So, you don't have date clothes?"

"No, but . . ." I fell back against my pillows. "It's way too early for this," I groaned.

"You're not backing out of it, are you?"

"No. I'm still hanging out with him . . . in three hours. And I'm wearing something from my bag. It'll be fine."

"Don't back out of this, Jazmyn."

"I'm not!" My voice was a mixture of amusement and annoyance.

"Good. Now, they just came to get me for breakfast, so I'll talk to you later. Text me his name and information. And a picture. And what you decide to wear."

"I will," I assured her. "Enjoy your breakfast and your time with Rose."

We said our goodbyes, and my lips pulled into a sleepy smile.

Even though she wasn't accepting visits from everyone, I was happy that she'd agreed to let Rose spend time at the facility with her.

I stretched my limbs, pointing my toes and extending my fingers. Yawning, I pulled the sheet over my shoulder and rolled onto my side. I was still a little tired, but I couldn't stop thinking about what Aunt Addy had said.

"Wearing jeans is fine," I grumbled as I forced myself out of bed and into the shower.

But Aunt Addy's words lingered in my mind as I cleaned, ate breakfast, and then stared into my suitcase.

*Shit.*

Except for the one dress I packed for church, I packed only jeans or yoga pants. When I visited Chance, I only planned outfits for our usual activities—movies, dinners, walks, and days in her garden. And while I'd been fully committed to wearing jeans and a cute top, I found myself in front of the full-length mirror in my green strappy sundress. I undid the top two buttons to show a little cleavage, and my look went from churchy to cheeky.

"The girls would be proud," I mumbled to myself as I pulled the flower charm from the crease between my breasts.

My locs were pinned back behind my right ear to show off my dangly gold earrings. With the gold sandals, gold bangle bracelets, and gold-rimmed sunglasses, I sparkled and shined as I twisted from left to right. The dress fanned out around me, showing off a glimpse of my thighs before settling at my knees. It wasn't too dressy, but it was nice.

I looked good, and my lips curled into a smile. I took a picture with my cell phone, and then it vibrated in my hand.

**Lamar Anderson:** The house with the flowers?

**Jazmyn Payne:** Yes. I'll be right out.

I went to grab my bag from the bedroom, and as I made my way to the living room, a knock stopped me in my tracks.

My stomach twisted nervously.

My last first date was nine years ago—when I was twenty-one years old. It was awkward with Tyson, and I should've never said yes to a second date, let alone his marriage proposal. After reflecting on my first date with Tyson and comparing that to the ease and effortlessness of my time with Lamar, my nerves dissipated.

Taking a deep breath, I opened the door.

*Gaaaaaaaaaaaahdamn*, I thought as my nerves came right back.

Lamar Anderson had looked good under the artificial lights in the sports bar. But with the sunlight beaming down on his mahogany skin, he somehow looked even better. From his thick dark eyebrows accentuating soft brown eyes to his full lips spreading into a bright white smile, I was mesmerized.

"Jazz! Wow."

My cheeks flushed as I stepped onto the porch. After locking up, I caught him staring. "Am I overdressed?"

"No." His eyes swept up and down my body. "Not at all."

I glanced down at my dress. "I know I'm just reviewing your business plan, but I didn't know what else the tour entailed."

"Jazz." His tone forced my eyes to meet his. "You're beautiful," he asserted softly.

"Thank you." I checked him out in his gray shirt stretching across his defined chest and biceps. His blue shorts displayed his muscular calves and expensive-looking blue, white, and gray sneakers. "You, too. I mean, handsome. You're handsome."

Seeming to smile at my awkwardness, he stated, "I'm going to show you around Spring Hill and then take you to lunch."

I nodded. "Okay."

He escorted me to his black SUV. I noted his license plate number as we approached. Opening my door, he smiled. "You need help?"

Without waiting for an answer, he placed one hand on the small of my back and took my hand in his, guiding me into the vehicle. I stepped onto the side rail and eased into the buttery leather seat, exhaling as he closed the door behind me. Glancing around, I noticed the clean burgundy-and-black interior.

Sending a quick text to my aunt, I gave her the make and model of the car with the Maryland tags.

"Your car is nice," I complimented him as he climbed into the driver's seat.

He flashed me a lopsided grin. "I appreciate that."

I slipped my phone back into my bag. "This interior is so . . ." I looked around again, unable to put it into words. "It's rich."

"Rich?" He chuckled, pressing the button to start the engine. "I mean, yeah, it cost a little bit extra because it's custom."

"I mean, it *does* look expensive," I told him. "But I'm talking about rich in color. This shade of red is so beautiful."

He sat back and assessed me.

Our eyes locked, and initially, I waited for his response. But after a few seconds of silence, we were just staring at each other. His cologne filled my nostrils. I inhaled deeply, realizing how long we'd been looking into each other's eyes. Inexplicably, I couldn't look away.

"Bordello," he said finally.

"Hm?"

"That's the . . ." His eyes dropped to my lips. "That's the name of the custom color." He tore his eyes from me and put his car in reverse. "You ready to see what Spring Hill has to offer?"

I exhaled. "I'm ready."

"So, Jazmyn . . ." He glanced over at me before driving away from Aunt Addison's house. "What did you get into yesterday?"

"Spent time with my aunt." I fidgeted with my seat belt. "How was the trip to get plants?"

He let out a dry laugh. "It was cool. They didn't have what the website said they did, so my mom switched up what she wanted. We were there for a lot longer than we were supposed to be. But it was fine."

We fell into an easy conversation about his mom's newfound love of gardening and my aunt's love of plants in general. I did more listening than talking, but we exchanged stories of their overzealousness. His mom sounded a lot like my aunt.

"She lost her mind in Richmond." Lamar laughed. "We went from the nursery to the hardware store and then back to the nursery until she had everything she wanted." He shook his head as he drove us out of Chance and entered Spring Hill. "I love my mom, but it'll be good for everyone when I head back."

"Why do you say that?"

"The longer I stay, the more she finds for me to do. And because Bill threw out his back, she got me doing everything she can think of."

"Who's Bill?"

"My stepdad." He glanced over at me. "You mentioned you grew up in Chance. Are your parents still here?"

I shook my head. "No. Well, yeah. But they spend summers and major holidays in Florida. They'll be back up this way in August."

"So they spend their summers at the beach in Florida . . . and you spend your summers in Chance." He paused. "Interesting."

I snickered. "I hear judgment."

"I'm not judging. I'm observing."

I pointed at him. "Aren't you also on vacation in Chance?"

"No," he disputed with a smirk. "I'm on vacation in Spring Hill."

I gestured around and comically peered out the window at the abundance of trees as we drove down the two-lane highway. "From the looks of things, we left the nothing in Chance, and we're headed to even more nothing in Spring Hill."

"Now who's judging?"

Innocently, I widened my eyes. "I'm not judging. I'm observing."

He let out a deep rumble of a laugh as he approached the first stoplight. "Well observe this." He smiled. "Spring Hill Square."

Spring Hill had evolved since I was a teen. There were stores and restaurants where trees used to be. Although they had modernized, it was still a small town and looked every bit of it. There was maybe a six- or seven-block assortment of buildings and then nothing but trees and farmland. But the sign that said WELCOME TO SPRING HILL SQUARE listed businesses below in fine print.

"There are thirty businesses over here," he told me, reading my mind. "This is like the downtown area."

"And three restaurants. Okay, I see you!"

"And a fourth one, the nice one, is down the street by the water." He pointed to the right proudly as he parallel parked on the street. He turned the engine off and shrugged his shoulders. "I know you're not used to the big city, being from Chance and all."

"This is damn near New York City," I joked, reaching for the door handle.

"Whoa . . ." His hand wrapped around my wrist. His touch sent a jolt of electricity through my arm.

Gasping at the unexpected sensation, I whipped my head around to face him.

"I'll get your door," he told me.

I swallowed hard. "Okay."

His fingers lingered on my flesh for a second longer than necessary as he held my gaze.

Licking his lips, he dropped his hand from me and climbed out of the SUV.

I exhaled loudly. Pushing myself up in my seat, I watched him circle the hood to get to the passenger side. When my door opened, he offered me his hand.

"You're quite the gentleman, aren't you?" I remarked, allowing him to help me out of the vehicle.

His lips spread into a slow smile without answering. Looking back and forth to make sure there was no oncoming traffic, he put his hand on my lower back and ushered me to the other side of the street.

"We're going to start here . . ." He smiled as we approached the first stop.

"A bookstore," I cooed as he opened the door for me.

It was called Edwina's. The bell announced our arrival, and we were greeted by an older woman with graying hair and a slow, dawdling walk.

"How can I help you?" she greeted us.

"We're just going to look around for a minute. We'll let you know," Lamar replied.

There were people milling around the store, but it was surprisingly quiet. I gravitated to the collection of journals on a shelf. I ran my fingertips over the leather-bound ones while I made my way down the aisle.

"Are we looking for anything in particular?" I wondered as I paused on a brown vintage journal with a rope closure. The hundred-dollar price tag helped me to move on from it. "Or are we just here for the tour?"

"You mentioned you taught English, so I planned for Edwina's to be our first stop." He headed down the first aisle. "They have rare books and a bunch of other stuff that might pique an English teacher's interest." He looked back at me. "And I already know you can't find books like this in Chance."

I snickered behind my hand, trying to keep quiet. "You're not wrong." Reaching up, I pulled a book off the shelf. "Have you ever read this?"

He read the title and then shook his head. "I don't think so. Should I?"

"For your program to help incoming rookies who are heading into the league, yes."

"And why is that?"

"Well, when I teach it, I tell my students that it's about the journey from a poor childhood into a privileged adulthood, and about how money and social status have the power to change you." I offered the book to him. "A lot of talent is found in people who don't have a lot, and when you don't have a lot and get thrust into that life, it can be overwhelming. So seeing it from an outside point of view could help them process it in a different way."

A small smile played on his lips. "You were thinking about my program?"

"Well, yeah." I lifted my shoulders, shrugging the question off. "You said you wanted to get together and talk about it today, so it crossed my mind."

He flipped the book over in his hand. "Okay, I'll get it." He paused for a moment. "Will you read something that I pick out for you?"

I eyed him suspiciously before I smiled. "Yeah. But if it's terrible, I won't take a book rec from you ever again."

He chuckled. "Oh shit, the pressure is on."

"And to be clear, *Great Expectations* popped in my head as a teaching tool for your business. My reading recommendation for you would be completely different."

We walked through the small store, discussing books, movies, and entertainment in general. Once we'd examined every inch of the place, we found ourselves back where we'd begun.

"Oh, hold on." He hooked his arm around me, his hand on my side when he squeezed behind me. His fingers skated over the extra fat on my side as he passed. "Wait right here. I'm going to get you a book."

Heat flushed my face, and I wrapped my arm around myself reflexively. I wasn't self-conscious about it; it was a mixture of surprise, curiosity, and attraction that jolted through me. He was on the other side of the store, and I could still feel his touch on that intimate spot.

My body stirred.

Pushing that thought out of my mind, I wandered back over to the journals and notebooks. I had a couple of blank journals at home, so it wasn't a necessity. But my eyes and hands locked with the brown leather-bound beauty that had caught my eye the moment I'd walked in. There was no way I could justify spending a hundred dollars on a notebook. But I imagined writing my first novel in that thing.

"Based on what I've learned about you today, I think I got a winner," he said as he appeared next to me.

I put the journal down and grinned. "What is it?"

He looked so pleased with himself. The gift bag he handed me was pretty, and the book inside was wrapped in brown paper. "You'll have to open it later and see."

"You just don't want me to know the title and determine right this second if I trust your book recommendations."

Letting out a stifled chuckle, he put his hand on my lower back and ushered me toward the exit. "You're not about to reject my book and embarrass me in front of Edwina."

With a giggle, I shook my head.

We spent an hour and a half window-shopping and exploring the square. Proving that Friday night hadn't been a fluke, we fell into an effortless conversation. He was funny and interesting, but it was his demeanor that made him easy to talk to. His energy and personality meshed so well with mine that I could exist in the moment with him without having to deal with any of the hardships of my life. I could just be.

"I don't know why you're laughing that hard," Lamar commented as he opened the door of the antique store for us to leave.

"That man bumped into you so hard. It's not . . ." Cackling, I waved one hand while wiping the tear from my eye with the other. "It's not funny. But why did he scream like that?"

The man hadn't been paying attention to what he was doing and had run directly into Lamar. Then he screamed as if Lamar jumped out to scare him. It startled both of us because that man was the one who'd come out of nowhere and then let out a shrill sound.

"The better question is why did the scream sound like that?" he retorted.

We were both still laughing as we made our way to his vehicle. After he opened the door for me, he circled around and climbed into the driver's seat. "Time for lunch," he announced, starting the engine.

We had been having so much fun, I hadn't realized I was hungry until that moment. My stomach rumbled, and I prayed he didn't hear it.

Clearing my throat, I shifted in my seat. "Where are we headed? One of the big four?"

He laughed. "I'm not going to let somebody from Chance—"

I shook my head. "I don't claim Chance."

Pulling out of the parking spot, he turned right and traveled down a long, winding road. In the seven minutes it took us to get to the restaurant on the water, we recapped the situation with the man in the last store, and I had literal tears in my eyes. We didn't compose ourselves until we were parked and heading into the restaurant.

"Your laugh is funny," he pointed out as we climbed the stairs to the entrance.

I made a face when I looked at him. "What's funny about my laugh?"

"It's just . . ." He grinned. "It's in surround sound."

"Are you saying I'm loud?"

He opened the door for me and waited until I walked inside. "I didn't say that."

Glancing over my shoulder, I eyed him suspiciously. "You implied it."

He put his hand on the small of my back. "I like that you're loud," he whispered.

I inhaled sharply.

Before I could fully process what he'd said, he moved toward the hostess. "We have a reservation for two under *Anderson*."

The hostess told a man in all black, who then escorted us to the second floor, to a table overlooking the water. The man attempted to pull my chair out for me, but Lamar sidestepped him and intervened.

"Thank you. I got it," he insisted, lining the chair up behind me and pushing it forward as I sat.

"Thank you," I murmured.

When he walked around the table and sat across from me, I couldn't help but smile. *Always the gentleman.*

"We are serving brunch until four," the man said, handing us oversized menus. "Your waiter, Gus, will be with you in a moment. Can I get you anything to drink while you wait?"

"I'll take a water, please," I replied.

Lamar nodded. "Water is good. Thank you."

We took a few minutes to review the menu, commenting on what looked good.

"I'm getting the steak-and-eggs brunch special," Lamar said. "What are you thinking?"

"I love chicken and waffles. But my eyes keep gravitating to the French toast casserole. I've never had that before, and I'm intrigued."

"I've had it and it's good. Would you like to order, or would you like me to?"

"Oh!" My eyebrows shot up. "Well, you can—"

"Hi, I'm Gus," greeted an older man with a slicked-back ponytail. He poured water into our glasses and then set the bottle between us. "I'll be your waiter today. What can I get you?"

"She'll have the French toast casserole," Lamar ordered as he stared at me. "What would you like as your side?"

I'd never had someone order for me before, so I was caught off guard. "Oh, um, bacon, please. Crispy."

"She'll have the French toast casserole with crispy bacon, and I'll take the steak and eggs, please. Medium steak, soft-scramble eggs."

"Very nice choices," Gus commented, taking the menus from our hands. "Your order will be up soon."

When we were left alone, Lamar caught me staring at him.

"What?" he wondered, sitting back in his chair.

"I was just thinking about how I've never had someone order for me before."

"How did you like it?"

Biting my lip to keep from smiling, I shrugged. "I don't know. I was too distracted by you ordering your whole meal halfway cooked."

He let out a light chuckle. "Please tell me you don't like your steak well-done."

"I sure do! It's the superior way to eat it. The praise is in the name." I emphasized my point with my hands. "Well done!"

He shook his head, amused. "You were my favorite person in Chance until just now."

After a few more laughs, I stared out toward the water. "This place is really nice," I told him. "Thanks for bringing me here. I would've never found it on my own."

"Because you don't venture out of Chance?"

"Because I don't venture out of my aunt's house," I blurted.

Curiosity flickered across his face. "You *did* say you don't come back often." He leaned forward, resting his forearms on the table. "So, when you're here for your one week in the summer, you're here for your aunt?"

"Yeah." I nodded, looking away momentarily. "So, where is this business plan I'm supposed to be looking at?"

He hesitated for a moment, seemingly confused by my sudden shift in conversation. "It's in the car. I mean, I have a copy on my phone, but . . ."

I reached over the table. "Let's see it."

A slow smile spread across his face as he unlocked his phone. "You have to be honest."

"I have no problem being honest. Part of my charm is that you'll always know where you stand with me."

His thumb flew over the screen, and then he handed me his device. "I like that."

I sat back in my chair and started reading the multipage document. I knew from our conversation at the sports bar that his idea was a good one. But reading a fully fleshed-out business plan that was smart, insightful, and innovative impressed me. From his mission plan, executive summary, and market opportunity, it was well thought out and cohesive. The information the new professional athletes would learn in the program would help them vet the professionals they'd hire to get what they wanted and needed out of their career.

"Wow," I commented, lifting my eyes to meet his across the table. "This is brilliant. This would help so many people, and it's just . . . so good. You have to do this."

"Really?"

I nodded. "You would change the game with this, Lamar."

"Are you sure? This is my baby right here. I put so much into it, but . . ." A flash of trepidation crossed his face. "I don't want to fuck this up."

"There's no way you could with this type of plan," I assured him. "When there's love and respect for what you're passionate about, you won't fuck it up. This executive summary is the definition of love and respect. This is amazing. I love the way you thought all this through. You are—your plan is incredible. You're about to do great things with this."

The crease of worry softened, and he smirked. "I may need you to hype me up like this before I pitch."

"And I'll do it. Even though we just met, I'm invested in seeing you make this happen. I'm invested in your success. So, if you need me to help you or to hype you, I will."

Holding eye contact, he licked his lips. "I believe you."

"You should," I replied softly. Squirming under the intensity of his gaze, I cleared my throat. "What are you looking for in the educators you bring on board?"

"People with experience who aren't actively practicing. What do you suggest?"

I smiled before launching into the list of ideas that had popped into my head as I read.

He nodded profusely with each point I made. "Yeah, that's good. *You're* good."

"And also reaching out to professors who teach sports law, contract law, sports management."

"I like that. A lot. Text that to me."

I pulled out my phone and sent him a text with my thoughts. As I held his phone, I looked between our phones until I saw my text notification pop up on his screen. He had me saved as *Jazz*, and for some reason, that made me feel warm inside.

"It's in your messages," I told him, finishing the section I was reading before handing him back his phone.

As soon as our eyes met, he shook his head. "You're smart. You're cool as fuck. You have good ideas. You look good in green." He set his phone on the table. "I knew there was something about you when I sat next to you on Friday."

"I'm a wealth of ideas."

"With ideas this good, just know you can get anything you want from me."

Fighting a grin, I bit down on my bottom lip.

"Here you are," Gus announced, placing our food in front of us. "The plates are hot, so please be careful."

We prayed over our meal and then immediately launched into

conversation as we ate. I gave him feedback, and he inquired about my thought process. I asked him questions, and he answered openly, honestly, and emphatically. The more we talked, the more impressed I became by him.

"The goal is to have the information readily accessible to help them put the best people around them," Lamar explained, after gulping down a huge swig of water. "Having the information readily accessible will help them decipher a contract and help them negotiate their worth. Too often they jump at the first offer they get because they don't know any better. Then, if they get hurt or flame out, they didn't invest their money well enough to hold them over until they figure out their next move. I want them to get it right the first time."

The passion in his deep voice, the expressiveness in his handsome face, and the conviction in his words were extremely attractive. So much so that when he licked his lips, my eyes followed his tongue.

Squirming in my chair, I looked away briefly to refocus. "I love it. I think that's exactly what's needed. Because even if the league does help with that, the league is going to look out for the league. A completely independent entity that prioritizes the players is necessary. Your idea is life-changing and empowering. Honestly, it's brilliant."

His eyes searched my face. "Thank you."

"I don't know what else you need, but it feels ready to launch before this upcoming season. Your mission, your summary, your breakdown . . ." I kissed the tips of my fingers. "Chef's kiss!"

"I appreciate that." Tapping his finger against his glass, he looked down before peering up at me. "I haven't really said much to anyone about this because it isn't ready yet."

"It feels ready to me. But if you don't think so, what do you think it needs to be ready?"

"Time," he answered. "I'd want this in place by the end of the year, so anyone thinking about entering the draft, anyone looking to make changes in the offseason will have this program. But I'd need time to implement it."

"Ah." I nodded in understanding. "So, your current schedule doesn't make time for it?"

"Not right now, but if I get some things in place . . ." He let out a huff. "I want to do this right. I want to make this happen. I don't half-ass anything I do, so I'm not putting this out in the world until I know I can do everything I set out to do."

"And you will. I can tell."

"Football has always been my life. Growing up, my goal—my dad's goal—was for me to make it to the league. But lately, my goal has been to make the league better. And the only way to make it better is to empower the players."

The passion in his words, in his eyes, in his expression caused goose bumps to prickle my skin. I was listening to him with my entire body.

"I love that," I murmured.

He silently held my gaze. Even though nothing was said aloud, the energy and the connection we shared stirred something within me. And, from the way he looked at me, I knew he felt it, too.

"I don't usually speak on what I have going on until it's official," he said in a low tone. "But with you . . ."

My stomach fluttered as his sentence trailed off. "Thank you for sharing with me. And here's my email." I watched him type it into his phone. "If you want me to take a look at anything, send it over. I'd be happy to help."

"There's something about you . . ."

I nodded. "I feel the same way. It's like we were meant to meet."

"That's exactly it." He stared at me, into me, as if he were trying to figure me out. "Because I don't usually trust people with my stuff like this."

"I get it." I cocked my head to the side. "I don't usually trust people period."

Running his tongue from one corner of his mouth to the other, he kept his eyes fixed on me. "Do you trust me?"

I nodded, the steady thump in my chest confirming what I'd already known. "I'm here, aren't I?"

"Good." He was quiet for a moment. "I have a mandatory work trip, so I have to head home tonight. Will you still be in the area this upcoming weekend?"

I nodded. "I don't plan on leaving until next Monday."

"Good." A slow smile stretched across his face. "I'll be back in Spring Hill to finish some stuff up for my mom on Saturday. I'd love to take you out again on Sunday." His eyes dipped to my lips. "A proper date if you're up for it."

I swallowed hard. "I'm up for it."

"Good. Let me get the check, and then we'll head out."

"Because he's a keeper, sweetheart," she continued. "Mark my words!"

There was a sparkle in her eyes and a lightness in her tone that reminded me of her normal self. I held her hand, and as I watched her, my eyes watered. It felt like old times. It felt like before she'd gotten sick.

*Well*, this *sick*.

I kissed her hand. "Aunt Addy—"

"Good morning, Ms. Payne!" a woman said as she strolled into the room. "Are you ready for physical therapy?" She looked at me and smiled. "And who is this young lady? Your daughter?"

"This is my niece, Jazmyn," Aunt Addy said proudly. "But she's like a daughter to me."

"Well, it's nice to meet you," the physical therapist acknowledged with a smile. "We're going to take good care of your aunt, and we're going to help her come home as soon as possible."

I nodded. "I like the sound of that."

"Sessions are usually ninety minutes, so feel free to wait in here," the physical therapist told me. "We have a full morning ahead of us."

Seeing Aunt Addy in pain was bad enough, but hearing her cry out as she was placed in her wheelchair gutted me. I had the decency to wait until they were out the door before I allowed tears to fall.

When Aunt Addy returned, she seemed exhausted. She slept until her lunch was delivered. Then we talked nonstop for about an hour. She left for her afternoon therapies and came back just as tired as she had earlier. She woke up twenty minutes after her dinner had arrived, barely ate, and then went to sleep again.

A few minutes before visiting hours were over, Aunt Addison opened her eyes.

"Start on your list," she whispered. "Don't waste a minute of your life."

"I won't," I promised.

She reached out for me with her right hand. As soon as I took it, she squeezed. "Live, Jazmyn. Live."

"I will."

# 6

". . . and then he drove me to your house," I concluded, trying not to smile at my aunt's grinning face. "When I got inside, I opened up the bag, and he'd gotten me a book about Nannie Helen Burroughs."

"That's perfect for you," Aunt Addy gasped.

"I know!" It took everything in me not to squeal.

"This is good. This is *real* good, Jazz." She looked as giddy as I felt. "Did you kiss? Did you"—she attempted to wiggle her eyebrows—"have some fun?"

I burst out laughing. "No, we didn't kiss *or have sex*, if that's what you're asking!"

"That's exactly what I was asking."

"Aunt Addison, you are too much!"

"I like hearing that you're getting out there and having a good time. It was your first date post-divorce."

"It wasn't a date." I leaned closer to her. "But when we go out on Sunday, it will be."

She squealed loud enough that one of the staff walking by paused and checked in on us.

"You're finally going to see a man about a horse," she said, before dissolving into a fit of giggles.

I couldn't do anything but laugh right along with her.

"He's young, but he sounds mature, like he has a good head on his shoulders," she commented. "That's a keeper."

"He didn't act or look four years younger than me, but I was really surprised that he's twenty-six. He's so together and professional." I shrugged. "I don't know. I don't want to get my hopes up. I've been wrong about a man before."

"Look a man in his eyes, and you can see the truth. If you really look and you really listen, the truth is right there."

Her words struck me.

Lamar *did* have kind eyes.

She closed her eyes, and a few minutes later, her grip on my hand loosened, and it was clear she was asleep.

"Good night," I murmured, before I left her bedside.

I held it together and didn't cry on the way home. I just kept thinking about Aunt Addy's words, repeating them in my head over and over again.

My phone rang right as I was sitting down to eat dinner.

"Hello?" I answered.

"Heyyyyyyy!" Aaliyah and Nina said in unison on a three-way call.

"How are you?" Aaliyah asked.

"How was the yoni steam?" Nina wondered.

"I was going to call you guys after I ate," I began, taking a deep breath. "Aunt Addy's hospital stint was more serious than I thought. She had a stroke." They gasped and I continued. "She's in a rehab facility for two weeks, and then she's coming home. Today was her first real day going through rehab, and it was hard."

"I'm so sorry to hear that," Nina said. "She's going to be okay though. She's tough."

"And she has you there," Aaliyah added. "You'll make this week fly by for her."

"I'm actually going to stay the full two weeks while she's in rehab." I got choked up. "I can't leave while she's in that place."

"Do you need anything?" Aaliyah sounded like she might cry.

"What can we do? I can order you something and have it delivered there," Nina offered.

"I love you both," I said softly, holding back my tears.

That was an understatement.

Even though there had been people I talked to in high school, they weren't friends. It was hard for me to get close to people in Chance once the bullying started. Aunt Addy encouraged me to go away for college and to be my full self. And within the first week of freshman year, I hadn't just made a bunch of friends—I'd met my best friends in the world.

"Tell me what you guys have going on?" I inquired. "I need to think about something else."

I listened to the happenings of their lives. Nina'd had another date and sexcapade with the man she'd met a few weeks ago during Richland Fashion Weekend.

"You're not worried he only wants you for fun and sex?" Aaliyah wondered.

"That's the only reason I want him," Nina countered.

I couldn't do anything but laugh.

Aaliyah reminded us of the memorial celebration for her sister that was coming up next weekend. And then she tried to breeze over the fact that she had circled back to have sex with her ex the other day.

"Matthew?!" I balked, almost choking on the name. "The blues singer? What?"

Nina howled. "Jazz called that man *Muddy Waters*!"

"It was a mistake," Aaliyah groaned. "I called Nina afterward, so she can vouch for me. I immediately regretted my decision. But in my defense, it had been way too long since I had sex. It had been six months, and I was getting restless. I don't know how you've been abstaining for two years, Jazz."

"It's been almost three years," Nina corrected, calling me out further. "Jazz just letting her coochie go to waste. Sad."

I laughed along with them. "My coochie isn't going to waste! You're acting like I'm completely against having sex again, and I'm not."

"You're just completely against dating and doing anything that will get you some dick," Aaliyah teased.

Nina sucked her teeth. "Like I said, coochie going to waste!"

My shoulders shook from laughter. "It's not! It's just . . . on break right now."

"A break this long is a sabbatical," Nina retorted.

"Stop it!" Aaliyah cried. "I'm weak."

I rolled my eyes even though I was still laughing. "Don't do me like this."

"And in her defense, Jazz is in Chance for two weeks. Who is she gonna fuck there?" Aaliyah argued. "When she gets back to Richland, she'll dip her toe in the water again."

"I can't wait to introduce you both to the streets," Nina proclaimed.

I frowned even though they couldn't see me. "I'll pass."

"Yeah, I'm not looking forward to that bullshit either," Aaliyah agreed.

"How are you going to meet anyone if you don't go outside?" Nina asked.

I was just about to tell them about Lamar, when Aaliyah yelped.

"I thought I blocked Matthew," she gasped. "How is he calling me right now?"

"Don't answer it. He might record the call and use it as the intro on his mixtape," Nina joked.

We went back and forth about that for a minute. And then we said our goodbyes, and I realized I hadn't told them about Lamar. But part of me felt it was for the best to wait before saying anything. I shared everything with Aaliyah and Nina, but I didn't even know what to say about Lamar. I wasn't sure what the situation was.

*I'll tell them about him if we actually go out next week.*

I was nervous just thinking about it.

Although there was no denying that I liked Lamar, I wasn't ready to tell anyone that. I was convinced that as soon as the words came out of my mouth, he would turn around and embarrass me.

*Like my ex.*

I shook my head thinking about it.

But as I dozed off, my gut told me that Lamar Anderson was different.

I woke up feeling good and optimistic, so I let that feeling carry me to the rehab center.

"What are we going to do first from your list?" I asked Aunt Addy as we chatted before her physical therapy session.

"After being locked in here, I think a spa day sounds like the right place to start."

I grinned. "That's a great idea—"

"Who is ready for some good hard work?" the physical therapist announced as she strolled into the room.

I watched my aunt get rolled out for another day of treatment when my phone vibrated with a text.

*Spam.*

It was almost embarrassing how badly I wanted it to be Lamar. For the next forty-eight hours, every time my phone chimed, I thought it was him. Excitement and nerves swirled in my belly with every text notification and then disappointment and confusion tugged at me when it wasn't him. The date we'd gone on was the best date of my life. It wasn't extravagant or over-the-top. It wasn't even the activity that made it so good. It was him. I'd never felt as instantly connected to a man, and it made me nervous that I felt something with him—and I wanted to feel it again.

So it was a little disconcerting that he didn't reach out to me until Wednesday night. But I played it cool.

**Lamar Anderson:** Would you prefer Jamaican or Italian food on Sunday?

**Jazmyn Payne:** Jamaican sounds good.

**Lamar Anderson:** How are you? How's Chance treating you since I left?

**Jazmyn Payne:** I haven't seen much of Chance since you left. But I'm doing well. How are you?

**Lamar Anderson:** Tired. But I'm cool. What are you up to?

**Jazmyn Payne:** Watching a movie with a frown.

**Lamar Anderson:** Why a frown?

**Jazmyn Payne:** Because this woman begged this engaged man to let the outcome of their one-on-one game determine if they'd be together and he basically took off his leg brace, tossed his crutches to the side and threw some flagrant fouls in order to beat her.

**Lamar Anderson:** Yoooooooooo! I'm weak!

I grinned, imagining his laugh.

**Jazmyn Payne:** What are you up to?

**Lamar Anderson:** Just got home from a three-day minicamp

and wanted to hit you up before I crashed. Can I call you tomorrow?

**Jazmyn Payne:** Of course. You don't have to ask.

**Lamar Anderson:** I didn't know what you and your aunt had planned so I wanted to make sure.

I felt a pit in my stomach.

As I read his text again, I was reminded that he had no idea what was going on with my aunt.

**Jazmyn Payne:** If you're free in the afternoon, that's probably the best time.

**Lamar Anderson:** Aight, I'm going to sleep, and I'll hit you up tomorrow afternoon.

**Jazmyn Payne:** I look forward to hearing from you. Have a good night!

Thursday morning, I walked into the rehab facility like I had every other day that week. The only difference was that while she was doing occupational therapy, I spent time talking to Lamar. When I heard her coming down the hall, I told him I'd call him that night. And when she entered the room, some of the joy I felt from the call dwindled.

"How was your session?" I asked, studying her as they got her situated in the hospital bed.

Her lips turned upward. "Good," she said weakly.

She was not good.

With each passing day, her energy depleted, and her light dimmed. I initiated conversation with hopeful optimism, and Aunt Addy replied with cheerful compliance despite how she looked. But by Saturday, it was harder for either of us to pretend.

"How are you?" I asked quietly.

With her eyes closed, she replied, "I'm fine. One week down, one week to go."

"How are you really?"

As soon as she opened her eyes, she shook her head.

Even though she didn't say a word, I knew the answer.

"I need to get out of here," she murmured, just before Rose walked in.

"Look at these two beautiful ladies," she sang with a flair.

"Rose!" Aunt Addy called out in response, flashing her a smile. "What did you do to your hair?"

"You like?" She did a little spin before she approached the bed. "As soon as you get out of here, I want you to meet my new stylist."

I offered my seat to her, and as soon as she sat down, they started exchanging stories. It sounded like when I got together with Nina and Aaliyah. My heart was heavy, replaying Aunt Addy's words, but I put a smile on my face, and I gathered my things. To give the two women time to talk, I went to the mall to pick up a couple of outfits since I was staying longer than expected.

*And maybe I'll find something to wear for my date.*

As a bottom-heavy size sixteen, looking for something cute and fashionable to wear in a small-town mall was going to take a little time. Pants were always ill fitting unless they were spandex or Lycra. Shirts didn't cover my ass. And some of the prints in stores were insulting. I had the pleasure of having two fashionable best friends—with one being a literal model, so I hadn't had to pick out my own clothes in a long time.

"Thanks," I mumbled as a man let the door close in my face.

He glanced back. "Oh, I didn't see you."

The woman he was with said something under her breath, and they both laughed. I was instantly irritated with them. I didn't want to assume they were talking shit about me, but the acid-like bitterness that seared through my belly all but confirmed it. Since I wasn't sure, I didn't call them out. Instead, I glared at the back of their heads as they walked toward the food court. When I lost sight of them, I became irritated with myself.

*I hate it here.*

Twelve years in Richland and a date with Lamar had put my guard down enough to think a quick trip to the mall would be fine. But I'd been quickly reminded of why I didn't venture out in Chance—nothing had changed. I would never feel comfortable or accepted in a place where I'd spent so long being either invisible or the target. I let a good night with Lamar make me forget where I was.

I rolled my shoulders back, held my head up high, and ignored the nagging feeling of dread that hovered over me.

*I'll check this store and then leave*, I thought as I walked into the nearest department store.

It was a small town, so I knew it was highly likely I'd run into someone. I was prepared for a familiar face treating me like Olivia and Morgan had at the sports bar. Mean girls, haters, and assholes, I could handle. I'd been handling them since middle school. But to have strangers treating me with disregard for no other reason than because of the way I look always cut deep. I'd worked hard to avoid situations that prompted that feeling inside me, but Chance had managed to force it all back to the forefront.

*Fuck this place!*

Standing in the middle of the aisle, I looked around in confusion. I took a few tentative steps to the left, searching for a sign to point me in the right direction so I could be in and out.

"If you're looking for the plus sizes, they're in the back, Jummy," said a grating voice from behind me.

I turned around to see Olivia Chapman with fresh microbraids and a smug look on her face. Two women I didn't recognize flanked her.

"If you're looking for a black eye, call me that again," I warned, glaring at her.

She lifted her hands in surrender. "Don't get violent, *Jazmyn*. I was just trying to help get you to the right department." She looked at my hand and then smirked. "Didn't you get married? Where's your ring?"

"You should be more concerned about the ring around your neck than the ring on my finger."

Her hand flew to her protruding collarbone. "There's no ring around my neck!" she protested indignantly.

Turning on my heel, I started to walk away from her when she began running her mouth again.

"Why were you talking to Lamar Anderson last weekend?" she asked.

I continued walking.

When I arrived at the back of the store, I saw the modest selection of plus-sized clothing and sighed. After scanning everything, I managed to find one sundress and one shirt that I liked. I took a picture and was just about to send it to the group chat.

"He acted like he knew you," Olivia stated from somewhere behind me. "How could *you* possibly know his fine ass?"

I didn't bother to turn around. "Why are you talking to me?"

"Why not?"

My lip curled in disgust as I turned to look at her. "Why not?!" I spat her question back at her in disbelief. "Girl, please."

She feigned confusion. "I know you're not still mad about what happened when we were kids. You're going to have to heal and let that go, sis."

"I'm not your sis."

"Well, then let me get to the point." She stepped up. "Lamar Anderson isn't active on social media, so he hasn't seen my DMs. Do you know how to get in touch with him?"

"Why would I tell you anything? I don't fuck with you."

"I didn't think so. It was a long shot to think you knew anything anyway," she said. "Were you two just next to each other randomly, or was it a Make-A-Wish situation?"

I snatched the garments I liked from the rack and stormed away.

"You have to know you could never pull someone like him, Jummy!" she yelled behind me.

Squeezing my eyes shut, I stopped in my tracks and took a deep breath. I'd taken kickboxing classes off and on since ninth grade and boxing lessons for the last five years. Everything in me wanted to throw my stuff down and roundhouse kick that arrogant look off her face. But I knew that was what she wanted. She wanted to be able to go back and tell everyone that I lost it on her "for no reason." Everyone would paint her as the innocent victim and me as the big, bad bully.

*I'm not going to give her the satisfaction.*

Forcing my feet forward, I went to pay for my items. I was cussing her out in my head the entire time. I was still irritated when I arrived at the rehab center, so I sat in the car for a while. It wasn't that I was holding on to childhood trauma. Therapy, relocation, my aunt, and time had me make peace with how I'd grown up, how my hometown disregarded me, and how being bullied had affected me.

But strangers in Chance treating me as if I didn't matter or didn't exist got under my skin. And Olivia and her friends were trying to piss me off in present day. On top of that, and much more importantly, my aunt was losing her spark with each passing day. I was already not in a good space, but to hear *Jummy* and to be taunted by the monsters of Chance had pushed me over the edge.

"Ahhhhhhhhhhhhhh!" I screamed at the top of my lungs.

Breathing heavily, I slumped against the headrest. I didn't know if I wanted to scream again or cry. It was all too much, and I just wanted the feelings to go away. So, when my phone rang, I almost didn't even look at it. I didn't feel like talking. I didn't feel like explaining to anyone what was going on. I didn't feel like feeling everything I was feeling. When I picked up the phone to end the call, I paused.

*Lamar.*

Everything disappeared with Lamar.

Breathing out the frustration and anger swirling within me, I quickly answered the phone. "Hello?"

"Hey, what's up?" Lamar greeted me. "You good?"

"I'm . . ." I exhaled. "I'm better now. I'm glad you called."

"What's going on?"

There was something about him that made me want to open up. But I loved the fact that he didn't know about my aunt, my ex-husband, or my childhood trauma. I loved that he didn't see me through the lens of my pain. I loved that he didn't treat me like I was wounded. He didn't see my baggage. He just saw me. And I wanted to hold on to that for as long as possible.

"It's just been a day," I answered, sidestepping everything I was going through. "I needed to hear a friendly voice, so I'm glad you called. What are you up to?"

"I'm on lunch break. We're almost done with my mom's garden. Once she figures out how she wants the walkway to look, Bill and I can knock it out and be done with it."

"You've been putting in work all week! I know you're going to be glad when you get a day off."

"Oh, you don't even know." He let out a light chuckle. "Tomorrow can't come fast enough. These next couple weeks are necessary."

"You have two weeks off? After being so busy, what are you going to do with all your time?"

"Well, I thought my vacation was going to start on Monday, but turns out, I have a real good day planned for tomorrow."

I smiled, staring out the window at the visitors walking toward the building. "Oh, really? What are these plans?"

"You'll have to wait to see."

"Oh, I like the sound of this."

"Good. I think you'll like it."

"I have no doubt that I will. It'll be the highlight of my week."

"What have you been doing since the last time I saw you?"

I shifted in my seat. "Like I told you the other day, my aunt and I have just spent the week talking, watching TV, catching up."

"But you haven't gone out in Chance?"

"If the mall counts. But my plan was to not do much in Chance. That's how it always is when I visit. What about you?" I changed the subject quickly. "You're the one with two weeks off. What are you doing with it?"

"I got a trip planned with the boys next week. We're flying out on Monday, spending ten days in Dubai."

"Oh, I love that! Special occasion or just because?"

"My boy Erickson is getting married, and he's always wanted to go, so that's what we're doing for his bachelor party."

"That's going to be a good time."

"Almost as good as the time we're about to have tomorrow."

I bit my bottom lip and ignored the butterflies that rippled through my belly. "Well, now you gotta come with it. You've just raised the expectations for tomorrow."

"Cool. I look forward to exceeding them."

All I could do was grin.

"But look, my mom just came in here like my break is over," he continued with a laugh. "So I'll hit you up later. And I'll definitely see you tomorrow."

"Take a picture of the finished product. I'd love to see it."

"I got you."

We said our goodbyes, and I sighed contentedly. The warmth that filled me cleared my mind and gave me the reset that I needed. He made me feel like everything was okay.

"Everything is going to be okay," I whispered as I got out of the car.

# 7

The botanical gardens tour forty-five minutes outside of Spring Hill was such a great surprise and a perfect way to spend Sunday morning. As much as I enjoyed learning about the flowers, walking and talking with Lamar through the gardens was the highlight. For lunch, we went to a Jamaican restaurant with the best oxtails I'd ever had in my life. Even though he made it clear that this one was a date, it felt the exact same as last week—effortless.

Everything between us was still comfortable and easy, flirtatious and fun. We'd spent four hours together, and besides his hand on the small of my back or our fingers brushing as we walked, we hadn't really touched. Our lips never met, but there were moments when I would be speaking and it felt like he wanted to kiss me. Our bodies never connected, but there were moments when we naturally gravitated toward each other. All day, every single lingering look, drawn-out laugh, playful teasing, and entertaining story felt so incredibly intimate.

And that scared me.

". . . and that's why I say *Love and Basketball* isn't a romance—it's a psychological thriller," I deadpanned.

His deep, rumbling laugh filled the car and turned me into mush. His voice was sexy, and his laugh was too. But when he was really cracking up, that sound made me giddy. I was so focused on him that I wasn't paying attention to anything else.

"Yooo, you're funny as shit," he commented through a chuckle.

"I'm serious!"

"That's what makes it so funny!"

"Because seriously, how do you show somebody you're in love?" I jutted my thumb over my shoulder as if the movie were in the backseat. "Because that ain't it!"

As his laughter died down, he answered, "Being in love to me is anticipating her needs, making sure she's good, taking care of her, making her life easier." He slowed to a stop and then looked at me. His eyes fixated on my lips before meeting my gaze again. "Whatever she needs to be good, I got her."

The air was thick in the SUV, and as we stared at each other, I forgot what question I'd even asked him. But hearing his answer immediately took me back to the night we'd met. He'd answered a similar question the same way. That night, the gleam in his eyes had been a little flirtatious. But, right now, the look was intense. There was something bubbling beneath the surface, and I felt it. It scared me because it wasn't just raw—it was real.

His tongue slid across his full lips before he broke the silence. "We're here."

He turned right, and I stared in awe at my surroundings as we drove down a dirt road. If I didn't feel so comfortable with him, I would've been more alarmed as we traveled deeper into the woods. Finally, the lush green trees opened up to a secluded spot near the river. Directly on the other side, small figures were all over the rocks, on the riverbank, and in the water. They were so far away, they looked like specks, yet they were so loud that they seemed close by.

Lamar pointed across the big body of water. "That's always been *the* spot in the summertime. When I was coming up, it was just the river. We'd ride our bikes over there and play games. It was cool. But now, over that hill is a parking lot where food trucks post up, so even more people show up." He looked over at me. "Spending the day at the river is one of the few things to do in Spring Hill during the summer."

"It's nice out here," I commented, taking everything in. "Crowded though."

"You don't like crowds?"

"Not around here. If I'm at a show or a festival anywhere else in the world, I'm fine. But crowds when I'm in or around Chance . . ." I shook my head and shuddered. When I met his gaze, my mouth went dry.

Lamar was sexy—that thick build, towering height, and flawless mahogany skin made him physically appealing, and I'd noticed that the moment I met him. But it was his intelligence, his eloquence, and his commitment to helping others that really captured my attention. He was easy to talk to, and that ease made me open up in a way that I hadn't felt compelled to do in a long time. The intimacy I felt with him was unlike anything I'd ever encountered.

And that was scary.

"So, there's nowhere you feel at ease in Chance?" he asked gently.

I swallowed. "My aunt's house."

"That's it?"

"Yeah. There used to be a gazebo behind the library. There was a storm a few years ago. When it was destroyed, they never rebuilt it. Not many people used it, but that gazebo was the only place where I could go to think, read, and relax. It was the only place in town where I felt safe. No one really went out there, but that was my spot," I explained. "Maybe that's *why* it was my spot."

He listened thoughtfully, nodding as I came to my realization. "I wish there were more spaces you felt safe."

I felt so exposed in front of him.

My stomach fluttered.

Clearing my throat, I shifted my gaze across the water and changed the subject. "If that's where the action is, what's this side over here?"

"This is where *I* come to think. Kind of like your gazebo." He did a three-point turn and then parked. Gesturing behind us, he continued. "This was never developed into anything, so it's out of the way. Stay right here." He got out of the car and walked around the back. The liftgate opened momentarily and then closed. When he opened the passenger-side door, my eyes went from his outstretched hand to the blanket slung over his arm. I slipped my hand in his as I eyed him suspiciously.

"What are we doing?" I wondered.

"You'll see. Just be careful," he murmured while he helped me out of the vehicle. With our hands still clasped, we walked about ten feet in front of his SUV. He held my hand tighter as he guided me down a short stone stairway. "Watch your step."

His grip on me didn't loosen until we were on a small landing on the riverbank. A huge stone jutted out, forming a bench. He covered the rock with the blanket and then gestured for me to take a seat.

"Thank you," I said, staring out at the water.

It was a heavily shaded area, and the water looked shallow. It wouldn't have been the ideal place to swim or fish or do any of the frolicking that was being done on the other side of the river. But I immediately saw what drew Lamar to it.

When he sat down next to me, I glanced over at him. "It's peaceful here."

Staring straight ahead, he nodded. "When you need to clear your head or just reset, this is the best place to come."

"Does no one else know about this place?"

"I'm sure they do, but they didn't hear about it from me."

"You keep it to yourself so it can stay peaceful."

"Exactly."

After basking in the solitude of it for a moment, I nodded. "This fits you," I murmured.

"How so?"

"Have you ever been told you have a calming spirit?"

He shook his head slowly. "I don't think so."

"Maybe it's just me." I chewed on my bottom lip. "But you feel calm."

"Thank you?" There was a questioning tinge at the end of his response, but I didn't elaborate. "What does that mean?"

It meant he felt like calm in the chaos that was my life. It meant it felt like his presence soothed every ache and pain bottled up in me. It meant that with him, I could just be me and escape everything else. But since I'd known him for all of five minutes, there was no way for me to say that he felt like a safe haven and not make things weird.

Heat crept up my neck. "I can't explain it . . ."

. . . *without looking delusional*, I finished silently.

"But it's a good thing?" he pressed.

Shifting my gaze away from him, I nodded. "Yes."

"Well, then I'm glad I feel calm to you."

We sat quietly, staring straight ahead for a minute, taking everything in.

"I can clear my head and think out here," Lamar said, breaking the silence.

"I can see why you'd keep it to yourself." I watched how the sun reflected off the surface of the water. "Are you worried I'm going to spread the word about your spot?" I asked jokingly.

"Nah, you wouldn't do that."

"Because you know I don't talk to anybody in the area?" I guessed, amused.

"Because I trust you." I felt him staring at me. "And I don't think you'd do me like that."

When I turned my face toward him, we locked eyes.

"How do you think I'd do you?" I asked, my heart beating faster.

"Right."

I licked my lips. "Is that why you invited me out?"

"Partly."

My stomach flipped.

Biting my bottom lip, I waited for him to elaborate. When he didn't, I pressed: "What was the other part of the reason?"

"When we first met, it didn't feel like we'd just met. Sitting at that bar with you felt like I'd known you for a while. I'd never met someone and just . . ." His tongue ran from one corner of his mouth to the other. "I felt it."

"Felt what?"

"You." His eyes bored into mine. "It's the way you look . . . the way you speak . . . the way you think . . . the way you make *me* think. I felt you, and I liked what I felt. I like being around you."

"I like being around you, too," I whispered.

His lips parted like he was about to say something, but then he tore his eyes from mine and cleared his throat.

"You know my passion project," he stated, staring across the river. "What's yours? I know you said you love teaching high school kids and tutoring college students, but what's your dream? What are you passionate about?"

"How do you know teaching isn't my dream?"

"Your eyes didn't do that thing when you talked about it."

"Do what thing?"

"When you were watching the game and talking about football, your face just . . . lit up. Same thing happened at the bookstore." He smiled. "The way you talk about football and books. *That's* what passion looks like."

My eyes slid over his handsome profile as the sun peeked through the trees to shine on him. I wasn't sure how he was able to read me so well. It was unnerving. *He* was unnerving.

I inhaled deeply before saying it aloud. "I want to write a book."

Lamar turned his head and stared at me. "That's what's up. What kind of book?"

"Contemporary fiction." I shifted my gaze back to the water as I continued. "I've been letting this idea bounce around my head for a few years now, and I'd love to write it one day. That's the dream."

"What's the story about?" I felt his eyes on me, but I kept my eyes forward.

"About a woman who overcame a bunch of different obstacles in her life to get her happily ever after."

"Ah, so it's a romance."

My lips curled into a smile. "I mean, yes. But the focal point of the story is that she's a private investigator. She's falling in love while getting help on a case. But the story would be equally focused on both aspects of her life."

"You should do it." He waited until our eyes locked before he inquired further. "What's stopping you from writing it?"

"I mean, yeah . . . you're right." I instantly thought about the list my aunt and I had made, and a small smile graced my lips. "I'm going to write over the next couple months. What about you? Do you make time for what's important to you?"

"My entire day is dedicated to football."

"Not today."

"You're right." His eyes dipped to my lips. "Not today," he repeated, his voice softer, sexier. When he met my gaze again, he cleared his throat. "So, why don't you make time for your book?"

I was unnerved by the moment we'd just shared and words started spilling out of my mouth. "When I first thought to write a book, I mentioned it to my parents, and they said less than ten percent of authors make a living from their writing. They said that statistically, I wouldn't make it, and I should pursue something reliable."

"Like teaching?" he guessed.

"Like teaching," I confirmed softly. "So, every time I think to start writing, I question if I'm wasting my time. I don't know if anyone would like it. I don't know if anyone would care about what I have to say. And somehow, I always manage to talk myself out of doing it because I don't know if it would be worth it . . . or if it would be any good."

"I can't imagine anything you do not being good."

My cheeks heated. "You've never heard me sing."

"You can't sing?"

"Not at all."

"With that laugh, I should've guessed."

"Hey!" I bumped him with my shoulder as we both laughed. "That's messed up. This is supposed to be a judgment free zone." I gestured around. "You can't bring me to this peaceful place and then judge me."

"Hey." He hooked his forefinger under my chin and turned my head to face him. "I would never judge you."

My stomach fluttered at the intensity of his stare. "I know," I murmured.

He licked his lips, and his thumb slid across my chin.

A distressed scream echoed from across the river, and the two of us whipped our heads toward the sound.

"Looks like the boat tipped," Lamar guessed. He pointed to a little shimmering red spot in the water. "There was a small red boat that looked overcrowded floating out there." He shook his head. "I hope they had life jackets."

Once I saw where he was pointing, I noticed some reflective orange jackets with heads bobbing in the water. "I think they did. I see some orange over there. I hope they can swim."

He shook his head. "I would hope so if they're playing around and doing dumb shit in the river. You know there are no lifeguards over there."

"No, I didn't know that." I frowned. "That's wild."

"You grew up down the street from Spring Hill and you've really never been to the river?"

"Never. I was working at the library or reading in the gazebo that used to be behind the library or watching football. I was a homebody." I shrugged. "Besides, bodies of water where I can't see the bottom freak me out. And not just because I can't swim."

He grinned. "Can't sing and can't swim. Got it."

I laughed. "Wait, tell me one of your flaws. You can't just be listing off mine without providing any of your own."

"Aight." He ran his hand down his beard before leaning over to me. "Between me and you, I don't really fuck with heights."

"You're scared of heights?"

"I wouldn't say '*scared*.' But . . ." He started laughing. "Don't judge me."

"I'm not judging! Heights can be scary. But it's just interesting because you're so tall. I would imagine everything is up high way up there."

"It is. But if I'm near a ledge or cliff, my center of gravity feels off. If I'm up here and the guardrail is down there"—he shook his head—"it just doesn't work."

I considered what he was describing. "That *does* make sense. Those railings are so low, if you were to topple over, they wouldn't be much help."

"Exactly." He emphasized his point with his hands. "So it's not really the height, it's the falling off the cliff. If that makes sense."

I nodded. "It does. I get that."

We both watched a bigger boat drag the capsized boat to shore. In the quiet that settled between us, something shifted. The clouds covered the sun briefly, and a gentle wind sent a chill down my spine. The crowd gathered across the river started shouting, and their cheers rang in my ears. But as I watched what was unfolding, I could barely focus on it.

Lamar was watching me, and I could feel it. I wasn't nervous, but the hair on the back of my neck stood on end, and a flutter swept through my belly. Warmth from his gaze heated my skin, and I basked in the feeling of him studying me. The longer it went on, the more apparent it was that I liked it.

"I'm curious about you," Lamar stated softly.

I glanced at him out of the corner of my eye. "What are you curious about?"

"Specifically . . ." He waited until I met his gaze before he continued. "I'm curious about the stuff you don't say."

I licked my lips and tried to steady my breathing. "Like what?"

"Like why you agreed to come out with me."

My lips curled into a slow smile. "Because I like the way I feel around you."

"And how do you feel?"

"Good," I answered simply.

With his eyes trained on me, he ran his tongue from one corner of his mouth to the other. "And what are you not saying when you bite your lip like that?"

My face heated immediately. "I don't always realize I'm doing it."

He looked me up and down before he met my gaze again. "I don't know if I believe that. But it's sexy, so I'll let you slide because I have another question."

*Sexy.* My stomach quivered.

"Ask me anything," I murmured.

A seductive smirk pulled at his lips. "Anything?"

I nodded again, slowly. "Anything."

"What's up with you and the two women from last Friday?"

My eyebrows flew up.

I didn't expect *that* question.

"Oh, that was . . . bullshit." I shook my head to try to minimize it, but as he continued staring, the words started to just flow out of me. "I went to school with them, and they were bullies—started in eighth grade and continued throughout high school."

"They seemed like the type," he acknowledged with a slow nod. "I knew it."

My face scrunched up in confusion. "What do you mean?"

"I knew they were full of shit when they said you were mean and you bullied them."

"What?" I screeched, the word coming out louder than I'd anticipated. "They said *I* bullied *them*?" My mouth hung open in disbelief. "*They* were the bullies! In eighth grade, the taller one liked a boy, and he wanted to be partners with me in our language arts class. So she decided that trying me would be her favorite pastime for the next five years, and she got everyone else on board with her bullshit. They're the reason I'm not a fan of crowds or of having a lot of attention on me . . . or being in Chance at all."

"Just based off the conversation I'd had with you in that short amount of time, I knew they were lying. And if you were mean to them, it was because they deserved that shit."

My eyes were wide. "I want to say that I can't believe they'd lie on me to someone they don't even know, but honestly, I can. They were shitty kids, and they grew up to be shitty adults."

"They even went as far as to say you beat them up."

I cringed. "Oh, well, uh . . ." I scratched my temple. "See, what had happened was . . ."

"Oh shit!" he bellowed, before bursting out laughing. "You beat them up?!"

"Wait, wait, wait, wait, wait!" I grabbed his arm in an attempt to stop his hooting and hollering. "Listen! Hear me out."

"I'm all ears."

"Senior year, Olivia and her minions were talking shit and then tripped me in the hallway and kicked my books. No one stepped in to help me, so I hopped up and beat her ass." My lips curled upward slightly at the memory. "They tried to jump me a few months later, but I handled business. So they wanted to press charges."

"And the school allowed that?"

I frowned slightly. "The school allowed Olivia to get away with everything she did."

*The* town *let Olivia get away with whatever*, I thought ruefully.

He nodded. "I can see why you don't fuck with Chance."

"They made school life hard, which in turn made life in Chance hard. And my parents . . ."

We sat in silence for a few seconds.

"Your parents?" he prodded.

"My parents expected perfection." I forced a smile. "Don't get me wrong, I love my parents. They're great—smart, successful, loving people. But they are perfectionists, and that's hard."

"Perfect doesn't exist."

Feeling his words deeply, I bit down on my bottom lip and nodded. "Exactly."

"Is that why you're so close to your aunt?"

"Aunt Addy has always related to me in a way my parents didn't. She always understood me. My parents . . ." My words got caught in my throat, so I just nodded until I could continue. "My parents understood perfection."

"I get that," he replied. "My dad wasn't the typical football dad. He instilled the love of football in me. I've been playing since I was five. But when I didn't have practice with the team, he had drills for me to run at home. I worked until I got it right. He'd always say to do the work so that when it matters, you get it right the first time. He wanted me to be perfect on the field. He wouldn't accept anything less." A small smile played on his lips as he shook his head. "It was tough growing up with that mindset. So I get where you're coming from."

"That made you closer to your mom?"

"Yeah." He paused. "But also, my dad died when I was fourteen, so all I had was my mom."

I gasped, grabbing his arm. "I'm so sorry."

He covered my hand with his, allowing his thumb to stroke my skin. "It's been twelve years. It's okay." He leaned closer to me, staring into my eyes. "But thank you."

"It makes sense." The words slipped out of my mouth before I realized it.

His eyebrows furrowed slightly. "What does?"

"It was your dad who fostered your love of football, and you work with football players. You're creating a program to help them, and you're passionate about making sure they get it right the first time. After all the pressure he put on you, you're helping to alleviate some pressure from others. I can't help but think that your dad's influence is all over that."

His fingers stilled, and he just stared at me.

He looked like he was going to kiss me, but instead, he leaned forward and pressed his lips against my forehead. He rose to his feet and then extended his hand toward me. "Come on. Let's go."

Grabbing the blanket, he held me tight to ensure I didn't slip on the stones as we made our way to the SUV. Even though we were on solid ground, he didn't let go of my hand. He hit a button on his key to open the liftgate. Just as we approached the vehicle, I had to break the silence.

"What I said back there . . ." I said quietly, squeezing his hand. "I'm sorry."

He tossed the blanket in the back and turned to me, pulling me in close. "Stop."

"I overstepped—"

Without warning, he leaned down, pressing his full, soft lips against mine. He stopped my sentence and my heart with that kiss. With my eyes closed and his mouth on mine, nothing else mattered. Nothing else existed. My mind went blank, and warmth coated and filled me.

I'd never experienced a kiss like it.

# 8

Pulling away slightly, he rested his forehead against mine. Even though the kiss had been brief, I felt it everywhere. Opening my eyes slowly, I met his heated gaze.

"You didn't overstep," he uttered.

"You got quiet and then wanted to leave," I whispered against his lips. "I thought it was because I said something wrong."

"No. Not at all." He sat in the cargo space and pulled me between his opened legs. With him seated, we were eye to eye. "What you said just . . . The way you see me . . . that's not something I'm used to, and it just . . ." He licked his lips. Placing his huge hands on my cheeks, he searched my face. "And I was trying not to kiss you."

"Why?"

"Because you seem like a good girl. I know you've been through some shit. And I didn't want to rush you or make you uncomfortable." His hands ran from my cheeks down my neck, over my shoulders, and down my arms until we were holding hands. "I want to spend more time with you. I'm feeling you, and I'm not trying to fuck this up."

I moved closer so my body was flush against his. He put his hands on my hips, and I wrapped my arms around his neck. Our noses were an inch apart.

"And you thought kissing me would fuck this up?" I murmured.

He nodded slowly. "Yeah, because I knew if I started kissing you, I wasn't going to want to stop."

My heart thumped in my chest as we stared into each other's eyes.

So, when I lowered my head, I made sure my lips were against his as I spoke. "Then don't stop."

All the air left my body when his lips seductively covered mine. The kiss earlier had been quick, soft, earnest. It had made my stomach flutter. But the slow, sensual, knowing way in which his mouth moved over mine now got me wet. I grabbed the collar of his T-shirt as his kiss swept through my body.

His hands slipped from my hips to my ass, and a chill ran up and down my spine. When he leaned back slightly, pulling me onto him, I felt his erection. And as our kiss deepened and our tongues met, I found myself attempting to climb into his lap.

Something within me snapped.

The combination of our passion, our conversation, our chemistry, and that bulge in his shorts had me ready to give myself to him. I was so shocked by the realization that I pulled away.

"I see what you meant earlier," I said breathlessly.

Still cupping my ass, he kept me pinned to him. "Which part?"

"About not wanting to stop."

"Then we should get out of here." His lips pulled into a slow seductive smile. "Because right now, all I want to do is tie you up, stretch you out, and bury myself deep inside you. I want to make you come . . . loudly . . . and repeatedly."

His words hardened my nipples, and I swallowed hard.

The good sense I'd been born with, that I'd cultivated through adulthood, left me as I stared into his eyes. "I want that, too," I told him.

"What?"

"All of it. I want everything you want." I loosened my grip on his shirt and allowed my hand to travel between us, moving down his firm chest and over his soft midsection.

Holding my gaze, he licked his lips. "Jazmyn, I want to know what you sound like when you come."

I moved my hand to the bulge that was straining against his shorts. "And I want you to make me come so you can hear me."

His eyes closed momentarily. "Jazz . . ."

The sexy way he dragged my name out made my toes curl.

"I like you," he said roughly. "I don't want to rush anything and mess up what we have going on. But if you don't stop touching me, I'm going to bend you over right now and make you come on my dick."

"I like you." Bringing our faces closer, I squeezed his erection. "And I want to come on your dick . . . I need it."

His mouth covered mine before the sentence had completely left me. We kissed with reckless abandon. Our hands were all over each other. I wanted him so bad that I was starting to lose control. The only thing I could think about was what it would feel like to be with him.

Breaking the kiss, I created enough space between us to be able to unzip his shorts.

His eyes dropped and watched me as I slipped my hand into his boxer briefs and wrapped my hand around his girthy dick. My eyes widened as I realized how big he was. And when I pulled it free, I sucked in a sharp breath.

*Ohmigod . . .*

Long, thick, hard, with a slight curve to the right. I was staring at a work of art.

When our eyes met, there was so much intensity in his gaze that I froze.

He grabbed the back of my neck and crashed his lips into mine. The force combined with his grip did something to me. I started stroking him, and he groaned into my mouth. Then he broke the kiss and pulled his wallet out of his pocket. The moment I saw the condom, another chill ran down my spine.

Once Lamar covered his nine-inch masterpiece with latex, he leaned forward. He bit one nipple through my dress and then the other. The wet heat from his mouth felt so good that my entire lower body clenched.

As he alternated between biting and sucking one breast and the other, he reached under my dress and tugged down my thong.

"Lift," he commanded, helping me out of the garment. "Now this leg."

He stuffed it into his pocket, and then he turned me around.

Trembling, I stared at the river. "Do you think they can see us?"

We were more hidden than we had been when we'd sat on the riverbank. Trees obstructed the view, and the angle felt like we couldn't be seen. But none of that mattered to me when his lips brushed my shoulder. He started kissing my skin, traveling up my neck.

With his lips pressed against the shell of my ear, he whispered, "I don't know if anyone can see us." Lifting the back of my dress slowly, he nibbled on my earlobe. "But if you'll feel more comfortable, we can slide over to that tree. Or I could bend you over in the trunk. Or I can make it look like you're sitting in my lap. Either way, they're not going to be able to see anything. I'm going to keep you covered. I'm going to keep you protected."

His voice was low, controlled, and sexy.

"Is that okay with you?" he asked.

"Yes," I breathed.

Honestly, at that point, I didn't care who saw or heard anything. I just wanted Lamar.

"Step forward and spread your legs," he whispered. "Put your hands on your knees."

I followed directions.

He gripped my hips firmly. "You're beautiful"—he kissed my left ass cheek—"and thick"—he kissed the other ass cheek—"and so fucking sexy."

Without warning, he licked my slit.

I gasped.

His tongue, wide and flat, skated over my sensitive flesh. My eyes shut tight, my legs locked, and I let out the loudest moan. His tongue massaged my clit, and my entire body started buzzing.

"You taste so fucking good," he groaned into my pussy.

"Yeah," I whimpered, trying to ride his face.

He stood and quickly spun me around. I had my hands in the cargo space and Lamar's body right behind me. My skirt was up, my ass was exposed, but as soon as I felt his dick playing with me, being filled by him was the only thing that mattered.

"Ohmigod," I exhaled.

I felt the pressure of his head at my opening, and even though it was just the tip, the way his dick split me in two caused the air to leave my lungs.

"Lamar, please," I begged.

The anticipation to have him fully inside me was like nothing I'd ever experienced. My heart pounded in my chest.

"You can't say my name like that," he uttered with a firm grip on my hips. "Do you know how fucking sexy you sound?"

The way the thickness of his head parted me had me ready to break down. I was shaking with desire. I tried to push my hips back, but he was in control.

"Please," I moaned. "Lamar, please."

He let out a guttural growl, and his fingers dug into my bare skin. "And that 'please.'"

The quivering in my belly and the desire that raced through my veins almost forced me to collapse.

I throbbed for him.

"Your pussy is so fucking wet." He let out a long, heavy breath. "And tight." He slid a few more inches in me. "I wish I could strip you, taste you, and fuck you properly."

"Ohmigod, ohmigoooooooooooooooooooooood."

"Don't worry, I'm going to make sure you come all over this dick." He gave me another couple of inches. "I'm going to take good care of this pussy."

"Please do," I moaned.

"Say 'please' again. I love how it sounds coming out of your mouth."

"Pleeeeeeeeeeeeeeeease," I moaned, just as he completely filled me up.

"Fuck . . ." He sucked in a sharp breath and then let it out shakily. "That's a tight fit. You good?"

"Yesssssssssssssss! God, yes."

"I love the way you're gripping me." Pulling almost all the way out, he took his time sliding back in. "Your pussy feels so fucking good."

"Lamar," I cried, feeling my orgasm building. "You're so deep. Please don't stop. Please!"

"I won't stop until you tell me to." He pulled out and then buried himself inside me again, filling me up. "I won't stop until this pussy can't take it anymore."

Moaning loudly, I was in heaven.

"Yeah, get loud for me, just like that," he uttered as he started sliding in and out of me. "I love the way you sound as you're taking this dick."

"Lamar . . ." My eyes shut tight as I quivered with want. "Shit . . ."

"I'm glad you can handle me, Jazzy. I'm glad you can take all this dick. Because there's nothing I want more than to make you come."

His words intensified his strokes, and I shuddered.

"La-Lamar, you're going to make me scream, and someone is going to hear us." I panted, trying not to be even more turned on by the prospect.

"Oh, you'd like that, wouldn't you? You want everyone on the other side of the river to hear you come on my dick?" He grabbed my hips as he picked up the pace.

My walls clenched, and heat spread throughout my entire body.

"Oh shit, that's a yes?" he groaned. "It's okay, Jazzy, I want it, too. I want them to hear how well you take this dick. I want them to know it's me making you moan like this."

"Pleeeeeeeeeeeeeeeeeeeeeeease," I begged wantonly, grinding myself against him. I took every inch he gave me.

"Fuck," he grunted. "You like that."

I did. A lot.

His dick, his hands, his words—everything about him stoked the fire inside me. I was just one exposed nerve in his hands, and everything he did stimulated me and drove me toward the most intense pleasure of my life.

My thighs hit the bumper, and the force of our bodies rocked the vehicle. The river rapids, birds chirping, and unintelligible dialogue from across the river barely covered the sound of our skin slapping, his ragged breathing, or my loud, lust-filled moans. I gave in to the ecstasy of being with him, and I didn't care who heard or saw.

"Please, please, please . . . Lamar, please don't—ohmigod," I whimpered. I felt like I was going to explode. He moved in and out of me until I hit the point of no return.

"Your pussy feels so fucking good." His voice was hoarse and needy. "*You* feel so fucking good."

The combination of his stroke and those words had me moaning, and I found myself tightening around his shaft.

"Oh shit," he groaned softly, picking up the pace. "Give it to me, Jazzy. Come on my dick."

As he continued to thrust his hips, I threw my ass back to meet him.

"Please don't stop," I begged breathily. "Please."

His dick with that delicious curve consistently hit the right spot, and my body was loving each and every second of it.

With a sexy growl, he let loose, ramming into me. "Fuck," he swore under his breath.

My muscles clenched. I dropped from my hands to my elbows as I started clamping down around him. My mouth opened but no sound escaped. Lamar losing control sent me over the edge in ecstasy.

*Oh! My! God!*

Quivering, I shut my eyes tightly and rode the wave. My body jerked against his as I came all over his dick.

He continued delivering long strokes as he talked me through it. "That's it, Jazzy," he groaned. "That's it. Give it to me."

Forcing me up, he turned us around so he could sit in the trunk with me sitting in his lap, still on his dick. He grabbed my breasts and forcefully thrust upward, bouncing me as he tweaked my nipples.

The new angle, the way he was fondling me, and hearing him pant in my ear rushed me toward a second orgasm.

"That's it," he murmured, moving one of his big hands to my throat and squeezing gently. "Just like that. Give me all of it. Let me feel it. Let me—fuuuuuuuuuuuuuuuuck!"

The ache deep inside me exploded, and my eyes rolled into the back of my head. Pleasure ripped through my entire body.

"Oh shit!" I moaned softly as I felt him pulsating inside me.

His entire body locked up, and his grip on me tightened while he emptied his load. But the guttural sounds that came out of him were what did it for me. I closed my eyes and committed it to memory.

Heart racing, I slumped against him. His arms were wrapped

around my middle, and his head rested against the back of my neck. Feeling his breath against my skin made me shiver.

"That was exactly what I needed," I told him as I climbed out of his lap.

He grabbed me before I could get too far away from him and pulled me in for the sweetest kiss. "That was really, *really* good."

"Yes it was." The evidence of that was currently coating my thighs.

"I'm going to need more of you."

"That can be arranged," I said with a grin. "Do you happen to have any napkins?"

"Oh yeah, I actually do," Lamar remembered. "My mom threw some wipes in the glove box yesterday."

We walked around the SUV so we could clean ourselves up. I watched him pull off the condom, clean up, and stuff his sizeable package back into his shorts.

"My eyes are up here," he joked.

Giggling, I looked into his handsome face. "My apologies. I was just . . . admiring."

"Oh, if you need me to pull it out again, I will." He helped me into the passenger seat and then dropped a peck on my lips. "Anytime."

My face was flushed as he closed the door and then got in on the driver's side.

As soon as he started the engine, he flashed a smile at me. "You surprise me."

"Because I was staring at your dick? In my defense, it's beautiful."

His hand fell off the gearshift, and he did a double take. "What?!"

I feigned confusion. "Oh, were you not . . . this wasn't about me staring at your dick?"

He let out a deep, hearty chuckle. "No!"

Warmth spread through me as I listened to his laughter. "Ohhhh, okay."

"I was talking about *you—you* surprise me." His amusement faded as he stared. "I didn't expect the afternoon to go like that. I knew you were a good girl but"—he licked his lips—"I had no idea how good."

My sore pussy throbbed.

The man had a way with words.

He put the car in drive and headed down the dirt road. When his phone started ringing through the Bluetooth speaker, he glanced at the display screen in the center of his dashboard. He looked around for something and then shook his head.

"I can't find my headphones. Excuse me for a minute," he said, before pressing the button to answer the call. "Hello?"

"Where are you?" a woman asked frantically. "Please tell me you didn't leave yet! Please tell me you're close."

# 9

I stared straight ahead, but I was all ears.

"Ma, what's up?" Lamar responded. "I'm about to head to Chance."

I'd tried not to jump to conclusions, but I was relieved to know it was his mother.

"Where are you?" she asked. "Are you close to the house?"

"I'm five minutes away."

"Please go to the house. Thank you. See you when you get there."

She disconnected the call before he had a chance to respond.

I looked over at him. There was no need to act like I hadn't been listening to the conversation. "What do you think is going on?" I wondered.

He shook his head, and his thick brows furrowed. "I have no idea. Do you mind if I stop by my mom's?"

"I don't mind at all."

We didn't talk during the five-minute trip. Every time I snuck a glance at him, there was a mixture of confusion and concern etching his handsome face.

"I don't know what I'm about to walk into," he said as we pulled up to a beautiful white Cape Cod–style home. "But you're more than welcome to come in. I'm going to see what she's talking about and grab my stuff. I'll just leave straight from Chance to get on the highway. It's closer anyway."

I suddenly realized I'd never put my thong back on.

I didn't even know where it was.

"I'll wait for you here," I told him.

"I'll be right back. If it takes more than five minutes, I'll come back out to get you," he assured me, squeezing my thigh affectionately.

He left the car running and the air-conditioning on as he jogged toward the house.

I rested against the headrest and sighed. *Who is this man?* I thought, replaying the events of the day. I bit my lip as the smile started to stretch across my face.

Lamar made me feel good. Lamar made me feel seen. And most importantly, Lamar made me forget.

I closed my eyes.

Seconds later, there was a knock at the window. My eyes flew open, and I saw an adorable brown-skinned woman with a flawless shoulder-length gray bob. I knew who she was immediately because she had Lamar's eyes and eyebrows.

Smiling, I rolled down the window. "Hi," I greeted her.

"Well, hello." She stuck her hand out. "I'm Gwen Brooks, Lamar's mother. Who are you?"

I shook her hand. "Hi, Mrs. Brooks. I'm Jazmyn Payne. I'm friends with Lamar."

"I would hope so, since you're sitting in his vehicle." She let out a little laugh before she stepped back and gestured to me. "Cut the car off, and come on inside. I taught him better than this." She shook her head and took a step back. "Come on."

I'd been raised with some sense, so I nodded. "Yes, ma'am."

I rolled the window up, pressed the button to stop the car, and followed Lamar's mom up the driveway. She had a grocery bag and an expensive purse in one hand. The other held her keys that she jingled with each step.

"Your dreadlocks are beautiful, Jazmyn. Who's your stylist?"

"Thank you! Her name is Oakley. Her shop is in Maryland."

"If you're ever looking for a local salon, check out Hot Comb."

"Thank you for the suggestion. Did they do your bob? I love it!"

"Thank you! You are so sweet! Are you from around here?" she asked.

"I grew up in Chance."

She gasped. "You did?!"

"Yes, ma'am."

"Well, that just tickles me! It's been a long time since Lamar brought home a *friend*—let alone a local friend."

We walked through the front door, and I felt the same welcoming energy that Lamar and his mother possessed.

As if on cue, Lamar jogged down the stairs with two duffel bags. As soon as he spotted us, he had questions.

"Ma, what was so urgent?" He jerked his thumb over his shoulder. "Bill had no clue what was going on, and you made it seem like it was an emergency."

"I never said the word 'emergency,'" she clarified as she headed down the hall. "Follow me."

Lamar and I exchanged smiles as she led us into the kitchen.

"I made you something, and I didn't want you to forget it," his mom stated, placing her grocery bag on the island. She went to the refrigerator and pulled out an aluminum foil–covered loaf of some sort. "A few days ago, you said you wanted a lemon pound cake, so after the early service of church, I came home and made you one."

"I appreciate that, Ma." He put down his duffel bags and went to hug his mother. "But don't ever call me sounding panicked again. I thought something was wrong."

"Something would've been wrong if I made this cake for you and you'd already hit the road." She crossed her arms over her chest and then winked at me. "I met your Jazmyn."

*Your Jazmyn.*

His eyes locked with mine, and a slow smile spread across his face. "I see that." He shifted his gaze to his mother. "I was going to introduce you, but you went ahead and did that yourself."

She laughed. "You left her in the car, so I *had* to do it myself. And while we're talking about it, don't leave her in the car again."

"I won't." He grabbed his bags and hoisted them onto his shoulders. "I have to drop Jazz off and then get on the road. But thank you again for this." He held up the foil-covered cake. "Love you."

"I love you, too." She shifted her gaze to me. "Oh!" Digging into her designer handbag, she searched for something. "I don't have a card on me. But either way, don't be a stranger, Jazmyn. It was lovely to meet you."

She gave me a hug.

"It was lovely to meet you, too," I told her.

The hug felt so motherly that I couldn't help but think about my aunt. Guilt stabbed me as I realized I hadn't checked on her for the last five hours.

We said our goodbyes and then Lamar drove to Chance.

The mood in the car was a little somber. If it weren't for his right hand resting on my leg, it would've been like we were in two completely different worlds. We listened to music and were lost in our own thoughts. I knew why I was in my feelings, but I didn't know why he was in his.

"Is everything okay?" I asked, turning the music down a little. "You've been quiet."

He squeezed the meatiness of my thigh. "I'm sorry. I just got in my head a little bit." He glanced over at me. "And it seemed like you needed a minute, too."

I gawked at his profile. *How did he know?*

"You tell me what's on your mind, and I'll tell you what's on mine," he offered.

I covered his hand with mine, interlocking our fingers. "You first."

With his eyes forward, he adjusted his grip on the steering wheel. "When Ma called and said to come home now, I thought something had happened with my niece or nephew. When I talked to Bill upstairs, he randomly asked me when was the last time I'd talked to Angel." He shook his head. "And it's been a minute, so . . . I was just thinking about that."

"Is something going on with your niece or nephew? Why do you think your first thought was that something happened?"

"I don't know."

We contemplated in silence as he pulled up in front of my aunt's house.

"Who's Angel?" I asked.

He put the car in park. "Bill's daughter, my stepsister."

I caressed his hand. "I didn't realize you had a stepsister."

"Stepsister and stepbrother. Angel and Will." Bringing my hand to his lips, he kissed it. "Don't move."

He opened the door and came to the other side to get me. He reached his hand out, and instinctively, I intertwined my fingers with his.

"Are you close with them?" I asked as we headed toward the house.

"We didn't grow up together, but yeah. Angel and I are a couple years apart, and she lived at the house until last year. Will had already joined the military when Ma and Bill got married. But Angel was pregnant at home, and I was in high school, so we saw each other more. We text every other week, but I haven't talked to her on the phone in a few weeks."

We stood on Aunt Addison's porch. I was on the top step, and he was two steps below, so we were eye to eye. I put my arms around his neck, and he wrapped his around my waist.

"Whenever I get that feeling like I need to reach out to someone, there's usually a reason. Call her."

His attention dropped to my mouth. "I will."

"Good." I placed a soft kiss against his lips. "Then you can start your week with a clear head." I kissed him again.

He pulled back slightly. "Now tell me what was on your mind." His hands ran up my back and then slowly worked their way back down, settling right above my ass. "I want to know."

"Honestly . . ." Biting my lip, I looked away. "I was just thinking about how when I'm with you, I don't think about anything else going on. I'm just able to be in the moment." I met his gaze. "I knew it when we met. I enjoyed it last week. But I didn't realize how much I needed it until today." I gave him a peck. "So thank you."

"Thank *you*." He paused, taking me in. "And I meant what I said earlier. I like you. I want to spend more time with you."

My cheeks flushed. "I'd like that."

"But my schedule is about to be crazy, so I may not be able to talk to or see you as much. With Dubai, training camp, preseason, and then the regular season, it's busy."

Disappointment tugged at my heart, and I felt the sting of rejection.

*I guess I don't fit into his real life.*

I knew he didn't mean it like that, and I hated that my mind went there. But I couldn't help feeling saddened that he was preemptively letting me know that he was too busy for me.

*We've known each other for only a week. What did I expect?*

I'd said I wanted a friend with benefits, and that's what I'd gotten.

"I understand being busy," I said finally.

He shook his head and pulled me closer. "Don't do that," he whispered, pressing his lips against mine. "I meant everything I said earlier. I'm going to be traveling, and then there are phone restrictions in training camp, so I'll be out of touch, but I'll reach out whenever I can. Every chance I can. And I'm going to figure out a way to see you as much as I can."

"Friends get busy and pick up where they leave off all the time." I hugged him tight so he couldn't see my face as I blinked back tears. When I felt like my emotions were in check, I plastered on a smile and looked him in the eyes. "You have a long drive, and I want you to get home safely."

"Call me before you go to bed," he said, just before his full lips covered mine.

He kissed me gently at first, and then our mouths and tongues collided with unfettered passion. Desire coiled in my belly, and any questions I had about what we'd shared over the last week melted. As we moaned our affection and our goodbyes, I held him tighter.

Seconds turned to minutes, and I had to break the kiss. "If we don't stop, you won't get home until after midnight."

"I know," he murmured, before kissing me again.

I smiled against his lips. "I'm going to miss you."

The words spilled out of me accidentally, and I froze.

My eyes opened slowly, and I found him staring at me.

His hands left my back, and he cupped my face. "I'm going to miss you, too." He planted a soft, sweet kiss against my waiting mouth. "You're going to call me later?"

I nodded. "Yes. Drive safely."

He waited for me to unlock the door and go inside before he left the porch. I waited until he pulled off to close and lock the door. As soon as I turned around, I felt an intense wave of emotion.

Anxiety hit me.

Fear gripped me.

Sadness crushed me.

Blinking back tears, I called to check on Aunt Addy, but she was already asleep. The silence in her home was deafening. I made dinner and tried to read a book while I ate at the kitchen table. When that didn't get me out of my head, I made my way to the shower. It wasn't until I was under the stream of the water that I broke down and cried.

While I was laying in bed, staring at the ceiling with tears still streaming down my face, I realized what was going on.

I liked Lamar; there was no denying that.

But I wasn't crying over Lamar because I had feelings for him. I was crying because of how Lamar made me feel. I was crying because being with Lamar had been the only thing that soothed the pain of watching Aunt Addy's health decline. I was crying because I was in Aunt Addy's house without her. I was crying because the thought of losing the first person who had ever fully understood me was heartbreaking. Something about him made me the version of myself that was unencumbered by the harsh realities of my life—my childhood in Chance, my divorce, my Aunt Addy's condition. He made me feel like the lightest, happiest, most unbothered version of myself. He saw me. More than that, he made me feel seen.

It was nice and I'd miss it.

He was nice and I'd miss him.

But it scared me.

So, with him being busy and unsure of when we'd see each other again and me not wanting anything resembling a relationship anyway, I needed to be realistic about our friendship.

And I silently reminded myself of that when I got his text an hour later.

> **Lamar Anderson:** Sis and her kids are fine. And she talked to bro last week and he was also fine. Call me if you're not too tired.

I reminded myself again that he said he was too busy for a relationship and that we were just friends before I called and talked to him for the remaining two hours of his drive. And I gave myself a third reminder when I woke up thinking about him Monday morning.

I had a pit in my stomach that grew every time he crossed my mind.

"You did it!" Aunt Addy exclaimed the moment I walked into her room at the rehab center.

I glanced at the nurse who was taking her vitals and then back at my aunt. "Good morning to you, too."

She laughed, and the sound made me smile.

"How are you?" I asked her. "How are you feeling?"

She looked tired, but there was excitement in her eyes. "I'll be better once you tell me about your date."

I waited until the nurse was fully out the room before I said anything. "So, he picked me up and took me to a botanical garden, and then we went to lunch. After lunch we went to the river to talk, and then we stopped by his parents' house so he could get his stuff, and he dropped me off before he headed out of town."

Her eyes widened. "You met his parents?!"

"I met his mom."

With a crooked grin, she gestured to her notepad on her tray table. "Get my paper for me, please." After I picked it up, she continued. "Go to your list, and put a star beside *dating*."

"It was a date, but we aren't dating. We're friends," I explained to her. "He has a busy schedule coming up, and I don't know what I want right now, so . . ."

"*Dating* means multiple dates," she continued, as if she didn't hear me. "When is the next one?" She nodded knowingly. "I have a good feeling about him."

Aunt Addison grilled me with questions about Lamar and the date, and I gladly answered, leaving out only the part where he'd bent me over and taken care of my needs.

She closed her eyes and exhaled. "I want to get started on my list as soon as I'm out of here."

"Absolutely. We can get the calendar out and plan out how we're going to execute your list by the end of the year."

When her eyes opened, she gave me a look. "*You* have until the end of the year. I need to do this by the end of the summer. The sooner, the better."

The physical therapist walked in before I had a chance to respond. My aunt flashed me a smile and then turned toward the medical team.

Silently, I sat down out of the way and shook off the undertones of our conversation. I rationalized why she'd said it, and I took a deep breath. We'd said we were making lists for the summer.

That's all.

She'd said I needed to get out of my comfort zone, and I agreed. She was going to check my list, and I was going to check hers. We were going to plot out how we were going to have the most memorable summer we'd had in years. We had plans.

Tears burned my eyes. I blinked rapidly as I pulled a book out of my bag. Pushing down my emotions, I focused on losing myself in the murder-mystery storyline.

Every day was different, but I tried to convince myself that Aunt Addy was getting better. I would peek over my book and watch her follow the directions as best she could. I would eat cafeteria food, play card games, and reminisce with her, and then I would go back to her house and get sad. Then I'd repeat the process the next day.

Addison Payne radiated light, and seeing her light dim broke my heart.

For the rest of the week, I didn't talk to Aaliyah and Nina outside of a few texts here and there. I didn't talk to Lamar because he was on the trip with his friends. I didn't talk to anyone as I watched my aunt decline in a few days' time.

On Friday morning, as I drove to the rehab center, it hit me that I hadn't heard from Lamar in days. He texted me to let me know he made it, and then a few hours later, he said they were going jet skiing. Unfortunately, I hadn't heard from him since. I knew he was with his friends, and he was under no obligation to keep in contact with me.

*But still.*

**Jazmyn Payne:** I hope you're having a good time! Don't forget to send me pictures from Burj Khalifa!

I squeezed my eyes shut after I sent that text. *Am I doing too much? Is this thirsty?*

He had been on my mind since he dropped me off, and while I was sitting in the car outside the rehab center, I couldn't help but check in with him. My body clenched with desire as the flashbacks hit me in waves, but last night's dream had been the most intense.

I'd initiated conversation because I wanted to talk to him. And while that was reason enough to reach out, selfishly, I also wanted the distraction.

*Even though he hadn't initiated contact since Monday.*

The way I felt about him triggered alarm bells in me. The calmness he provided made me nervous. The comfort he offered made me uncomfortable. The desire he invoked in me made me reckless. He made me feel so good, and *that* made me feel bad.

I was still pondering Lamar's radio silence when I walked into Aunt Addison's hospital room and froze. A doctor and two nurses were gathered around her bed. Nurse Monica was standing off to the side, but she was close enough to hear what was going on. I stood in the doorway with my mouth agape, unable to process what I was seeing.

"Jazmyn," Monica called out to me.

I forced my feet to move in her direction. "Is . . . everything okay?" I asked the room as I focused on my aunt's face.

Her eyes were closed, and she looked peaceful.

*No, she can't be.* My stomach dropped, and I instantly felt faint.

"Ms. Payne is resting," the doctor informed me. "She had an

eventful morning. She got quite spirited during the conversation, and I think she just wore herself out. She closed her eyes maybe three minutes ago, so either it's a nap, or she'll awaken in a couple of minutes. Are you Jazmyn Payne?"

"I am."

The doctor stepped toward me and started to speak. ". . . the two clots . . . thickened heart muscle . . . heart function is at forty-seven . . . no progress . . . keep her comfortable."

I heard him, but I was in a daze.

Monica thanked them as I just continued staring at my aunt, praying she'd wake up in the next couple of minutes.

The doctor and nurses left the room.

"What's going on?" I asked Monica, pulling the chair close to my aunt's bed.

"They were discussing her progress." She sighed loudly. "Or lack thereof."

I gently took Aunt Addy's left hand in mine, and I continued praying she'd wake up.

"She's not responding to physical and occupational therapy, and they've seen a slow decline in her overall functioning. Addison's doctors agree that since she wants to be home and this place isn't helping, we should take her home."

I nodded. "Okay. Will they be coming to the house to do therapies?"

"If she wants that. Apparently, she said she didn't earlier. With her decline, it may be for the best to not force anything."

"So she's on hospice again . . ." I clarified. "For the fourth time."

"Yes. And as always, we're going to make sure she has everything she needs to be comfortable. But she has requested to be in her own home. I tried to explain to her that she can't be home alone in her condition, and she wasn't hearing it." She pushed her glasses up the bridge of her nose. "Is there anyone who can stay with her if she returns home?"

"I can stay for another couple of weeks," I assured her.

*Two more weeks would be mid-July, and I could do that.*

She gave me a tight smile. "From the looks of things, we're thinking she's going to need someone with her for longer. Is there anyone else who could stay until mid-August? I know your parents will be back by then, but is there any other family in Chance?"

There was no one else who could do it. She didn't have any children. I was the only one she'd trust to be there. I was the only one she had.

"I'll do it," I whispered, my eyes welling with tears. "I can stay for the summer."

# 10

Aunt Addison's health had gone downhill around the same time as my marriage, and that seemed to bring us even closer. She began feeling sick, and I started listening to my gut about the man I shouldn't have married, but we persevered. When shit hit the fan in both our lives—she had a cardiac event, and I found out Tyson was cheating—it was in the exact same month. Nothing had been the same from that moment on.

"The only way to keep a man is to get a man who wants to be kept," Aunt Addy said from the recliner in the living room on Wednesday afternoon.

With a laugh, I snapped my fingers and nodded in agreement. "Facts."

After her doctor had ordered a battery of tests to be done before she could leave, Aunt Addy was released from the rehab facility on Sunday afternoon. She'd been home for three days, and she was in much better spirits. She was back to her old self—personality wise.

Physically, she was different.

She got around in a wheelchair for the most part because her left side was weak. But she was still relatively mobile, and with assistance, she could slowly walk short distances—from her bed to the recliner, from the bathroom to the hallway, from the couch to her chair. She kept her arm propped on a pillow or the armrest. Despite those physical changes, her spirit, her joy, and her attitude were quintessentially Addison Payne.

"People who hate themselves will always make you pay for loving them," Aunt Addy warned.

"Preach," I cosigned, amused by the steady stream of life advice that poured out of her.

"Write that down."

I nodded, fully intending to. "You should take all your advice and put it in a book."

She gave me a look. "You should be writing *your* book."

I laughed. "I knew as soon as I opened my mouth that you were going to say that. I started already. I don't have much, but I did start."

She gave me a singular nod. "Good. Now, what's the update with that man? You've been avoiding that subject, too."

I shrugged. "Nothing to avoid. Nothing going on."

She gave me a skeptical look. "I saw that smile on your face last week. That didn't look like nothing."

Amused, I shook my head. "I don't know what you want me to say. It was a date." I pointed at her. "Per the list, I did everything I was supposed to do."

"Per the list, you're supposed to go on *dates*. Plural. Let's not forget the reason we're doing this."

"Let's focus on *your* list. Is tomorrow going to be too much?" I wondered. "I wouldn't have scheduled the spa day on the same day as your hair appointment."

"But the salon had a cancellation and could get us in early. And the spa would've made us pay for a cancellation. And once my hair is done and my nails are done, we can schedule my photoshoot." My aunt nodded. "It'll work out."

I looked at Monica. "But is it too much?"

"I don't think we're changing Addison's mind, so we'll see tomorrow," she answered with a dry laugh.

Aunt Addy and I spent the rest of the evening talking about the photoshoot. I took notes, making sure not to miss a detail. After we ate dinner, Monica helped her with her nighttime routine. And I went to bed thinking about what she'd said about Lamar.

I hadn't heard from him in over a week. It had been days since I'd sent that text. He was supposed to be back on Thursday, and I truly hoped he'd had a great time. But the fact that he hadn't reached out got under my skin.

Even still, waking up to the sound of my aunt cackling put a smile on my face.

"Good morning!" I yelled out.

"I hope I didn't wake you up," she said over the subtle squeak of her wheelchair moving down the hall. "But now that you're up, what do you want for breakfast?"

Sitting up in bed, I tossed the comforter off me. "Bacon, please."

"You always want bacon."

"And do."

I wasn't going to think about Lamar and his return from Dubai. The focus of the day was making Aunt Addison feel special and beautiful. It was our first time knocking something off her list.

"I've heard nothing but good things about Hot Comb," Aunt Addy said as we pulled into the parking lot of the salon. "I've never gone because you know I'm loyal to Liz. But Liz doesn't do color."

"The reviews are outstanding," Monica commented as she parked.

We got Aunt Addy in her wheelchair, and then we entered the reasonably busy salon. I grabbed the door, and Monica wheeled her in.

"Welcome to Hot Comb," a woman greeted us. "Name please?"

"Addison Payne."

"You're here for a coloring appointment." She smiled. "You two can follow me." She turned to me and pointed. "Our waiting area is over here."

Aunt Addy gasped. "Oh! That means I can do a grand reveal."

I laughed as Monica took her back to her stylist. Just when I got comfortable in the waiting area, a woman walked in with the cutest little girl. She looked to be about two years old and had bows all over her short hair. With a huge smile, the little girl toddled right up to me as if she knew me.

"Well, hello," I greeted the little one.

"I'm sorry!" The woman who I presumed was her mother strolled up to us.

"It's fine. She's so cute," I remarked as the little girl touched my knee.

"My daughter thinks every Black woman with locs is my sister," she said with a little laugh.

When I opened my palm, the little girl started patting it. I looked up at her mother, and her smile faltered.

Confusion and shock puckered her face. "Jazmyn Payne?"

My brows creased. I had no idea who she was. "We know each other?"

She sat in the seat next to me. "No, not really. I mean, my name is Decca." She gestured down her plump body. "I, um . . . look different than I did back then, but we, um . . . we went to high school together."

"Oh." With pursed lips, I just stared back at her.

"I never knew what happened to you," she said softly. "I wondered for years. I even searched for you on social media."

I was intentionally hard to find online because I didn't want anyone from Chance or any of my students to find me on the internet. But I was surprised and curious as to why someone I'd had no interactions with would be looking for me.

"Why?" I asked aloud.

Her daughter climbed into her lap and started humming. Decca glanced at her and then back at me. "I used to see you around school and the library. I thought how they treated you and what they used to say about you was really messed up. Whenever I'd see you in the library, I always thought about inviting you to my book club or just . . . saying hi."

Sitting back in the chair, I maintained eye contact. "So why didn't you?"

She was quiet, and a flicker of shame crossed her face. "Because I didn't want to go through what you went through. I didn't want to lose the little social capital I had. I was lanky and awkward and kind of shy. I didn't have many friends, and I didn't want to lose the ones I had. So it was easier to just not . . ."

My brows furrowed. "It was easier to just not say anything?"

She nodded. "It was easier to do nothing than to stand up for you or offer you friendship. Especially after that flyer thing. I always wanted to apologize for never doing what I knew was right. Because I *am* sorry. And you didn't deserve that."

"Decca, your stylist is ready," the woman from the front announced before I could respond.

With a small smile, Decca gave me a nod as she scooped up her daughter. She walked away, and for the next few minutes, I thought about what she'd said. Being a social pariah because of something I did would've been one thing. But it being based on a lie, jealousy, and a group of mean girls with a vendetta was maddening. To finally hear someone admit that they had seen what was happening, known it was wrong, and distanced themselves from me anyway was truly disheartening.

*I hate it here.*

Ninety minutes later, Monica came out to get me. "Addison and the stylist hit it off. They didn't stop talking this whole time."

I grinned. "That's good! She makes a friend wherever she goes."

"Come see her hair."

Standing, I said, "Lead the way."

I followed her down the hall and around a wall. It opened to a large styling room with six stations. My eyes zeroed in on the wheelchair sitting next to the station on the far right. I couldn't see my aunt. I could see only the back of the stylist.

"I can't believe we haven't met before. But I'm glad you have my number now," the stylist was saying as we walked toward them.

"And we'll have to get together soon. Because I *will* be at that jazz festival in a few weeks."

"I know that's right!"

My aunt sounded like her old self, and that put the biggest smile on my face.

*She's going to be okay*, I told myself.

"We're here and we're ready," Monica called out as we approached.

"Presenting to you, the new and improved Addison Payne," the stylist announced as she spun the chair around.

My aunt's long locs were such a vibrant blue. I couldn't take my eyes off them. She was always so creative and stylish, but dyeing her hair such a bright color was one of the coolest things she'd done.

"I love it!" I couldn't stop staring as I got closer. "You look so good!"

"Jazmyn?!" the stylist exclaimed.

When I looked over, I saw a familiar face and a fantastic bob. "Mrs. Brooks?!"

"You know my niece?" Aunt Addison asked with a huge grin.

"I met her a couple of weeks ago when she stopped by my house with my son."

My aunt's head whipped around. "Your son is Lamar!"

The two of them squealed and started talking at the same time as my stomach dropped. My face flushed with embarrassment at their excitement.

Aunt Addy knew that he was out of town, but she didn't know he'd ignored me for almost his entire ten-day vacation.

"He's in Dubai, right?" she asked, even though she already knew.

I stared daggers at her. *Girl, what is you doing?*

Mrs. Brooks didn't miss a beat. "Yes, and he gets back today. I only talked to him once the whole time he's been gone." She shook her head and then turned my aunt to see her reflection in the mirror. "He lost his phone while jet skiing! My husband's birthday was a couple days ago, so he called to say happy birthday from his friend's phone. Fortunately, he was able to order a new phone, and it'll be waiting for him when he gets home today." While Monica was assisting my aunt back into her wheelchair, Mrs. Brooks turned to me. "It is so funny running into you like this!"

"When you mentioned Hot Comb, I didn't realize you worked here. I just liked your hair, and when I checked the reviews online, I knew I needed to get my aunt in for her color."

She smiled, tilting her head to the side. "I knew I liked you."

"She's a wonderful woman," Aunt Addy complimented.

"I believe that," Mrs. Brooks agreed with a smirk. "Lamar never brings women home, so she must be."

Everyone was staring at me.

I had no idea what to say. Heat crept up my neck as the seconds passed.

"Gwen, your one o'clock is here," someone called from behind me.

"We have to get to our next appointment anyway," Aunt Addy stated, before reaching out to take Mrs. Brooks's hand. "Gwen, it was so nice talking to you today."

"It's been my pleasure. And don't forget about me with the jazz festival. I'd love for us to do that."

"It's a plan. Talk to you soon."

We said our goodbyes, paid for services, and then climbed in the van. The moment Monica pulled out of the parking spot, the two of them started questioning me about Lamar.

"You made it seem like you met his mother in passing," Aunt Addy cried, looking at me giddily. "But the way she reacted made it seem like you two spent some time together! Like her son was introducing her to someone special in his life."

I stared out the window so I could avoid the way she was looking at me. "I spent five minutes with her. And she was just being kind. Lamar and I are friends."

"So you've been on two dates with him, and he already introduced you to his mother?" Monica asked. "That doesn't sound like 'just friends' to me."

My aunt sucked her teeth. "She claims that first date wasn't a date, but you should've seen the way her face was lit up talking about their outing."

Monica slowed to a stop. "I always think that if you meet people who light you up, they are worth keeping around."

"And you get along with his mother." Aunt Addy made a humming noise. "Match made in heaven."

I shook my head. "Are you two done? This is too much!"

They just laughed.

We went to the spa and spent the afternoon getting a massage, facial, manicure, and pedicure. Between the hair appointment and the spa day, we were starving. We stopped at a fast-food restaurant to pick up an early dinner and then headed back to the house.

"Let's eat in front of the TV so we can relax a little more," Aunt Addy suggested.

We agreed without hesitation, and the three of us got set up in the living room. I knew it was more comfortable for her to be in her recliner. As hungry as I was, my food was going to be finished in no time, so I didn't care where we ate.

"This is delicious," my aunt gushed.

"Yes, indeed," Monica replied.

I nodded as I popped a fry into my mouth.

When we were done, we were all exhausted.

"I'll clean up," I announced, grabbing the trash from everyone. "I'm going to take a shower, and then I'll be back."

"Thank you, Jazz."

I showered, put on my pajamas, and then walked in on Aunt Addison and Monica cackling over a reality TV show.

"Oh! I just noticed my phone has been on silent all day," Aunt Addy told us as Monica helped her into the wheelchair.

I went to the kitchen to throw everything in the trash, and I heard Rose's voice coming from her voicemail. Aunt Addy checked her messages on speakerphone, and I laughed to myself as her best friend accused her of being a harlot because of the book she suggested for their book club. The next couple of voicemails were from other friends. The fourth was from the rehab facility to schedule an outpatient home visit. The fifth message was her doctor's office, reminding her of her appointment tomorrow. As I was walking through the living room, the next voicemail stopped me in my tracks.

*"Hello, Ms. Payne. How're you doing? I know this is a bit unusual, but my name is Lamar Anderson. You met my mother, Gwendolyn Brooks, at her salon this morning, and I hope you don't mind, but she gave me your number. I lost my phone in Dubai, and I lost everything in it—including your niece's number. My number is the same, so if you could please ask her to call me, I would appreciate it. Thank you."*

My heart thumped in my chest, and I stared at her phone as if looking hard enough would make him appear. The message ended, and it switched to another message from Rose, but I didn't hear a word. I couldn't stop thinking about the message from Lamar.

And they couldn't stop talking about it.

"I'm going to my room," I announced, backing out of the living room.

"I know what you better be doing," Aunt Addy teased. "Calling Lamar!"

"Oh absolutely!" Monica chimed in.

I shook my head and closed the bedroom door behind me.

Taking a deep breath, I called Lamar.

"Hello?" he answered on the second ring.

"Hi. It's Jazz."

"Jazz." His smile was evident. "It's good to hear your voice."

There was a slight flutter in my belly, and my lips curled upward. "It's good to hear yours, too."

"How are you? Last I heard, you were getting your ass kicked in gin rummy."

I let out a loud laugh. "First of all, I wasn't getting my ass kicked. I lost with dignity. And my aunt has almost three decades of experience on me. Second of all, that's very rude."

"How is it rude to point out the facts? Didn't you say she had just beaten you three times in a row? That's what kicking ass looks like."

"See, now you're just using things I've told you against me, and I don't like that."

He let out a deep chuckle. "Well, I don't want to do anything that you don't like."

I reclined back against my pillows and ignored the innuendo in his tone and how it made me feel. "Is that right?"

"The only reason you haven't heard from me is because my phone is in the ocean. I forgot I had it in my pocket, and I hit that wave . . ." He made a noise in the back of his throat. "I didn't even realize I'd lost it until we were heading back to the hotel. I went to text you the itinerary, and I realized I'd lost that shit."

"You were gonna text me the trip itinerary?"

"Yeah. You told me before I left that you wanted pictures from the Burj Khalifa, and when I saw the itinerary Erickson's fiancée put together, I wanted you to know when to expect them."

Warmth spread through my body, and I paused briefly before I commented, "I love that Erickson's fiancée put together an itinerary. Did y'all do it all?"

"Yes. Every single thing on that list. It was cool though. Apparently, she'd been putting together a list of all the things he'd mentioned he wanted to do over the last couple years, and that's what we did. He was surprised. He loved it."

"That's so sweet. That's . . . I love that."

"Yeah. He's been through a lot, so this was a long time coming. We had a good time. And I was mad that I lost my phone. Not just for everything that was in it, but because I wanted to hit you up. I thought about you . . . a lot."

"Really?" I grinned. "What about?"

"Everything. I thought about what you said about my business plan. I thought about how cool you are. I thought about how much fun it is to be with you. I thought about how you . . . Just know you were on my mind a lot."

I bit my bottom lip just imagining how he'd wanted to complete that other sentence. "I'm glad to hear it. You crossed my mind a time or two. I was hoping you were enjoying yourself and wondering what you were doing while you were traipsing around the UAE." I smiled. "It's funny, every time I've gone out with you, you've managed to make me forget I was in Chance."

"That's a good thing?"

"That's a real good thing."

"Good. Speaking of Chance, I thought you were heading back to Maryland last week. What made you stay another week?"

"My aunt . . ." Clearing my throat lightly, I rolled onto my side. "And I'm going to be here for longer than anticipated."

"You good?"

My stomach knotted. "In Chance, nothing is good," I joked, sidestepping the question. "But I'll be here for a minute."

He snickered. "Well, what's a minute?"

"August."

"August?!"

"Yeah. My parents get back from Florida in August."

"Oh. Okay. Hm." He seemed to be contemplating something. "That's going to make things a little more complicated."

"How?"

"I start training camp on Monday, and then right after that it's the preseason. I thought you were going to be in Maryland. Richland is about an hour from Baltimore. It would've been easier to carve out some time to see you. But with you in Chance . . . damn."

"That's six hours," I pointed out. "On a good day with no traffic."

"Exactly." He exhaled loudly. "This isn't how I thought this conversation was going to go."

"What were you thinking?"

"I was thinking your aunt was going to call you and tell you to call me. You were going to be at home, reading or running through football schemes."

I laughed as he kept going.

"And I was going to ask if you had plans this weekend because I wanted to see you—I *want* to see you."

"And I want to be seen." I hesitated. "By you, if I didn't make it clear."

He chuckled lightly. "This is what I'm talking about. This is why I like you. You're funny and different and . . . not boring at all. I was hoping to spend some time with you."

"To do what exactly?"

There was a pause. "Anything you want."

I inhaled sharply, squeezing my thighs together.

The sexy tone of his voice as he said it was intoxicating. I closed my eyes and let it replay in my mind two more times before I spoke.

"Anything?" I replied.

"Come on, Jazmyn, you know that you can get anything you want from me."

When he'd said it a couple of weeks ago, it had sounded friendly. When he'd said it just now, it had sounded like a sexual invitation.

"Lamar," I sighed, shaking my head. "Don't you try to seduce me."

He chuckled lightly. "I should be saying that to you! You gave me a taste, and now you're gone for the summer."

His words sent shock waves through my entire body.

"I'm exactly where you left me," I said softly.

He made a noise, and I couldn't take it. I had to change the subject.

"I saw your mom today," I blurted out.

I knew I'd killed the vibe from his silence followed by the way he stammered.

"Y-yeah, um, yeah, she told me," he sputtered.

"She suggested Hot Comb, but she didn't tell me she works there. My aunt wanted to get her hair dyed, I looked up the place and the reviews were amazing."

"She co-owns it with her business partner."

"Oh, that's cool."

We talked for most of the night about his trip, my time with Aunt Addy, and our reviews of each other's book. The conversation was fun and flirtatious but never teetered on sexual again. We laughed a lot, and when we finally said good night, I had a smile on my face.

When I woke up, I was home alone with a text from my aunt.

> **Addison Payne:** I took an earlier doctor's appointment, and I didn't want to wake you. Let me know if you need anything. Be back by ten o'clock.

I showered and dressed for a chill day of games, movies, and conversation. I was just finishing my breakfast when I heard the front door open.

"You said you wanted a movie day," I yelled out as I finished washing my dishes. "I've picked out two movies. I hope you picked out yours." I turned when they entered the kitchen. "Because it's been . . ." My eyes bounced between the two of them. "Everything okay?"

"Yes," Aunt Addy answered, before pointing to Monica. "We got popcorn and candy."

I knew something was off, but I didn't push it right then and there. I figured I would follow up after we got settled in for the movie.

When Aunt Addy went to the bathroom, I turned to Monica. "What's going on?" I asked in a low tone.

"The tests came back, and she's declining. All we can do is make her comfortable," she answered quietly.

I glanced in the direction of the hallway. "Outside of the effects of the stroke, she seems fine."

She gave me a sympathetic look. "I know."

I was confused, mostly because I didn't want to understand what she was saying.

Monica left an hour later.

When Aunt Addy and I were alone, she waited until a commercial break to turn to me. "I love you."

I reached over and grabbed her hand, giving it a firm squeeze. "I love you, too."

"I think I can get my list done by the end of July."

"Three weeks is pushing it."

She held my gaze before she spoke. "I need to get my list done by the end of July. Let's make it happen."

The seriousness in her expression made my eyes water, and I nodded. "Let's make it happen."

# 11

**Lamar Anderson:** I know this is last minute, but what if you met me in Richmond tomorrow? It's the halfway point between us and I'd like to see you before work gets crazy.

I stared at the message before closing my eyes and remembering what it was like to be with him, next to him, around him. I took a minute to remember his kiss, his touch, his dick. I allowed myself to get lost in how everything disappeared around him.

*I could really use that right now.*

**Jazmyn Payne:** I'd love to see you tomorrow, but I can't. I'm sorry.

**Lamar Anderson:** No, it's cool. It was a long shot.

**Jazmyn Payne:** My aunt and I just finished making all these plans.

I stopped typing as the weight of everything started to crush me.

**Lamar Anderson:** I get how it is when you're visiting with family. Just hit me up when you get some time. You've been on my mind a lot and so I thought I'd toss it out there.

**Jazmyn Payne:** I'll call when I can. I do miss you.

**Lamar Anderson:** I miss you, too. And even if we can't link up, I hope we get a minute to talk.

I didn't have a response as tears filled my eyes all over again. Shaking my head, I put my phone down. I wasn't in a good space.

Aunt Addison's health issues weren't unfamiliar territory nor was her being on hospice. Usually, I kept my tears to myself and processed her illness away from her. But as I listened to her accept that she had less than six months to live, I was thrust into new territory. We spent the weekend planning out her July schedule as if she wouldn't make it into August, and it took a toll on me.

"It feels like you're giving up," I told her after lunch on Sunday.

"Jazmyn, sweetheart," she started, reaching for my hand. "This is it."

"You can keep fighting. You told me to never stop fighting for myself. Never stop fighting for what I want. Never stop fighting—period."

She tipped her head to the side and stared at me with watery eyes. "And I want you to hold on to that." She squeezed my hand. "Fight for what you want, fight for what's right, fight for *you* . . . because you matter. So much. So, so much, Jazmyn. Fight and keep fighting."

"That's what I need you to do," I said, weeping.

"My heart has been failing for the last few years, but I fought because I had the fight in me. I did what I needed to do, and I defied the odds because I knew in my soul it wasn't my time." She let out a shaky breath. "And now my soul is telling me that this is the end of the line for me."

My chin dropped to my chest. "I don't understand."

"Jazmyn, this isn't like the other times when they didn't know if I'd survive the surgeries or the recoveries or the complications. This isn't me giving up. This is me knowing." She paused. "I know."

Just hearing the clarity and certainty in her voice forced my head up and made me lock eyes with her.

"Here's something I want you to remember about fighting," she verbalized earnestly. "You have to know when to stop. You ask yourself if it's worth the fight. If it is, you fight. If you feel it in your heart, your soul, your bones, you fight. But if you don't . . ." She shook her head. "Then stop." She paused as if she were waiting to make sure the message had sunk in with me. "Fighting for yourself also looks like letting things go."

A fresh wave of tears streamed down my face as I silently looked at her. For the first time all weekend, I truly heard what she was saying, and I couldn't stop crying if I tried.

"I'm scared," I choked out.

"I'm not. Faith over fear. We have faith in God's plan, and we don't let fear control us."

"I'm not ready for you to . . ." I couldn't even complete the sentence.

"I'm at peace with it," she assured me. "You need to be at peace with it, too."

"I can't lose you," I said through sobs.

"Sweetheart, you're not losing me. Everything I am, I poured into you."

We spent the rest of the day together, watching her favorite show. When I woke up Monday morning, I was in a different headspace. I'd heard my aunt, and I'd needed to sleep on her words. I didn't feel *better* but I felt a sense of understanding. My heart hurt because I didn't want to be without her. I cried because I was going to miss her. But after everything Addison Payne had done for me in my thirty years, I refused to not do everything I could for her.

> **Aaliyah James:** Hey Jazz, how are you? I know you have a lot going on but call me and let me know how you're doing. You haven't been answering calls, and I want to hear your voice. We miss you!

> **Nina Ford:** In case you needed a laugh, this old man approached me and said I looked like I smelled like cookies and cakes, and I told him he looked like he smelled like frankincense & myrrh. Love you!

> **Lamar Anderson:** I know it's been a while. Training camp is kicking my ass. But I came across a couple of people I might approach about working with me. I emailed you their names and bios just to get your thoughts.

I'd figured training camps were tough, but I'd assumed the coaching staff, trainers, and those in support roles had it easier than the players. It made sense that everyone had to go hard during camp because football truly was a team effort. But I had never considered how intense it would be for everyone involved.

Even still, I didn't text him back.

I didn't text Aaliyah or Nina back either.

It was hard enough to process my aunt dying, but there was no way I was going to be able to talk about it. And I didn't have time to dwell in my sadness or distract myself from what was happening. I had too much to do, and I needed to embrace and appreciate the time I had with Aunt Addy. The only thing she wanted to plan by herself was the party. Everything else, she left in my hands.

So, when I wasn't writing my novel, I was working on the items on my aunt's list.

The book club meeting was scheduled for the first of August because that would allow three weeks for people to read. Rose helped Aunt Addy spread the word, and I loved watching the two of them together. Their relationship reminded me that the love between friends wasn't just powerful—it was medicinal.

"No," Monica said definitively, pushing her glasses up the bridge of her nose. "I do not advise you to get a tattoo. There's too much risk involved. Absolutely not."

Aunt Addison looked up at her incredulously. "Risk?"

"The risk for infection for people in your condition . . ." She shook her head. "Addison, no. Endocarditis is serious, and it could—"

"Kill me?" she interrupted, making a face. "I'm dying whether I get the tattoo or not. So I'm getting a tattoo."

They were fussing back and forth in their typical playful way, but they were both serious. Their relationship reminded me that the care and consideration between friends is vital.

"What if we do the tattoo at the end of the month?" I suggested as a compromise. "We're doing the book club meeting the first of August. Why don't we get it on July thirty-first?"

Aunt Addy nodded. "I can agree to that."

The photoshoot was scheduled almost immediately, and since she had lost a few more pounds, she insisted on going shopping to find a new dress. After twelve stores and almost four hours at the mall, she found three dresses she loved, shoes she'd never wear, and a handbag just because.

"Never let unpleasant circumstances keep you from enjoying life," Aunt Addy said as she examined the bag. "Treat yourself."

I thought about that advice for the next couple of hours.

"I still think this white one looks bridal," I commented when we got back to her house and I hung up her dresses.

"I'm going to wear these two for the photos." Aunt Addy pointed to the blue-and-purple dress and the black dress. "The white one I'm saving."

"Saving for what?"

She winked. "You'll see."

"I like that the blue-and-purple dress goes so well with your hair!" Monica commented.

And it really did.

During the photoshoot, Aunt Addison looked radiant. There was only one time when she looked like she was getting weak, but the photographer was so good with her.

"And that's it," the photographer concluded with a big smile. "That was great, Addison. You will have these back in two weeks."

I helped her into her wheelchair as she peppered him with questions.

"You'll be able to hang these beauties up in your home no later than the first week of August," he continued.

As they finalized things and shook hands, I caught the tail end of the conversation.

". . . we will see you out there in a couple weeks," Aunt Addy said to him with a wave.

I waited until we got outside to ask, "Where will we be seeing him? When we pick up the prints?"

"He's going to be at the jazz festival!"

As per the schedule we had created, we'd knock something off her list and then take a day or two to rest in between. On those days we'd talk, we'd tend to her garden, we'd take walks, and we'd play games. Her energy didn't seem to be depleting, and she didn't seem any sicker than she had before. But there was a sacredness to those moments that reminded me that time was a luxury.

It was a reminder to not take one minute for granted.

When I took her to the botanical gardens that Lamar had taken me to, we had a picnic. It was the perfect temperature, and Aunt Addy wanted to see the flowers. We were only halfway through our

Philly cheesesteaks when an unexpected storm moved over us. I was pushing Aunt Addy in her wheelchair, and Monica decided to get the van so she could pull up to the front. But in her haste, she slipped and fell in a puddle.

I tried not to laugh, but Aunt Addy kept crying out, "Lawd have mercy!"

By the time we made it to the van, we were all soaking wet.

It was quiet when we first climbed in. I had tears in my eyes from holding in my amusement.

"I busted my ass," Monica blurted out.

"You sure did! Now, Monica, if you need to take a minute and let your knees rest, let's do that," Aunt Addy joked.

I was weak.

We laughed the entire way home.

"I've always wanted to have a picnic," Aunt Addy told us with a contented sigh.

"I'm sorry it didn't go as planned," I said sympathetically.

She turned to look at me. "It was better than planned. It was picture-perfect, and then the rain came, and I haven't laughed this hard in ages. Made it memorable in a different way." She relaxed against the headrest. "I don't think it could've gone better."

Two days after that, we were still laughing about Monica's fall. We were telling Rose about it while in the lobby of the spa.

"Welcome to your first yoni steam," a woman greeted us, after reading our paperwork. "A yoni steam is a cleanse for your vagina and uterus. The benefits include"—she looked at me—"balancing hormones, detoxification of the uterus"—she looked at Rose—"fewer headaches, stress and depression relief"—she looked at Aunt Addy—"increased energy, and overall pain relief. The vagina is a self-cleaning organ, so this yoni steam isn't about *cleaning*. It's about *cleansing*."

I looked at Aunt Addy. *What the hell do you have us doing?*

When it was my turn to squat over a bowl of plant-based herbs in a room covered in beautiful drapery and crystals, I had that same thought running through my head again.

*This is some wild-ass shit.*

When our sessions concluded, we waited for Monica to pick us up.

"It's been a while since I've had that much action," Rose joked, causing us all to laugh.

When we climbed into the van, Monica kept looking at us and shaking her head. "You know there are no medical benefits to getting a yoni steam, and in fact, you could hurt yourself if you're not careful."

I smiled, listening to Monica lecture Aunt Addy and Rose while the two of them made jokes like teenagers in the car with their parents.

"I've hurt myself squatting over more dangerous things," Aunt Addy quipped. "I'll be fine."

"My first husband didn't have medical benefits, but I let him blow off steam between my legs," Rose added with a giggle.

"The two of you are exhausting," Monica complained good-naturedly. "I hope it's not going to be like this at the drive-in this weekend."

"It'll be worse," the two women said in unison.

And they weren't lying.

The horror movie they were showing at the dilapidated drive-in theater wasn't anything Aunt Addy particularly wanted to see. But it was the only film they were showing, so Aunt Addy called a bunch of her friends and created a drinking game.

"Anytime someone falls down, we drink," she instructed.

And we did.

The entire group had this youthful energy about them, but their ages ranged from forty-five to seventy-five.

My aunt's friend winked at me. "When you really live, age ain't nothing but a number."

"I know that's right!" Aunt Addy chimed in, and the two cackled.

I looked around at everyone hugging Aunt Addy before leaving. Having a network of people was important, but having close friends who showed up for you when you needed them was everything.

*She's blessed.*

I loved watching my aunt interact with her friends. But I had to admit that it made me miss my best friends. I'd been so consumed with my time with Aunt Addy that I hadn't talked to Nina and Aaliyah. Watching my aunt's friend open the door for his wife reminded me that I hadn't really talked to Lamar either.

But I'd been working on his business plan.

Twice a week he'd update our shared document with notes, and in turn, in the middle of the night, I'd read the updates, respond, and make comments of my own. In his business plan, I didn't feel any guilt for communicating with him. I was helping a friend while my aunt was resting. There was no harm in that.

We didn't have phone conversations.

We had his business plan.

We exchanged letter-like commentary on how to make his passion project the best it could be. Sometimes our remarks were funny, but most of the time it was serious, and I was deeply impressed by how smart, how dedicated, and how inspiring he was. But it was the summary that I'd anticipate the most. The way he shared himself and his reason for the update compelled me to share mine. Even without conversing, I felt like I knew him better.

Jazz, let me know what you think about the addendum to the financial literacy piece. My mom and stepdad were the ones who taught me, but I realized in college that everyone didn't get the same lessons. This one time . . .

Lamar, splitting the classes up so credit, investments, and taxes are not quick financial footnotes, but actual separate courses is smart. I learned the hard way about taxes when I had my first job at the library and that little check wasn't what I thought it was going to be . . .

Jazz, I think you're right. The addition of a professional development course is necessary. The better you are as an athlete, the more you're given and the less work you have to do. Everything becomes about the sport and that's it. My mom wasn't playing that, so I had to make a plan for life after football. Back in high school . . .

Lamar, when I was in high school, I spent so much time lost in a book or in boxing classes, one of the librarians worried I didn't know how to talk to people. She came out to the gazebo and suggested a communications class . . .

Jazz, another by-product of being a star athlete is that sometimes they get away with talking to people any kind of way. My homeboy got sucker punched one night . . .

I felt closer to him than ever, but I hadn't heard his voice in weeks.

"What's going on with you and that boy?" Aunt Addy asked as we headed back to her house. "I can't think of his name."

"Lamar," Monica answered.

With wide eyes, I looked between the backs of their heads. *Was it that obvious I was thinking about him?*

"Nothing's going on," I replied with a shrug. "We're friends."

"The way he was on my voicemail begging for you to call him and the way you ran to your room to make the call sounds like more than friendship to me," Aunt Addy teased before giggling.

I stared out the window. "It's not like that. We're still friends though."

They let the subject go.

But once we were in the house and Monica had gone home for the night, Aunt Addy called me into her room.

"What's really going on with you and Lamar?" she asked me from underneath her covers.

The question was unexpected.

"Nothing," I replied, lifting my shoulders. "He's busy. I'm busy. But we're friends. I'm helping him with his business plan."

"But you want to be more."

I shifted from one foot to the other. "Actually, I want to go to sleep."

She let out a light laugh. "Good night."

"Good night, Aunt Addy."

I thought about that conversation as I pulled out my laptop and looked over the shared document and the changes Lamar had made. I laughed to myself as I read the note he'd added to one of my suggestions.

*He's so funny*, I thought with a grin.

I wasn't sure if it was because of my aunt's comments or the jokes he'd made in the document, but when I saw Lamar's mom at the jazz festival the following weekend, I got nervous.

I hadn't been nervous when I met her.

I hadn't been nervous when I saw her at Hot Comb.

But when Gwen and her husband, Bill, approached our section at the festival, all I could think about was her asking me about her son. There were twenty of us in the section, and I didn't want to be put on the spot in front of Aunt Addy's friends and their dates.

Gwen immediately came over and gave me a hug. When she stepped back, she gestured to her husband. "Bill, this is Jazmyn," Gwen introduced. "She's the one Lamar brought home last month."

"Oh yeah! Hey, nice to meet you," Bill said, shaking my hand. "I've heard nothing but good things."

And that was the last mention of Lamar.

The artist lineup was stacked, so we spent most of the time singing and dancing to the music. I walked around the festival, taking everything in, and then, when I saw a group of similarly aged people staring my way, I immediately turned around.

I didn't know who they were, but as soon as the hair on the back of my neck had stood up and my stomach had lurched, I'd known I wasn't safe. For the sake of my aunt, I'd spent more time in and around Chance than I had my entire senior year. With my jaw clenched and my blood boiling, I took the long way back to my aunt and her friends so I could shake off the negative energy.

*Fuck those people. Fuck this town. I'm here for Aunt Addy. Nothing else matters*, I reminded myself as I headed back to the group.

As I approached, I noticed my aunt grimacing when no one was looking. When she caught sight of me, she flashed me a bright smile.

"Are you okay?" I wondered.

"I'm good, I'm good. But I'm ready to go," Aunt Addy told me. "But feel free to stay. I don't want to rush you."

"These are songs from your youth, not mine!" I assured her. "I'm good."

My aunt's head fell back as she laughed. "Jazmyn!"

Aunt Addy, Monica, and I said our goodbyes to everyone.

"I like you more and more each time I see you," Gwen stated, giving me a big hug.

"I feel the same way," I returned.

It was easy for me to see where Lamar got his kindness. It was hard for me to remember why I had been nervous and why I'd thought it would be awkward. Lamar had barely been mentioned.

Until we climbed in the van.

"You get along well with your in-laws," Aunt Addy joked.

"Haha," I replied dryly. "Lamar and I are friends."

When Monica got out of the car at the gas station to fill up the tank, Aunt Addy turned around and looked at me. "You're friends?" she asked skeptically.

"We're friends."

"Does he know that?"

My eyebrows flew up. "Ye-yeah," I stammered. "What? Why?"

*Did his mom say something?*

"Just thinking about the way he sounded on my voicemail *begging* for you to call him."

"Oh." I swallowed hard. "He was just . . ." I couldn't think of anything to explain it away. "We're friends."

She tilted her head to the side. "Is that what you want?"

"I enjoy having him in my life."

"Jazmyn . . ." She paused, eyeing me carefully. "That sounds like a cop-out."

"It would be too complicated."

"That sounds like an excuse, not an answer."

"I don't—I'm not—I—" I sputtered, unsure of how to even respond to that. "It's not an excuse."

"I saw you after your dates. I heard you after that phone call. Seems to me like you wanted more." She gave me a look. "Seems like it *was* more."

I looked down at my hands. "Well, everything is not necessarily what it seems." I raised my head and continued. "And I'm still figuring things out."

She stared at me silently for a moment; a sympathetic expression crossed her face. "Are you figuring out what you want, or do you know what you want and are afraid to stand in it?"

# 12

Aunt Addy stared at her African violet tattoo on the inside of her wrist. "I love it."

I held out my arm next to hers to showcase my temporary tattoo that matched her real one. "It's so cute," I agreed.

"I still can't believe you did that yesterday," Monica complained, shaking her head.

"I can't believe you haven't finished the book! The meeting is in a couple hours, and I know you haven't made it to the end yet."

"I'm almost done," Monica replied. "If I weren't up worrying about you and this risky behavior—"

"Risky behavior?!" My aunt balked. "I got a tattoo. If you think I've never noticed that lower-back tattoo you have, you'd be mistaken." She looked at me. "Monica has a little . . . what do they call it? A slag tag? A tramp stamp?"

I laughed out loud. "Yeah, a *long* time ago, they called those tramp stamps. I've never even heard of a slag tag."

"It was something I heard when I was living abroad," my aunt quickly explained.

Monica turned around and lifted her scrubs to show off a butterfly with expansive wings. "Leave my tramp stamp alone! I was twenty-one when I got this, and it still looks pretty good."

"It looks great!" Aunt Addy exclaimed. "But you can't talk about my little flower when you got your whole lower back covered."

She turned back around and put her hands on her hips. "It's not my whole back. And you have some nerve calling me a tramp when your book club pick started with sex on the first page! I mean, really! What kind of mess is that?"

Aunt Addy pursed her lips. "And I see you kept reading."

"I sure did!"

They cackled, and all I could do was shake my head.

When we arrived at the library a little later, it was evident that if Monica hadn't finished the book, she wouldn't have been alone.

"Wow," I breathed, looking at the turnout.

More than fifty people who either knew my aunt or knew about the book club had shown up. Only about thirty-five of them had read the whole book, but everyone participated in an amazing discussion. The bakery that provided refreshments was a hit. The photographer donated a thirty-minute headshot session, and Lamar's mom donated a gift card to Hot Comb as door prizes. After three hours, the library told us we had to shut it down and everyone begrudgingly left.

"Excuse me, Ms. Payne," the petite librarian with the tiny afro called out. "This was such a big hit. Would you consider doing this again every other month? We would love to make this a regular thing."

My aunt's smile grew even though she shifted uncomfortably in her chair. "I would love to have this be a regular thing. Is there someone who could take lead in case I'm unable to do it?"

The librarian shifted her eyes to me. "You're Jazmyn Payne, right? You're the one I worked with to set this up?"

I nodded. "Yes."

"Would you be willing to do it?" She put her hands together in prayer form. "Please. We could meet next month to get things started."

"No, I don't live here, and I'm leaving before the month is out," I answered.

"What about you?" Aunt Addy questioned the librarian. "Would you be able to do it?"

Her face lit up. "I'd love to! Just let me know what you need."

They exchanged information, and then the librarian turned to me.

"Jazmyn, I just need you to sign some paperwork. But can I show you something first? It'll take five minutes."

"Yeah," I told her. Turning to Aunt Addy and Monica, I could see she was uncomfortable in her chair. "I'll meet you two in the van," I told them.

I followed the librarian to the back of the library. As we took the same route that I'd taken all those years ago, a sad smile pulled at my lips at the memory.

*It's too bad they—*

"When you called to schedule this book club meeting, I knew your name sounded familiar," she said, interrupting my thoughts. "And then, when you said you were leaving soon, I knew I needed to show you this before you left town." She pushed open the back door. "You're the first of the public to see it."

My hands flew to my face, and I gasped. "The gazebo!"

Bigger and better, the structure was at least twice the size of the one before it.

"After they finish painting it, we're going to announce the grand opening in time for this upcoming school year," she said excitedly.

"This is beautiful."

She nodded. "It's much nicer than the one we originally were going to go with, but with the money we received, we were able to really make it special. We were told that this was your favorite spot in Chance."

"It was." I looked around in awe. "It's beautiful."

"Now, hopefully, this will be enough to get you back for the next book club meeting!"

We laughed.

Heading back inside, we stopped by the information desk so I could sign the paperwork to confirm that we'd left the space the way we found it. I thanked the librarians and other workers for their help in making the event a success, and then I left.

"And when Barbara said . . ." Aunt Addy was midstory when I climbed inside the van.

I listened to her excitement as she relayed the whole conversation to Monica. Hearing the happiness in her voice struck a chord in me, and my eyes watered. Blinking back tears, I wanted to commit the sound of her glee, the sound of her laugh, the sound of her joy to memory.

We made it back to her house, and we were sitting down for dinner an hour later. She still had that well-earned, self-satisfied smile on her face.

"I'm proud of you," I told her. "That was a really good turnout."

"Yes, it was," she said, her smile growing. "And the library keeping it going is . . ." She nodded. "That's a blessing."

"It is. All my life I've seen you do things like that. You decide you want to do something, and you just do it. And every single time, it ends up being epic."

"Your legacy is in your impact." She tapped the table as she said it. "And I want to make sure I leave mine in everything and everywhere I can."

I stretched across the table to put my hand on her hand. "You've done that and so much more."

"Everything I've ever done with my life has left a mark, has left *my* mark." She paused, taking a deep breath. Her eyes were watery but bright, like happy tears were forming. "I lived my life. I left my mark. And I'm very happy with that."

"I'm happy that you're happy."

She gave me a soft smile. "Jazmyn, I want the same for you. I want you to be happy. I want you to leave your mark. And I want you to live your life."

"I am. I will," I whispered, choking up. "I will."

"I love you."

"I love you, too." Trying not to cry, I changed the subject. "When are you going to let me in on your party plans? It's the last thing on your list."

"You'll get the invitation with everyone else when it's time," she answered coyly. "I want your parents to be here for it."

"I thought you wanted to knock everything out by now."

"Everything but the party. That's coming." She tilted her head to the side. "You've made sure that I got through my list. Now it's time to get through yours."

"I know. I am." I lifted my wrist. "I've mapped out my tattoo."

"Do you remember why I asked you to do this?"

As I studied the seriousness in her face, I put my arm down and my eyes started stinging. "Yeah."

"Honoring who you were and acknowledging who you are . . . it informs who you're going to be. On the other side of this list is your fire."

I nodded, unable to speak.

"You go back home in three weeks," she reminded me gently. "You go back to work a few days after that. I want us to focus on your list. I want to focus on you for the rest of your time here."

"And I want to focus on *you* . . ."—I swallowed around the lump in my throat—"for the rest of your time here."

The next day we picked up her prints from the photographer. She'd insisted that we couldn't check out the digital copies until we saw the prints first.

"Lawd have mercy," my aunt cried when she saw them.

I literally gasped.

She'd looked good on the day of. She'd looked beautiful and regal. But in the photos, he captured all of that and then took it to the next level.

"You look incredible," I gushed.

"I do," she agreed without taking her eyes off the images. "I should've done this a long time ago. I could've put these on the internet and had these photos all over my house."

I laughed. "You still can."

"And I will."

We joked the entire way back to her house.

"I think I'm going to lie down for a bit. I'm tired," Aunt Addy said.

"Okay." I pushed her wheelchair down the hallway. "Feeling okay?"

"Just tired."

"Do you need me to call Monica? She should be here in an hour."

"No, no. I just need to rest. It's been a busy week." I watched her move to the bed. "But I'd like for you to head down to the rec center and sign up for swim lessons."

"Aunt Addy . . ."

"You said you wanted to do whatever I wanted to do. And I told you that I want to make sure you're tackling your list." She pointed at me. "Swim lessons."

"But I don't want to—"

"Would you really deny me?"

"Fine," I sighed loudly. "I'll go sign up."

She smirked. "Good."

My phone vibrated and I checked it. Seeing an email alert from Lamar curled my lips upward. When I glanced back up, my aunt gave me a knowing look.

"What?" I laughed awkwardly.

"I didn't say a word," she said in a singsong tone. "We'll talk when I wake up."

I left the room so she would stop analyzing me. My phone vibrated again just as I sat on the couch. It was a text. And as soon as I saw who it was from, my heart skipped a beat.

> **Lamar Anderson:** I uploaded the final draft of the business plan into a new shared document and emailed you the link. It has all the changes we talked about. I'm meeting with my lawyer and my accountant next week to finalize it. Thank you for all your help. I couldn't have done this without you. I know you were busy this month and I appreciate everything you did to make my idea better. I appreciate you. And if you ever need anything from me, and I mean anything, you got it.

I reread his words. Almost as if my brain were malfunctioning, I didn't know what to say. He didn't really ask a question. There was nothing that mandated a response. But as I sat in the quiet of my aunt's house, I wanted to say something. We hadn't talked in weeks outside of the shared document. Because I couldn't settle on how I wanted to respond, I typed and deleted words until Monica walked through the front door.

Her presence brought me back to reality.

Dropping my phone in my bag, I greeted her.

"It's way too quiet in here. Where's Addison?"

"She wanted to take a nap, and she's making me do something from my list, so I'll be back." I paused before heading toward the door. "She said she was tired, and she seems like she might be in some pain. I've been noticing that she's been getting tired and having less energy. She seems achy and uncomfortable sometimes. She says she's okay, but . . ." I shook my head. "Is that normal?"

Monica gave me a kind smile. "Yes. Tiredness, discomfort, and pain are all normal for what Addison is experiencing. For the last week and a half, she's declined medication to help with her pain, said she wanted to get through her list first."

My heart sank. "She's in pain from everything we've been doing?"

"She's in pain from her heart failure." Looking me in the eyes, Monica stepped forward and put her hand on my shoulder. "You being here and going through that list with her did wonders for her health. She's doing what she wants to do, and you helped make that happen for her."

"Thank you," I whispered, squeezing my eyes shut so tears didn't form. "I should head out so I can tell her I'm making progress when she wakes up."

"When she loses her appetite, that's when we need to worry. Until then, you keep doing what you're doing. You're doing a great job."

I'd spent all of July focused on tasks to make sure Aunt Addy was able to do everything she wanted to do. I spent my nights reading or working on ideas for Lamar's business plan. I didn't let myself get consumed by sadness because just the thought of not being able to call her for advice, hear her voice, or spend time with her was too heavy. It had been easier for me to pretend that it was like every other time she was on hospice.

But it wasn't.

I went to the rec center to sign up for private lessons and tried to forget the thoughts that were plaguing me. Once I told them when I was leaving town, they arranged for my swim lessons to be held over the next twelve business days. On the drive back to Aunt Addy's, I considered how I would manage to complete my list as soon as possible.

"What did they say?" Aunt Addy asked the moment I closed the door behind me.

"They had a two day a week, six-week program that they're condensing into twelve days over the next two and a half weeks to turn me into a swimmer. *But* class is at six o'clock in the morning."

"Good! You got a swimsuit? You need a couple of them. When do you start?"

"I stopped and got a cheap one on the way home because tomorrow is my first day."

"Why swim classes?" Monica asked.

"Because I allowed people to rob me of the experience in eighth grade, and Aunt Addy reminded me that the longer I put it off, the longer I let them win."

"I'm confused." The nurse glanced between me and my aunt. "Are you telling me you were bullied out of swimming?"

I nodded. "The bullying started in eighth grade, and when swim instruction happened during PE classes in eighth and ninth grade, I never felt comfortable wearing a swimsuit to participate. And once I got to college, learning to swim fell further down my list of priorities."

Monica's eyes were wide, almost in disbelief. "Really?"

I nodded again.

"I just . . ." She shook her head. "I'm sorry that happened to you. I just have such a hard time believing you were bullied. Your personality is just so . . . Addison."

"Yeah, *now*." I let out a dry laugh. "But back when I was twelve, thirteen, I let them get under my skin. I didn't get my Addison-like personality until later."

Addison grinned. "And I couldn't be prouder of every stage of you." She turned to her nurse. "And that's what the lists have always been about. To remind us of who we were, who we are, and who we'll become." She fixed her eyes on me. "What's next on your list? What else can you do while you're here with me?"

"What have you done already?" Monica asked, looking between the two of us as she shuffled the deck of cards.

"Not much," my aunt answered for me.

"I started my vegetarian diet on August first. I just signed up for swim lessons, and I made my tattoo appointment. I went on a date in June," I argued theatrically in the middle of the living room.

Aunt Addy cocked her head to the side. "Like I said, not much."

I put my hands on my hips. "I completed my date and my tour of a new city."

*"Dates."* She emphasized the word. "You were supposed to go on *dates*. And Spring Hill barely counts as a new city!"

I lifted my finger in the air. "But it counts!"

Monica leaned forward. "Oh! While you were out, a package came for you." She tapped the box on the table. After I picked it up, she continued. "You know, if you're looking for someone to go on a date with, there's a man who started at the agency four months ago who is around your age and single. He's a travel nurse, so he's only here for two more months."

"No thank you," I told her, taking a seat on the other side of the couch with my box in my lap.

"No thank you to dating or no thank you to Pierre? Because he's really quite handsome," Monica declared.

"No thank you," I replied, feeling my aunt's eyes on me. "I'm just not interested."

"You know why she's not interested?" Aunt Addy chimed in.

"Oh yeeeeah!" Monica feigned surprise, reacting dramatically. "Lamar!"

I rolled my eyes at the two of them. "I'm changing the subject."

"When was the last time you talked to him?" my aunt asked. "You like him. He likes you. His parents like you. I've never met him, and I like him. What am I missing?"

My eyes bounced around the room, going from picture to picture to avoid looking at them. "Our schedules just didn't align. He's busy. I'm busy. But it's okay. We're friends." I jumped to my feet. "I'm hungry. Are y'all hungry?"

I heard the two of them giggling as I rushed to the kitchen with my package. Away from their prying eyes, I smiled at the name above the return address.

*Anderson.*

Opening it carefully, a gift box with the words "Thank You" emblazoned on the top was inside. I removed the lid and found a card placed delicately on a bed of tissue paper.

*A place for all the stuff you don't say.*

I gasped when I saw the brown vintage journal with a rope closure. The beautiful journal that I'd coveted in Spring Hill weeks ago, the one I would've never purchased for myself because of the price. Lamar had it sent to me as a thank-you. Clutching it against my breasts, I let my head fall back.

*Ohmigod!*

"Jazmyn!" Aunt Addy called out.

"I'm coming," I yelled, putting the journal back in the box and taking it to my room.

Hours later, Monica had gotten Aunt Addy ready for bed and left for the night. I was sitting in the chair in the corner of her room, laughing at something she'd said.

"Okay, on that note, I'm going to bed," I told her as I rose to my feet.

"Before you go to bed, I want to talk to you about something," Aunt Addy said, her jovial expression changing slightly.

"What's going on?"

"We had so much going on in July that I didn't notice. But now I realized I haven't heard you talk on the phone—not to Lamar, not to your friends, nothing. Why aren't you talking to anyone?"

I hesitated, looking down at my hands before taking a deep breath and answering, "I just felt like it was important to be here for you. Yeah, maybe I put everything else on the back burner, but I wanted to spend every minute I could with you before . . ."

She reached out for my hand. When I took it, she said, "I appreciate that so much. I really do. But you have a life."

My eyes started watering. "You've always been my inspiration, my role model, and the person to make sure I'm good. I can't imagine my life without you."

She paused. "I know you love me, and I love you more than you could possibly know. But your world will not end when I'm gone. You don't have just me. You have so many other relationships. That's why I don't want you to avoid your friends, Lamar, or any of the others in your life."

I nodded, fighting back tears. "I mean, I'm not avoiding my friends. I texted Nina and Aaliyah."

"What about Lamar?"

I got quiet.

"What about Lamar?" she repeated.

"I can't," I whispered. "We're still friends. But I just . . . can't."

"Why not?"

"I feel guilty," I admitted, letting my head fall back.

"Why would you feel guilty?" she asked.

"He makes me feel like everything is going to be okay, and everything is *not* okay," I cried.

I hadn't fully realized why until that moment.

Lamar made me feel good, made me feel as if everything was okay. And while my aunt, my favorite person in the world, was dying, I didn't want to feel good. It didn't feel right. Working on his business plan was a distraction, and it was work. I liked doing it. But talking to or seeing Lamar made everything else disappear, and I couldn't afford to disappear from what was happening. Aunt Addison deserved my undivided attention.

She let out a shaky breath. "You have nothing to feel guilty about, Jazmyn. Nothing," she whispered emphatically. "You *should* be surrounded by people who make you feel good. And if he makes you feel good, you *deserve* that. You are deserving. And you have such a bright future ahead of you. There's so much you've yet to do, and you can't let me dying be the reason you don't live your life. If you want to be inspired by anything I've ever done, be inspired to live your life on your terms, fully and completely."

Wiping the tears from my face, I hugged her. "I love you," I choked out softly.

She rubbed my back with one hand. "I love you, too."

# 13

Aunt Addison's words didn't eliminate the guilt I felt, but it made me feel at ease enough to send a text.

**Jazmyn Payne:** Thank you so much for the journal, Lamar. I don't know how you knew but I can't tell you how much I appreciate your thoughtfulness. And I know I said it in the comments I made on your business plan, but you are brilliant. I hope you'll keep me updated with what your lawyer and accountant say about your business plan because it's ready. I'm sorry it's taken so long for me to reply via text or to call. I know I haven't been a good friend over the last several weeks, but I hope preseason is treating you well.

**Lamar Anderson:** Why are you texting me like you're going away? Did you deploy?

I laughed out loud.

**Jazmyn Payne:** That's hilarious! Why would you say that?

**Lamar Anderson:** You disappeared for weeks. I thought you might be in basic training or some shit.

**Jazmyn Payne:** I'm so weak right now! I gave you a compliment and sent you good vibes and this is the thanks I get?

**Lamar Anderson:** I'm just messing with you.

**Jazmyn Payne:** You haven't called me either so we're even. I've been busy. You've been busy. It's the nature of adult friendships.

My phone vibrated in my hand, lighting up the darkened room as his name flashed across the screen.

"Hello?" I answered quietly.

Even though my door was closed and Aunt Addy had been asleep for half an hour, I kept my voice low.

"Did I wake you?" Lamar's deep voice tickled my eardrums, and warmth swept through my entire body.

"No." My voice was breathy. I swallowed hard and regrouped. "Just in bed because I have to wake up early. How are you?"

"I'm good, tired. How are you? It's been a minute."

"Yeah, it has," I acknowledged.

"Why do you have to wake up early?"

"I have a swim lesson."

"A swim lesson?! That's what's up. I thought you were scared of the water."

"I never said that." I giggled. "But you see how I told you something and you used it against me?"

He chuckled. "I didn't use anything against you! I'm just asking! When did you decide to face your fears?"

"Mm-hmm, I'm choosing to ignore the shade," I replied, grinning. "My aunt and I came up with lists of things to do this summer, and learning to swim was one of mine. So my last couple of weeks here will have some very early mornings."

"That's what's up." He paused. "Wait, you're going to be in Chance for two more weeks?"

"Yeah. Two and a half, actually."

"You moved back?"

I scoffed. "Absolutely not. Even though my property manager probably thinks so."

"You've been gone all summer. You need somebody to check on it? Make sure it's still standing?"

I snickered lightly. "I'm more worried about paying rent at a place I'm not staying than I am that Richland Hills is still standing."

"Richland Hills," he repeated. "Is that the place that—"

"That's the one," I interrupted.

We both laughed.

"So, you're still in Chance . . . ?"

I sighed. "I am."

"Everything okay?"

I rolled over to my side, pressing the phone to my ear.

Everything about his tone and his energy put me at ease, but when I opened my mouth, the words wouldn't come out. It wasn't because I didn't trust him or because I didn't feel like I could. But I didn't want the lightness between us to disappear. Sickness and death were so dark and heavy. I needed his light, and I needed things between us to remain light.

But I also couldn't lie to him.

I swallowed hard. "I decided to spend the summer with my aunt," I told him, choosing my words carefully. "I wanted to help her get through her list, and she wanted to see me get a start on mine."

"How's it been going?"

"So far, so good."

I ran down the list of things we'd accomplished. He laughed when I recapped our picnic and when I told him how my aunt and her friends got down at the drive-in movie. I described the blue hair and the tattoos. I filled him in on the jazz festival, and he asked questions about the photoshoot, the book club, and the mystery party. But he was in a stunned silence when I told him about the yoni steam.

"She wanted to do what?" he balked.

I snickered into my pillow. "It was an interesting experience."

"What made her want to do— You know what, never mind. I don't want to know!" He let out a laugh. "But it sounds like you two knocked a lot off her list. No wonder I couldn't get you on the phone. You were busy as hell."

"Just like you! You went to training camp, and I barely got a call."

"Training camp ran from six o'clock in the morning until nine o'clock at night, then lights out at eleven. After a shower, I was crashing around ten."

"Wow, I didn't realize it was that intense."

"Yeah, it's a rough few weeks. But I did try to hit you up here and there when I had a little more energy. Definitely not on the days we had two-a-days. But I did call you—not that you picked up when I did."

"I know, I know. I'm sorry."

"Don't apologize. Family is important, and after hearing how you and your aunt were moving, I know you were busy. And I can't complain too much—every time I had a chance to update my business plan, I checked before bed, and you had tweaked and added things to make it better. I'm *this close* to hiring you on the spot."

"So what I hear you saying is that I wasn't the most present friend, but I was pretty great. So great, in fact, that you'd hire me to be a senior partner!"

He chuckled, and that deep, rich sound put a smile on my face. "Yeah, I think I'll keep you."

"Good. I like being kept."

"You'll have to let me take you out again when our schedules free up. I'm off tomorrow, but then practice picks back up, and the first preseason game is coming up."

"Yeah, I'd like that. I won't be back in Maryland until the regular season is about to start. But we should definitely get together."

"The way you talked about Chance, I just knew you'd be back up here already. It's clear your aunt means a lot to you."

"She does. She's . . ." I sighed a little thinking about why we'd gotten so much done so fast. "Aunt Addy was the first person to show me that life was more than Chance. She lives her life to the fullest. She's always been my inspiration."

"That's why you're getting the same tattoo?"

My lips tugged upward. "Yeah, that's one of the reasons. For my first tattoo, I—"

"Oh, this will be your first one?"

"Yeah, I was always curious about tattoos, but I thought they'd hurt, so I never got one. Do you have any?"

I'd checked out his arms every time I saw him, and I hadn't noticed any.

"Yeah, I have one on my back," he told me. "It goes from one shoulder to the other, and it's pretty detailed."

My phone pinged and I ignored it.

"Did it hurt?" I asked.

"Hell yeah."

Remembering what he looked like from behind, I smirked. "You have broad shoulders, so I bet! What's it of?"

"It's angel wings and a cross with my dad's name, date of birth, and death. I just sent you a picture of it."

"Oh, let me check."

I'd just opened the text when he continued. "That was from Jumeirah Beach in Dubai. I got the tour guide to take this of me about fifteen minutes before I dropped my shit in the ocean. It was the last picture that had backed up."

*Well, damn!*

I couldn't even respond verbally to what he was saying because I was gawking at his sexy-ass image splayed on my phone. I definitely saved it to my photo album and continued staring. The different shades of blue between the water and the sky were beautiful, but water droplets adorning Lamar's brown skin as he stretched his arms to the side showing off his tattoo and his wingspan really stole the show. His tall, thick build, muscular arms, and intricate wing tattoo only made him sexier.

"Oh wow," I breathed finally. "It's beautiful."

"You can't really see all the details, but I'll show it to you the next time we see each other."

The thought of seeing him again made my stomach flutter. But the thought of seeing him again at least partially naked for me to see the details of his tattoo sent a wave of heat through my body. My mouth went dry for a moment.

"I'd like that," I murmured. "To see you—it. I'd like to see it." I put my hand over my face. "Okay, it's late, and my brain just malfunctioned. I should go to bed."

"It's not even eleven o'clock," he pointed out in a teasing tone, ignoring my attempt to get off the phone. "Now, were you saying you'd like to see me or the tattoo?"

I let out an embarrassed laugh. I wasn't embarrassed by my admission. It was the way I'd stumbled over my words that had my face aflame.

"Okay, what I was *trying* to say is that I'd like to see the tattoo," I clarified. "What came out was that I'd like to see you. Both things are true. I just don't know why I got so tongue-tied there."

His soft chuckle was seductive. "I liked it."

"You like that my brain and my mouth weren't on the same page?"

"I like your brain and your mouth."

My stomach flipped. "Oh?"

"Yeah, you're smart. You think outside the box. I like the way you make connections in your head. I like that I never know exactly what you're thinking or what you're about to say. I could go on, but I'll just say that, for a lot of reasons, I like your brain and your mouth . . . a lot."

The air left my lungs.

His words hit my ears, my heart, and my pussy simultaneously.

He cleared his throat. "You told me about your fake tattoo, but you didn't send me a picture of it."

Grateful for the distraction, I sent him the picture I'd taken right before the book club meeting. I was sitting with my fist against my cheek and the inside of my wrist facing the camera. I was smiling, but the purpose of the photo was to show off my tattoo.

"Nice," he reacted. "That purple looks good on your skin."

"Thank you. I hope it shows up like that when I get the real thing. I've always thought the African violet was pretty, but"—I looked at my wrist in the dark—"I didn't know what I was going to get tattooed on me when I put 'get a tattoo' on the list. But the moment Aunt Addy got hers, I knew I wanted to get a matching one."

"So, if you didn't know what you wanted to get, what made you put it on the list?" he questioned.

I rolled onto my back. "I wanted to do something painful."

He was completely silent for a few seconds. "Are you—are you a masochist?"

The concern in his voice made me laugh out loud.

"No, I . . ." I hesitated for only a second, and then my truth poured out of me. "Everything on the list my aunt and I came up with is symbolic of where I was, where I am, and where I'm going. Getting a tattoo after being scared it would hurt is me facing the pain head-on. It's me proving to myself that not only can I take it, but I can also survive it, and something beautiful can come out of it. It represents pain I've overcome. And after Aunt Addy said it didn't hurt, she said that she would look at it and remember that pain doesn't last forever. And that was really powerful for me." I realized how I must've sounded and closed my eyes. "My bad, I was rambling."

"No, you're good. I love when you get going. You give me a peek at what's in that head of yours. It's even better when it's something personal and you really open up. So thank you for sharing."

"You're easy to talk to."

"You're easy to listen to." He paused. "And I like when you let me in."

My lower body clenched. *I'm trying to let you in again.*

I bit my lip to keep my thoughts to myself, but I felt my truth about to bubble out of me.

A thump in the other room crashed me down to reality.

*Aunt Addy!*

"Hey, I need to check on my aunt," I said in a rush, pushing the covers off me and scrambling to my feet. "I have to go."

"Let me know if you need anything."

My heart thudded in my chest. "I will, thank you, bye."

Guilt weighed me down. I'd been so busy swooning on the phone that I'd gotten distracted from what mattered most—being there for my aunt.

Ending the call as I opened my aunt's door, I found her sleeping soundly and the TV remote control and her Bible on the floor. In the glow of the reruns on the screen, she looked peaceful. I picked up everything from the floor and then watched my aunt carefully. Her cheeks were hollowed and her body looked frail, but she was just sleeping.

*Thank God*, I exhaled heavily.

Blinking back tears, I quietly backed out of the room, closing the door.

The thought of something happening to her was terrifying, but the guilt of being distracted and happy while she was in the next room hurting, or in pain, or dying was soul crushing.

Climbing into bed, I remembered what Aunt Addy had said about not feeling guilty. But I couldn't help it.

**Lamar Anderson:** Everything okay?

**Jazmyn Payne:** I heard something fall and I was worried. But it was just some stuff she had on the bed.

**Lamar Anderson:** Okay good, I'm glad to hear it. Your voice sounded off, so I just wanted to make sure.

**Jazmyn Payne:** Thank you for checking on me. I'm going to try to get some sleep now. I have to wake up in five minutes.

**Lamar Anderson:** You don't ever have to thank me for checking on you. And if you need anything, let me know. Even if I can't be there, I can send whatever you need. Get your rest.

**Jazmyn Payne:** Thank you, Lamar. I appreciate you saying that. Good night!

**Lamar Anderson:** I mean it. I got you. Whatever you need, whenever you need it, I'm here. Good night.

I momentarily closed my eyes and took a deep, shaky breath. His words swam in my head and my heart. Trying not to think about the way he affected me, I connected my phone to the charger and then pulled the sheet over my shoulders. I didn't have the words to fully describe how his energy made me feel. All I knew was that I wanted to go to sleep and forget the conflicting feelings that stirred within me.

*Go to sleep*, I chastised myself as I tossed and turned.

Waking up early for that first class was tough, but the happiness on my aunt's face when I returned made it worth it. The warmth I felt wasn't riddled with guilt, and I let that keep me too busy to have phone conversations with Lamar. Fortunately, or unfortunately, preseason kept him too busy to call until two days later. I told him I couldn't talk, but I could text. That was my excuse for the next few days because I couldn't bring myself to get on the phone with him. Even though I texted with him every night and thought of him every day, hearing his voice would be too distracting.

And I couldn't afford to get distracted.

"What do you have going on over there?" Aunt Addy asked as I'd just texted a goodnight message to Lamar.

"About to go to bed so I can be ready for my lesson on techniques in the morning."

Her smile grew. "You seem so much more confident about your lessons now."

I nodded. "I am."

By the end of the first week, I felt like I had become much more comfortable in the water. When I told Aunt Addy over Sunday dinner, she said she wanted to see me swim. So, on the Monday of my second week, much to Monica's displeasure, Aunt Addy was in attendance. It was the first time she'd been out of the house in a while. Other than us sitting in her backyard, enjoying the garden, she hadn't wanted to leave the comforts of home until now.

"You're getting good," Aunt Addy complimented me as I climbed out of the pool. "You have one week down, and you're already looking like a mermaid."

Laughing, I wrapped my towel around me. "A mermaid?"

"Yes, very beautiful. Very little leg movement. All arms."

I cackled. "Okay, but I'm getting better! I'm convinced I'll be able to swim before I leave Chance. Me and the water are becoming one."

"I believe it! Speaking of water, have you talked to your friends? I thought after our talk last week, I would've heard you on the phone with someone."

I froze, caught off guard by the question. "Um, I've sent some texts."

"Have you told your friends or Lamar that you're a swimmer now?"

"Yeah . . ." I studied her face. "Where did that come from?" I asked, confused.

She reached out for me. "Relationships, all relationships, need water to grow."

"I'm watering my relationships." I took her hand, squeezing it. "I've been a little . . . sad, so I haven't talked to them that much, but I'm watering them."

"I'm not just talking about them," she said gently. "*You* need water, too. Don't close yourself off from people who love you because you're sad. Let people in. Let yourself be watered." She squeezed my hand. "Let yourself be loved on."

"You did a good job in there," Monica said, interrupting Aunt Addy's stirring words.

I took a small step back, blinking the tears away. "Thank you."

Monica flashed a quirky smile. "Addison said you looked like a mermaid, and I couldn't unsee it."

I snickered. "Yeah, she told me. I'm going to work on kicking my legs tomorrow."

"She was all arms out there, but she was moving!" Aunt Addy added as the two ladies laughed a little too hard. "Monica and I are going to head home. I'll make you some bacon."

"I can't eat bacon," I reminded her. "Temporary vegetarian."

"Oh shoot, that's right!" She shook her head. "I know you wanted to prove you can do hard things, but when you come back and the house smells like bacon, that'll be the real test."

I nodded. "And that's a fact!"

We said our goodbyes, and I headed to the locker room to get changed.

Thinking about what Aunt Addison said about my friendships, I got to the car and looked at all the unanswered texts from my friends—even my work friends. Only Aaliyah and Nina knew what was really going on, and I didn't have the energy to fake it with everyone else. I reread my last text conversation with Lamar, who knew nothing about my aunt's condition and yet I didn't have to fake anything with him. I didn't have to pretend to be happy or in good spirits; he made me happy and put me in good spirits. On the drive to Aunt Addy's house, I thought about all the messages and a knot formed in my belly.

*I really haven't been a good friend.*

I parked beside Monica's van, and I replied in the group chat with my girls. I then reread the last text from Lamar, realizing I'd never texted him back. Not really thinking about how it was before eight o'clock in the morning, I sent a message.

**Jazmyn Payne:** I owe you an explanation.

**Lamar Anderson:** About what? What are you doing right now?

**Jazmyn Payne:** Just finished my swim lesson. I'm sorry to text so early. What are you doing?

**Lamar Anderson:** I'm heading into the gym now.

**Jazmyn Payne:** I hope you have a good workout, and that work goes well today. Can you give me a call tonight?

**Lamar Anderson:** Yeah, it'll be good to hear your voice.

My stomach fluttered.

**Jazmyn Payne:** Okay, talk soon!

I squeezed my eyes shut. It didn't matter how many times I called him a friend or tried to play it cool, he gave me butterflies.

And that scared me.

I tucked my phone into my bag and went into the house. Aunt Addy was back in bed, so after a shower and changing into comfortable clothes, I went to sit in her room to watch TV with her. When she fell back asleep, I went to get something to snack on when I got a text.

**Nina Ford:** GIRL! Eleven o'clock! URGENT three-way call!

The capitalized *girl* told me everything I needed to know. Nina didn't usually request an urgent conference call, so when my phone rang at eleven, I went to my room and was ready to hear whatever was going on.

And it was worth it.

Besides the belly laughs that I'd needed more than anything, Nina damn near confessed her love for a man. She didn't say it with her words, but she didn't have to. It was evident that it was different with him. Nina kept a roster for her own reasons, and she enjoyed the company of all the men she entertained. But I'd never heard her talk about a man the way she talked about the Fun One, as she called him.

It made me happy to hear her happy. It also made me curious because she was deviating from her multi-man plan.

*What changed?* I wondered as I listened to her gush.

"How about we focus on the fact that Aaliyah is turning thirty and the three of us will be reunited in a couple weeks," Nina said, trying to get us off her back.

"It'll be good to see you guys." I sighed. "It's been a long summer."

We talked for the next twenty minutes. Aaliyah had to abruptly get off the phone because she was being summoned at work.

"Where are you now?" I asked Nina. "It's almost time for your meeting."

"I'm in the parking deck across the street. I'm meeting with Sasha in HR at noon. I have ten minutes before I need to head over."

"Okay, good." I went and stood by the window. Staring toward the neighbor's yard, I suddenly got nervous. "So . . . I have a question."

"What's going on?" Nina asked carefully.

We went back and forth for a minute before I asked her what I really wanted to ask her. "Even if you like the person, how do you end it with someone you slept with?"

"Jazz . . ." She dragged my name out. "Are you sleeping with someone?"

My jaw dropped. "I didn't say that!"

"You didn't have to say it!"

"Your meeting is at noon, right? Because you have only seven minutes to get in there."

"I'm crossing the street now. But back to you—"

"Back to you," I countered, trying to throw her off my scent. "You stopped talking to the Romantic One because things were changing, but it sounds like things are changing with the Fun One, too. Are you planning on ending things with him?"

"No. Are you deflecting so I won't ask about the mystery man you've been getting busy with in your hometown?"

I let out a dry laugh. "I'm getting off the phone."

"Well, while you sit in denial, I'm going to give you some real talk. It's about time you got them cobwebs cleared out. And don't be more worried about hurting someone else's feelings than you are about hurting your own. If it needs to end, end it. But don't end it just because you're scared."

I froze.

My heartbeat was loud as the word *scared* vibrated through my entire body.

"Jazz?" she called out.

I cleared my throat. "I'm here."

"Don't be scared," she repeated.

I bit my bottom lip. "You don't be scared either."

"I'm feeling really good and confident about today," she declared. "Now that I'm here, I'm excited. Oh, I might lose you in the elevator."

"I didn't mean about the job," I clarified. "Have a great first day! You got this! Bye, girl!"

I ended the call and tossed the phone on the bed behind me.

Still staring out the window, I just kept hearing the word *scared* echoing in my head.

Because I was scared.

Lamar scared me.

# 14

Being "just friends" with Lamar meant eliminating the feelings that would complicate that friendship. We genuinely clicked, so friendship with him was easy. And because he was such a gentleman, he never made the conversation sexual or even referred to our sexual encounter. If it weren't for my feelings for him, I would've been able to convince myself that we had a regular friendship.

But when I started to explain to him why I'd been MIA, my throat closed up, and I lost my nerve. I wasn't able to say anything else for a myriad of reasons, and instead of pressuring me, he sat in silence with me. After a few minutes had passed, he told me I didn't owe him anything and we could sit on the phone for as long as I needed.

"If you need a distraction or if you want to talk about it, I'm here either way," he told me gently.

That twenty-minute call changed everything.

We texted all week, but he didn't call me again until Friday. Aunt Addy, Rose, and a couple of others were in the living room cutting up while Lamar and I spent two hours talking about our childhoods, our families growing up, and our passion for his project.

On Saturday evening, while my aunt had visitors, I lay across the bed and talked to Lamar about his lawyer and accountant obtaining the necessary licenses and permits. I cheered about him officially registering his business name. He was still months from an official launch, but I was so proud and wanted to celebrate him. My cheeks hurt from how hard I was smiling. With the faint sound of my aunt's laughter in the background, it was easy to feel like everything was normal. It didn't hit me until Sunday, when I didn't get a call from him, that the guilt that had plagued me for weeks had faded.

But when I answered his call on Monday night, the house was quiet, and I'd been tossing and turning in bed for an hour. The light, fun energy of the weekend had been replaced with a contemplative, vulnerable silence that made it impossible for me to rest. "Hello?"

"Why are you whispering?" Lamar asked.

Covering my mouth, I let out a laugh. "My aunt went to bed early, and the TV is off, so I'm just keeping my voice down." I reclined against the pillows on my bed. "How are you?"

"Tired. But I'm good. How are you?"

"I'm okay," I sighed. "Tell me about your day."

"You know you can talk to me about anything, right?"

A small smile pulled at my lips at the kindness in his words and the care in his voice. My eyes stung a little because I knew he was being sincere.

"Thank you," I murmured. "Tell me about your day."

"For preseason, it's pretty much the same: workout, meetings, practice, game day, repeat."

"You're never very specific," I pointed out.

"Neither are you," he countered.

"What do you mean? I've talked to you at length about my job and the joy and pain of teaching teens."

"Yeah, but I'm not talking about your job."

Nerves tightened my belly. I didn't know exactly what he was going to say next, but the way my body stiffened, I was bracing myself for it.

"You like me, and that's why you act like this," he said in a low, sexy tone.

I couldn't help but giggle. "What?"

"Is that you denying you like me?"

"No, I'm not denying it," I replied, trying to laugh it off. "I just . . . What does that have to do with anything?"

"Tell me something, and I'll tell you something."

Swallowing hard, I wondered aloud softly, "What do you want to know?"

"Everything. Whatever you want to tell me."

I hesitated for a moment. I almost told him about Aunt Addy's prognosis, but I couldn't bring myself to say it. "I was married," I blurted.

"What?" He sounded shocked.

I scoffed, feigning offense. "Why are you surprised that someone wanted to marry me?"

"Nah. If anything, I'm surprised that someone would let you go."

Grinning, I turned onto my side. "He didn't have a choice. I divorced him."

"I don't doubt it. But I can't believe he let it happen. You're the whole package."

"You lose what you don't value, and he didn't value what he had."

"You gonna tell me the story, or you gonna keep being vague?" he challenged.

I nodded. "You're right. But keep in mind that my parents drilled perfection into my head, so even though I left Chance, that misguided mindset came with me, and it took me a little while to grow out of that." I took a breath before continuing. "I met my ex in undergrad, and he asked me to marry him right after grad school. I said yes not because I thought he was the one but because it fit the perfect narrative. We separated three years later because I caught him cheating." I shrugged even though he couldn't see me. "As soon as I saw the messages and the pictures, I called my aunt, and she connected me with her friend who's a divorce lawyer."

"So, you just saw the messages and left? You didn't talk to him about it, you just left?"

"There was nothing to talk about. But yeah, two days later, after I spoke with the lawyer and found an apartment to move into, I let him know that I was done."

"Oh shit, that's cold! I love it."

"You love it?" I questioned skeptically.

"Yeah, too often people stay in shit they need to leave. You knew your worth and got up out of there. I love it."

I smiled. "Thank you. Not everyone sees it like that, so I appreciate you."

"Who wouldn't have seen it like that?"

"My parents. A divorce doesn't fit with their idea of perfection."

"Ah. Understood. Parents can put some shit in your head, and it takes a long time to shake."

"Yeah, exactly that." I sighed, rolling onto my back. "You can relate?"

"My dad always talked about me getting to the league. And since there's no family connection to get me in, I had to play a perfect game. So that's how I've approached football my whole life. I'm proud of what I do, but when I got my job, for a long time, I downplayed it because it wasn't my dad's idea of perfect. But then I realized perfect doesn't exist and my dad would've been proud, and I let that shit go."

"Good. I'm glad you let it go and realized your dad would be proud of you regardless."

"Yeah, I mean, there's the fifty-three-man active roster and then the practice squad, but it's all the same team. Anyone can get activated from the practice squad at any time and—"

I looked around the room incredulously because I wasn't sure I heard him correctly. "Wait, wait, wait, wait, wait . . . *what*?"

"I'm part of the scout team, the practice squad for the Maryland Monarchs. Well, it won't be official until the end of the month, but yeah. I've been on the practice squad for the last few years."

"You play professional football?"

He let out a light chuckle. "Yeah. Defensive tackle."

I immediately thought about how when we'd met, I'd been talking shit about how the starting defensive tackle needed to tighten up. *Well, damn.*

"So, I knew you worked for the Monarchs. This whole time I thought you were a consultant or something. But you are a *football player*. That's wild!"

"Okay, you sound a little *too* shocked. I don't look the part?"

I snickered. "No, you look like a football player. I told you when we met, you look like you play defense. But it's just funny to me that when you said your day consisted of working out, meetings, and then practice, it never crossed my mind that you were on the field." I paused. "Probably because we spent the summer going over your business plan. It was giving front-of-house consultant job."

"I can see that," he conceded with a chuckle. "And I'll get there. That's what I'm moving toward because I'm a twenty-six-year-old practice-squad player. Even if I stay healthy and beat out these young boys coming in for my spot, I could get released at any time. Coach Rice likes me, but it's a week-to-week job. I could get released and picked up by another team, in another city at any time. So I have to have my backup plan ready. All it takes is one injury, and then you're done. You never know what might happen."

I nodded. "Any given Sunday."

"Any given Sunday," he agreed.

"You've been with the Monarchs the whole time?"

"Yeah, that's been the good thing. I was activated last year when the backup was in an accident."

"Did you play?"

"Nah, Channing is the starter, and he was healthy, so I rode the bench."

"The fact that you were activated shows they see your value," I pointed out.

"Yeah. But anything can happen at any time, so I'm meeting with some investors tomorrow, and we'll see what happens."

"There's no way they can't see the vision. There's no way they won't want to help you bring this to life. It's incredible."

"That means a lot coming from you. Thank you."

"You're welcome." I smiled. "Lamar Anderson . . . professional athlete. Why didn't you say anything?"

"I never bring it up. I like to keep it private."

"Why?" I wondered, incredulously. "It's a pretty awesome job."

He let out a light chuckle. "Yeah, I like it. Love it actually. But it, uh . . . falls short of the expectation."

"Whose expectation? You get paid to play professional football. There are not a lot of people who can say that. You won."

"I need to carry you around as my personal cheerleader."

"I'm more of a coach than a cheerleader."

"For me, you could be both."

Grinning, I closed my eyes momentarily. "For you, I could do that."

"You've been single for two years?"

It was such an abrupt shift in subject matter that I hesitated momentarily. "Yes . . . the divorce was finalized two years ago." Wanting to turn the tables on him, I asked, "When was your last relationship?"

"It's been a minute," he answered.

"Does that mean you're afraid of commitment? Or are you for the streets? Or you got out of something yesterday? Or does that mean you—"

"Hold up! What?!" He chuckled. "Why are *those* the reasons you're assuming?"

"Because you were intentionally vague with your answer."

"I swear I'm not being intentionally vague." His amusement was evident. "There's just not much to tell as far as relationships go."

"Well, let's try," I probed.

"I'll try if you try," he countered. "I'm not the only one being vague."

"What—"

"My last real relationship was in college," he started, interrupting my protests. "Her name was Milan. We dated for a while, but soon after I started on the practice squad, we broke up."

"Oh wow. I'm sorry. Were you two in love?"

"We were young, and I thought it was love. But even at the time, I knew it wasn't that deep. So it worked out for the best for both of us. I need something real, and she only wanted to be with a pro baller."

I furrowed my brows in confusion. "But you *are* a pro baller . . . ? You literally play football as your *profession* . . . That's the definition of a pro baller."

"She didn't see it that way." He chuckled. "I got a professional schedule without the perks. And the schedule *is* demanding. During the regular season, we practice four days a week, one day is for meetings, conditioning, and training, and then there's game day."

"That's why she broke up with you?"

"Officially, she left because she said I didn't have enough time for her. But unofficially, yeah. I have a league schedule without the big contract, the money, or the fame."

"And that's what she was after?"

"Yeah. That's what she told her people. She meant to send the text to them, but she accidentally sent it to me."

My eyes widened. "Wow . . . that's messed up," I murmured.

"It worked out the way it was supposed to. We weren't friends. We weren't compatible. Turns out, she didn't like football. She liked the idea of being with a football player. Those are two completely different things. My life is football, and I can't be with anyone who doesn't love it." He paused. "It was a good lesson to learn."

The knot in my belly tightened. "Anytime you can learn and grow from a situation, it's a good look. But still . . . that sucks."

"Yeah, but it ended three and a half years ago. That's why I said there's not much to tell."

"You haven't dated in three and a half years?!" I exclaimed.

"I've dated and talked to women since then. But you asked me about relationships, and I haven't had a relationship since then. I don't have a lot of time, so I haven't invested in anyone. Have you dated since your divorce?"

"No, I haven't," I answered sheepishly.

*That's why I couldn't control myself around you the last time we saw each other*, I explained silently.

"Why not?"

"After what I went through, I just didn't have the energy. I'd rather spend my time with people I genuinely like than to spend my time on dates with strangers."

"Valid. But everybody was a stranger to you at one point in time."

I rolled my eyes. "You sound like Aunt Addy."

"My mom said that at any point of the relationship, anyone can be a stranger to you. Whether you've just met them or you've known them for twenty years."

I reflected on that. "That's deep. That's that old-school mom wisdom."

He paused. "So now I sound like your aunt *and* my mom."

I laughed. "That's not a bad thing!"

"I mean . . ." He yawned.

"Aight, it's time for bed. I have to wake up early for my swim pre-test, and you have your meeting tomorrow," I told him.

"Yeah. It's not until the afternoon, so I'll probably try to sleep in, but hit me up and let me know how you did."

"I will. You, too!" I put my hand to my chest. "Have a good night."

"Goodnight, Jazmyn."

I exhaled as I ended the call.

Within minutes, I was fast asleep.

I woke up in a good mood and did well on my swim pretest. I knew my conversation with Lamar had a little to do with that. My mood was brightened even more when I told Aunt Addy, since she insisted on being present for my official testing on Wednesday. The fact that she was feeling up to it made me happy because her energy levels had been dwindling. So, on Wednesday, I swam from one end of the pool to the other with my aunt and Monica beaming as they watched.

"I'm so proud of you," Aunt Addy told me when I ran over to her. "You did it! You overcame the past. You should be proud of yourself."

With water still dripping from me, I resisted the urge to hug her by pulling my towel around me tighter.

*I* am *proud of myself.*

"Thank you for pushing me to do it. This feels good."

"What time did you say your parents were coming over?" she asked.

"Noon."

"Are they bringing lunch?"

I laughed. "I think so, but I'm not sure."

She shook her head and then looked at Monica. "Remind me to call them at nine o'clock. It's too early right now."

"It absolutely is too early," Monica responded. She turned to me. "But I am glad to witness you accomplish this."

I grinned. "Thank you!"

I said goodbye to them and got back into the water. I practiced my stroke on my own and marveled at how good I'd gotten in two and a half weeks.

*I'm still not going to the six-foot side*, I thought, looking over at where my instructor was working with a couple of kids in the deep end.

An hour later, I was sitting at that same tattoo parlor I'd visited with Aunt Addy, getting my African violet tattoo and my belly button pierced. I didn't tell her I was doing it. I planned on surprising my aunt with three things off my list instead of one when I returned to her house. So, when I entered the living room, I wasn't expecting to be the one surprised.

"Not a cake!" I cried, staring at the sheet cake with *You can swim!* scrawled in icing. "Thank you."

"Now we have to wait until your parents get here to cut it since they're bringing lunch," Aunt Addy told me from her chair. "But we just wanted you to know how proud we are of you."

I squatted beside her to give her a hug instead of leaning down like I'd normally do. "Thank you, Aunt Addy." After giving her a squeeze, I turned to Monica, who had picked up the cake to take to the kitchen. "Thank you, too, Monica."

"What took you so long to get back here?" Aunt Addy asked. "We had that cake sitting for an hour and a half."

Rising to my feet, I laughed. "Well, actually, I have a surprise for you, too." I extended my arm, showing her my wrist and the tattooed flower in the exact same spot as hers. As she oohed and ahhed, I lifted my T-shirt so she could see the L-shaped bar that went through my reddened skin. The jeweled ends sparkled when the sun hit it. "I knocked three things off my list today."

Aunt Addy's eyes widened. "Oh wow! You really did it."

She tried to lean forward to get a better look, but I could tell she was struggling. So I stepped forward.

"Jazmyn, it's beautiful," she murmured, inspecting the piercing. "I'm so proud of you." A sentimental smile tugged at her lips as she met my gaze. "Twelve-year-old you is proud of you, too."

Hearing that choked me up. My eyes watered, and I blinked rapidly. "Thanks."

"Lookin' good, Jazmyn!" Monica commented as she strolled back into the room.

The distraction kept my tears at bay and I smiled. "You like?"

She nodded. "I had one when I was your age."

"I bet you did," Aunt Addy commented comically.

We all laughed.

She turned her attention back to me. "Did it hurt?"

"It didn't *hurt*, but it felt weird," I explained, dropping my shirt and taking a seat on the couch.

"Just make sure it doesn't get infected," Monica warned.

I nodded. "That's why I had to wait until after my swim lessons."

"Twenty-five years ago . . ."

Aunt Addy and I chuckled as we listened to Monica's story of her "wild" youth. Hearing my aunt and her nurse go back and forth about who had more wild adventures in their twenties was hilarious and heartwarming at the exact same time. But it really made me think about my twenties, what I'd done, and the stories I'd have to share about my life.

*I'm really the most boring person in the room right now.*

Monica had just helped my aunt into the recliner when there was a knock at the door. I got up and opened it. I'd been so caught up in their shenanigans, I hadn't mentally prepared for the reunion with my parents.

I loved Mom and Dad, and they were fundamentally good people. But their preoccupation with perfection and with what other people thought of them had done a number on me growing up. In my adulthood, they weren't the most supportive when ideas or lifestyle choices didn't align with what they perceived to be the best option. They would worry and offer help in an overbearing and oppressive way if I diverged from their path. But I never doubted they had my best interest at heart. They just never really saw me for who I was.

*Or who I am.*

"My beautiful daughter," my mom greeted me as soon as her eyes landed on me. She looked me up and down in my black yoga pants and my BACKFIELD IN MOTION T-shirt. "In her crude shirt choice."

I rolled my eyes as we hugged. "Mom, it's not crude."

She walked in, and my dad looked at me and laughed. "Jazmyn!" He gave me a tight hug with one arm. The other arm held a bag of food. "It's a football reference," he explained to Mom.

After he came in, I closed the door behind them.

The house suddenly felt crowded.

Mom and Dad hadn't seen Aunt Addison in a wheelchair before.

They fussed over her, and she fussed at them for treating her like a child. They asked Monica a million questions, and she patiently answered each one. It was fascinating, but it was the perfect representation of how they operated. Their love was evident, but their methods were domineering.

"Why didn't you tell us about this?" Mom asked me as we sat around the living room eating lunch. "We could've come back early."

"Because you would've come back early," Aunt Addy answered for me.

I burst out laughing and almost choked on my greens.

"We are not surprised you didn't say anything, Addison," Mom replied with pursed lips. She shifted her focus back to me. "Why didn't *you* say anything, Jazmyn? When we talked, you said you two were shopping and gardening and reading a book for a book club. You didn't say anything about this." She gestured to my aunt.

I lifted my eyebrows. "What was I supposed to say?"

"That your aunt wanted to dye her hair blue!"

I laughed again. "What's wrong with blue hair?"

"You're not some teenager, Addy," Dad pointed out. "Don't you think this is a little young for you?"

"What is everyone going to say?!" Mom exclaimed.

"Everyone who has seen it loves it," Aunt Addy told them. "And the only person whose opinion matters on the subject"—she pointed to herself—"loves it."

"I just don't want you to need something, and they treat you poorly because they're judging you by your appearance," Mom explained. "If you have to go to the hospital, I don't want them to not try to save you."

My aunt looked from my mom to my dad. "Miranda. Richard. I'm on hospice. I won't be going to the hospital."

"Speaking of hospice," Dad started, scooting to the edge of his chair and leaning toward his sister. "Jazmyn is heading home on Friday. We wanted to know how you felt about staying with us."

Aunt Addy shook her head. "No thank you."

"Addison," he protested. "We want to take care of you and make sure you're okay. You can't be here alone."

"Then you can come see me right here. In my home. Where I'll be."

*I know that's right!*

"How would it look for us to leave you here alone?" Mom asked. "We have the space." She pointed to Monica. "You can bring your nurse."

As they went back and forth, I really didn't understand how my parents thought Aunt Addison would want to leave her home and live with them. They meant well, but they missed the mark.

"Her speech and her enunciation are a little off, but that mind of hers is sharp as a tack," Mom pointed out later, when we were alone.

Aunt Addy had gone to her room to rest, and Monica and my father were discussing her care in the kitchen.

"It's tough seeing her not moving around on her own though," she continued, pulling a frown.

"Yeah, it is. She was moving a lot better when she was fresh out of rehab. We did a bunch of stuff in July, and she'd get out of her chair. But she started declining again. Her energy seems to be decreasing." My voice cracked, and I bit my lip to keep my emotions in check.

My mom pulled me in for a hug. "I know you're looking forward to getting back home. Aaliyah's birthday party is this weekend, right?"

"I'm looking forward to the party, but I've enjoyed spending this time with Aunt Addy," I admitted, releasing from the embrace. "It was an unexpected stay, but I think it was necessary."

She patted my knee. "You're a blessing. We were ready to come right back up here if we had to."

"I know. But I was already here, and I didn't have work, so it worked out."

"School starts on Monday?"

"On Tuesday."

She was quiet for a moment. "Are you happy?"

"I mean . . ." I gestured in the direction of Aunt Addy's room. "Not with this situation."

"Of course not. I just worry about this being the second significant loss in the last couple of years."

"Second?"

"First your divorce and now this. You're up in Richland, and I know you have your friends and your job, but I worry about you."

"My divorce doesn't compare to losing Aunt Addy . . . at all."

"But it was a loss. He was your *husband*."

I rolled my eyes. "Mom, please."

"I worry that when Addison passes, you will shut down like you shut down after your divorce."

My eyebrows furrowed. "I didn't shut down. I just . . . took the time to heal from the situation and to unlearn what I'd been taught."

As if she hadn't heard anything I'd just said, she continued. "And when we lose Addison, who has always been your closest confidant, will you shut out your friends? The rest of your family? I don't want you to be lonely."

"Why would you think I'd shut my family and friends out?" I looked around the empty room in confusion. *What is she on?*

"Because that's what happened after your divorce," she said emphatically. "You abruptly cut ties with Tyson, no questions asked. And then you abandoned the idea of marriage and relationships."

Making a face, I shifted uncomfortably. "That's not exactly what happened."

"Then why haven't you dated again? Why do you insist on being alone?"

"I never said I was abandoning relationships. *Abandoning* means to give up completely. I said I was not interested, and that means I was not concerned with it. There is a difference, and that difference matters."

She brushed her hand over my locs and then cupped my cheek. "I'm afraid you aren't processing your pain and—"

"Mom, I'm fine. My pain has been processed. The healing I had to do was from thinking I had to live a perfect little life that didn't fit me with a man who wasn't worthy of me. It wasn't the breakup with Tyson that I needed to heal from. I had to heal from the realization that striving for perfection, living up to other people's expectations, had taken a lot from me. Because if we're being real, I never should've married that man in the first place."

"You didn't *have* to marry him, honey. I mean, he seemed perfect for you, so we were happy to see you married."

"No, he didn't seem perfect for me, and he wasn't."

*And if you knew me better, you would know that.*

"But I married him anyway, so that's on me," I continued.

She gave my shoulders a squeeze. "What I would recommend, to help you during this time—"

"I'm going to hold your hand when I tell you this," I interrupted as I clutched her hand. "You're my mom; you're not my therapist."

"Honey, I'm not treating you like one of my clients."

"You sure about that?"

My dad and Monica came back into the living room, and we changed the subject.

Aunt Addy woke up, and the five of us had dinner. My parents made a plan to come back the next day and coordinated care with Monica. I retreated to my room, still thinking about what my mom had said.

*Abandoning the idea of relationships and marriage is not the same as not being interested*, I argued to myself.

And I kept repeating that thought anytime my mind strayed.

Picking up my phone, I called Aaliyah.

"Hello?" she answered.

"Do we *all* have to have a date for Saturday or just you?" I asked.

"Well, hello to you, too." She snickered. "Yes. But your date doesn't have to be a *date* date. It can be anyone you want to bring."

I cleared my throat. "Okay."

"Is there someone you have in mind?"

"Is there someone *you* have in mind?" I countered. "Your party is in forty-eight hours, and last I heard, you were into Lennox. Is he still the one?"

"Lennox is no longer a contender."

My eyebrows shot up. "What? Since when?"

"Officially last night," she said, before giving me a quick rundown of what had happened over the past week.

*The bartender*, I thought with a rueful smile. *I know more about him than the men she's actually going on dates with.*

"Lennox went out of town for work or something. He'll be back on my birthday. But I'm going to let him know it's not going to work the next time we speak," she continued.

"Interesting . . ."

We spent twenty minutes discussing her birthday-date dilemma and her upcoming date. When she turned the conversation to me, I didn't plan on saying anything, but it burst out of me.

"So, I was talking to my mom, and she basically said that she thinks I haven't 'processed my pain' from Tyson," I told her.

"From Tyson?!" Aaliyah screeched. "What?"

I laughed. "Exactly!"

"Why would she think you were still hung up on him?"

"She said I abandoned the idea of relationships and marriage because I 'lost' my husband. And I never abandoned the idea, and I certainly didn't *lose* my husband."

"He lost *you*!"

"Okay!" I agreed.

"Where did that come from?" she wondered.

"She was saying that she was worried about how I handle significant losses since Aunt Addy is . . ." I swallowed hard, unable to say it—especially when that wasn't the focus of the conversation. "My mom basically was saying that she's worried about the way I handle loss because I haven't had a man since the divorce."

"I don't think Tyson had anything to do with that. But . . ." She dragged the word out. "I *do* think the experience jaded you. I mean, it would've jaded me, too. That asshole had been cheating the whole time! But I think the experience made you apprehensive to trust and open up to someone."

I slowly nodded even though she couldn't see me. "Yeah," I sighed.

"You're going to meet someone who is going to make you comfortable enough to try again. Until then, you said you were going to have sex this summer. So maybe take a page out of Nina's book and get back on the horse."

I giggled lightly. "That's the same exact thing Aunt Addy said." I closed my eyes, and I saw Lamar. A quick flashback of our time near the river washed over me. "Mm."

"Who are you thinking about bringing to my party? Maybe whoever you bring will help you get back on the horse."

A throb between my thighs sparked an idea.

"I have someone in mind," I told her. "But if he can't come, I'll figure something out."

"He? Who is he?"

"I met him in Chance, actually. But he lives in Maryland."

"What? How cool is that?"

"Yeah, he was only here visiting family, but we became friends."

"And he's just a friend?"

"Suddenly, I gotta go," I told her.

"Hmm. Interesting . . ."

We burst out laughing.

"This is the longest I've gone without seeing you," she told me. "I'm going to give you the biggest hug."

I smiled. "I'm looking forward to it."

We said goodbye, and then I made another call.

"Hey, what's up?" Lamar answered over the commotion in the background.

"Hi, are you busy? I just have a quick question."

"I have a few minutes for you. You good?"

"Yeah, I'm good. I was just wondering if you were busy on Saturday?"

"Practice in the morning, but free after three o'clock."

"Well, my best friend's thirtieth birthday party is Saturday. It's an overnight thing. I know it's last-minute, but would you want to go with me?"

"Is this you asking me out?"

My face got warm. "Yes. Was that not clear?"

He chuckled. "I wouldn't mind seeing you. I've only been trying all summer."

"You've been in training camp all summer," I argued with a grin.

"Yeah. But I've been wanting to see you all summer, too. So text me the details." He yelled something to someone in the background. "We just found out we made the cut, so I gotta go, but I'll hit you up tonight."

Grinning, I bit down on my bottom lip. "Congratulations! Talk soon."

**Jazmyn Payne:** Anyone up?

**Nina Ford:** Not Jazz sending a "you up?" text like one of these trash ass men Aaliyah's matching with on Tender-Fish!

**Aaliyah James:** You know I can see your text too, right?

I laughed out loud.

**Jazmyn Payne:** Just confirming I'll be bringing a date on Saturday.

**Nina Ford:** Is it that man you fucked in Chance?

**Aaliyah James:** You fucked somebody in Chance?! Is it that guy you said you made friends with?

**Nina Ford:** Sounds like she made more than friends! Sounds like she made it clap!

**Jazmyn Payne:** I made a friend and there may have been some benefits. But we're friends so I asked him to come with me to the party. And I'm just preparing y'all now, so you don't embarrass me and make it something it's not.

**Aaliyah James:** Nina, you hear this? Jazz thinks we're going to embarrass her in front of her boyfriend.

**Nina Ford:** He must've knocked the Mario coins out her pussy if she's giving us this type of warning days in advance.

Cackling, I changed the subject.

**Jazmyn Payne:** Aaliyah, which man did you decide to bring? Or are you still in denial like Nina is about her dating situation?

**Nina Ford:** I'm not in denial. I'm just making questionable decisions.

**Aaliyah James:** I'm not in denial. I'm under duress.

**Jazmyn Payne:** I'm so weak! I needed these laughs. I can't wait to see you two this weekend.

# 15

It was hard saying goodbye to Aunt Addy on Friday. I'd packed my car early in the morning, but I planned to hang around until at least lunchtime.

"What's going on with your party?" I asked as I watched her eat bacon. I looked down at the vegetarian sausage on my plate and sighed. "Why are you being so secretive about it?"

"You'll see." She winked. "So, tell me, I heard you giggling and sniggling on the phone yesterday. What was all the congratulations about?"

"Oh, I was, um"—I let out an embarrassed laugh—"congratulating Lamar. He had a good work-related meeting, and he's going to take things to the next level. I'm sorry, I didn't realize I was so loud."

She smiled, slightly tilting her head. "Don't be sorry. It was nice hearing you sound so . . . happy."

"I'm going to miss you."

"I'm going to miss you, too. Thank you for spending the summer with me."

"I wanted to be here with you. You don't have to thank me."

Seconds later, my mom and dad burst through the door. The four of us talked until it was time for me to get on the road.

"What is that on your wrist?!" Mom exclaimed.

Aunt Addy laughed. "My new tat."

"What are you doing getting a tattoo?" Dad asked, confused and amused at the same time. "You're too old to be doing stuff like this!"

"And in your condition," my mom added. She turned to me with her hands on her hips. "Did you know about this?"

I turned to better show the inside of my arm. "I sure did."

"Oh my God!" Mom gasped dramatically. "How are you going to be able to teach with tattoos all over you? How are you going to become a principal one day?"

"She's going to quit the school system and write books anyway," Aunt Addy answered for me.

"What?!" Dad gasped. "Teaching is such a respectable career."

My mom's hands flew to her cheeks. "Jazmyn! You can't quit this close to the school year!"

"She's kidding." I laughed. "But I am going to publish a book—"

"She's almost done," Aunt Addy interjected.

"Yes. I'm finishing it in the next few weeks. So, if on Tuesday they fire me for the small tattoo on the inside of my wrist, I have a backup plan."

"What am I going to do with you two?" Mom fussed, pulling me into a hug. "I love you, and I just want what's best."

"Bye, Mom, I love you, too," I told her, giving her a squeeze.

I hugged my dad next. "I love you. Season starts next week."

"I know. I got the first game in my calendar."

When I got to my aunt, we both had tears in our eyes. I bent down and hugged her silently for a moment, not wanting to break down and cry.

"I love you," I choked out.

"I love you more," she replied. "Remember to never stop fighting."

Tightening our embrace, I murmured, "You either."

Wiping the tears from my eyes, I told them all goodbye and headed outside. Monica was parking as I approached my car. I waited for her to come up the driveway, and then I gave her a hug.

"You have my number," I told her. "If anything changes, if you think she's about to go, call me. I will drive down here. I don't care what time it is. Call me and let me know."

"I will," she assured me. "I promise."

I gave her a wave. "Take care of her."

"Always."

I didn't make it down the street before I started crying. I'd only been driving for ten minutes when my phone rang.

It was Aunt Addy.

"Hello?" I answered, fully prepared to turn around.

"Don't forget to send me a picture of you and Lamar at Aaliyah's birthday party tonight. I didn't want to say anything in front of your parents because they would've asked all types of questions."

"Thank you." I laughed. "The party is tomorrow, but I will absolutely send you pictures."

"Live your life."

We said our goodbyes, and I dried my tears. With my music turned up, I didn't get consumed with sadness. I just got introspective and gave myself space to think.

When I arrived home, I had a white envelope taped to my door. I grabbed it as I walked into my cute little one-bedroom apartment. Frowning at the stale scent that greeted me when I entered, I carried my bags to the bedroom. The lack of movement and warm weather for almost two months forced me to immediately open my windows and get to cleaning. By the time I finished, I was exhausted. But before I showered and prepared for bed, I remembered the letter from the door.

*Shit*, I internally groaned as I recognized the Richland Hills letterhead and the two-week-old date emblazoned on the top.

I was expecting the worst as I started reading, and then I stopped in my tracks as I realized a mistake had to have been made.

"I wish," I muttered as I saw that there was a credit on my account that covered my rent through the rest of the year.

*I'll send her an email.*

Shaking my head, I headed to the bathroom. After a shower, I called Nina, and at midnight, we called Aaliyah to tell her happy birthday. Talking to them was a great way to wind down, and when I fell asleep, I slept hard.

**Lamar Anderson:** If I leave straight from the facility, I can get to you at four o'clock. If I go home, I can get to you by five, five-thirty. Let me know what you want me to do. I have my stuff with me.

**Jazmyn Payne:** We have to be there at six and we can't be late so I'd rather you just come straight here. You can get ready with me and then we'll head out to Dowdy Lake.

I sent that text when I woke up and then rushed to my nail appointment. I hadn't been since the spa day with my aunt. I got my eyebrows threaded, and I got a wax because I hadn't had one since June. I couldn't get a hair appointment until next week, so when I showered, I took extra time to wash my locs.

"Braless?" I mumbled out loud as I stared at the black gown. The backless halter with two sheer pieces that hung long like a train was a sexy choice that Nina and Aaliyah had picked out for me. But I was only just now realizing that due to my summer in Chance, I'd never purchased the breast tape necessary for a dress like that.

I tied my silk robe tighter and reached for my phone. I was going to call Nina to ask what she would suggest since I didn't have tape. But I saw the time and freaked out because I still needed to sit under the dryer to dry my hair.

To kill two birds with one stone, I set up my hooded hair dryer in the living room, and I moisturized my body while sitting under it. I wanted to have everything done and be dressed before Lamar arrived at four o'clock.

**Lamar Anderson:** Are you home?

**Jazmyn Payne:** Yes, sitting under the dryer so texting is easier.

**Lamar Anderson:** Is it okay if I come up? I'm a little early.

Panic swirled in my belly as I still needed fifteen more minutes until my hair was dry.

*There's nothing I can do about it now.*

I crossed the living room to unlock the door and then got back underneath the dryer.

**Jazmyn Payne:** Of course, come on up. It's unlocked.

I hadn't seen Lamar in so long, I got nervous when he knocked. I made sure I was covered up completely and retied the belt of my robe just as the handle started to turn.

"Hey," I greeted him when he walked through the door in basketball shorts and a T-shirt. "Come in."

"What's up?" he said, noticing what I had on. "Is this the move for the night? Because if so, I'm going to be overdressed."

Grinning, I rolled my eyes. "I'm getting dressed after my hair dries."

"I'm not complaining. I like it." He tilted his head to the side. "That's a short-ass robe."

"I have about fifteen more minutes under here, and then I'm getting dressed," I replied, swatting at his arm as he came close. "You can put that"—I pointed to his duffel and garment bags—"in my room. It's at the end of the hall. And the bathroom is right next to it. I have a towel and washcloth out for you."

"Thank you." He grabbed my hand and then leaned down to kiss it. "It's really good to see you."

"It's good to see you, too."

Fifteen minutes later, the dryer stopped, and the shower turned off. I had just gotten in my room when Lamar exited the bathroom.

*Well, damn.*

Lamar Anderson's fine ass was wrapped in just a towel.

He stopped when he saw me.

At six feet five inches with broad shoulders and muscular arms, he filled the doorway with his thick body. The water droplets speckling his mahogany skin dripped down his firm chest and soft belly. The outline of his terry cloth–covered bulge held my attention and seemed to become more pronounced as the seconds ticked by.

My nipples tightened against the silk at the sight of him. I ripped my eyes up to his and flushed when I realized he'd caught me staring. "I, um . . . did you—is the bathroom steamy?" I stammered.

His gaze slowly scanned my body, lingering on my breasts. "Yes."

"Okay, I'll give it a few minutes," I mumbled distractedly, sweeping my eyes down his body again.

He licked his lips and started to cross the room toward me. "How much time do we have?"

The way he looked at me sucked the breath from my body. His gaze left me exposed, inexplicably vulnerable.

I exhaled shakily. "Um, we need to leave in an hour and fifteen minutes."

"So there's time."

"For what?" I whispered.

Without a word, he gently wrapped his hand around my neck and backed me up against the wall. His face hovered over mine. Seconds ticked by, and my heart started racing. His eyes bored into me with such a fierce intensity that it reduced me to nothing more than raw nerve endings. The want and need etched into his handsome features assured me he was just as far gone as I was.

"There's time for me to show you what's been on my mind," he said softly.

His mouth was so close, I thought he was going to kiss me. But he hovered just out of reach, leaving me waiting, wanting. The electricity crackled between us.

"If you want that," he whispered. "Do you want that?"

As he stared into my eyes, his fingers flexed against my throat. I knew my pulse told him my truth.

"Yes," I breathed. "I want it."

He let his hand slowly slide down my throat and drift between my breasts, parting my robe in the process. His fingers skated over my belly, unraveling the belt on the descent. He continued over my soft flesh until he reached his destination between my thighs.

He sucked in a sharp breath. "Is this for me?"

I nodded as his fingers played in my wetness. "Yes."

He closed his eyes for a second as if he were letting my answer wash over him. "Is your pussy always this wet?"

"When I think about you," I admitted.

Groaning, he crashed his lips into mine.

There was a passionate, almost-frenetic energy in the long-overdue kiss. Things heated up quickly. We had our hands all over each other, and when his tongue met mine, I felt it everywhere. I was so consumed that I didn't even realize his towel and my robe had pooled at our feet.

My hands moved down his firm chest and the soft thickness of his midsection. The moment I dipped below his belly button, the kiss became more passionate. I wrapped my fingers around his dick and lightly ran my hand from the base to the tip.

Gripping my hips in response, he groaned, pulling out of the kiss. "Jazz . . ."

"Yes?"

He pressed his lips against mine. "I want you to ride my face until you come for me." He palmed my ass. "And then I'm going to put all this dick"—shifting forward and pressing himself against my belly—"deep in your pussy, and I want you to come for me all over again."

"Yes," I breathed.

He kissed me hard while he lifted me by my ass and carried me to the bed a few feet away. He released me, making sure I felt every inch of him as he slid me down his body. When my feet touched the floor, he sat on my bed and pulled me between his open legs.

Lamar looked up at me, licking his lips as he scanned my naked body. "This is sexy," he murmured, staring at my newest piercing. "Is this new?"

"Yeah," I breathed. My face flushed as he examined it, his eyes taking in my midsection.

"I love the way it looks on you." With his hands on my hips, he leaned up to kiss above the belly jewelry. "I love the way you look." He kissed to the right of it. "I love the way you feel"—he kissed to the left of it—"and the way you taste." Moving his hands to my ass, he kissed me from one hip to the other. "I want every inch of you."

"You can have anything you want," I told him, my voice barely audible.

"Sit on my face," he whispered against my skin.

His heated gaze was trained on me as he lay back. I bit my lip while I climbed onto the bed and straddled his head. The moment I got comfortable, he wrapped his arms around my thick thighs and went to work.

Lamar Anderson was not playing with me.

His skillful tongue knew exactly what to do, and my body reacted in kind. His beard tickled my ass as he ran his tongue the entire length of me. I'd been fantasizing about him eating me since the first time his tongue touched me, so I wanted to savor the feeling. But that time had been an appetizer, and this was the main course. I wanted to relish being devoured. But I was close to the edge, and he kept flicking and sucking my clit with the perfect amount of pressure.

I didn't last two minutes.

Writhing above him, I couldn't take it anymore, and I came hard.

"Oh my God." I panted as I rolled off him.

I landed on my back in the middle of the bed. With my eyes closed, I put my hand to my chest.

"You look as good as you taste," he whispered into my neck.

His lips skated down my jaw, and when he kissed me, it was with reckless abandon. Our mouths moved as if we couldn't get enough of each other.

"I can't get enough of you," he groaned into my mouth as I rolled on top of him. With his back pinned against the bed, he gave me a heated gaze.

I reached down for his nine thick inches, wrapping my fingers around his girth. I trembled as I moved over the curve, remembering how it felt inside me. "Good."

Egged on by the sounds he made as I stroked him, I looked into his eyes and licked the length of him.

"Jazz . . ." he uttered, desire dripping from the way he said my name.

The way his face twitched made me do it one more time before resting it against my lips. He inhaled sharply. I knew he was bracing himself for what was about to happen.

"Is this for me?" I asked, overenunciating so my lips purposely brushed against the sensitive tip.

"Hell yeah—"

Stopping his sentence in its tracks, I engulfed the head of his dick in my mouth and swirled my tongue around.

"Oh shit!" Lamar gasped, putting his hand on the back of my head.

I sucked hard and sloppily as I worked my way down his shaft, taking as much of him as I could to the back of my throat. He growled so loudly that I was certain my neighbors heard.

"Goddamn, Jazz . . ." He closed his eyes as if it were too much for him, and that just turned me on more.

I pulled off him and pumped him with my fist. When he opened his eyes, I smirked before slipping him between my lips again. Moving my mouth up and down on him, I gagged slightly every time he hit the back of my throat. I gently played with his balls, teasing him to heighten his pleasure.

He growled, gripping my locs at the root.

I could sense that he was being rushed to his orgasm when he started to rock his hips and force my head to meet him.

"Fuck! That mouth," he groaned sexily, pulling me off him. "You're trying to make me come."

Wiping my face with the back of my hand, I nodded. "Mm-hmm."

He licked his lips and then rolled us over so that he was on top of me. "I'm not coming in your mouth yet." He kissed me and then kissed his way down to my breasts. He sucked one nipple and then the other before he uttered, "Not when I've been thinking about coming in your pussy all summer."

*Oh shit.*

It was the perfect storm of what he'd said, how he'd said it, and the way he stared into my eyes that caused me to clench. I was momentarily pinned under him as he got situated, and I loved the way it felt. I couldn't move, and the thought of him restraining me gave me butterflies. I kept thinking about how he'd said he wanted to tie me up, and I almost came at the thought of it.

He kissed up my sternum. "You wrapped those soft, sexy lips around—"

Our mouths collided as we devoured each other. He caged me with his arms, and the kiss deepened. He was between my legs, and without thinking, I wrapped them around his waist. I felt him hot and hard, pressing against me. Still covered in my saliva, his dick slid across my slit enticingly.

I moaned.

I let my lashes flutter open as I broke the kiss. Staring up at him, my heart thumped against my chest. The way his eyes glinted with unbridled lust did something to me.

"I want you so bad," I admitted breathily.

"Where do you want me?"

"I want you inside me," I told him as I slid my hands up his muscular arms. "I *need* you inside me."

He made a noise before his lips met mine. He sucked my bottom lip into his mouth before kissing me deeply. It sent chills from my head to my toes and ignited the fire between my thighs. The pull deep in my belly caused me to clench tightly and throb with anticipation.

Wrapping my arms around his neck, I pulled him as close as possible and caressed my tongue against his. When he pulled away, he searched my eyes.

"I want to feel that tight little pussy of yours gripping me," he growled, grinding against me. "I want to feel you come on my dick."

"Yes, please," I moaned, rubbing myself along his shaft. "Please . . ."

He closed his eyes tightly.

I touched his face before bringing his lips to mine. "Please . . . please make me come on your dick," I begged between pecks.

"Jazzy . . ." My name was barely a whisper as our mouths moved over each other. His breathing was as erratic as my heartbeats. We were barely holding on to our self-control.

He moved so the head of his dick could experience my wetness, and then he paused. Feeling his restraint only added to the sexiness of the moment.

"I should get a condom from my bag," he uttered thickly.

I held his gaze. Twenty seconds of lust-filled silence passed between us.

"You should get a condom," I murmured as I rolled my hips, forcing his dick to part my lips fractionally.

"Yes." His voice broke sexily as he moved his body forward. "Being responsible . . ." He pushed himself off me and went to his bag.

I watched his athletic body move across the room, and I licked my lips watching him roll the condom over his big dick.

Instead of meeting me in the middle of the bed, he grabbed my legs and pulled me where he wanted me. I'd never been manhandled like that before, and I let out a little giggle of surprise.

"You okay?" he asked, spreading my legs and climbing between them.

"Yes," I breathed, tweaking my nipples.

He used his dick to spread my wetness over my clit, causing me to moan. "Good."

I quivered.

I ran my hands all over my breasts and belly before reaching between my legs and grabbing his dick. Using it to play with my clit, I got myself worked up. The sound of my wetness punctuated the air. The way his eyes pinned me as he watched me use his dick to play with myself forced me to moan.

"Fuck," he grunted, grabbing my hips. Tilting me so my ass was slightly off the bed, he flexed his fingers against my skin as he lined his dick up.

My breathing was heavy, anticipating what was to come. "Please."

He slowly parted my lips as he pressed his head into me. We moaned in unison.

He squeezed his eyes shut as he held himself in place.

"Please fill me up," I begged. "Please, please let me feel y—"

My sentence dissolved the moment he sank into me.

He let out a rumbling noise in the back of his throat.

Inch by inch he stretched me out deliciously. Digging my nails into his shoulders, I moaned loudly. The yearning deep in my core spread through my entire body as he worked his way into me. Once he was buried inside, he paused, adjusting to the tight fit.

"You're so fucking tight." He put his hand around my neck and then leaned down so his mouth was against my ear. "But you take me so fucking good."

Chills ran down my spine.

"Lamar," I whimpered.

"Fuck," he swore, before slowly pulling out of me. He bit down on my earlobe before he thrust forward.

I gasped, clenching around him.

A groan from the depths of him rumbled through his body and tingled mine. The sexiness of that sound and knowing I'd caused him to make it made my heart flutter. I ran my nails down his back and then pulled him closer, wanting all of him.

I moaned.

"I love the way you sound," he whispered.

He sat up, letting his hand slip from my neck, over my breasts, and down my belly. He spread my thighs wider and watched himself move in and out of me. Hearing him, seeing him, feeling him heightened the experience.

"This pretty pussy looks so fucking good," he murmured. "You taking that shit, Jazzy."

Incoherent words rolled off my tongue as he started strumming my clit with his thumb.

"That's it, Jazzy," he groaned. "That's it. Give it to me."

With each stroke, I got louder and more responsive. I didn't recognize my own voice. And the louder I got, the rougher he became. The more my body responded, the louder he became. The sound of my wetness invited him in deeper.

"Oh fuck," he panted as he drove himself into me.

My lashes fluttered closed. "Please don't stop, please don't stop, please don't stop . . ."

"Look at me. Open your eyes, Jazzy. Let me see you."

My eyes opened, and as soon as they locked with his, my orgasm snuck up on me. I gasped as I clamped down around his dick.

He grunted, fucking me through it. He held my legs open and never broke his rhythm. He fell forward, and his mouth covered mine. The new position of his body caused his dick to hit a spot that had never been hit before.

"Oh my God," I cried out as another impending implosion built.

Grunts and moans poured out of us as he began succumbing to his own pleasure. Feeling him lose control, watching the way his face contorted, and being so stretched and full of dick pushed me over the edge. A silent scream left my mouth as my legs locked and my back arched violently. For the third—and most powerful—time, I came hard, trembling and free-falling into pleasure.

I had no control of my pulsating body as he bucked against me. Cursing under his breath, he stiffened and shuddered. His mouth found mine, and we shared heady, passionate, out-of-breath kisses.

My heart was pounding in my chest, and both of us panted, completely exhausted. Pulling out of the kiss, he rested his forehead against mine. I reached up and gently scratched his beard.

"I'm really feeling you," I whispered, staring into his eyes.

He brushed his lips against mine. "I'm really feeling you, too."

# 16

After the first time we'd had sex, I met his mom. After the second time we'd had sex, he met my best friends. I didn't have much dating experience, but I knew we weren't doing things the typical way. It was just my luck that my attempt to get back out there ended up being the best sex I'd ever had with the best man I'd ever met. He made me feel so many different emotions—all of them good, but scary.

*What is this?*

I wasn't sure what was going on. But when I looked over at Lamar, I couldn't help but smile. I liked him, and I wanted to see him, but I'd asked him to be my date only because Aaliyah had said we *had* to bring one. Yet, after being reunited, the date felt more significant.

"You are so beautiful," Lamar whispered, running his hand down my exposed back. His fingertips danced over my skin and sent a chill down my spine. "And sexy."

"So are you," I complimented him back as we stood off to the side of the party. I ran my hand down the lapel of his sleek black suit. "I like this look on you."

The black-on-black double-breasted tuxedo suit was tailored to perfection. Because of his measurements, he had only a handful of suits, and each of them was custom-made to fit his proportions.

"You like this?" He stepped back, opening the suit jacket to show off the complete look.

I nodded. "A lot. I prefer you naked, but this is a close second."

*Clothed and unclothed, coming and going, the man looks good.*

Licking his lips, he let go of his jacket and grabbed my face. "Is that right?"

"Yes," I murmured, staring into his eyes.

And I meant it.

He leaned down and pressed his lips against mine. It was a soft, sweet kiss. I wrapped my arms around him and melted into his body.

I sighed contentedly into his mouth before pulling away. "I'm glad you're here."

"I'm glad you invited me." He kissed me again and then looked around the lake house grounds. "This is cool."

"You're having a good time?"

"Hell yeah. Did you taste that food?"

I laughed. "The dinner was perfect."

Chef Tiana Mason cooked some of the most delicious vegetarian dishes known to man, and Lamar had raved about the chicken from the first bite on. The sit-down dinner had been an intimate gathering of Aaliyah's closest friends and family—and their dates. I knew a lot of the people there, and I was worried that it would be uncomfortable for Lamar. But I was pleasantly surprised at how well he fit in, the ease with which he engaged in conversation with the people around us—particularly my best friends and their dates. I knew how smart, funny and charismatic he was, but we had spent only a couple of days together, and we were mostly alone. It had been eye-opening in the best way to see him with a bunch of people he didn't know.

"This used to be my shit," he commented as the DJ played a song from ten years ago.

The DJ had been playing hit after hit for the last three and a half hours. More than a hundred people were spread about the lake house grounds in celebration. Although the music had been good, Lamar and I alternated from the dance floor to the lake to sitting in the tent talking. It was our first date that wasn't a quiet one-on-one, and yet, we still carved out pockets of time to make it so.

". . . so it takes me twenty minutes to write a work email in total," I explained as we stood by the lake. "Two minutes to write it. And eighteen minutes to go over it with a fine-tooth comb so I don't call someone *mama* when I meant *ma'am*."

He burst out laughing. "Yeah, that's tough. Has that happened?"

I gave him a serious look. "Yes. In a reply-all message that went to the principal, the vice principal, the guidance counselors, and the other teachers in the English department." I put my hand on his arm. "I considered walking out mid-class and just transferring schools."

Amused, he shook his head. "Damn."

"Now, what about you?" I asked, looking up at him.

"Something embarrassing that I learned from," he mused, rubbing his beard. "Okay, so, it's my first year with the Monarchs. There's ninety of us in training camp. They make cuts in August, and when I get the call, I'm hype. I pull up to the practice facility, we call it The Lab. I park, hop out the ride . . . and am immediately humbled."

"Why?"

He shook his head. "Practice squad parks in the back—past the dumpsters." When my jaw dropped, he continued. "You have to earn your spot in the main lot."

"Damn."

Maybe it was the signature drinks running through our systems, but we simultaneously burst out laughing.

"I came to steal Jazz for a minute, but it looks like I'm interrupting a good time," Aaliyah commented as she appeared with a glowing smile on her face.

"A good time is definitely being had," I said.

"You did the damn thing with this party," Lamar told her, gesturing around. "Thanks for letting me be here."

"I'm glad to have you." Aaliyah cocked her head to the side. "And I'm glad to have you putting a smile on Jazz's face."

His palm crept up my spine. "And I plan to keep a smile on her face."

My stomach fluttered.

"Oh, I like that," she cooed, shifting her eyes between us. "I like him."

"Yeah." Biting my bottom lip, I peered up at him. "I like him, too."

Aaliyah squealed giddily, and Lamar grinned, letting his fingers dance up my back.

"I'll go get another one of those drinks and let you two talk," Lamar stated before walking away.

As soon as he was out of earshot, Aaliyah wiggled her eyebrows. "I thought you said you two were friends."

"We are friends," I said, unable to stop smiling. We made our way to the dock. "There are some definite benefits that have come with the friendship though."

"I bet!" She stuck out her tongue and then laughed. "But let's be real, you two are *not* just friends. That man looks at you like you hung the sun, the moon, and the stars."

I directed my attention over to where he was getting a drink. "He does?"

"Yes. And it's not just him. The way the two of you look at each other is so beautiful. I think he may be the one."

Stopping on the dock, I rolled my eyes. "Girl."

"What?"

"How many drinks have you had?"

"That doesn't matter. I'm telling the truth. I'm calling it now. He is the one!"

"How many drinks?"

"A lot, but that's not why I'm saying that."

I laughed loudly. "You're one to talk. You've been grinning since your Cinderella moment." I touched her hair that had mysteriously gotten sweated out early on in the night. "And didn't you start the night with a blowout?"

She put her hands on her hips. "I've been on the dance floor all night."

I pursed my lips. "Yeah, okay," I replied sarcastically. "That's not the only thing you've been on."

We cracked up.

Spotting Nina, we tried to wave her down, but she was too enthralled with her date.

"Nina!" I yelled, right when the DJ switched to a different song.

She heard and made her way over to us.

I saw all thirty-two of her teeth as she approached us.

"The two of you look happy as hell," she remarked when she was a few feet away.

We teased Nina about her situation, and then she turned the heat on us. Aaliyah didn't deny that the man who'd swept her off her feet for her birthday was her man, but she said nothing was official.

*Yet.*

Nina claimed her date wasn't her man because of a technicality.

*But that's not how it looks.*

And I told them that Lamar and I were just friends because that's what we were—even though the whole night felt like more.

*And if I count the first time we hung out, it's only our third date.*

It was possible I was just as delusional as my friends.

"What are you scared of?" Nina asked.

As the alcohol coursed through my system, my mind sent me back to a realization I had weeks ago.

*Lamar*, I answered silently. *Lamar scares me.*

Maybe I was scared of my own feelings. Maybe I was scared that it was just a fling for him. I knew I liked him, and I didn't doubt that he liked me. But his career didn't allow for a relationship, and I wasn't really interested in putting myself in a position to get hurt.

"I am enjoying myself," I admitted after they started double-teaming me. "That doesn't change the fact that we're friends. It's only our third date. And the first time we've seen each other since June."

"So?" Aaliyah countered. "I saw the way you two were looking at each other."

"And you think we didn't notice how you two kept sneaking off?" Nina pointed out. "Making out behind the tent. Fucking behind the house."

"No, we didn't!" I protested over their laughter.

Nina shrugged. "Before the fireworks, I just assumed you took his fine ass around back and climbed him like a tree."

"That sounds like something you would do," I countered.

She nodded. "And would!"

"He's good-looking, big and tall, charismatic, interesting." Aaliyah started listing some of Lamar's qualities. "You both love football and he looks like a football player."

I nodded. "He is."

"He makes you feel good, and I haven't seen you smile like you've been smiling in a really long time." Nina squeezed my shoulder. "It looks good on you."

"You already admitted you like him," Aaliyah said.

"And you already admitted you fucked him." Nina held up two fingers. "Twice."

The birthday girl cocked her head to the side. "You definitely downplayed this 'friendship' because from where I'm standing, it's true love."

Nina and I groaned in unison.

I rolled my eyes. "You want everybody to be in love so bad."

We were laughing and joking when Aaliyah's cousin Tamara and her wife came by with a tray of drinks.

"We want to toast my cousin," Tamara said after we all had a drink in our hands. "Where are your dates?"

We all gestured to the three handsome men huddled together in conversation. Her wife took the rest of the drinks and went to go get them. When she got back a couple of minutes later with the men in tow, we were all weak with laughter.

Lamar slid beside me and put his arm around me. I automatically leaned into his warmth. I inhaled his cologne, and the mixture of bergamot orange, cedarwood, and musk caused me to nuzzle my face into his chest. When I realized what I was doing, my eyes flew open.

*What is in these drinks?*

I glanced around to see if anyone noticed, and Nina was staring me dead in my face.

Heat traveled to my cheeks when she winked at me.

I looked away before I burst out laughing.

Tamara lifted her cup and gave a sweet and funny toast.

"To Aaliyah!" we cheered in unison.

Tamara and her wife walked off, and Mecca, another one of Aaliyah's cousins, took a picture of the couple. Once done, she headed our way.

"Aaliyah, her best friends, and their dates," she stated as she got closer to us. "Can you get together for a picture?" Mecca asked.

The six of us huddled together and posed.

"Got it," she said.

Someone toward the edge of the lake called her name, and she ran from the dock without a goodbye.

Nina gestured with her thumb. "I can't remember if she's the nosy one or if—"

"It's her," Aaliyah interrupted.

We all laughed.

The six of us talked for a few minutes, and it wasn't lost on me how well we all meshed. We probably could've stood there and talked for the rest of the night, but the DJ put on a song from our college days, so we scrambled toward the dance floor. After fifteen straight minutes of high-intensity dancing, I was done.

"What's wrong?" Lamar asked.

"My feet are killing me," I admitted. "Will you sit with me?"

Lamar and I got drinks and then went in one of the tents to sit down on a bench.

"Your friends are cool," he said.

"Yeah, they are," I agreed, smiling toward the dance floor where they still were.

"I didn't know what to expect."

"Why?"

"The way you were in Chance. And whenever I asked you what you were doing, you were at your aunt's house." He smirked. "I had no idea y'all would be this lit."

I laughed. "You can't judge me by my days in Chance."

"Oh, don't get me wrong, I fucked with you in Chance. I like that version of you, too." He gestured around. "But I like seeing this side of you, as well."

"You like seeing me tipsy."

He shook his head. "No, even before these drinks—by the way, what is this shit? It tastes like punch."

"Right!" I took a sip. "It's so good. It's a Malibu Sunrise with a twist. Something Ahmad came up with for her a couple of months ago."

"It's good as hell." He paused, taking me in. "But even before the party and the drinks. The side of you I saw at the dinner table when you were talking, on the dance floor when you went to support your friend, when you wanted to make sure everyone had cake. I mean, yeah, I did enjoy how after you got a couple of drinks in you, you were grinding on me and talking reckless like you wanted me to take you up to that bedroom." He chuckled to himself. "But really, I'm talking about the whole night. I like seeing you happy."

I took a sip of my drink, letting his words wash over me. "You didn't think I was happy in Chance?"

He seemed to consider his words before he answered, "You were preoccupied in Chance."

"I hope you didn't feel that way when we were together, because I was very much *occupied* with you." I placed my cup on the table and scooted closer to him. "No matter what was going on in Chance, when I was with you, I was able to be in the moment."

"I never felt like you were being rude or you weren't fully there," he explained. "But I knew from the moment we met that you were carrying something heavy."

"I was," I admitted softly. "I am."

"You can talk to me about anything. You do know that, right? After everything you've done for me, I got you."

I closed my eyes. The alcohol was making it really easy to admit things, and I wasn't sure I was ready.

"Hey, look at me," he said, taking my hand and bringing it to his lips.

When I opened them, my eyes locked with his and automatically started to water. I wasn't completely inebriated. But that last drink had me tipsy enough to face my fear.

He shook his head. "You don't have to tell me anything you don't want to tell me."

Worry had my heart racing. "It's not that I don't want to tell you," I started, feeling my truth welling up inside me. "It's that I don't want you to look at me differently after I tell you."

Concern flickered across his face. "Why would I look at you differently?"

"I like you. A lot. And I have from the beginning. You saw me for me. You didn't see my hurt or my pain. You didn't look at me like I was going to break. And I loved that. I was able to be with you and forget everything else because you didn't know . . ."

His eyes begged me to tell him, but he didn't say a word. He silently held my hand, running his thumb over my knuckles.

"My aunt Addy has had health issues for a while. But a few hours before we met, I found out she had a stroke," I whispered after an extended silence. "The stroke and the rehab that followed took a toll on her, and she is . . ." I couldn't bring myself to say the word. "I stayed in Chance to be with her because they wouldn't release her to be in her home alone. My parents came back earlier this week, and now they're with her. But I'm going to lose the person closest to me any day now, and it is crushing me."

He squeezed my hand comfortingly, and I squeezed his back.

"So being with you and having you not know was nice because I could pretend it wasn't happening," I continued. "Aaliyah and Nina knew Aunt Addy was on hospice and declining, so it always felt like they were worried about me. And sometimes it was too much. Which sounds ridiculous, I know. How dare I have amazing friends who care about my mental and emotional health?" I gave him a rueful smile before sighing. "But because I knew that they knew, I couldn't pretend it wasn't happening. So, when I met you and you didn't know, and we just clicked . . . I wanted to hold on to that for as long as I could. I'm sorry I didn't tell you sooner. Especially as we got closer, I should've told you. I just wanted you to see *me* for as long as possible."

"Don't be sorry." He kissed my hand again. "You don't owe me an apology. But you need to know that I see you, and I like everything I see. Every part of you that you've shown me, I've liked it, and I've wanted more of it. You don't have to hide any part of who you are with me. You're funny. You're sexy. You're perceptive. You're deep. I like all that shit."

"Thank you for saying that, but I want you to still see me as happy, too. I don't want you to look at me as sad. I don't want you to look at me differently—"

"I don't. I haven't."

"—because being around you makes me happy."

His words overlapped my own.

My brows furrowed as I repeated what he'd just said in my head. "What?" I whispered in confusion.

"Your aunt told my mom that she was dyeing her hair as part of a list of things she wanted to do before she's gone . . . and that she's on hospice. And when I called my mom after I got back from Dubai, she told me. She thought I knew. I told her that you'd tell me when you were ready."

My eyes widened. "Wait, wait, wait, wait, wait . . . you've known for two months?"

"Yes. And I never looked at you as anything other than the beautiful, smart, intriguing woman who got me to order a burger instead of wings. Who made an ordinary trip home . . . more than that. A woman who had a lot going on and still made room for me, still made my business idea a viable plan." He leaned forward, holding my gaze. "I knew you were carrying something heavy, and nothing changed. I found out what it was, and nothing changed. And now you know that I know . . . and nothing has changed."

Blinking back tears, I was overwhelmed by his words. I could only manage to utter his name. "Lamar."

"You want me to see you, and I do." He put his arm around my shoulders and his mouth against the shell of my ear. "I see all of you."

Shivering, I leaned into him before turning to crash my lips against his. I wrapped my arms around his neck as our tongues gently teased each other. I pulled out of the kiss as abruptly as I'd initiated it. One more second and I was prepared to climb into his lap and show him how much his words meant to me.

I stared into his eyes. "I like you."

His lips spread into a smile as he pulled me close. "I like you, too."

"Tomorrow is the last Sunday before school starts. Would you like to spend the day with me?"

He ran his fingertips down my back. "I would love to."

When the DJ announced that the party was over, most people headed to their cars. Lamar and I went straight to one of the three bedrooms upstairs that Aaliyah had assigned to us upon arrival. I took a shower and slipped into a silky nightgown. Then I climbed into bed to wait for Lamar to finish his shower—and fell asleep.

Between the way Lamar had put it on me before the party, all the action during the party, and those delicious-ass drinks, I was knocked out cold. It wasn't until the wee hours of the morning that I was cognizant of his arm draped across my midsection and his body pressed against my backside. His breath tickled my neck as I roused from slumber.

Turning carefully until I was face-to-face with him, I watched him sleep. I reached up and caressed his beard. The soft coarse hair was well moisturized and perfectly framed his mouth. His full, kissable lips turned slightly downward at the corners as he slept. His long eyelashes rested on his blemish-free cheeks, hiding the most soulful brown eyes.

Lamar Anderson was so incredibly handsome.

And for all the shit I'd been talking on the dance floor, I woke up next to that sexy man well rested and unfucked.

# 17

"Oh my God," I huffed, trying to catch my breath as I collapsed on the bed. I ran my hands from my belly to my breasts, tweaking my nipples. My body was still vibrating from the intensity of my orgasm. "That felt so . . ." I shivered. "So good."

The first time Lamar and I'd had sex, it was an unexpected, lust-fueled quickie in the woods. The second time, it was passionately rushed in my bedroom prior to the party. So, when he woke up and found me caressing his face, he pulled me close. His hard dick pressed up against me, and seconds later, our clothes were off, and we had been slow fucking and kissing leisurely.

"You take care of me in a way that I've never experienced before," I confessed softly. "I feel you everywhere."

"All I want to do is take care of you." Lamar kissed from my belly to my neck before hovering over my face. "I know I said perfection doesn't exist. But that was before I had your pussy."

I giggled, pulling his lips to mine. "I can't believe you picked me up and did all that."

"I can't believe you thought I was going to drop you."

"I weigh a good amount."

"And I deadlift six hundred pounds." He dropped a peck on my lips. "You're light work."

I'd never been called *light* before. I'd been big my whole life, and I had to admit it felt nice to feel so dainty with him. My entire childhood, I had been one of the biggest kids in my grade. In college, I dated a string of average-height, skinny men before marrying an average-height, skinny man. I'd never been manhandled before. I'd never had someone make me feel weightless. I'd never been picked up and fucked against a wall, let alone above the bed.

I'd never felt like the extra fat on my body was the thing that prevented me from being beautiful. But it definitely kept me from being seen as desirable in Chance—at least openly. The mean girls targeting me and making me public enemy number one made it difficult to make friends, let alone date. Antagonizing me with fat jokes was par for the course, but there were boys who would steal glances and try to proposition me when no one was around. So I knew my weight wasn't the sole issue. But that environment had kept me from ever asking a man to pick me up, spin me around, and handle me like I'd just been handled.

*And there's no way I can go back.*

"How much time do we have?" Lamar asked. "If I weren't rushing to get to your place after practice, I would've remembered to grab my ties and really give you a demonstration."

With the biggest, goofiest grin on my face, I giggled. "Lamar—"

My words were interrupted by a knock at the door.

I scrambled out of the bed, wrapping myself in the sheet. Looking over my shoulder, I saw Lamar was covering himself with the comforter.

I cracked the door, smiling when I saw Aaliyah. "Heyyyyyy."

"Hey," she said distractedly. "We have to be gone by noon. The cleaning crew is here." She swept her eyes down my sheet-laden body. "I'll have them start downstairs."

"We're packing up now."

She gave me a look as she walked toward the stairs. "Mm-hmm."

Laughing, I closed the door and spun around.

"We have to go," I announced.

Lamar took a shower while I quickly packed, and then he packed while I showered. We were walking out of the bedroom thirty minutes later.

"Are you hungry?" I asked as he opened the door of his SUV for me.

He grabbed my ass as he helped me inside. "Hell yeah."

I waited until he walked around and climbed in the driver's side seat.

"Do you want to find a place that is more of the vibe of the place you took me to in Spring Hill? If so, we could go back to my place, and I could change." I gestured to my jeans and T-shirt. "Or do you want to eat something right now?"

"Let's eat now, and then we can change and go somewhere nice for dinner."

I nodded. "Okay, I know just the place."

I hadn't had beef in a month, so I gave him the address, and then I sent a text to my aunt with a photo attached.

"I have to make a call," I told him. "Do you mind?"

He reached over and squeezed my thigh. "Nah, you're good."

I went to my aunt's contact and then pressed the button.

"Hello?" she answered.

"Aunt Addy!" I greeted her. "How are you?"

"I'm good now! I've been wondering how the party went, and I've been waiting for a picture of you and your date."

I glanced over at Lamar and smiled. "I sent you a picture. Check your phone."

"Hold on." Seconds ticked by and then she gasped. "You look beautiful! And that's Lamar?! Goodness gracious! You two look good together. When I told you to get back on the horse, I didn't realize he'd be a stallion!"

I burst out laughing. "That is a wild thing to say."

"I can't wait to meet him."

"I'm sure he'd like that."

"And I haven't seen that smile on your face in a long time. Maybe on your graduation days. But it is really good to see you smiling like that. You just look so happy! Everything you've been through . . . you deserve to smile this big and be this happy. I know y'all had a good time!"

"We did! It was a great party and"—I looked over again—"I had a great date."

He smiled as he switched lanes.

"You two look good together," Aunt Addy stated. "Is that still your friend, or is he your boyfriend yet?"

There was no way I could answer the question. I tried not to smile, but I couldn't help it.

"We're actually in the car now. Heading to get lunch," I answered, hoping she'd get the hint.

"So, you stayed the night together? This is getting serious! Tell him I said hello!"

I snickered and changed the subject again. "How are you feeling?"

"Tell him! Would you really deny me—"

"Oh my God," I complained with amusement. I turned to Lamar. "Aunt Addy says hello."

"Hey, Aunt Addy!" he said loudly.

"You heard him? Now, how are you feeling?" I repeated the question.

"He's got a nice deep voice, don't he? Got some bass to it."

My eyes started watering from holding in a laugh. "How. Are. You?"

When she finished laughing, she answered, "Oh, I'm fine."

"I need more information."

"You didn't give me more information," she teased.

"Aunt Addy!"

"I'm fine. I'm tired," she sighed. "Monica is in the kitchen preparing lunch. I'm going to find a movie. There's not much to tell. Your parents are coming by tonight to get on my last nerve."

I laughed. "Not on your last nerve!"

"I love them. I appreciate them. But yesterday, Richard decided he was going to tend to my yard, and he completely destroyed the flowers I planted in the back—"

"The rosebushes?" I interrupted, shocked.

"The rosebushes!" She sucked her teeth. "They didn't even have the opportunity to grow in good."

"Oh no! I'm sorry!"

"He didn't mean to do it, but . . ." She sighed. "Fortunately, that's the last cut for the season. But I can tell you about all this later."

"It's not a problem. If you want to tell me about it, I want to hear about it."

"You said you were in the car with that handsome man, so get off this phone with me and enjoy him. Tell him I said I look forward to meeting him."

"Aunt Addy—"

"Jazmyn, sweetheart, live your life. I'm fine. You have fun on your date. I love you. Bye!"

"I love you, too. Bye."

I ended the call, slipping my phone into my handbag.

"Aunt Addy said she looks forward to meeting you," I informed him.

"When you talk to her again, tell her I look forward to meeting her, too. How's she doing?" Lamar asked.

"She says she's fine." I planned to check in with Monica to verify, but I didn't mention that. "Thanks for asking."

He grabbed my hand and kissed it.

"How's your family?" I wondered, shifting the focus.

When we arrived at Al's Diner, we ordered cheeseburgers and fries. We sat across from each other and talked about music. We argued over lyrics and the lyrical prowess of different artists. After leaving, we walked up the street. We listened to the songs we'd discussed in the diner while I showed him parts of Richland.

He was a step behind me, and when I stopped to point out something, he gripped my hips, pulling me into him as he listened. Feeling his fingers flex against me had my stomach quivering in excitement. I looked up and over my left shoulder.

My heart skipped a beat.

I loved the way that man looked at me.

"Are you paying attention?" I asked, trying not to smile.

"You're beautiful," he commented. "So I'm a little distracted. But I'm listening."

With a giggle, I rose up onto my toes to kiss his lips.

Once he slipped his arm around me, we continued the tour.

"This is it," I remarked after we'd made it to the park on the other side of the downtown area. "I don't think I was ever meant to be in a small town."

"I don't think you were either."

"I got here twelve years ago, and it was like . . ." I gestured around. "I was finally home. I knew it was the place for me. That's why I built a life here after graduation. I found my place. When I met Aaliyah and Nina, I knew I'd met my people. So that's why I'm still here."

"Would you want to stay here permanently?"

"I would. Unless there was a really, *really* good reason for me to go elsewhere." We turned and started walking back toward Al's Diner. "Is Baltimore like that for you?"

He shook his head. "Nah. The only thing that's like that for me is football. I mean, home is home. Spring Hill is where I was born and raised. And Baltimore has been cool for the last few years. But if I'm playing ball, I could make almost anywhere work."

"So, you'd move to Wyoming if they had a team?" I asked, picking a state randomly.

"If that was the only place that I could play, hell yeah. And crazy enough, that could happen."

My eyebrows shot up. "What?"

"You can be with one team for one week and then be across the country with another team the next week. As long as you get released early enough in the week, another team can pick you up for the practice squad."

"Wait, wait, wait, wait, wait . . . don't you have a place in Baltimore?"

He nodded. "Yeah."

"What if, God forbid, you get sent to a new team? What happens to your apartment?"

"I have a townhouse. I know guys who live out of a hotel because that's more cost-effective for them." He shook his head. "But I couldn't do it. I need a home base. So, financially, it might not make sense to some people, but—"

"No, I get it," I agreed quickly. "Having a place to call home makes complete sense to me. And fortunately, it's been working out."

He nodded. "Yeah, it has. You should come check it out."

"Your place? Or Baltimore."

"My place. But I'll show you around Baltimore, too."

My lips twitched, trying not to grin up at him. "Is that an invitation?"

"Yes." He smirked, running his hand over his beard. "An open one."

"With the season starting next week, I figured you'd be busy."

"Yeah. I am." He shrugged. "But I'd still want to see you."

*I'd want to*, I repeated silently as we walked.

I didn't want to read too much into it. But *I'd want to* was hopeful. It wasn't definitive. Our connection was electric, and our feelings were real, but from the beginning, I'd known what it was. Even if I'd let the way he handled my body skew the reality of our relationship for a moment, the fact remained that he was too busy for more with me, and I was too scared to admit I wanted more with him.

I cleared my throat lightly. "I'd want to see you, too."

"Good." He draped his arm around my shoulder and pulled me into him. "We'll have to figure something out."

Nodding, I put my arm around his torso as we walked through downtown Richland. "Are you off tomorrow?"

"No. They don't give a damn about a holiday since the regular season starts this week. It's a half day though."

"And school starts Tuesday, so I guess we should get back to my place and enjoy the rest of this Sunday."

He kissed me and caused butterflies to ripple through my belly. When he pulled away, he whispered, "I like the sound of that."

We got to his SUV, and he pulled his phone out of his pocket. "Excuse me for a minute," he told me, before answering the call. "What's up, Ma?"

He opened the door for me and then climbed into the driver's seat.

"Yeah, I know. I'm going to miss it. But depending on what they have us doing on Tuesday, I might drive down and bring her gift because I won't be back down for the rest of the season." He started the engine and turned the air-conditioning on. "Yeah, I'll let you know tomorrow after the morning session if I'm driving down. Yeah, okay. Love you, too. Bye."

He disconnected the call and looked over at me. "My bad."

I shook my head. "You're fine."

He pulled off from the curb and made his way to my place. "My niece's tenth birthday party is this weekend, and they're having a party at my mom's."

I noticed the disappointment in his voice. We'd talked about our families before, and I knew he was a big family man. "You're going to miss it?"

"I'm going to try not to. I usually miss it and it's fine. I send a gift. But my nephew's birthday is in May, so I was at his party. And apparently today my niece said something to my mom about me never coming to hers."

I reached over and intertwined my fingers with his. "I want to say that she'll understand, but she's ten." I squeezed his hand. "*But* because she's ten, and I know you'll make it up to her, she'll be okay. Everything you've ever told me lets me know that she knows you love her."

"Yeah. I might drive down there on her actual birthday. I don't know. I'm gonna figure something out."

"Yeah, you will. You have a way of making everything better, so your niece is going to be fine. Everything is going to work out."

He brought my hand to his lips and kissed it. "I appreciate you saying that."

We got back to my place, and even though the plan had been to dress up and go to dinner, we holed up in bed for the rest of the day. We got up only to eat Thai delivery, and then he packed up to leave my place around seven o'clock.

"Thank you for spending the weekend with me," I said as I walked Lamar to the door, slightly limping and fully drained. I tightened the belt of my robe before looking up into his eyes. "It was fun."

He dropped his bags at his feet. "Thank you for inviting me to spend it with you," he replied, pulling me flush against him. "I had a real good time."

"Me, too." I reached up to clasp my hands behind his neck. "I almost didn't ask. But I'm glad I did."

"You weren't going to ask me?" he scoffed, grabbing my ass through the robe and giving me a light spank. "Why not?"

"When it occurred to me that I needed a date, we hadn't seen each other for almost two months. We didn't really talk in July and talked when we could in August. It was last-minute. I didn't think you'd have the time to come. I didn't think you'd *want* to come." I lifted my shoulders. "I guess I just felt like I was asking for too much."

He stared into my eyes, and I felt like he was piercing my soul.

He brought his face close, allowing his mouth to hover over mine. "You can get anything you want from me."

I swallowed hard. "Well, what if what I want is something you can't give me?"

"Tell me what you want, and let me determine what I can and can't give you."

*More time.*

*An upcoming date.*

*One more orgasm for the road.*

"Okay," I whispered.

"You know what I noticed?" he asked, rubbing the tip of his nose to mine. "You open up more when we're touching," he said, just before his lips covered mine.

As our tongues touched and the kiss deepened, I realized he wasn't wrong. My feelings for him always felt like they were about to spill out of me when we were together.

We said goodbye, and after closing the door behind him, I immediately showered and went to bed. I hadn't had regular sex in years, so to have been so thoroughly taken care of had taken a lot out of me. I wanted to sleep in on Monday, but because I'd been gone all summer, I had to wake up early to set up my classroom first thing in the morning. I was only able to get in for three hours because the principal had cookout plans that afternoon. So I did a lot of work in a limited amount of time. Between that and my time with Lamar, I was exhausted. I was halfway to sleep before eight o'clock and still sore Tuesday.

"'Education is the passport to the future, for tomorrow belongs to those who prepare for it today,'" I quoted Malcolm X to my students as I did at the beginning of every school year. "Raise your hand if you're ready to prepare."

They quietly looked around the room. But then slowly, everyone lifted an arm in the air.

And that was the last moment of silence I had for the rest of the day.

**Lamar Anderson:** How was the first day of school?

**Jazmyn Payne:** It's seven-thirty and I'm already in the bed.

**Lamar Anderson:** Damn! That bad?

**Jazmyn Payne:** It was loud. Half the kids didn't do the summer reading. And it was a lot of yelling for no reason.

**Lamar Anderson:** Why were you yelling?!

Pulling the covers over my shoulder, I snickered into my pillow.

**Jazmyn Payne:** Not me! The students! How are you feeling about tomorrow? It's the first game practice, right?

**Lamar Anderson:** Yes. Wednesdays and Thursdays are the longest days so I'm sure I'll feel like you do now.

**Jazmyn Payne:** You've been killing it all summer. The fact that the season is starting, I know practices are about to get more intense. But you got this! Even if it's late and I go to sleep early, let me know how it goes please.

**Lamar Anderson:** Thank you, I will. I know you're tired. Get your rest and I'll hit you up tomorrow.

I started to put my phone on the charger when I realized I had an email.

"Oh shit!" I exclaimed in a whisper, sitting straight up in bed.

The property manager emailed me a confirmation. It wasn't a misprint or a wrong address; the credit on my account was real. My rent was paid for the next four months.

# 18

**Jazmyn Payne:** What type of workout is this, Nina? I said I wanted to increase my flexibility not do a floor routine in the Olympics!

I sent a photo of my sweaty face to the group chat after a failed attempt to do the last move.

**Nina Ford:** I am so weak right now!

**Aaliyah James:** Ever since you got home, you've been glowing! I love that for you. You deserve these wins!

**Nina Ford:** Right? Jazz got her rent paid and she got her back blown out. What's next? A raise? A book deal?

**Jazmyn Payne:** After a trip to Chance, Richland always feels good. But this week feels different.

**Nina Ford:** Because you got dicked down and extra money in your pocket. A great start to the month!

Amused, I shook my head. *She's not wrong.*

**Aaliyah James:** Because you're in love!

I froze before ignoring Aaliyah's comment.

**Jazmyn Payne:** With everything going on, I still can't wrap my mind around my rent situation!

**Nina Ford:** Maybe you've been overpaying for a one-bedroom, one-bath for too long and they decided they owe you.

**Jazmyn Payne:** You've met the property manager . . . She'd rather burn this bitch to the ground for the insurance money than to make it more affordable. This is definitely not her. The leasing agent said she's heard of people coming in to bless accounts, so I just chalked it up to that.

**Aaliyah James:** Oh, I've heard of that too! And if anyone deserves an extra blessing, it's you.

**Jazmyn Payne:** With everything going on, this came right on time.

**Nina Ford:** From the way you talked about Lamar, you also came right on time.

**Aaliyah James:** I just laughed so loud Ahmad came in here asking what was so funny.

**Jazmyn Payne:** Don't tell him what Nina said!

**Nina Ford:** Don't be ashamed now, Jazz! You needed a special workout to calm your muscles down after Lamar turned you every which way but loose!

**Jazmyn Payne:** You don't take nothing seriously!

**Aaliyah James:** From what I understand, Lamar took you very seriously and that's why your body hurts.

My head fell back as I laughed.

**Nina Ford:** That's hilarious!

**Jazmyn Payne:** Congratulations on getting under my skin!

**Aaliyah James:** We're just playing! We're happy for you Jazz!

**Nina Ford:** Congratulations on getting the kind of dick that requires a deep stretch!

Cackling, I tossed my phone on the couch and struggled to get up after those exercises. It was Saturday morning, the first week of school had been rough, and my body ached for Lamar in an unhealthy way. I was sore from the positions he'd put me in. But the throbbing between my thighs was agonizing.

And I had no idea when I was going to see him again.

Fortunately, we talked every night.

Sometimes it was for ten minutes, and sometimes it was for an hour, but since the party, we'd made a point to talk every night. It wasn't something that was stated or planned. It just happened that way. But due to our nightly chats, I found myself dreaming of him and waking up with a smile.

*This is a problem.*

After cleaning, doing laundry, and making lunch, I spent the rest of the day grading assignments. When my phone rang, I welcomed the break.

"Aunt Addy, I was starting to think you were avoiding my call," I answered.

"Hey, Jazmyn," she replied, sounding lethargic. "How are you?"

I scooted to the edge of the couch and turned the volume up to hear her better. "How are *you*?"

"I'm okay. When are you going to see Lamar again?"

A nervous laugh jumped out of me at the quick, unexpected shift. "Um. The season has officially started, so . . . I'm not sure."

"Do you want to see him again?"

"I do," I admitted.

"Then do it."

*If only it were that simple.*

I cleared my throat. "Okay, what about your party? I haven't seen my invitation in the mail. Are you trying to uninvite me? Because I'll just show up."

She laughed, sounding slightly winded. "No, no, no. It's coming though. Where are you on your list?"

We talked for a little while longer, and then we said good night.

Closing my eyes, I slumped into the cushion because I could hear it in her voice. I wasn't in denial, but I wasn't ready for her to go.

*I need to work on my book*, I thought, before pushing myself up and getting to it.

I woke up early on Sunday to write before going to the sports bar up the street. I was still thinking about my storyline up until I watched the Monarchs jog out onto the field to start the game.

"Hey!" Aaliyah greeted me, touching my back as she took the seat next to me.

I hugged her. "Hey, Liyah! I love these glasses!" Smiling at her man, I hugged him as well. "Hey, Ahmad!"

"What's up?" he said, before taking the seat next to Aaliyah. "We didn't miss anything, did we?"

"The first quarter just started. Monarchs lost the coin toss so they're getting the ball first." I'd caught them up. "You didn't miss anything."

The game came back on, and the Monarchs ended up scoring. So, when the Wasps were on offense and the Monarchs were on defense, I paid close attention.

"Something is going on with Channing," I pointed out as Channing missed a tackle. "Watch the way he moves on the ball. He used to be quick. There's something wrong. I'm telling you."

"He got hurt last year," Ahmad reminded us. "Maybe he never fully recovered because his ass be on the field limping."

I laughed. "It *is* a limp!"

"Who are you talking about?" Aaliyah asked, looking between us.

"Number ninety-nine," Ahmad answered her, pointing at the screen.

"On the Monarchs?" she wondered.

I looked at her with my brows furrowed because they'd just showed the replay twice. "Girl!"

"Baby, take those glasses off, and you might be able to see something," he teased.

She looked like she was holding in her amusement. "I need my glasses to see, thank you very much!"

"Those glasses ain't got the first bit of prescription in them." Ahmad chuckled. "They might as well not have lenses!"

Aaliyah was trying not to laugh as she pushed her glasses up the bridge of her nose.

I, on the other hand, was weak.

Tears were in my eyes, and my body quaked. I almost missed the next play because I was laughing so hard.

"Jazz, don't encourage him. He doesn't know how to act. Just bad!" She turned to Ahmad. "You had silver teeth as a toddler, huh?"

He burst out laughing.

She put her hands on her hips. "Y'all ain't about to sit here and talk about my fashion-statement glasses!"

"*Y'all*?!" I reacted with wide teary eyes. "What do you mean *y'all*?! I didn't even say anything! How did I get in this?"

"You laughed a little too hard. It felt like laughter of agreement."

"Those glasses don't have prescription in them though! He wasn't lying!" I argued. "You have twenty-twenty vision, and you still missed multiple replays."

"Your glasses look beautiful on you." He leaned over and kissed her cheek. "But now use your *eyes* to watch number ninety-nine on this play. He's playing defense."

"In *my* defense, I was watching the offense." She giggled, snuggling against him.

Watching them, I couldn't help but smile. They were so cute and playful with each other. They had spent every day together since her party. For the past week, Aaliyah had been in the healthiest, happiest, and most hilarious relationship, and I was thrilled for her. She deserved it.

"That should've been a flag!" I exclaimed, throwing my hand up in the fourth quarter.

I'd been ignoring my group chat with my work friends, Ben and Alexa, since halftime. The game was close, but it shouldn't have been. The Monarchs defense was letting the Wasps make plays on them because they'd located the weak spot—Channing.

"He's going to have to come out if he keeps letting people run by him," I commented.

"I think whatever injury he had last year, he reinjured it," Ahmad mused.

Aaliyah frowned. "Did he trip on that last play?"

I nodded with my eyes fixed on the screen. "Yeah, I— Oh shit!"

Channing got to the running back first, and two other defensive players tackled him, too. Channing attempted to get back up for the next play and couldn't. He ended up being carted off the field, with a towel over his face and trainers protecting his right leg. It was later announced that he experienced a severe knee injury and that he would be transferred to the hospital.

"I wanted him out, but not like this," I said, making a face.

"How is this guy?" Aaliyah asked, gesturing to Channing's backup who came onto the field. "Bennett?"

"He might've subbed a few times, but I don't remember it. I've never seen him play with the game on the line," I responded distractedly.

"Game over," Ahmad pronounced as the quarterback for the Wasps scrambled and then dumped the ball to the tight end. "The Monarchs need to step their defense up." He turned to look at me. "Lamar said he works with the Monarchs, so tell him to help them on defense."

I laughed but said nothing.

I knew he hadn't told them he played, so I wasn't going to say anything either. He preferred to refer to his role as a help to the fifty-three men on the active roster—which was the truth. But he was a player—a defensive player. And there was no way for me to tell Ahmad that his exact role was directly related to helping the Monarchs on defense.

*The irony.*

Ahmad got up, and as soon as he was a few feet from the table, I glanced at Aaliyah.

"I love him for you," I told her.

She grinned. "Me, too."

I started to say something, but a trick play pulled my attention, and my eyes widened.

"What happened?" Aaliyah asked. "I missed it."

"They're about to show a replay," I told her.

Everyone in the bar got loud as the twenty-yard play captured everyone's attention. I glanced over at her, and she was staring at Ahmad, who was talking to our waitress.

"You know what I can't get over," Aaliyah mused.

"What?"

"We alternate between his place and mine, but I haven't slept alone in a week. And I don't want to ever sleep without him. And not just for the sex even though mm-mm-mm-mm-mmmmm."

"Oh wow. You got it bad." I pulled my eyes from the screen to look at her. "He's amazing, and you two are the cutest." My vision darted to the screen to make sure the game wasn't back from timeout before returning to her. "I love this for you, Aaliyah."

"Thank you." She swooned. "And you know what I love for you?"

"My team could still come away with a win?"

"Yes, *and* you meeting someone who looks at you like you hung the moon and the stars."

I rolled my eyes. "Liyah, please."

"I'm serious! Like I've said at least three times since my birthday, Lamar is your future husband."

"Husband?!" The commentators announced that the timeout was over, but I was still staring at my best friend in shock. "You saw us together once!"

"And that's all I needed to see."

Trying not to smile, I rolled my eyes. "You know you're projecting, right?"

Lowering her voice as her boyfriend approached the table, she said, "And you know you're in denial!"

"You see that play?" Ahmad asked as he took his seat, slipping his arm around Aaliyah. "I can't believe that shit worked."

"I know!" I exclaimed. "I really thought Martin was going to kick it!"

"Same, same," Aaliyah added, her lips pursed thoughtfully.

Amused, I shook my head. She'd missed the whole play, but I opted not to call her out. Three minutes later, the entire sports bar erupted into a mix of cheers and boos as the Wasps won the game.

The waitress stopped at our table. "Do you need any to-go cups or anything?"

"Just the check for me, please," I requested.

She pointed at Ahmad. "He's already taken care of the bill."

I turned to him. "Thank you! You don't have to pay for mine though. What do I owe you?"

He shook his head. "You don't owe me anything. I'm not going to pay for ours and not pay for yours, too."

I was going to argue to reimburse him, but the kindness in his smile forced me to relent. "Well, thank you."

After a round of hugs, they insisted on walking me to my car. We said goodbye for a final time, and I went home to mentally prepare for the work week.

. . .

"Hello?" I answered the phone a couple of hours later when I saw Lamar's name flashing on the screen.

"What's up, Jazz?"

"Not much," I replied, putting the last of the graded papers in a folder. "Just finished uploading the grades in the system. What are you up to?"

"Just got home from Vinnie's place—well, his girlfriend's place. We watched the game over there."

"He's on the practice squad, too?"

"No, not anymore. He didn't make it out of camp. Got cut last week."

"Oh wow, I'm sorry to hear that."

"Yeah, it's part of the game. He's trying to figure out what he's going to do next. He's waiting to hear back from Florida."

"I hope it works out for him."

"Yeah, me, too. But I want to know if you watched the game."

"I did."

"What were your thoughts?"

I launched into my analysis of the game while he listened, agreeing periodically. "What do you think?" I asked in conclusion.

"I think you're smart as hell and you know your stuff," he responded softly.

"I do."

"That was the second thing I noticed about you."

"What was the first?"

"Your beauty. It was the locs, the eyes, the smile. Not to mention you're thick as fuck. So I noticed you before I even sat down good."

I grinned. "Ahhh, so *that's* why you sat next to me."

"That's not why I sat down, but it's definitely why I stayed."

"I'm glad you like what you saw."

"I like what I saw, heard, smelled, felt, tasted. You were hitting all my senses. And you do it every single time I see you."

Butterflies swirled in my belly, and the words were flying out of my mouth before I could overthink it. "Well, I hope I get the chance to do it again soon."

That was the best I was going to do. I wasn't going to ask him out. I wasn't going to beg him to see me.

*If it's going to happen, he'll have to—*

"What about Saturday?" he suggested, interrupting my internal dialogue.

"Saturday sounds great," I answered, trying to temper my excitement.

"I would get to you by four at the latest. Or if you want to come up here, I could be at my place by two, two thirty."

"I don't mind coming up there."

"Okay, here it is. I'll put a plan together for Saturday. And you can let me know what you want to do, and we can do that on Sunday."

There was only one thing I could think about doing while in Baltimore.

*Lamar Anderson.*

I cleared my throat. "Whatever you want to do with me in Baltimore works for me."

He groaned. "Don't say it like that."

"Don't say it like what?" I asked innocently.

"I know your sexy ass is doing this on purpose."

"All I said was that whatever you want to do with me this weekend, I'd be open to doing." I paused. "Wide open."

He groaned again. "Jazz, I think you're trying to get my dick hard."

"What?" Trying not to laugh, I feigned confusion. "I'm just trying to confirm our weekend plans."

"Two can play that game," he said in a sexy, warning tone.

My lower body clenched.

We talked for about fifteen more minutes, and then we said good night because we both had early mornings.

*The life of a high school teacher is not for the weak.*

I was physically tired when I woke up in the morning. But every time the conversation with Lamar crossed my mind, I got a little burst of energy.

Ben Riker, the government and history teacher, knocked on my open door a few hours later. "Ms. Payne?"

"Come in, Mr. Riker," I called out from the chair in the corner of the room.

"I see you're hiding in the blind spot," he said, laughing as he walked in.

"It's my free period, and I decided I wanted to take a break."

"Is it because of that fight?"

My eyes bulged. "Yes! It hasn't even been a full week of school yet. How is there an issue already?"

He crossed his arms. "Apparently it's something that rolled over from camp."

"If they were beefin' at a camp, then they should've been beefin' at that camp. Why would they bring this to my classroom? That's sad."

"Was it upsetting you and your fellow educators?"

"Yes because it's like damn, if you can't go to school, where the hell can you go?" He started laughing, which caused me to laugh.

"No, but seriously, it is sad," I continued. "They could've gotten hurt. They could've hurt someone else." I shook my head. "I just need it to not happen again."

"I'm glad it was just hair pulling and name-calling."

"Fights these days get scary real quick."

"Yeah, because people want to bring guns and knives and bags of rocks. No one wants to use hands. And it's not a real fight if it's not hand-to-hand."

"Bags of rocks?" My brows furrowed and I made a face. "What did you have going on in school that 'bags of rocks' came to mind?"

"You're focused on the wrong thing! But for your information, when I was coming up, we did what we had to do." He chuckled. "I know you don't know anything about fighting."

Olivia Chapman and her crew popped in my mind.

I got up from the chair and crossed the room to my desk since the bell was going to ring any minute. "I just hope they work things out because when something like that happens, no one wins."

He nodded. "Speaking of wins"—his grin widened—"I just came in here to let you know the Wasps won." He rubbed his hands together. "So I believe you owe me a dollar."

I rolled my eyes and pulled a dollar out of my wallet to hand to him. "The Monarchs will come back from this. By the end of the season, they'll have a better record than the Wasps."

"Yeah, yeah, yeah." He held the dollar up toward the light, pretending to check to see if it was counterfeit. "We'll see," he said.

"Yes, we will."

He was almost out of the classroom when the other English teacher, Alexa Rae, popped her head in the doorway. "I see Mr. Riker came to collect his dollar from you, too," she stated.

"The Wasps get one win, and here he comes," I replied as he ignored us.

She lifted a fist in the air. "Go Monarchs!"

"Go Monarchs!" I returned.

By the time I got home from work, it was after six. I was hungry, tired, and ready to go to sleep. I ate quickly, showered, and was climbing into bed when I got a phone call from Lamar.

I wiggled my toes under the covers. "Well, hello," I answered cheerfully.

"Well, hello to you," he returned, sounding just as cheerful. "What are you up to?"

"I just got in bed."

He laughed. "I knew I needed to try to catch you before eight! Something told me to call now instead of waiting to get home."

"Well, I'm glad you did because I was just about to text you."

"How was your day?" he asked.

"It was eventful. I mean, mostly it was a regular day. But two kids were fighting in my classroom, so it was hectic."

"Are you okay?"

"Oh yeah, it wasn't anything too wild . . . it was open-hand slaps and hair pulling. But it was startling to me because it hasn't even been a full week of school! So now I'm having to write incident reports and converse with the parents about the suspension." I shook my head. "Just extra work."

"Extra work at the school leaves less time for you to write your book."

"I know."

"You gotta find a way to make time for it," he stated. "You should always make time for what's important to you."

"You're right."

"And selfishly, I want to know if the private investigator finds what she's looking for."

My heart thumped in my chest. *He remembered.*

I hadn't realized how silent I'd become until he said, "That *is* what it's still about, right?"

"Yeah," I answered softly. Warmth washed over me. "I just . . . You remembered?"

"Of course. I can't wait to read it. And according to Aunt Addy, you have less than four months to get it done."

I put my hand to my chest and closed my eyes. "I'll get it done." I swallowed the lump in my throat. "How are you? What are you up to? How was practice?"

"Practice was really good. They put me to work. My body is tired."

"You have tomorrow off, so you can actually get some rest."

"Oh yeah . . ."

We talked for twenty more minutes before we said good night. I plugged my phone into the charger and just stared at the ceiling for a few minutes. I didn't know why him remembering what my story was about had hit me the way that it did. But the way it made me feel momentarily short-circuited my brain.

*I can't wait to see him this weekend*, I thought as I drifted to sleep with a smile.

> **Lamar Anderson:** I have some news. Give me a call as soon as you can.

I saw his text as I was leaving school after an ordinary Tuesday. It was almost three o'clock, and the text had come in around lunchtime. It was his off day, but he'd never texted me during the school day before. I made the call as soon as I backed out of my parking spot.

He answered on the first ring. "Jazz!"

Just hearing his voice put a smile on my face. "Hey! What's going on? Everything okay?"

"I'm good. I'm *real* good." He let out an enthusiastic laugh. "How are you?"

His excitement was infectious. "I'm ready to hear your news!"

There was a dramatic pause. "I'm being elevated to the main roster for Sunday's game!"

I gasped and started banging the steering wheel. "What? Oh my God, Lamar! That's amazing! Congratulations!"

"Thank you! I mean, I'm hype. I didn't think it was going to happen, to be honest. This is just some wild shit. I'll be the backup's backup now that they've activated me."

He was talking so fast, I giggled.

"This is amazing!" I exclaimed. "You put in that work, so it makes sense that they would call you up and activate you. You should be so excited and so proud of yourself. I know I am, and I know your family is!"

"Oh, they don't know. Nobody knows."

I scrunched my face in confusion. "Wait, wait, wait, wait, wait . . . what?"

"It's taken everything in me not to call everybody I fucking know and tell them. I don't even be on social media like that, and I wanted to post something. But it's Tuesday. Sunday is a long way away. Things change all the time. I've been activated, but I don't know if I'm second or third on the depth chart. It's unlikely I'll get any time on the field, so I'll let them know at the end of the week. I wanna keep this thing to myself for a minute."

"But you told me?"

"I know I can trust you."

Feeling all fluttery inside, I bit my lip. "Yeah."

"That's why I told you. That, and since I'll be traveling with the team Saturday, I have to cancel our date," he continued.

My flutters dissipated. *Damn.*

# 19

Lamar was a professional athlete. He worked his ass off, so his elevation to the active roster didn't change his schedule. We still talked every night, and he was prominently featured in my dreams. Even though I was disappointed I wasn't going to see him, I was ecstatic that he was getting the opportunity of a lifetime. So, on Saturday after he landed in Florida, he sent me a text.

> **Lamar Anderson:** We landed and now we're on a bus to the stadium for a light practice. Then we check in to the hotel and have a position meeting and then I can call you. And I promise no jet skiing.

I snickered to myself.

> **Jazmyn Payne:** Yes, please keep your phone away from any water. I'm glad you made it safely, #90. How do you feel?
>
> **Lamar Anderson:** I feel good. I feel ready.
>
> **Jazmyn Payne:** You are good. You are ready. I'm here if you need a pep talk. Have fun and do what you do. You got this!
>
> **Lamar Anderson:** Thank you, I'll call you tonight. How are you? You good?
>
> **Jazmyn Payne:** I'm good! Excited for you!

Jay Channing was going to be out for the season with a severe meniscus tear and a Grade III ACL tear. They'd taken him to the hospital for surgery immediately after the game. The second-string tackle, Hoyt Bennett, was starting for the first time against the

Florida Crocs, and the commentators speculated that he would be targeted because of his youth and inexperience. The rookie had been a standout in college, but from week one's performance, they had concerns. Not one on-air personality mentioned Lamar, the now second-string defensive tackle and the man who had me weak—in every sense of the word.

"I cannot!" I laughed hard and loudly that night while on the phone with him. Holding my stomach with one hand and the phone with the other, I doubled over. A tear formed in the corner of my eye from laughing so hard. "Stop!"

"I'm serious," Lamar said as he walked back from picking up dinner. "I thought for sure I had the room to myself. He came out the bathroom like a ghost, and it took everything in me to not knock his ass out."

Amused, I collapsed back on my bed. "So, you didn't hear him at all?"

"No! I was on the phone with Bill when I came in. I put my shit down, sat at the desk, finished the conversation with him. Turned around, and this dude was just easing out the bathroom like a cat burglar. The toilet ain't flush, the shower wasn't on, I was at that desk on the phone with Bill for at least five minutes. I don't know what the fuck he was doing in there. I just know he came out on some creep shit, and now I gotta go back in there and sleep in the bed three feet away."

My head fell back, and a whole new round of laughter erupted from me. "That is too funny! This cannot be true!"

"It's true." He chuckled. "Everything but the creep part because Leon seems cool. But he did come out that bathroom like a ghost, and when I turned around, I jumped a little bit and threw my fist up. I was about to square up with a ghost. Scared or not, he was going to feel these hands."

I was still cracking up when he got to his hotel room.

"I'm walking in now. It looks like Leon is still out," he informed me.

Checking the clock, I saw it was almost ten o'clock. "He has an hour before lights out."

"Yeah. They take that curfew shit serious, too. If . . ." The muffled sound of him getting undressed made his voice far away. ". . . wouldn't be sleep right now."

"I missed that last part," I interjected.

"Oh, I said if we had our date tonight, we wouldn't be 'sleep right now."

My entire body perked up at his words. "Oh?" I licked my lips. "What would we be doing?"

"There's a concert happening in Baltimore tonight. I wanted to take you."

My nipples were hard for nothing.

"Oh." Realizing I sounded disappointed, I tried again with a more upbeat tone. "Oh wow! That would've been cool. The last time I saw live music was at that jazz festival with my aunt and your mom. Next time, let's do it."

He was quiet for a moment. "Why'd you say 'oh' like that at first?"

"I do-don't know . . . um, like what?" I stammered.

"What did you think I was going to say?" he asked softer, sexier.

"I didn't know," I whispered, tweaking my nipples to alleviate some of the tension.

"Because if you wanted me to tell you everything I wanted to do with you this weekend, I could."

"I'd like that a lot. Because as happy as I am for you, I was really, *really* looking forward to being with you."

Pinching my nipples again, I swallowed hard.

"I wanted to be with you, too." As if he could see me, Lamar groaned. "You don't even know how bad I want you."

"Because you don't tell me," I blurted.

"Jazz, I think about you in general all the time. I think about how good you are, how funny you are, how much I like you as a person. And I like to keep that at the forefront because I think about your pussy, how you feel, how you taste, how you look, how you sound almost just as much. The only reason I don't bring up sex with you is because I don't want you to think that's the only thing I want from you. Since the first time we had sex—" He interrupted himself. "Shit. Leon's back."

Seconds later the sound of the door hitting the wall followed by a goofy chuckle filled the background of his space.

"What's up, man? Damn! Why'd you open the door like that?" Lamar greeted him.

"I wanted to make sure you heard me this time," Leon said loudly. "Didn't want to scare you again."

Lamar and I burst out laughing at the same time. The sexual tension that had been brewing between us dissolved into chaotic amusement as he went back and forth with his roommate.

"Nah, your creep ass was hiding in the bathroom!" Lamar retorted. "I'm on the phone."

"Oh, my bad, LA," Leon said.

"Jazz?" Lamar focused his full attention back on me and our conversation. "You still there?"

"I'm still here," I answered.

"How far along are you in your book?"

"I'm almost done. I don't know if it's any good or not, but I'm writing it."

"Are you going to let me read it?"

A mixture of nerves, embarrassment, and discomfort swept through me. "Maybe! I don't know!" I squeaked, putting a hand over my face. "You sound like Aunt Addy. She was asking me to send her chapters as I finish."

"Did you do it?"

"No. I told her once I got to the halfway point, I would."

"And you have more than that?"

"Yeah, but I'm just going to finish it and send her the whole thing."

"That's what's up. Well, I look forward to reading it when you're done. Or right now. Either way."

I laughed, shaking my head even though he couldn't see me. "The only thing you need to be reading in the immediate future is the Crocs' offense."

The Florida Crocs had been a decent team last season, mostly because their quarterback was slippery.

"You're right," he said with amusement. "You're going to be watching the sideline for me tomorrow?"

"I'm going to be glued to the TV. I'm watching from home so I don't miss a thing."

Leon was in the background, making a lot of noise. "My bad, LA. I'm almost done."

"You good," Lamar replied, before redirecting to me. "I'm gonna get off the phone and get my mind right for tomorrow."

"I understand completely. Get your rest, and do big things tomorrow. Quick question though . . . do the guys on the team call you 'LA'?"

"Yeah, one of the running backs is named Lamar, and Anderson is the last name of the starting tight end. So it's just been LA since I got here."

"That's cool!"

"Is it? Because when they're talking fast, it definitely sounds like Ellie."

I laughed. "That's alright though. You know what it is. And you got this, LA!"

"No," he uttered firmly. He lowered his voice to continue. "I like when you say my name."

My body reacted to every part of that statement. "Lamar."

"Yeah, just like that."

There was so much I wanted to say in response because his words reverberated through my body. I knew without a shadow of a doubt that there was a damp spot in my panties. All I could manage to do was let out a slightly horny sigh.

"I can't wait to hear your analysis of the game tomorrow," he said at his regular volume.

"And I can't wait to give it to you."

He inhaled and exhaled audibly. "Good night, Jazmyn."

It wasn't until I heard how his breathing changed that I thought about what I'd said. Smiling at the thought of me having an effect on him, I rolled over to my side and squeezed my thighs together. "Good night, Lamar."

We ended the call, and I immediately got up to get a snack. I wasn't typically a late-night snacker, but I needed the sugar high. The short-term boost from the glucose was going to help me focus on writing a bit more. Because there was no way I was going to be able to sleep. Not with the explicit thoughts that kept running through my mind.

"What was he going to say?" I mused aloud as I walked from the kitchen with a small bag of chocolate candies.

Although Leon's shenanigans and Lamar's storytelling had provided the best laugh I'd had in a while, I resented Leon for coming back to the room when he had. Because my imagination was running away with itself, and I knew that my best bet would be to channel that energy into my novel. And I ended up staying awake writing until one o'clock in the morning.

I woke up for church at seven o'clock and made it on time for the nine o'clock service. I had a lot to be thankful for and a lot to pray about. But I knew I was meant to be there when the pastor started preaching about fear and faith. On the way home, I kept thinking about the message.

*Operating in faith is trusting the process. Operating in fear is halting the process.*

I called Aunt Addy immediately.

"Good morning," she greeted me with a little more energy than she'd had on Saturday.

"Good morning! How are you doing?"

"I'm doing," she replied. "How are you? Tell me something good."

"I just left church, and the message was about faith over fear."

"Amen! And how do you feel about that?"

"I feel like I better understand some of the things you were telling me this summer."

"Does that mean you're gonna stop being scary with that boy and that book and that school district?"

I cackled. "First of all, I'm not being scary! I told Lamar I hoped we could see each other again soon, and he set a date. The date was cancelled—"

"Because he's in the game! I told Monica to order pizza and wings because we're going to be watching."

"Good. And that sounds good; I might do the same. Anyway,

I also wrote more in my novel. And I can't do anything about the school district rules, so I'm not scared, I just need my job."

"Still sounds like you're being scary to me!"

I laughed and hearing her laugh made my heart swell.

"How are you feeling?" I asked her again. "You sound good."

"I'm good, sweetheart. Don't worry about me. Because I'm not worried."

We talked for fifteen more minutes, and when I walked into my apartment, I told her I'd call her after the game. While I was taking off my dress, I looked at the clock and realized two people I cared for were about to have the biggest moment of their careers. So I sent a couple of inspirational texts.

*Lamar.*

> **Jazmyn Payne:** I know you probably won't get this until after the game but just know that you are living your dream right now. God has blessed you with talent and now with this opportunity. Take everything in and bask in it. Be proud of what you've done and the work you've put in. I'm proud of you. Your mom and Bill are proud of you. And I know your dad is smiling down on you from Heaven right now.

*Nina.*

> **Jazmyn Payne:** Twenty-four hours from now, you're going to be walking down a runway! Okay super model! I see you! I'm so proud of you Nina. You've put in the work and now your dreams are coming true. Love this for you!
>
> **Nina Ford:** You got some dick, didn't you? A bitch gets some dick in her life and becomes an inspirational speaker.

I laughed out loud.

> **Jazmyn Payne:** I can't stand you! I just came back from church!

**Nina Ford:** See, I thought you were filled with dick and whole time, you were just filled with the Holy Ghost. My apologies.

**Jazmyn Payne:** I'm done!!!!

**Nina Ford:** I'm about to walk into rehearsal but seriously, thank you for your words and for this laugh.

**Jazmyn Payne:** Go kill it! Can't wait to see the pictures!

I ordered a pizza, and my food arrived just as the game was about to start. My stomach knotted with anxiousness as the Monarchs ran onto the field. I scanned the players as quickly as I could, but the camera operator switched to a view of the crowd. When the game officially started, I was grinning. I loved football anyway, but it felt different.

It *was* different.

Lamar was out there—on the sideline, but out there nonetheless.

Crocs won the coin toss and deferred the ball. So, when the Monarchs offense jogged out, I relaxed a bit and ate some pizza. The Monarchs drove the ball down the field and scored relatively easily, methodically shaving time off the clock with running plays. My phone dinged, and I knew it was going to be my group chat with my work friends.

I was focused on the game, but every time the camera would catch a glimpse of the sideline, I searched for number ninety. The Monarchs defense came onto the field, and I leaned forward, literally on the edge of my seat.

And everything Ben had predicted was right.

The Crocs kept going at Hoyt Bennett, and they were winning the matchup. He was missing every other tackle and didn't pressure the quarterback or *anyone* on the offense.

*Maybe he's nervous*, I thought as they jogged into the locker room at halftime.

**Jazmyn Payne:** I think Bennett is nervous. That's gotta be it. Because they drafted him in the first round for a reason. THIS can't be the reason.

**Alexa Rae:** I don't want to say this is completely Bennett's fault, but I don't think it would make a difference if he was there or not. He's adding no value. There could be a cardboard cutout in that spot, and it would be just as effective.

**Ben Riker:** No, it's his fault. And what's going on with the safety? Does he know he's not supposed to make the other team feel safe?

Snickering, my eyes went back to the TV as the third quarter started. After a field goal put points on the board, the Monarchs were still losing by ten points. When the defense came out, I wondered if they were going to be able to make any adjustments.

"Oh my God," I breathed as I saw number ninety.

In place of Bennett, Lamar Anderson was lining up on the defensive line. I turned the TV up and rose to my feet. My heart was thumping in my chest, and knots formed in my belly. I was not expecting to have such a visceral reaction to seeing him on-screen. I was excited for him, but at the exact same time, I was extremely nervous. Pacing from one side of the room to the other, I anticipated the ball being snapped.

I held my breath when the quarterback pitched the ball to the running back and he ran to the right. Almost immediately, Lamar tackled him for a two-yard loss.

"Yes!" I exclaimed, bouncing on my toes.

The next play, two other defensive players tackled the running back after a gain for three yards. The third play was a blitz, and because of how the quarterback fled the pocket, Lamar sacked him.

"Yes!" I cheered.

The Monarchs stopped the Crocs, got the ball back, and scored.

With Lamar in, the defensive line was stronger than ever as he rushed the passer several times, resulting in two sacks. He was also in on a bunch of tackles and one forced fumble. The Monarchs won by three points, but more importantly, Lamar was a rock star on the field.

I picked up my phone to see Alexa and Ben raving about how the change in personnel on defense had made all the difference. I wanted to be cool about what I'd just witnessed without making it seem like I had feelings for the man.

**Jazmyn Payne:** Anderson should be the starter.

I started watching the next game, but I couldn't stop thinking about Lamar and how well he'd done. He'd never *said* he was good. I'd assumed he was good. But to watch him be excellent was sexy. To see him capitalize on the opportunity he'd been given and chase a lifelong dream was so deeply attractive. It was the culmination of his hard work, his dedication, and his drive.

"Hello?" I answered my phone when I saw him calling. "Is this *the* Lamar Anderson?

"Jazz." He chuckled over the commotion in the background. "Chill . . ."

"You did your big one on that field, you hear me? You killed it! You held a defensive clinic. It was everything! You were a machine out there," I gushed.

"Thank you." He let out a light, almost-bashful chuckle. "I appreciate you. And I really appreciated that message you sent me this morning. It came right when I was about to put my phone in the locker. It was the last thing I saw before we headed out."

"Oh, I hope it wasn't too heavy. I would've hated to have thrown you off your game."

"No, it wasn't. It was . . ." His sentence faded sentimentally. "I needed that. Thank you."

I smiled. "It was from the heart, so I'm glad you appreciated it."

Two masculine voices started talking so loudly in the background that it sounded like they were on the phone with us. Then it turned into a chant to which Lamar laughed.

"What are they saying?" I asked curiously.

"Hollywood," he answered with a light chuckle. "They gave me a game ball and said I was no longer LA—I'm Hollywood because I'm a star."

"You *are* a star! That's so cute!" I let out an excited yelp. "I'm so happy for you!"

Someone turned the music up, and I could barely hear him.

"It's a lot going on here, but I just wanted to call and thank you. We're about to get on the bus to head to the airport. I'll probably get home around midnight. I know you'll be asleep, so I just wanted to say good night."

My stomach fluttered. "Good night. Send me a text when you get home. I'll be asleep, but at least when I wake up, I'll know you're good."

"I'll do that." He paused. "I think we get directly on a plane when we get to the airport, but I'm not sure. I don't know how this works. I just . . . wanted to give you a call and hear your voice."

"Well, I'm glad you did," I told him. "And I know I texted it, but as a football lover, as a Monarchs fan, and as your . . . friend, I just want you to hear me say I'm proud of you and happy for you. Byeeee, Lamar." I sang the goodbye and his name.

"Bye, Jazz."

The call disconnected while I still had the phone pressed to my ear. *Giddy* was the only word that could describe how I felt.

I called Aunt Addy to talk to her about the game, but my mom answered and told me she was sleeping. We talked for about ten minutes, but I couldn't tell her anything about Lamar because she would've asked a million questions. I wanted to call my best friends and tell them, but Nina was preparing for the biggest event of her career, and Aaliyah was introducing Ahmad to her family. My work friends would've been excited to hear that I knew Lamar, but I didn't want them in my business like that. So I grabbed my laptop and channeled all my giddy energy into my novel.

I went to bed a little later than usual, so when I woke up feeling groggy, I wasn't surprised. I reached for my phone to turn off the alarm, and I saw a text that had come in while I was asleep.

**Lamar Anderson:** Me not telling you how often I think about you and how bad I want to see you, touch you, taste you, and fuck you is just me trying to be respectful. If you want me to be a little less respectful, I'd tell you that I liked you before I had you. And since I've had you, I can't even beat my meat without thinking about you. I'm home and I need to see you soon.

That woke me right up. It was a good thing I was on my way to take a shower because my panties were soaked.

**Jazmyn Payne:** Can you meet me at my place tomorrow please?

**Lamar Anderson:** Yes.

# 20

I woke up Tuesday morning a few minutes before my alarm like a kid on Christmas. *Excited* didn't even fully encapsulate how I felt about seeing Lamar. When I walked into the school, I had an extra pep in my step.

The school day dragged a little bit because I kept checking the clock. I found myself randomly smiling between classes as I thought about how I wanted to celebrate his big game. My body was almost vibrating in anticipation of a reunion with Lamar. And when the final bell rang, I grabbed my bag and damn near ran to the parking lot. I dug my keys out of my handbag, and in the process, my phone fell between the seat and the middle console.

"Shit," I muttered, sticking my hand in the space to see if I could feel it. Knowing I was going to have to move my seat back, I decided to just worry about that when I got home.

I pulled out of the teachers' lot, fully intending to speed to my apartment complex. But in my planning, I didn't account for the fact that school buses would be dropping kids off on my route.

And I got caught behind one.

It was a quarter to four when I finally pulled into my parking spot. Lamar was going to be there any minute, so I was pressed for time. Moving my seat, I was able to access my phone. While checking it for scratches, I noticed the text notification and missed call from Lamar. Grabbing the rest of my stuff, I hurried to my apartment. Dumping my bags in the living room, I opened his texts. And froze.

> **Lamar Anderson:** I'm sorry Jazz. A four o'clock meeting came up that I can't reschedule. If it's over at five, I can make it down there by six.
>
> **Lamar Anderson:** Call me as soon as you get this. Please.

Disappointment punched me in the gut. I didn't realize how bad I wanted to see him until the chance had been snatched away from me. I looked at the time, and it was five minutes before his meeting. I contemplated texting instead of calling since it was about to be four o'clock, but before I knew what I was doing, the phone was ringing.

"Jazz, I'm so sorry," he answered in a hushed tone.

Just hearing his voice tugged at me. I swallowed my emotion. "Hey, is everything okay?"

"More than okay. Very okay. Shit is getting wild. But I'm sorry I'm not there."

"I'm sorry about that, too."

"My agent set a meeting, and I can't get into all the details now, but I'm sorry about our plans. I was really looking forward to being there with you right now. I meant what I said. I want to see you. I *need* to see you. I'll call you when it's over."

"Okay, talk to you soon. Good luck with your meeting."

We said goodbye, and I just stood in the middle of my living room for a minute. I shut my eyes tightly and let my head fall back. I reminded myself that he'd told me he was busy from the beginning. I wasn't trying to take it personally. I wasn't trying to make a big deal out of nothing. But that sting that I felt was still stinging.

*And this is exactly why you shouldn't have gotten your hopes up*, I chastised myself.

Exhaling loudly, I had to acknowledge that me getting hurt would be my own fault. Lamar's back-to-back missed dates weren't intentional. He'd been up-front with me and told me he was busy. He'd told me his schedule was why he wasn't in a relationship.

*This is on me.*

It wasn't just about the sex even though I'd been craving that man since the last time we'd been together. I wanted to see him. I wanted to spend time with him. I wanted to feel the way only he could make me feel. The disappointment was heavier than I'd expected it to be. My feelings were deeper than I'd expected them to be.

*No, no, no.* I put my hand over my heart. *This is not happening.*

He'd said he was too busy for a relationship from the beginning. Even though we had crazy chemistry, an amazing connection, mind-blowing sex, and genuine affection for each other, he and I were technically just friends.

*No matter what it feels like.*

From my innate reaction to his missed date, it was clear my feelings were deeper than I'd intended for them to be and that Lamar could hurt me if I let him.

*Because how do I look getting upset about something he already told me?* I asked myself. *He's busy. He doesn't have time for anything. Enjoy it for what it is.*

I was just sitting down to eat dinner at six o'clock when Lamar called. I squared my shoulders and mentally prepared to keep it cute.

"Hey!" I answered on speakerphone with a little more enthusiasm than I felt.

"First and foremost, I'm sorry," he said. "This is the second time work has messed up a date, and I don't want you to think I don't want to see you. Because I do. Bad."

Despite my best efforts, I folded.

Butterflies fluttered haphazardly throughout my belly, and I had to fight to keep myself in check. "I accept your apology. I know you're busy." Taking a bite of my salad, I tried to chew as quietly as possible. "How was your meeting?"

"Jazz."

The way he said my name gave me pause. "Hm?"

"Talk to me. Are you upset with me?"

"No. I'm not upset with you." I planned to stop there, but my truth came tumbling out. "I'm just . . . disappointed that we didn't see each other. But it's not on you. You don't owe me your time. You told me from the beginning that you were busy. So, I promise, I'm not mad. I just . . ." I stabbed at a cucumber. "I got ahead of myself."

"What do you mean?"

I put my fork down and stared at my phone as if I could see him. "Asking you to come on your only day off from practice. We were only going to be able to spend a few hours together before you would've needed to go back home. We both have early mornings. If I'm tired, I can push through the workday. But if you're tired, you could get hurt. I shouldn't have asked you to come."

"I'm glad you asked. I wanted to be there. I *want* to be there with you. So yes, you should've asked. *Anytime* you want to see me, let me know."

*I did.* I pursed my lips. *Twice.*

As if he could read my mind, he continued. "I can't guarantee it won't happen again, but I'm going to make it up to you. Okay?"

I bit my lip and shook my head. The earnestness in his tone and the sincerity of his words got me. "Okay," I murmured.

"So, you forgive me?"

"Yes."

"Thank you." He sounded relieved.

"Now can you please tell me about this meeting?" I insisted, taking another bite of food.

"The Crocs are interested in picking me up to bring onto their active roster—"

My eyes bulged. "That's incredible, Lamar! Wh-what are you going to do? What did you say? Is that allowed?" My questions came at him in rapid succession.

He chuckled lightly and continued talking. "My agent and my manager asked me what I wanted. I told them I wanted to play, but if I could stay in Maryland, that's what I would want to do. So the four-o'clock meeting was with the Monarchs' front office. We used the Crocs as a bargaining chip because you can't deprive a practice squad player the opportunity to go to a team and be on the active roster. So we talked about what that would look like, especially with Channing being on injured reserve for the rest of the season. And long story short, I have a contract. As of tomorrow morning, I'll officially be number one on the depth chart for the Monarchs."

"Lamar!" I gasped, dropping my fork. Even though I'd known where the story was headed, hearing him confirm that he was taking over Channing's spot as the first string defensive tackle made me want to shout. "Congratulations! I'm so happy for you! This is so cool! How do you feel?"

"Thank you! I feel good. I feel ready for the opportunity. I'm not even going to front like this ain't a dream come true. I had my exit strategy ready, my business is almost ready, and I was ready for it not to happen. I didn't think it was in the cards for me, but I guess it is."

"When it's your time, it's your time! This is so exciting!"

"I told you it was an important, can't-miss type of meeting. I wouldn't miss seeing you for some bullshit."

I smiled. "Not you hitting me with an *I told you so* after burying the lede!"

"No, I led with what was most important. It was the second time work interrupted our plans. I'm not trying to waste your time. I have every intention of following through when I make plans with you, so I needed to let you know I was sorry first."

My stomach fluttered. "I know it wasn't intentional. And I appreciate the apology and the fact that you handled it the way that you did." I shook my head, in awe. "This is such a big deal. It wouldn't have taken away from your apology. This is major, Lamar. I'm so happy for you. You should do something to celebrate tonight . . . but not too much because you have practice and a contract to sign in the morning."

"I can't do the only thing I want to do," he whispered.

My lower body clenched.

It wasn't just what he'd said; it was the way he'd said it. I knew I could either feed into the sexual undertone of it, or I could keep the conversation friendly. I stuffed salad in my mouth to give me time to think.

"What are you eating?" I asked after swallowing. "You could celebrate with a nice dinner."

He scoffed. "You want me to celebrate with the wings I'm going to throw in the air fryer?"

"Nothing wrong with air fryer wings." I paused. "Except the lack of grease to make it taste the way it should. Outside of that, you're good."

He burst out laughing. "In the offseason, I fry chicken. During the season, I bake it or air fry it. But don't sleep on my air fry chicken until you've tried it."

"Let me find out you do your thing in the kitchen."

"I have skills."

"Yes, you do," I blurted without thinking.

*Shit.*

"That's what got you that contract, *Hollywood*!" I exclaimed, trying to cover my admission. "What did your mom and Bill say?"

"I haven't told anyone else yet. You were my first call."

My heart leapt into my throat momentarily. "I'm the first one you told?"

"You're the only one I've told. I'm about to call them and then Erickson in a couple minutes."

"Oh wow, that makes me feel special."

"You *are* special."

I grinned, feeling flushed. "Lamar . . ."

"What time are you going to sleep? Nine?"

"You know it." I giggled.

"I'm going to make these calls and let my people know, then circle back to tell you good night."

"Yes, of course. We'll talk later. Congratulations again!"

We said goodbye, and I finished my dinner with a huge smile.

I felt so inspired by his achievement that I immediately took a shower, put on a cute cami set, grabbed my laptop, and got to work. I decided to write until bedtime. I channeled my emotional roller coaster of an afternoon into the characters of my story, determined to complete the chapter I was working on.

I was coming up on the end of the final paragraph when I thought I heard knocking. It was eight o'clock, so I knew it had to be my neighbors' door. I continued working until I heard it again, louder. I turned down the music on my phone and listened. When I heard the third round of knocks, I got up and tiptoed toward it. I'd made it only to the end of the hall when my phone vibrated.

It was Lamar.

I stopped in the middle of the living room and answered in a whisper. "Hello?" I quietly kept walking.

"I just wanted to tell you good night," he said.

When I looked through the peephole, the air left my lungs, and my heart skipped a beat.

"Jazz . . ." Lamar said my name so sexily that I was immediately overwhelmed.

With a shaky hand, I unlocked the door and opened it. My eyes were wide as I stared at him.

Lamar flashed me a smile. "What's up, Jazz?"

"What . . . ?!" I exhaled, trying to wrap my mind around what I was seeing in front of me. "Hi!"

His smile grew. "I'm sorry to show up unannounced. But can I come in?"

"Yes, of course! Sorry, come in." Almost in a trance, I moved backward until the back of my legs hit the couch. My eyes were glued to him as he approached me. "What are you doing here?"

"This."

Grabbing my face, he crashed his lips into mine. His touch was gentle, yet his kiss was rough. The contrast between his thumbs stroking my cheeks and his mouth moving over mine made me tremble with want. My nipples hardened, and desire coiled in my belly. I grabbed his T-shirt and pulled him. Our bodies were pressed together, and his kiss spread through me like wildfire.

His hands slid from my face down my neck as he kissed his way to my ear. "I'm here because I like you." He squeezed my throat as he kissed his way back to my lips. "A lot." His hands moved from my neck over my shoulders, tugging down the straps of my cami as he kissed down my chest. When he reached the cami bodice, he looked up at me. "I'm here because I want you." He dragged his lips across the fabric until he reached my nipple. Biting down and licking it through the thin material, he made me moan. "So fucking bad."

"Mmmmmmmmmm."

With our eyes locked, he tugged the cami down, freeing my breasts as he lowered me to the couch.

"I'm here because I want to make it up to you," he murmured.

As soon as my ass hit the cushion, he situated himself between my legs. Kneading my breasts, he wrapped his lips around each nipple in turn.

Feeling his warm mouth against my bare skin caused me to gasp. "That feels so good," I said breathily as he captured a nipple between his teeth and bit softly.

He licked and sucked each protruding peak, alternating back and forth until I felt that pull deep in my gut. He hooked the back of my legs over his forearms and pulled me to the edge of the couch.

"Oh!" I yelped, surprised by his strength.

"I'm here because . . ." He rocked me back, lifting me so he could pull at my shorts; once he worked them over my hips, they came off easily. ". . . you asked me how I wanted to celebrate . . ." When he spread my legs again, my ass was hanging on the edge of the couch. ". . . and what I wanted for dinner."

Panting, I watched him watching me. I was fully exposed, naked except for my cami bunched at my waist.

Dragging his lips along the inside of my thighs, he oscillated between the left one and the right one until he was face-to-face with my hot flesh. "And this is the only way I wanted to celebrate," he uttered, his breath tickling my skin. "And the only thing I wanted to eat."

My heart thumped loudly as I stared at his gorgeous face between my legs. I'd fantasized about being with him off and on since we'd met. But nothing compared to the real thing. Nothing could replicate the softness of his lips, the power of his hands, or the skill of his mouth.

"Ohmigod," I cried out as he kissed the crease.

"So tell me how I can make it up to you," he groaned, his lips brushing across the hood of my clit with each word.

I didn't even recognize my own voice as I let out a whimper that was partially a cry for release and partially an announcement that he could do whatever he wanted with my body.

"Open your eyes," he demanded. "Use your words."

I inhaled sharply as electricity shot through me. "I—I want . . ." I swallowed hard. "I want to . . . come."

His eyes darkened as my words hit him. The intensity in his gaze caused me to grab the arm of the couch.

"I can do that," he growled, before running his tongue along my slit. "You taste so fucking good."

"Please. Lamar, please," I begged.

"I'll make you come, Jazzy. Don't worry." Without hesitation, he flattened his tongue and licked every inch of me before he stopped at my little bundle of nerves.

"Yes, yes, yes, yes," I cried out, as his tongue skillfully swirled in a circle around my clit. My hands found the back of his head, and my hips bucked against his face. "Ohmigod, yes!"

When I felt like I couldn't take it anymore, he sucked my clit and slowly slid two fingers inside me.

I moaned loudly, and so did he, right along with me.

Every time I looked at him buried between my legs, my impending orgasm got closer. I tried to continue watching him take care of me, but it felt too good to keep my eyes open. His fingers curled upward into my G-spot as he continued his expert assault on my clit.

I was panting. My heart was racing, and my skin was on fire. The sound of my wetness reverberated through the room, and I was starting to lose control. My hips moved uncontrollably to meet the movements of his tongue and fingers.

"Lamar, Lamar, Lamar . . ." I gasped his name, closing my eyes.

I could feel myself getting close.

He flicked his tongue over my sensitive flesh, and then he suctioned his lips around my clit. I tried to hold it together. I wasn't trying to force his face into me, but my hands held his head as I lost control of my hips. My eyes rolled back, and a wave of heat washed over me as I started my descent into ecstasy.

"Right there, right there, right there . . ." I moaned as my entire body shuddered.

He locked my thighs with his arms, but since he never stopped flicking his tongue, a second orgasm ripped through me and left me quivering.

My mouth was open, but sound didn't come out. I was momentarily frozen with my hips in the air and my body rigid.

It took a solid minute for my nervous system to finally calm down.

"That felt so good." I panted, slowly opening my eyes. My body slacked, and I let out a ragged breath.

He pulled his fingers out of me, and while maintaining eye contact, he licked the length of my slit and then planted a kiss on my mound.

"I love the way you sound, the way you look, the way you taste," he groaned as he gently took my legs off his shoulders. "Everything about you." He rose to his feet. Grabbing himself, he took a step back and eyed my body. "You're so fucking sexy, Jazzy."

His dick was rock-hard. And while I was sexually satiated, I wanted all of him.

"I love . . . everything about you," I admitted quietly as I pushed myself up into a seated position. "I've never . . ." A rush of feelings flooded my system.

*I've never felt like this before.*

He searched my eyes. "You've never what?"

"I never"—I swallowed hard—"expected to see you tonight. I'm really glad you came, but you didn't have to. I really did understand."

"I didn't like disappointing you." He reached out to me. "I never want to disappoint you." Once I put my hand in his, he pulled me to my feet and continued. "And you seemed surprised earlier when I said you were special. I didn't like that." He leaned down to kiss me. "Because I need you to know you're special to me."

"You're special to me, too," I admitted softly.

Our arms wrapped tight around each other as our mouths and tongues gently wrestled. Tasting myself on his lips, I melted into him. Each kiss was a reminder of how he satisfied me, and my stomach fluttered in remembrance. His hands traveled over my bare skin, giving me goose bumps.

"How much time do we have?" I asked, pulling out of the kiss.

He looked at his watch and then put his hand back on my bare ass. "I should probably go in the next fifteen minutes," he whispered in my ear.

"There's a lot we can do in fifteen minutes."

"I didn't come here for a quickie." He squeezed the fleshiness of my bottom before letting it go and cupping my face. "I like you, and I wouldn't disrespect you like that."

*Disrespect me.*

I slipped my hand in between us, sliding over the bulge in the front of his pants. "I want more of you," I whispered.

He licked his lips. "You can see how bad I want to take you up on that." He took a small step back so I could see his print for emphasis. "Because I want you." He cupped my cheeks and kissed me. "And I like you"—he kissed me again—"and you're special"—his tongue gently met mine—"and you deserve more than a quick fuck."

"Lamar," I whined.

His fingers coasted down my face and wrapped around my neck. "Don't say my name like that." He drew me into him, and his mouth covered mine. "Do you know how hard it is to resist you?"

*Then don't.*

"Mmm," he groaned, pulling out of the kiss slowly. He let his fingers slide from my neck down my chest as he took a step back. "I'm going to go . . . because if I keep kissing you, I'm not going home."

My body and my feelings were laid bare in front of him. Even though he wasn't outright rejecting me, I wasn't getting what I wanted tonight. And it stung.

I was battling myself internally, because on one hand, I wanted to tell him how bad I wanted him, how I needed to feel him inside me, how I craved him. On the other hand, if he slid inside me, there was no telling how long we'd spend pleasing each other. If he got home late and did terrible at practice, that could jeopardize his opportunity. And as bad as I wanted him, I didn't want to come between him and his dreams.

I swallowed hard.

"I understand," I whispered, pulling the straps of my cami back onto my shoulders, covering at least the top half of my body. "I'm glad we got a chance to see each other."

"So am I." His eyes dropped to my lips. "I needed to see you."

"I needed to see you, too."

He drew me into an embrace. I rested my head against his chest, and I hugged him tight. We were quiet, rocking back and forth leisurely. I listened to his heart beating. I closed my eyes as the seconds ticked by. The moment I felt my eyes watering, I pulled away.

We silently walked to the door.

"I'm proud of you," I expressed softly. "Congratulations again."

His lips pulled into a smile, and his eyes lit up. "Thank you." He brushed my cheek with the back of his hand. "That means a lot to me. Especially coming from you."

Butterflies moved through my belly as I held his gaze. "You have a big day ahead of you. Get home safely, and get a good night's sleep."

He put his hand on the doorknob and paused. He turned to me, and his lips parted as if he were going to say something. Instead, he leaned down and pressed his lips against mine.

"Good night, Jazz."

"Good night, Lamar."

When the door shut behind him, I put my hand to my chest and exhaled.

# 21

*I'm falling for Lamar.*

I winced as I admitted it. Fear, anxiety, nerves, and apprehension swirled in my belly because friends with benefits was impossible to navigate when real feelings were involved. Every conversation, every date, and every moment between us had only amplified that. But it was clear to me only in that moment that I wanted to be more than friends.

*Since when do* I *want a relationship?*

After being cheated on by my ex, a relationship with a professional athlete felt like setting myself up. And with his busy schedule and his new contract, if he hadn't wanted a relationship before, it was unlikely he'd want one now.

*So I can either tell him I want to be with him and lose him as a friend, or I can just not say anything, make the whole thing weird, and lose him as a friend.*

Either way, I'd end up losing him, and I'd end up hurt.

*Nope.*

Grabbing my phone, I was going to take my predicament to the group chat when I saw I had texts from Lamar. But I couldn't open them until I had a handle on my thoughts. I needed to be in the right mindset to respond to whatever he said. So I skipped over his name and noticed the group chat was already active that morning.

I glanced at the clock and then back at my phone because it was early.

**Nina Ford:** Is this who I think it is?

A photo was attached to the text.

**Aaliyah James:** Is that Jazz's man?

**Jazmyn Payne:** To answer Nina's question, if you think this was my date to Aaliyah's party, then yes.

**Aaliyah James:** Just a date? Because you two looked like more . . .

So it hadn't just felt like something more at Aaliyah's party—other people had seen it, too.

**Jazmyn Payne:** Despite what it looked like, we're friends. Friends with benefits but friends, nonetheless.

**Nina Ford:** Now I know a lie when I read it.

My stomach lurched. If I couldn't convince my best friends that Lamar and I were just friends via text, I knew I wasn't going to be able to convince him that I wanted to be just friends.

**Aaliyah James:** It looked real friendly the Sunday morning after my party . . .

**Jazmyn Payne:** It's way too early for you two to be double teaming me!

**Aaliyah James:** Then just admit that you and this apparently famous man are more than friends. And why didn't you tell us you were dating a celebrity?

**Jazmyn Payne:** I definitely told you both on your birthday that he was a football player.

**Aaliyah James:** He was so cool and laid back. I didn't think he was in the league. I thought you meant he was a football player as in he played football for fun, or he played back in college.

**Nina Ford:** He looks like a football player. That's what I thought you meant. I thought you were describing those broad ass shoulders. But you meant his job is professional athlete?

**Jazmyn Payne:** Yes, he plays for the Maryland Monarchs.

**Aaliyah James:** I'd never heard of him before, but you know I don't know much about football.

**Nina Ford:** I know enough about football to know Jazz told that fine man to put her backfield in motion!

**Aaliyah James:** She said go deep!

Rolling my eyes, I put my phone down and went to get ready for work. I was in distress, and those two had jokes. I sprayed conditioning tonic in my hair, gathered my locs in a half-up, half-down style, and then put on my clothes. My phone kept going off, so I picked it back up to read what I'd missed.

**Nina Ford:** Jazz let him go . . . ALL . . . THE . . . WAY!

**Aaliyah James:** Jazz said he could tackle her any day of the week!

**Nina Ford:** I know he's impressed with Jazz's ball handling!

**Aaliyah James:** Touchdown!

**Nina Ford:** It's a game of inches!

**Aaliyah James:** Let's play ball!

I laughed. *Girl. Wrong sport.*

**Nina Ford:** Aaliyah, no. You ruined it. That's baseball.

**Jazmyn Payne:** Are you two done?

**Aaliyah James:** I am, apparently. It was between "play ball" and "goal" and I wasn't confident about either.

**Nina Ford:** I have tears in my eyes. This was the laugh I needed this morning!

**Aaliyah James:** Same!

I shook my head. I was glad they'd had a good laugh, but I needed advice. I'd come to the group chat with a serious concern, and they were making jokes. I was going to have to talk to them about my problem later.

> **Jazmyn Payne:** I can't stand either one of you.
>
> **Nina Ford:** Jazz got a famous boyfriend and now she can't stand us.
>
> **Aaliyah James:** Can't do nothing with money!

Still slightly amused by their commentary, I shook my head. "I can't stand them," I muttered, dropping my phone in my handbag and scooping up my workbag.

On the drive to work, I called Aunt Addy.

"Good morning," she greeted me, sounding weary.

Alarmed, my eyebrows shot up. "Aunt Addy, how are you?"

"Tired."

"Oh no, I'm sorry. I didn't mean to wake you."

"Not that type of tired, sweetheart."

There was a pain in my chest. "Oh," I whispered, understanding what she meant. "I'm sorry about that, too."

"Don't be. Just tell me something good."

"Um." It was hard to think of anything good right in that moment.

"How's Lamar?" she asked.

"He's doing really well. If all goes according to plan, he'll be playing in the game on Sunday."

"Oh, how nice! Tell him I said congratulations."

I smiled. "I will."

"How are you and Lamar?"

"I don't know . . . Our friendship is good." I gripped the steering wheel tight. "We had two dates planned, and he had to cancel them both because of work. He told me from the beginning that he was busy, so he didn't have a lot of time and that's why he doesn't invest in relationships. But . . ."

"But what?"

"I think I'm in love with him," I blurted.

She made a noise that sounded like her laugh, but different, weaker. "I think so, too."

"Why do you think so?"

"The way you talk about him. The way you wrote those words."

"What?" I gasped.

After Lamar had left, I'd emailed half the story I was writing to my aunt. I had more chapters written, but since I wasn't done, I didn't want to give her the whole thing. It had been only nine hours since I'd sent it. I'd had no idea she would've gotten to them so fast.

"You already read them?!" I exclaimed.

"I did and I loved it. It makes me want to know who did the crime. But it's no mystery that the woman is in love." She laughed again. "I just know he's going to be helping her in more ways than one."

I laughed. "In the story, yes, that's how it's going to go."

"Not just in the story. It happens like that in real life, too."

"But in the story, he didn't tell her he was too busy for a relationship."

"Yet every time we talk, you've seen him or talked to him recently," she countered.

I opened my mouth and then closed it.

She wasn't wrong.

"Okay," I conceded. "But having feelings for someone while knowing it can't go anywhere is a setup."

"Tell him how you feel, and find out if it can go somewhere or not."

"If I do that, either I'm going to get hurt, or it's going to ruin the relationship we have. I value his friendship, and I don't want to lose it."

"What if you're not alone in this?" my aunt questioned. "What if he's in love with you, too?"

"Who's in love?" my mom asked in the background. "Who are you talking to? Is that Jazmyn?"

"I just pulled up at work," I said quickly. "Tell Mom I said hi! I love you! Bye!"

Aunt Addy let out her weak laugh. "I love you, too."

I ended the call.

The last thing I needed was my mom psychoanalyzing the predicament I was in. She meant well and I loved her, but I would only tell her something I was solid on. And the situation with Lamar was liquid.

Parking my car, I picked up my phone so I could read Lamar's messages before entering the school.

> **Lamar Anderson:** I made it home a little while ago. My dick was hard the whole ride because I could still taste you. Leaving your place tonight was one of the hardest things I've ever done. Thank you for letting me stop by and see you. Goodnight Jazz.

I was thankful for the foresight not to open that text while walking into the school. I pulled my cardigan a little tighter over my chest as I read the message again. Closing my eyes, I exhaled and let the shiver work its way through my body.

> **Jazmyn Payne:** Good morning! I'm glad you made it home safely. Thank you for coming to see me. I enjoyed you very much. And if it was that hard for you to leave, you should've stayed. Messages like this are the reason why I wanted to sit on it last night.

I reread his message again, and when I was about to put my phone away, he replied.

> **Lamar Anderson:** Good morning. I just wanted you to know that I didn't make that decision lightly and as soon as I got in the car, I regretted it. I stand by leaving because you deserve so much more than a quick fuck. I didn't have much time, so I wanted to focus on you and take care of you. I wasn't going to disrespect you by showing up late and not having much time and still trying to have sex with you. But trust, I've been thinking about everything I wanted to do to you since I left.

**Jazmyn Payne:** I wouldn't have felt disrespected because I wanted you so bad I couldn't rest. Dick deprivation had me tossing and turning all night. I would've been fine with a quickie. I just needed you.

**Lamar Anderson:** I needed you too. I needed you so bad that when I got home, I put my fingers under my nose because your scent was on them, and I beat my meat, imagining you riding my face.

Squeezing my eyes and my thighs together, I let out a trembling breath. The mere thought of him masturbating did it for me, but to know exactly what he'd been fantasizing about and imagining how he'd looked while doing it was overloading my system. I had only two minutes before walking into that building, and I needed to get it together.

**Jazmyn Payne:** I can't continue this conversation. I need to go shape the minds of the youth. Are you at The Lab yet?

**Lamar Anderson:** Yeah, I'm just finishing my workout. I'm about to get dressed for the meeting. And then I'll have practice.

**Jazmyn Payne:** Today is your first official day at practice as a full-blown active roster team member. I'm so happy for you! Kill it today! You got this!

I made sure my phone was on silent, and I dropped it in my workbag. Closing my eyes, I took a second to clear my mind.

*I don't know what I'm going to do about him, but right now my mind needs to be on work. I will—*

The sharp rap at my window scared me.

"Ah!" I let out a short shriek seeing Alexa's face was damn near mashed against the glass.

"Oh my God!" I complained as I opened the car door with my stuff in my hands. "Why would you do that?"

"I wanted to make sure you weren't dead!" She put her hands on her hips. "Your eyes were closed. Your head was back. It looked like something was going on!"

"I was thinking!" Laughing, I hit the button to lock my car. "Why was your face against the window like that?"

"I was trying to see if you were breathing!"

Snickering, I shook my head as we headed into the school. "Alexa!"

"You're always here early. I'm usually the one walking in with the bell. So, when I looked over and saw your body in the car—"

"Not my body!" I interrupted, reacting to her dramatics.

The workday was busy, so I didn't even have a chance to overthink everything I was feeling. But as soon as I drove off the school grounds, I did just that. And my aunt's question rolled around in my head.

*What if he's in love with me, too?*

The thought twisted my gut.

I tried to distract myself with work. So, when Nina called around six o'clock that evening, I welcomed an entertaining distraction. I'd barely said hello when she interrupted me.

"Jazz!" Nina exclaimed.

My eyes widened. "What's wrong?"

"What have you been doing?"

I walked from the kitchen to the living room with my water bottle. "After I got home, I started grading these assignments, and you know what? I'm one assignment away from just not assigning homework anymore, and school just started."

She laughed. "I don't know how you do it."

"Having the entire summer off helps."

"I bet! But listen . . . did you see what I texted you earlier in the group chat? Because you didn't say anything, and I wanted to make sure you were okay."

"You mean when you and Liyah were practicing your standup routine while my personal life was in shambles?"

"First of all," Nina started, amused, "this level of dramatic response is hilarious. I'd expect that from Aaliyah, not you. Second, why is your personal life in shambles?"

I paced from one side of the room to the other. "So, you know how I was saying I liked Lamar? Yeah, well, turns out I . . . more than like him." I took a deep breath. "I think I fell in love with him."

Nina was quiet for a moment, and then she cleared her throat. "Jazz, I'm going to hold your hand when I say this . . . no shit."

My mouth dropped. "Nina!"

"I'm sorry, but Jazz . . . it's as clear as day! But I'll give you a pass because we've all been in denial before. I get it."

"I don't think I was in denial. I honestly didn't realize it until last night."

"What happened last night?"

I gave her a quick recap of how the day had played out.

"Oh yeah," Nina intoned. "No wonder you're in love."

"Nina!"

"I'm serious." She paused. "Have you told him how you feel?"

I shook my head. "No! Of course not."

"What's stopping you?"

"I don't to ruin anything. I don't . . ."

*I don't want to tell him and lose him*, I continued silently.

"You don't what?" she probed gently. When I didn't answer, she asked, "Do you want to be with him?"

"I . . ." I stopped the yes from rolling off my tongue, and my answer faltered.

After a few seconds of my stunned silence, Nina continued. "Okay, so real talk . . . you need to decide what you want first. If you want to be with him, tell him how you feel. If you don't want to be with him, don't tell him. Keep it how it is. But you figure out what you want first."

I chewed my bottom lip.

I knew what I wanted. I wanted to be with him. I was scared to admit it aloud because if I admitted it, it became real.

And if it was real, I'd have to deal with it.

"But listen," Nina demanded, reclaiming my attention, "the main reason I called you is to see if you saw the link I sent."

"Oh, I'm sorry. When you asked me if I saw it, I thought you were talking about the jokes from this morning."

"Those were hilarious, but no. This is something else."

Sitting on the couch, I put the call on speakerphone and then went to the group chat. I saw a link and opened it in my web browser.

*Maryland Monarchs Has a "Hollywood" Breakout Star.*

The title alone pulled my lips into a smile.

I read the article, and it highlighted Lamar's agility, physicality, and ability to get to the ball. It mentioned that he'd been on the practice squad until his standout performance earned him a starting position on the active roster. It closed by saying that if Sunday were to be believed, Lamar "Hollywood" Anderson would be a star right now but a legend in the making.

"Aww, this article is great," I said. "I'm glad he's getting praised for how well he played. If he hasn't seen it, I should—"

"No, not the article! That's what Aaliyah sent when we were realizing you were dating a celebrity. Look at what I sent!"

I looked back at the group chat and saw the link from Nina. I clicked on it, and my eyes bulged. "What is this?"

I couldn't process what I was looking at. I could see it, but it didn't make any sense.

The social media post was captioned, *Everyone is talking about Hollywood on the field, but I'm talking about Hollywood off the field! The man isn't active on social media, but he's clearly active in these streets. Out and about, potentially boo'ed up? Who is the Maryland Monarchs' new superstar that they call Hollywood Anderson? What do you think? Sound off in the comments.*

The photo attached was the group picture of me, Lamar, Nina, Russ, Aaliyah, and Ahmad. A second photo had cropped all of us out and just focused on Lamar. The post had two hundred thousand likes and thousands of comments.

I stared at the image. "This is the picture from—"

"Aaliyah's party," Nina interjected. "That's the picture that—"

"Mecca took," I finished her sentence. "Why would she post this?"

"I don't know. I'm still waiting for Aaliyah to call me back and tell me if she cussed her cousin out yet."

I clicked on the profile picture, and my brows furrowed. "Wait, wait, wait, wait, wait . . . who is Lemon Drop?"

"She's a content creator who focuses on good-looking men in sports," she patiently explained.

"But Mecca took this picture. How would a content creator who apparently lives in Atlanta have this picture? *We* don't even have a copy of this picture!"

"Exactly. But here's the thing, the picture is apparently everywhere. It's been shared around. A lot."

I was legitimately shocked. "What?"

"I don't know the full extent of it, but one of the models I work with saw it on his friend's social media page. It became a whole thing. I'll tell you about that later. But I just wanted you to be aware." She paused. "And prepared."

The hair on the back of my neck stood up. "Prepared?" I murmured.

"I know you're not big on having lots of attention," Nina stated carefully. "And the internet is the internet."

I looked at the number of followers Lemon Drop had. "There are millions of people who follow that Lemon Drop page."

"Yeah." She was quiet for a moment. "Are you okay?"

"I'm more confused than anything . . . about everything."

"Figure out what you want, and then talk to him about it," Nina advised. "If you want to be friends, tell him that. If you want to be more, tell him that. But you need to say something."

"I will. I'm just . . ."

"Scared," she guessed. "But, Jazz, real talk . . . whether you're calling each other *friend* or not, you're into him and he's into you. And now that he's the internet's flavor of the week, there will be people wanting to know if he's available. So you decide if he is or if he isn't."

"I wish," I scoffed. Her confidence and decisiveness were admirable, but those things didn't apply to my situation. "I don't think I'm the deciding factor. His career is."

I could hear the smile in her voice as she said, "You'd be surprised . . ."

My feelings for Lamar were real, and I didn't need to be real with just him about that—I needed to be real with myself. The more I fought it, the more it fought me.

*I'll talk to him on Friday.*

Wednesdays and Thursdays were Lamar's longest practice days. Fridays were shorter days, and he usually got home at a more reasonable time. I knew I needed to have a real conversation with him, and I didn't want it to be after a long day. So, Friday morning, I sent him a text asking him to call me when he finished practice. And then I proceeded to go over my plan in my head so I would be prepared.

Nerves started getting the best of me as the day went on.

Lamar had struck a chord in me, and I couldn't imagine not having him in my life. And even though my loved ones didn't think there was anything to worry about if I told him how I felt, they didn't understand what Lamar meant to me. They didn't understand how losing him would affect me. They didn't understand how at times his voice, his touch, his conversation felt like the only thing tethering me to reality. So it was a risk to tell him my truth. But seeing as how I'd almost told him when he was eating me, it was going to come out one way or another. My best bet was to do it in a controlled environment. I needed to do it in a way to salvage the friendship if he wasn't interested in a relationship.

*But how do I do that?*

I'd been home for no more than fifteen minutes when my phone rang.

Sitting on the couch, I stared at his name flashing across the screen. Breathing in deeply, I rolled my shoulders back.

"Hey, Lamar," I answered, my voice squeaking in the process.

"Hey, what's up?" Lamar responded. "Everything okay?"

I cleared my throat. "Yeah, everything is fine. How are you?"

"Nah, Jazz. Talk to me. I can tell something is going on. *And* you said you wanted to talk."

"Okay." Letting out a nervous giggle, I stood up. "So, the weekend of Aaliyah's party, something happened . . ."

"Are you talking about that picture?" he guessed.

"Uh . . . yeah," I answered, allowing the subject to change.

I rationalized that since I wanted to talk to him about the photo anyway, it wasn't a complete deviation from my plan.

"Nina texted me a link to this woman's post on social media," I continued. "After Nina told me it had gone viral, I looked, and . . . there it was. Aaliyah's cousin must've posted it, and then it got shared.

I hadn't been online much because I've been writing, so I had no idea this was going on."

"I've had some people text me about it. I was surprised, but it's cool. It's a good picture."

"It is. So . . . you're cool with it? I didn't know if you felt like your privacy was violated."

"I mean, yeah, it was, but it's fine." He paused. "Is this what you wanted to talk to me about?"

"Partially. I didn't know if you saw it . . . or how you felt about it. I didn't want you to feel like you couldn't hang out with me and my friends because someone might take a picture and put you on the internet."

"*That's* what you were worried about?" He let out a relieved chuckle. "You had me worried. I thought . . . something was wrong."

My stomach knotted. "What did you think?" I asked slowly.

"I don't know, the last couple days . . ." He hesitated. "I thought maybe popping up on you didn't work in my favor. I don't typically show up somewhere uninvited. So I'm sorry if—"

"No, that's not it at all." I had cut him off quickly, shaking my head even though he couldn't see me. "First of all, you were invited. You were later than we originally planned, but you were invited. And second of all, I love that you showed up. I love . . ." My heart raced as the words got caught in my throat. "I love being around you. I love spending time with you. I love our relationship."

*I can't tell him over the phone.*

I wanted to tell him.

I *needed* to tell him.

But I had to do it in person.

I needed to be able to look him in the eyes and see his reaction and response. I needed to see if he was going to reciprocate or reject me. I needed to read him. My aunt had said something at the beginning of the summer about looking someone in the eye to see the truth, and this was one of those moments.

"I love that you came over," I continued. "I don't want you to doubt that for a minute. Do you have plans tonight?"

"Nah, I'm just going to shower, eat, watch a movie, talk to you. What about you?"

"If I were to come talk to you in person, would that throw you off your pregame prep? I know this is your first official game as a first-string starter, so I don't want to mess up what you have going on to get in the right mindset."

"Yo." He laughed. "It's funny because I wanted to ask you to come up here, but I didn't want to ask you to get on the road in that Friday traffic. I swear I almost asked. We fly out around lunch tomorrow, so I have to be at the field in the morning. But if you're down, I want you here. I *want* you here."

Even with the knot in my belly, his words gave me butterflies. "Okay, I'm going to put a bag together. I'll call you when I'm about to leave. I'm looking forward to seeing you."

"Mm, you have no idea."

# 22

"This is niiiiiiiiiiiiiiiiice," I mumbled under my breath as I pulled into the gated community.

It was half past seven by the time I arrived at Lamar's townhouse. I parked, and then I sat there for a few minutes. Closing my eyes, I said a quick prayer that I wouldn't embarrass myself, and then I headed to the door.

Taking in a deep breath, I rolled my shoulders back. *Here goes nothing.*

The seconds ticked by, and anxiousness crept back up my neck. Looking down at my white tennis dress with my colorful sneakers, I had second thoughts. While in my closet, the casual yet cute dress had seemed perfect. But as I waited, I felt like I was doing too much and not enough at the same time.

Before I had time to pull out my mirror from my handbag to give myself one last look, the door swung open.

"God, you're beautiful," Lamar greeted me, taking a step back. "Come in."

With my cheeks flushed, I tugged at my pleated skirt. "Thank you," I murmured, eyeing him in his basketball shorts and white T-shirt.

It didn't make any sense for him to look that good.

"I'm glad you're here," he said, checking me out as I entered his garage.

"I'm glad to be here," I said nervously. Taking another deep breath, I prepared myself to launch into my speech. "I—"

My sentence had barely begun when he scooped me up in his arms and hugged me close.

I gasped before melting into him, wrapping my arms around his neck. He held on to me tight, and closing my eyes, I squeezed him back. He kissed the top of my head and whispered something I couldn't hear.

And he just held me.

Having his body pressed against mine erased any and all worry, doubt, anxiety, and fear. The longer we stayed in that embrace, the easier it was for everything to fade away.

It was just me and him.

He dropped his head, nuzzling his face against mine. "I got you," he whispered against my skin.

A shiver ran down my spine.

I lifted my head, and as soon as our eyes locked, warmth washed over me. My heart thumped loudly while his face hovered over mine. It was as if he were seeing me, reading me, and I was fully exposed. I inhaled shakily, and my knees felt weak.

Nodding as if answering a question I hadn't asked aloud, he leaned down, and his nose met mine. He paused momentarily, searching my face, and then when his lips brushed mine, time stopped.

His mouth moved over mine with slow, dawdling kisses that cleared my mind but flooded my body. I wasn't thinking at all, just feeling. The way his beard tickled my face as he overpowered me and the way his hands ran up and down my back so slowly was soothing. The way his tongue danced with mine and the way he grunted his approval when I sucked on his bottom lip was so sexy. But it was the way he seemed to sense that I needed him to be there for me first and then to desire me second.

It had been only a couple of minutes, and I'd cycled through distress and had arrived at desire by the time we pulled apart. My nipples were hard, my panties were damp, and my plan completely flew out the window.

He cupped my face with his hands. "Can I show you around before we talk?"

I nodded, unable to find my words.

He placed a sweet kiss against my lips and then grabbed my hand. "This is the garage." Pulling me past a four-door luxury sedan, he walked me through a door. "And this is the den . . ."

Looking around, my eyes were wide. "Oh, my goodness. This is so cool." A big-screen TV, football paraphernalia, and brown leather furniture created a footballer's dream space. "Is this where you watch the games?"

He chuckled. "Yeah. Or movies." He pointed to the bar in the back and showed me the bathroom around the corner. "If I have anybody over, this is where we chill." He pulled his phone out of his pocket. "Excuse me for a minute."

"You're good," I told him. "I'll look around."

I made my way to a bookshelf, and I eyed the titles. Almost all of them were sports books or biographies by sports figures.

"Tuesday is the only day I have off, so I can make it work, but it's last-minute," Lamar explained, before he burst out laughing. "I get it, I get it. But damn, E. Nah, I'm going to make it work." He paused. "I'm going to ask her. Well, it's not like you gave me time to plan it out. Your ass just told me about it!" He let out a loud laugh. "Yes, she's real!"

With my interest piqued, I glanced over my shoulder at him.

"Uh-huh," he mumbled. "Yeah . . . oh . . . true, true . . . oh, word?"

Figuring the conversation had shifted from me, I turned back toward the bookcase, and that's when I noticed the bookends.

He had photos inside block-shaped frames. Pictures of him with his mother, Bill, and other members of his family were displayed. Gingerly, I picked up a Little League photo of Lamar and a man I instantly knew was his father.

*They look just alike.*

The proud looks on their faces said so much as little Lamar held up a trophy almost as big as he was. The way his dad was smiling, that trophy could've been a Super Bowl ring.

"I'm going to ask her, and then I'll hit you back," Lamar said, again grabbing my attention. "Aight, hold on." He hit a button and then looked up at me. "I muted the call." He held it up to show me. "Erickson and Tara are flying in on Tuesday, and they want to have dinner with us. I know it's last-minute, so I'd understand if you can't make it. But I'd love for you to be there."

I grinned. "I'd love to be there."

"You sure? I don't want you tired on your way to work on Wednesday."

"If you can go to work tired on Wednesday, so can I," I reasoned. "Besides, I'm looking forward to meeting your friends."

"They're looking forward to meeting you, too." He smirked and unmuted the phone. "She said she'll come." His shoulders shook as he laughed. "Aight, I'm gonna get back to her, but I'll see you Tuesday."

He ended the call and then shook his head. "I'm sorry about that."

I walked back toward the couch. "It gave me a chance to check out your photos." Jutting my thumb over my shoulder, I widened my eyes. "Boy, you look just like your daddy!"

Lamar chuckled. "Yeah, that's what they say."

"I really like this space," I told him, taking everything in. I ran my fingers along the back of the couch. "And this looks comfortable. May I?"

"Of course." He smirked, folding his arms over his chest as he watched me. "Anything you want."

I sat down on the couch and then the love seat. "This is really nice."

"Thank you."

I ran my hand over the seat next to me, gliding my fingertips over the buttery-smooth material. Part of me wanted him to sit next to me while I shared my truth with him. But the other part of me wanted him on the couch so I could have more space between us and I could look him in his eyes.

*If we're touching, I might forget what I need to say.*

"I like this spot. Where's your spot?" I wondered.

His smirk gave way to a smile. "Where you are now."

My eyebrows shot up. "Are you serious?"

"Yeah." He licked his lips. "I guess that's just one of the many things we have in common."

I found myself grinning.

"Sit so we can talk," I insisted. "I'll let you get your spot back."

"It can be yours."

"Oh really?"

He nodded. "When I said you can get whatever you want from

me, I meant it. So, if you want my spot, it's yours." He walked over to me, but he didn't sit. "But let me give you the rest of the tour first." He reached out to me.

"Oh! I'm sorry." I placed my hand in his and he helped me to my feet. "I thought this was where you chill when you have anybody over."

Pulling me close so I was flush against his body, he held my gaze. "You're not just anybody."

My stomach fluttered. "That's good to hear."

After a swift kiss, he placed his hand on the small of my back. "Now here's the real tour," he said as he escorted me to the door that took us to a set of stairs.

When we got to the landing, I looked around in awe. "Wow."

His home was beautiful.

As he showed me around, I couldn't help but be impressed with the three-story townhome. The downstairs alone was almost the size of my entire apartment, and it was just a den, a bar kitchenette, a bathroom, and the garage where his other car was located. The next level had the kitchen, dining room, and the living room. The third level had his bedroom, a guest bedroom, and a sitting room. I thought we were done, but then we climbed another set of steps to a loft floor where his office and a roof deck were located. When he opened the door for us to go onto the deck, I was speechless.

Or so I thought.

"I can't even imagine what your rent would be," I blurted as I stared toward the skyline.

"I own it."

My head whipped around toward him. "What?"

"It's mine. I bought it."

"When you said you live in a townhouse, I didn't think you meant you *own* it. This is amazing." Awestruck, I shook my head. "Are you a Gates? A Carter?" I asked jokingly.

Laughing, his brows furrowed. "A Carter?"

"Shawn and Bey," I clarified as I peered over the railing. "Is this typical practice squad living?"

"Hell nah!" Still laughing, he shook his head. "Most people on the practice squad live in a hotel so they can have that flexibility because we can get dropped at any time."

"So, what made you buy?"

"I know myself well enough to know that I needed a home. A place to come back to. In the back of my mind, even if I had to go to a different team, if I got a nice enough place, I could rent it out or later on, I could sell it. But I knew it would be a good investment."

I nodded. "And I do remember you saying you needed a home base, and you said you had a townhouse, but I didn't expect this. I mean, this place makes sense with you being on the active roster and getting at least the league minimum. But you said practice squad gets paid weekly because you could be gone the next week. How . . . ?" I put my hands to my face as I realized I was rambling. "It's not my business. I'm sorry. I shouldn't be—"

"No," he interrupted, grabbing my hand and tugging me. "You can ask me whatever you want."

"I'm being nosy."

He put his hands on my hips and pulled me into him. "Ask me."

"How did you buy a home with a week-to-week job? Is that not risky? Obviously, it worked out now because you have a contract." I let my fingers dance up his arms before resting on his shoulders. "But . . . how?"

"I didn't use the money from football for this. My mom invested my dad's life insurance, damn near tripled it, and put it in a trust that I couldn't get until after I graduated college. By that time, it was more than enough for me to get this."

"Your mom is smart."

He nodded. "Yeah. So, if I did get traded or go to a different practice squad, I could do something temporary like a hotel or a month-to-month lease, and in the offseason, I'd come back home."

Something about the way he said *home* jogged a memory for me. Reaching up, I touched his face, lightly scratching his beard. I pulled him down to me so our lips could touch before I whispered, "Did you make Baltimore your home because of your dad?"

His fingers stilled, and he just stared at me.

A few seconds passed before he answered.

"Yeah," he uttered. His eyes searched mine. "Every time you do that, it makes me want you more."

"Do what?"

"See me," he answered softly, before pressing his lips against my forehead and then against my lips.

Pulling out of the kiss, I stared into his brown eyes and felt a stirring within me. His sincerity and earnestness always managed to soothe my mind, endear my heart, and set my body on fire.

"I . . ."

*Say it now*, I encouraged myself. *Tell him how you feel.*

Cupping my cheeks, he searched my eyes. "Do you trust me?"

"Yes," I answered without hesitation.

And it wasn't just my body talking—I meant it. I trusted him. I'd trusted him since the day I decided to climb into his SUV and let him drive me to a different town twenty-four hours after we'd met.

"Come here," he whispered, grabbing my hand and leading me back inside.

As soon as we made it down the steps, he spun me around and covered my mouth with his. He guided us down the hall to his bedroom with our lips engaged and our tongues caressing. He backed me into a wall and kissed me harder, his dick pressing against me.

I quivered with want.

Breaking the kiss momentarily, he stripped me out of my tennis dress and unhooked my bra. As he pulled the straps from my arms, desire and lust flashed in his eyes. As I stood before him in just my G-string and sneakers, he made me feel so incredibly sexy.

"I love when you look at me like that," I murmured.

He pulled the shirt from his body and tossed it in the pile with my belongings. "Like what?"

"Like . . . you want me."

Under his gaze, he had me discombobulated. To say that he looked at me like he wanted me was the most simplistic way for me to describe it. Because it was more than just him wanting and desiring me. It was him seeing and understanding me. It was him getting me. It was him knowing what I wanted and what I needed in the moment. It was him needing me in the same capacity that I needed him.

*But what's the word for that?*

His eyes swept up and down my body before he met my gaze. "I do want you."

"Good. I want you, too."

I gasped when he scooped me in his arms and his bare chest met mine. It was like our bodies were charged and the electricity between us was crackling.

"Do you remember me telling you what I wanted to do to you?" he asked as he set me on my feet in front of his bed. Leaning down, he rested his hands on my hips and his lips against the shell of my ear. "What I've thought about doing to you since I laid eyes on you."

My breathing hitched. "You want to tie me up."

His eyes were trained on me. "Yes. I do." His hands ran up my sides, over my breasts, and around my neck. "If you'll let me . . . If you want me to."

"Yes."

Squeezing my throat slightly, he licked his lips. "Say it."

"I want you to tie me up."

"Good," he breathed, sliding his hands down my breasts, over my belly. When he got to my hips, he ran his fingertips along the waistband of my G-string before cupping my ass. He pulled me firmly into the bulge in his shorts. "Let me take care of you. Let me show you how much I want you."

"Yes, please," I murmured.

Without warning, he crashed his mouth into mine, causing me to moan.

Our hands were all over each other. I found myself pushing his shorts and boxer briefs off his hips, freeing the erection I'd felt but had yet to see.

Thick, long, and hard with a slight curve to the right, his dick was beautiful. I wanted to look at it, but I wasn't ready to end the kiss. Instead, I wrapped my fingers around his girth and squeezed gently. The low groan that escaped him made my lower body clench.

He pulled out of the kiss, and his heated gaze took me in. "You are so sexy."

"So are you," I replied, running my hand over the length of him.

"I've thought about this since I asked you for your number." He took three steps backward before he turned and went to his chest of drawers. "In our first conversation, you said you had a lot going on. And all I wanted to do was lighten your load. Most of that was because I liked you immediately." He reached into the top drawer before pulling out a blindfold and a box. He turned, approaching me with his dick leading the way. "But I'd be lying if I said it wasn't also because of how sexy you are. How your ass moves to its own rhythm when you walk. How your nipples harden with the slightest touch. How your mouth opens wide when you laugh. How your lips spread when you smile. How your eyes burn into me when you're listening. How just your scent does it for me." He put the box on the nightstand. "I've wanted you since the moment I laid eyes on you." He put the blindfold on me, sliding it to my forehead so I could still see. "I've wanted to tie you up since the moment you said you had a lot going on."

I gasped as he trailed his lips down my neck and chest.

"Because I might not be able to control how you feel about anything else in your life . . ." He attached his hot mouth around my left nipple and then my right, sucking as he yanked my G-string down. After I stepped out of it, he kissed his way up to my lips. "But I can control how you feel in here."

I moaned into his mouth.

"Can I take care of you?" he asked me softly. "Can I show you how bad I want you?"

I bit my bottom lip. "Yes."

"Get in the middle of the bed," he commanded.

I did as I was told.

The California king–sized mattress was firm yet soft. It was exactly what I'd expect of an athlete his size. When I pulled back the comforter and felt the bamboo sheets, that was a pleasant surprise.

*Who put you on to bamboo?* I wondered as he went to his box and pulled out two sets of wristband cuffs.

After attaching something to the mattress, he put the cuffs around my wrists and tied me to the bed. My heart rate ticked up as he did the same thing to my ankles. Swallowing hard, I found myself fully exposed and in the X position as Lamar stared at me.

He ran his hand over his dick as he appraised me and his work. "You look so fucking good," he marveled.

I would've imagined I'd be self-conscious in such a vulnerable position. But I wasn't at all. The longer he stared at me, the harder he stroked. The harder he stroked, the wetter I became.

When his eyes met mine, he whispered, "Even better than I imagined."

He went to his closet, and when he came back, he had a metal rod in his hand.

My brows furrowed. "What's that?"

"A spreader bar," he answered, bringing it to my face so I could see it closely. "I'm going to unlock your ankles from the bed and connect them to this bar. It's going to keep your legs open nice and wide for me. But you won't be pinned to the bed with this."

After he explained it, he attached the bar to the cuffs around my ankles. Once I was attached, he lifted the bar and my legs in one foul swoop as a demonstration. Licking his lips, he inspected his handiwork.

"Are you comfortable? These are all new, so let me know if it's good. I don't want it scratching your skin."

"I'm good."

Once satisfied, he climbed on the bed between my open legs and kissed just below my belly button.

My entire body felt it.

"This looks so good on you," he said as he kissed right above my belly ring. "It fits you." He kissed his way between my breasts, then up my chest and neck before hovering over my lips. "Are you ready?"

I wanted him to kiss me. When I lifted my head, our lips brushed. "Do I need a safe word?"

Looking into my eyes, he brought his nose to mine. "You're always safe with me," he assured me softly. "At any point you want me to stop, I'll stop. You don't have anything to worry about."

I nodded, rubbing the tip of my nose against his. "Okay."

He kissed me, and when he pulled away, he smiled. "You ready for me?"

"Yes."

I bit down on my bottom lip as he slid down my blindfold.

I couldn't see anything, but I could sense his presence and feel his eyes on me.

With my wrists cuffed and bound to the bed and my legs forced apart by the spreader bar, I was completely at his mercy. My nipples were taut with desire, and I was dripping with want. The silence was loudly punctuated by my heart pounding in my ears. I wouldn't have been surprised if Lamar could hear it, too.

Seconds ticked by, and Lamar hadn't touched me yet.

Just as I was about to call out his name, I felt fingers skating over my belly. He was making slow, dawdling figure eight patterns. My body tingled with anticipation.

"Oh shit!" I gasped as he captured a nipple in his mouth.

I'd been so distracted by his fingers, I hadn't expected his tongue to swirl around my nipple the way that it did. He moved closer and took care of the other nipple, causing me to sigh blissfully. He alternated back and forth, and then he licked his way up to my mouth and kissed me. Just as his tongue parted my lips, his hand dipped its way between my spread thighs.

A sharp intake of breath filled my lungs as he gently explored my wetness. Sliding his fingers between my lips and up to my clit, he just barely grazed it.

I moaned into his mouth as he teased me.

Lifting my hips in an effort to control where he touched me, I was disappointed when he pulled away.

"I'm in control," he reminded me as he caressed my slit again.

"I can't help it," I said, panting.

"I know. That's why I'm here."

Just as he brushed against my clit, my hips lifted, begging him to do it again.

He put his mouth against my ear and allowed his breath to tickle my skin. "I would hate to have to punish you for not following directions," he threatened, before biting down on my earlobe.

I moaned.

My body was on fire, and when his fingers teased my clit again, I did my best not to roll my body upward.

"Good girl," he groaned, before running both his hands up my body. He kneaded my breasts, using his thumb to toy with the hardened peaks.

I gasped when his warm, wet mouth clamped down on my right nipple. "Yes," I hissed as his tongue moved in small circles.

Forgetting about the spreader bar temporarily, I tried to squeeze my legs together to alleviate the throbbing between my thighs. When I realized I couldn't do anything about it, I let out a whimper.

"I don't think you understand how bad I want you," he said as he bit down, focusing all my attention to his talented mouth. "So let me be clear . . ."

Without warning, he grabbed my legs and pushed them almost all the way to the headboard.

I sucked in a sharp breath, but I didn't have time to react before the first smack against my ass filled the room.

"Oh shit," I moaned.

My body was on fire.

"When I first saw all this ass, having you like this crossed my mind." He slapped the top of my thighs so I could feel it in my pussy. "Then we had a conversation, and I got to know you . . . and I just wanted you around." He slapped my ass again. "I thought about you every single day." He ran his fingers down my slit. "Then you gave me a taste of this pussy . . . and I haven't been able to get you off my mind since."

"Lamar." I exhaled his name.

He smacked my ass. "But you knew that would happen, didn't you?" He dragged his fingers over my pussy and then slapped the back of my thighs. "You knew what you were doing to me."

"You were doing the same thing to me," I admitted breathily.

He spanked me. "You made me like you . . . made me want you . . .

made me think about you . . . made me work with you . . . made me need you." With each statement, he made sure his fingers caressed me as he set up for the next slap. Five times in a row, he did that, stoking the fire that radiated from where his hand kept connecting.

And then he stopped.

I clenched and squirmed, anticipating a smack that didn't seem to be coming. His hand just rested against my mound.

"Please," I begged.

He let my legs down, and I felt him reposition himself on the bed. I wanted to touch him. I wanted him to touch me. But he wasn't doing anything.

And I was throbbing.

"Please what?" His fingers slid into my slick folds, finding my clit and teasing it. "Please what?" he repeated.

"That," I gasped. "Please do that."

One finger pushed inside me, penetrating deep. "That?" he whispered, moving so slowly that it made me ache for more.

I wished I could touch him.

I wished I could touch myself.

"Yes, please," I begged, pulling on my handcuffs.

He slid his finger in and out, never going any faster. "How bad do you want it?"

Even though he hadn't changed his pace, the way his thumb kept bumping into my clit was adding fuel to an out-of-control fire.

"I'm willing to do whatever you want me to." My words came out in heavy breaths as I started moving my hips to meet his finger.

"Let me know when you're at the point where the only thing you can think about is getting off. That's when you want it so bad that it's the only thing on your mind and you can't take any more . . ."

As the pleasure mounted, I felt myself heading toward the point of no return. "I'm there. I'm there. I'm—"

And then he stopped.

"No," I whined, shaking with desire as he removed his finger.

"Do you feel that?" I felt his breath on my face as he asked the question. "Do you feel how bad you wanted me to get you off? How close it was?"

"Yes."

"That's how bad I want you all the fucking time," he said, just before he kissed me.

Tasting myself on his lips made me kiss him harder. Knowing that he'd taken his finger out of me and licked it clean made me moan. His tongue probed mine, asking questions he already knew the answer to.

"You can have me," I blurted. "I'm all yours."

"I can have you?" He kissed me one more time before he kissed his way down my body. "All of you?" He licked my slit.

I almost came right there on the spot.

"Yessssssssss." I dragged the word out as I forced my hips up, trying to find his mouth again. Realizing he was intentionally out of reach, I slumped against the bed, defeated. "Lamar."

"So that's a yes?" he said, placing a kiss against my thigh.

"Yes. You can have anything you—ohmigod!"

His tongue flicked my clit.

"Tell me again," he demanded, teasing and toying with me.

My hips jerked as his tongue made slow circles on my sensitive bundle of nerves. As he slid two fingers inside me, it was clearly his intention to drive me crazy. My breathing got faster, and I couldn't keep myself from moaning.

"Yes," I cried out, feeling I was going to give in to my orgasm any minute. "You can have anything you want. Anything. Any . . . thing."

He took his free hand and pinched my nipple. I felt my orgasm building, and even if I'd wanted to try to stave it off, I wasn't sure I could. I struggled against my restraints as his tongue and fingers took me to the edge.

And then he stopped.

"Lamar," I huffed sharply.

My entire body was going to explode. All I needed was to be touched once, and it would be over for me. He had never denied me an orgasm before, and I was hating it and loving it at the same time.

"As good as you taste, you think it was easy for me to stop?" he asked quietly as the bed dipped. "But the first time you come . . . tied up and spread out on my bed . . . it's going to be on my dick."

"Oh, yeah, yeah." I nodded. "I like that. Yes, please."

"You know it's not just your body that I want, right?"

I heard what sounded like a condom wrapper, and I nodded. "Yes."

"Stick out your tongue," he demanded seconds later. "I want you to feel the condom."

I did what I was told, and his latex-covered dick slid across it. I tried my best to suck it, but he pulled away. Planting a quick kiss on my lips, he repositioned himself.

He grabbed my thighs, hoisted my lower body up, and had me at an angle.

"You still okay, Jazzy?"

"Mm-hmm."

With my legs in the air, he kissed my calves.

I moaned as I felt the pressure of his thick head against my opening.

"You said I could have whatever I want," he stated in a low tone. "You mean that?"

"Yesssssssssssssssssssssss." My entire body screamed my answer as he slowly pushed his head in.

"Damn, your pussy is wet," he whispered. "Fuck."

My body started to tremble. Hearing the hoarseness of his voice as he tried to work his way into me was just enough to push me to the point of no return.

"Oh my God," I cried out as he moved in and out of me. With the way he was giving me long, hard strokes, the orgasm he'd been teasing me with was coming fast. "I'm gonna come."

His hands moved all over me. "That's what I want. I want to feel you come all over my dick. I wanna watch this pretty pussy give in to me. I wanna watch you give in to me."

"Yes, yes, yes, yes!" I cried out as he pushed me over the edge.

"That's it, Jazzy. Take it. That's it, baby. Feel it. I want you to feel it. Just feel . . . don't think, just feel. Let me do this for you. Let me take care of you. Let me—Fuck!"

He grunted, picking up speed. His breaths were coming out in short bursts as I started clamping down around him.

"Oh shit, oh shit, oh shit, oh shit . . . yessssssssssss!" I yelled breathlessly.

The heat that had coiled deep in my core exploded, and my body started convulsing. I came hard, and because I wasn't able to close my legs, he didn't stop. Spread wide, I was vulnerable to his strokes. Something about the way he was fucking me overwhelmed me, and I felt my eyes water. He thrust in and out of me, turning me into a ball of nerves. It was so intense that it teetered between pleasure and pain for a few seconds, and then, unexpectedly, another wave of pleasure rippled through my body.

"That's it, Jazzy. This pussy gets so wet for me. I want it. I want you."

"Pleaseeeeeeeeeeeeeeeee." I started bucking against him.

"That's it," he groaned, losing control. "God, I love to hear you beg for it."

Each moan grew louder, and I didn't recognize my own voice.

"Oh, please, please, please, please, please." I twisted wildly as he made incidental contact with my clit, extending my pleasure. The combination of him stretching me out, giving in to his pleasure, and stimulating my clit had me breathless and seeing stars.

Letting out a guttural growl as he came, Lamar dug his fingers into the meatiness of my thighs. "Fuck," he swore.

His body stiffened, jerked hard, and then shivered.

Our heaving breaths filled the bedroom as we basked in the afterglow.

*Three times*, I marveled. I hadn't even known I was capable of coming back-to-back-to-back like that.

He uncuffed my legs first, kissing the spots where they had been bound and then massaging them as he put them down. He kissed his way up my trembling body and then uncuffed my wrists. His mouth found mine, and he kissed me passionately before removing my blindfold.

I struggled to open my eyes, as the light seemed extremely bright. But when Lamar came into focus, my heart skipped a beat. With me still flat on my back, my sore body and tender pussy reacted to the sight of him.

"You okay?" he asked softly, searching my face. "How do you feel?"

Reaching up, I placed my hands on his cheeks. "I feel good . . . and weak . . . and thoroughly satisfied. I loved every minute of it." Bringing his face down to meet mine, I kissed him. The delicious feeling of his body weight pinning me to the bed made me deepen the kiss. "I just wish I could've watched you," I murmured into his mouth.

He rolled to the side of me and propped himself up on his right elbow. Gazing down at me, he allowed the fingers on his left hand to dance across my skin. "I wanted to rip the blindfold off you," he whispered. "I love watching your face and looking in your eyes when you're about to come."

I bit my lip. "Why didn't you?"

"Because I just wanted you to feel it. I wanted you to feel me."

I reached down, pulled the condom off his dick, and then wrapped my hand around his girth. Even when he was soft, he was still big and thick.

I shivered.

"I wanted you to feel how bad I want you," he continued. "And I mean that in every way imaginable." He ran his fingers over my left thigh, dragging them over my swollen, wet lips on his way to my right thigh. "And it's not just because of this." He patted my pussy. "It's because"—his hand skated over my belly and fondled my left breast—"of this." His palm flattened over my rapidly beating heart. "And"—his hand wrapped around my neck, squeezing gently before running his thumb over my lips—"this." He brushed my cheek with the back of his hand and then tapped my temple. "And this."

My breathing hitched as his words overwhelmed me. "Lamar."

"And I wanted you to feel that," he concluded, holding my gaze.

"I want to be with you," I blurted.

He leaned down and kissed me. "You are with me."

"No, I mean . . ." Heat traveled up my neck and flushed my face. "I, um . . . I want to be in a relationship with you." When he didn't immediately say anything, I rushed to keep talking. "That's what I wanted to talk to you about. And I understand your situation, and we don't have to make this a big deal. We can absolutely just be friends. I just couldn't *not* tell you how I felt and—"

"Jazz," he interrupted gently.

My cell phone rang from inside my handbag somewhere on the floor. Although it startled me, I didn't break eye contact. I wanted to hear what he was going to say. I *needed* to hear what he was going to say. So, when he didn't say anything, my gut twisted.

Staring into his eyes, seeing so much tortured emotion in them, made the silence deafening.

*I said I wanted to be with him, and I almost said* I love you, *and all he's doing is looking at me.*

I needed a second to collect my thoughts, and I couldn't think clearly while he was staring at me or touching me. I also didn't want him to see that my eyes had gotten glassy.

"Sorry, I thought I had that on vibrate," I said, breaking eye contact and scrambling off the bed. "Please forget I said anything."

Finding my bag, I pulled out my phone to turn the ringer off, but then I noticed who it was.

Glancing up at him, I mouthed an apology.

"Hey, Aunt Addy," I answered, thankful for the brief intermission of embarrassing myself.

"Jazmyn, it's Monica," my aunt's nurse replied.

My stomach dropped.

# 23

I stared at Aunt Addy as she slept. I'd arrived in Chance a little after two o'clock in the morning. As soon as Monica said that Aunt Addison had declined significantly, I'd thrown on a pair of Lamar's sweatpants and a T-shirt before speeding out of town.

*"Jazz, earlier, I—"*

*"We're good." I interrupted, knowing I didn't have the emotional bandwidth to deal with the fallout of my admission. "Please forget I said anything. I was caught up in the moment, and right now, my mind is all over the place." My voice broke. "I can't."*

*He cleared his throat. "I'm sorry. You're right. Drive safely. Call me when you get there. Let me know what you need. I got you."*

I replayed that painful conversation with Lamar in my mind to drown out Monica's explanation of what was going on with Aunt Addy.

*Broca's aphasia . . . continued decline . . . suspects a ministroke . . .*

I repeated the words, trying to make sense of it all because I'd just talked to her. Thursday evening, we'd talked for only ten minutes, but she sounded okay. She sounded tired, weak, but okay. She asked me about the last portion of my book. I asked her about her party. There was no indication that the last time I'd heard her voice would possibly be the last time I'd ever hear her voice.

"She was napping, and she woke up and said your name," Monica had explained upon my arrival. "She picked up her phone, and . . . there was a panicked look on her face, and she was making noises instead of words. She tried speaking, and the words wouldn't come. She got upset, so I took the phone. That's when I talked to you. I gave her something to calm her down. Your dad ate soup with her and sat with her for a while, and then she went back to sleep. She's been sleeping since."

I hadn't cried since I'd laid eyes on Aunt Addy. Even though she was sleeping, actually seeing her made me feel better.

*Maybe this is what she meant by making peace with losing her.*

"Get some rest," Monica suggested about an hour after I'd arrived. "It's three o'clock in the morning."

I got out of the chair in the corner of my aunt's room and followed the nurse down the hall. When we got to the living room, she turned and looked at me. "She's comfortable. You had a long drive. Try to get some rest, and if anything changes, I'll wake you up."

"What happened?" I asked, getting worked up. "Between you and my parents, I thought I knew everything that was going on. And I know she's been spending most of her time in bed. Does she need to get out more and get moving, or does she need activities—"

"Jazmyn," she interrupted. Walking over to me, she placed her hands on my shoulders. "There is nothing that can be done. She hired me to care for her at the end of her life, and I am here. Your parents are here every day to sit and talk with her. She allows Rose to visit. She doesn't get out of bed because she can't tolerate activity. But there is no correlation between her being in the bed and her symptoms now." She searched my face for understanding. "This is just what her condition is. We're approaching end of life."

Blinking rapidly, I shook my head. "I just . . . I talked to her yesterday."

She hugged me, and I hugged her back tight. "I know. I know. It's hard to watch someone you love die." She took a step back and grabbed my hands. "But hear me, nothing has been out of the ordinary. When she takes her medication, she's not in any pain. The only day she experienced some discomfort was the day she postponed the pain medicine to stay up late to read your book."

I knew she was trying to make me feel better, but that made me sad. I didn't want my aunt to be in pain. I also didn't want her to die without me completing it.

*She hates a cliffhanger*, I thought with a quivering lip.

"Please be real with me, Monica," I pleaded tearfully. "What do you think? Not as a nurse to a patient's family, but as two people who love her. Just between me and you, what do you think is going on?"

"Addison is dying," she said gently. "As I tried to explain to you on the phone, her aphasia could be from a ministroke, and it could be Broca's aphasia. She was having difficulty speaking, and when she did speak, she wasn't finding the right words. I believe that upset her, and she stopped trying to speak."

"You think she's not speaking because of the difficulty and *not* because she can't?"

"We won't know for sure. But I've been with Addison for a long time now, and I'm speculating based on her personality. I'll assess tomorrow and follow up with the doctor on call."

"So there's a chance."

"Only God can have the final say. So, if He sees fit, she could very well wake up in the morning and say something. But from doing this work for as long as I have, I think you should prepare yourself for the fact that she may not speak again." She took a step back and pushed her glasses up the bridge of her nose. "Now get some rest. She'll be happy to see you in the morning."

I nodded. "Thanks, Monica," I mumbled as I headed to the room I always claimed as my own.

The reality of Aunt Addy dying hit me like a freight train. I'd had months to prepare. I'd spent the summer with her. But as I collapsed onto that bed, I realized I wasn't ready.

*And there's nothing I can do about it.*

I didn't dream that night. But when I woke up to the smell of bacon wafting through the air, I was pulled into a childhood memory of a six-year-old me waking up like it was Christmas morning because Aunt Addy was coming to visit for the weekend. My whole life, I'd looked up to her for support, for guidance, for inspiration. She had been the first person to truly see me.

*And I'm losing her.*

Opening my eyes, I stared at the ceiling for a while before I grabbed my phone.

**Lamar Anderson:** Just checking on you. Give me a call whenever you can. We're flying out in a couple hours. If I miss your call, I'll call you back as soon as I can. I just want to hear your voice.

My emotions swelled.

That message pulled at me, but I didn't text him back or call him. Instead, I put my phone in my pocket and went directly to my aunt's room.

"Good morning," I greeted her as I walked in.

Her eyes widened when she saw me. She didn't try to speak, but she dropped her piece of bacon and reached out her hand. I rushed to her side and gave her a squeeze.

She'd lost more weight. I'd noticed it last night, but seeing her sitting up with pillows propped up behind her and feeling her frail body, I found it was even more noticeable.

I sat down in a chair next to the bed, then put my hand on hers. "Aunt Addy, I just needed to come and put my eyes on you. Monica told me that you're doing okay but you're having trouble speaking, so I just wanted to see you for myself."

She nodded and pulled her lips into a crooked smile.

"I'm going to take a shower and get dressed for the day while you finish your breakfast. Then maybe we can watch a movie. Does that sound okay?"

She gave a singular nod.

"Okay." I squeezed her hand again. "I love you, Aunt Addy."

She squeezed my hand back as if to say she loved me, too.

By the time I returned to her room, my aunt was taking a nap with Monica monitoring.

My dad was in the living room.

"Hey, Dad," I said after our hug.

After I sat down on the couch beside him, he asked, "How are you?"

"I'm okay. How are you?"

"I'm okay." He shook his head. "No, I'm not okay."

I reached for his hand, and we sat quietly on the couch for a few minutes.

"Your grandparents had me in their early twenties and had Addison ten years later," my father started. "*I* looked after her while they worked. *I* was her protector. *I* made sure she was okay." He let go of me to reach for his coffee. After taking a sip, he continued. "But I couldn't make this okay."

"No one could make this okay. What matters is that you were always here. Getting on her nerves like big brothers do."

He smiled. "Did she tell you what happened when I cut the grass?"

I twisted my lips to keep from smiling. "She might have mentioned it."

"She was hot about that! I didn't do it on purpose. I was trying to help her out!"

I laughed. "I know. And she knew it, too. But she had put in work on that garden."

"Yeah, she did. Before your mom and I went to Florida, we helped with the garden every other weekend. We'd come by to see her, and she was out there, and she put us to work. I knew what the layout was. How was I supposed to know you two planted some more stuff this summer? Who plants flowers in the summer?"

I snickered. "She planted them a few days before I got here, and she did it at night when the forecast called for cloudiness the next day. The perfect conditions," I said, quoting her exact words.

He threw his hand up in faux exasperation. "You sound just like her."

"Because that's how she explained it to me when I asked the same thing!"

We let our amusement fade out. He drank his coffee, and I stared at the pictures on her mantel.

"As much as I worried about Addison, I envied her," Dad admitted quietly. "She had a spark and a fearlessness that allowed her to do whatever she wanted. Don't get me wrong, I love my life. Some of the things she did, I couldn't imagine doing." With a scoff, he stared into his coffee cup. "Some of the things she did, I wouldn't do even if I *could* imagine it. But I always envied her spark." He turned to look at me, holding my gaze. "You remind me so much of her because you have that same spark." He paused, his lips pulling down slightly at the corners. "But instead of fearless, did your mom and I make you fearful?"

It was the first time he'd ever said anything like that to me, and it caught me off guard.

Seconds later, the front door opened, and my mom walked in.

"Jazmyn!" She placed her bags on the floor as I stood to hug her. She held me for an extended period of time, and I let her. When she pulled away, she looked at me.

"We're going to be okay," she murmured.

I nodded. "I know."

She kissed my cheek and then went to kiss my dad. I grabbed the bags she'd left at the door and carried them into the kitchen.

I made my way back into the living room, where my parents were talking.

"The other day I overheard a conversation where it seemed like Addison was indicating that you were in love," Mom commented, the minute I sat down.

"Oh, um—I—um, what?" I stammered, completely blindsided.

My parents were two for two with the unexpected questions.

"Are you sure she wasn't talking about the character in my book?" I asked, sidestepping what she was inferring. "Because she read some chapters, and we were talking about that the other day."

"You writing this book isn't getting in the way of your teaching, is it?" she wondered. "I have a contact in Maryland who knows of a program that prepares you to be a principal. Wouldn't that be nice?"

"I'm not interested in being a principal," I told her.

"You should talk to Mr. Robinson and just hear him out. He could get you in—"

"I'm good, Mom. Thanks, but no thanks."

She leaned forward. "I just think that would be good for someone like you. And it's a more obtainable goal than getting a book published."

Rising to my feet, I said, "I have some things to take care of."

"Jazmyn, no, hear me out. Being a principal would—"

Dad put his hand on Mom's knee. "Let's not do this."

"Do what?!" Mom exclaimed. "I just want the best for her!"

I walked to the bedroom, closing the door behind me. I got my laptop out of my bag and immediately realized that, in my haste, I'd forgotten the charger. But in my defense, I'd thought I was just going to be at Lamar's overnight.

*I guess I'll just write until the laptop dies.*

Before I started typing, I pulled my phone out and responded to the messages I'd gotten from Aaliyah and Nina to let them know I was okay. And then I called Lamar.

"Jazz," he answered, his voice louder than the noise around him.

"Hey." I glanced at the time. "Oh, sorry, you're at the airport, aren't you?"

"On the plane. We're about to take off, but I didn't want to miss your call. How's Aunt Addy?"

I closed my eyes, allowing the sound of his voice and the care in his words to wash over me. "She's not talking, and she looks smaller than she was when I left. But she's still here."

*But I don't know for how much longer.*

That thought nearly took me out.

"I'm glad you're there for her," he said gently. "Is there anything I can do? Let me know how I can be there for you."

Overwhelmed, I put my hand to my chest.

"You can play your ass off tomorrow," I answered.

"I can do that. We're about to take off. But if you need anything, I need you to tell me, okay?"

"Okay."

"I'm serious. Anything you want, anything you need, just let me know."

"I will. Thank you." A small smile pulled at my lips. "Now have a safe flight and text me to let me know you landed."

We exchanged goodbyes, and after ending the call, I put the phone over my heart and exhaled.

*That man.*

I knew he had feelings for me. He'd made a whole show of letting me know all the ways he wanted me. But when I'd said I wanted to be in a relationship with him, he'd hesitated. And even though I knew he said his schedule didn't leave time for a relationship, his silence stung.

I knew he felt what I felt, but I wasn't going to bring it up again. The last thing I wanted was to lose him. There were only four people who I let fully see me, and I was already losing one of them.

Picking up my laptop, I walked to my aunt's bedroom and made myself comfortable in the chair in the corner. While Aunt Addy slept, I wrote. I was determined to complete the story as soon as possible.

*She will know how the story ends*, I thought with my fingers flying across the keys.

> **Jazmyn Payne:** It's late. I know you're probably asleep. I didn't call you back because I didn't want to wake you. But I'm looking forward to watching you play tomorrow. It's been a long time since I've watched the game with my dad and my aunt, so it'll be nice to be here with people I care about watching someone I care about live out his dreams. I just wanted to let you know that I'll be watching and rooting for you. Your friendship means the world to me and I'm excited for you. Your first league start is a huge deal! Have a good night and talk to you tomorrow.
>
> **Lamar Anderson:** I was just about to hit you up to see how you were because I'm about to go to sleep. Leon is snoring his ass off.

I was about to text him back, but my phone rang.

"Hello?" I answered.

"What's up, Jazz?" Lamar's deep voice was a sexy, gravelly whisper that sent a chill down my spine.

My toes wiggled under the covers. "Hi."

"You okay?"

"I'm okay. You okay?"

"Yeah. I just wanted to check on you," he said with a yawn. "I needed to hear your voice before game day."

My lips curled into a smile.

"I'm glad you called," I murmured, placing my hand to my chest.

He was quiet. "Are you sure you're okay?"

"I'm sure. Hearing from you helps. You make everything better."

"You make *me* better." He paused. "I'm glad I got a chance to talk to you."

"Me, too. Now get some rest because it's late and tomorrow is a big day."

He let out a sleepy chuckle. "Okay."

"And, Lamar?"

"Yeah?"

"Just focus on how talented you are. You're excellent. Don't worry about perfection. Be yourself. Be excellent. Play *your* game tomorrow."

He was quiet for a second. "I like that. I got you. Good night, Jazz."

"Good night."

Lamar was a balm for my soul. I didn't forget my pain existed, but he made me momentarily forget how bad it hurt.

*Momentarily.*

I knew Aunt Addy wasn't getting better. But when I woke up Sunday morning and went to her room, she smiled at me. She was weak and she didn't say anything, but she smiled. Monica hadn't noted any change in her condition. We all knew what was happening, but we didn't know when it would happen. I was ready to just call in to work and stay in Chance. But I knew I needed to save my bereavement days for when it was time. So, instead, I packed my stuff and planned to leave after the game.

Dad and I gathered in Aunt Addy's room so the three of us could watch the game like we had when I was a child. After Dad mentioned I looked extra excited for kickoff, I felt compelled to text Lamar.

> **Jazmyn Payne:** To see you live out your dream is inspiring and beautiful. You are inspiring and beautiful. You don't have to be anything but you out there and it's going to be enough. Play your game.

"When was the last time you went to a Monarchs game, Jazmyn?" Dad asked.

"It's been a while. Maybe five or six years ago," I answered, putting my phone down.

"Addison and I were supposed to go a couple years back. It's so hard to drive all that way and then be at work on Monday." He turned to his sister. "Ain't that right?"

She looked at him and gave a small nod.

"Aunt Addy said something about wanting to go to a Monarchs game this summer."

She closed her eyes and smiled.

I stared at her for a minute, waiting to see if she was awake or not. I glanced at my father, and he was doing the same thing. When our eyes met, we shared a forlorn look. The football commentator announced kickoff, Aunt Addy's eyes opened, and we all shifted our attention to the TV.

Monarchs lost the coin toss, so their defense was up first against the Illinois Iguanas.

"Defense is looking good this year," my dad commented. "Tough and aggressive like they were ten years ago. Watch the new kid. Ninety."

I couldn't help grinning. "Yeah, Anderson is really good."

As if on cue, for the first play of the game, the Monarchs' defense executed an all-out blitz. Lamar strip sacked the quarterback, and the middle linebacker, Reed, recovered the ball.

"Monarchs' ball!" Dad cheered.

Right after the play, Aunt Addy reached over and grabbed my arm. I looked at her, surprised. At first, I assumed it was excitement from the turnover. But the way she looked at me, I knew she knew it was Lamar who sacked the quarterback.

"Yeah, that was him," I told her. "He's making a name for himself in the league with that play right there."

"He sure is," Dad chimed in. "I don't know much about him, but if he keeps playing like this, Channing ain't getting his job back!"

"Wow, that was a way to start the game! Let's check the replay," the commentator announced. "You can see Coach Rice and the Maryland Monarchs are making a statement by starting the game with an all-out blitz. They really went big, and it paid off. Defensive tackle Lamar Anderson blows past the O-line and gets to the quarterback in seconds. Look at that—he doesn't even have time to secure the ball because he doesn't see Anderson coming. Wow! What a hit! And then the speed of middle linebacker Jalen Reed to get on that loose ball and recover it for the Monarchs. If the Monarchs keep playing like this, the game is theirs. Now let's see if the Iguanas have a defensive answer to that."

"It's still early in the game," my dad pointed out. "The offense now has to do something and put some points on the board." He gestured to the TV. "But this is why you can never underestimate the importance of a good defense."

I nodded. "Defense wins games."

The Iguanas did their best to contain the Monarchs' defense, but their offensive line couldn't handle it, running backs couldn't get yards, and wide receivers couldn't get open. The entire defense played hard, but I kept my eyes on number ninety. He was rushing the passer, stopping the run, and tackling everybody all game.

Aunt Addy fell asleep early in the second quarter but woke up for a minute during halftime. Dad had gone to the kitchen, so I took the time to fill her in.

Taking her hand in mine, I lowered my voice. "I took your advice, and I talked to him. We both admitted to having feelings for each other, but when I told him I wanted to be with him, he hesitated." I paused, anticipating her asking me what I did next. "I told him that I just needed to get it off my chest and I was cool just being friends."

Her long blink indicated displeasure—or sleepiness. Because I knew she wasn't bored by my story, I felt compelled to explain myself. "He's become one of my best friends and one of my favorite people. Doesn't matter if it's a bad day or a good day, when I have some news, I reach out to you, Aaliyah, Nina, and Lamar."

She squeezed my hand, so I squeezed back. Her lips turned up in a small smile, so I continued. "I've known from the beginning that he didn't want a relationship. And that's okay. I can respect it. So now I just have to pray my admission doesn't ruin our connection. What if it does?"

I studied her face, willing her to give me advice and trying to interpret any facial tic, blink, or squeeze as a substitute for her comforting words.

"I don't regret telling him though." I sighed. "I'm glad he knows. I'm glad I tried. Now, if we can just move past it . . ." I put my hand on her cheek, and she leaned into it gradually. "You know what I mean?"

She nodded.

"Thanks for listening. Thanks for always being there."

I missed her voice.

Not just the vocal cadence, but her unique personality, her worldview, and how she applied it to what she'd say.

"What are you two talking about?" Dad asked as he came back into the room.

"I was just thanking her for all her guidance and wisdom," I answered.

The game started again, and sometime in the third quarter, Aunt Addy fell asleep, but she woke up late in the fourth quarter. While Dad started telling her what she missed, my eyes were fixed on the TV—especially when the Monarchs defense was on the field. So, when the game came to an end, I was grinning when the camera panned over to him and a couple of other defensive players.

"This is a defense to watch," the commentator said. "Anderson has been a game changer in both his game appearances . . ."

"What time are you getting on the road, Jazmyn?" Dad wondered.

I looked at Aunt Addy, whose eyes were closed, and rose to my feet. "Now."

"We'll call you if there's a change," he said gently.

I leaned down and hugged my aunt. "I'm heading home, Aunt Addy."

She opened her eyes and touched my arm, but she didn't say anything.

"And don't worry," I continued, "I'll be finishing the book this week and getting it to you."

She gave me a small smile.

Staring at her, seeing her tired eyes and her light dimming, a wave of sadness hit me. "I love you."

She opened her mouth but no words came out. I chose to believe she was saying *I love you, too*, and I hugged her again to hide my watery eyes.

Blinking rapidly, I pulled away and flashed a big smile. "I'll call you tomorrow."

She nodded and lifted her hand. I took it and squeezed.

"I'm going to take Jazmyn's stuff to her car for her," my dad told her. "I'll be right back."

Silently, we walked down the hall, stopping only to pick up my bags. We didn't speak again until we got outside, and I unlocked the car doors.

"What made you ask me that question yesterday?" I wondered, before I tugged on the handle. "About you and mom making me fearful?"

He walked around me, placing my bag in the backseat. "A conversation with Addison. We were talking about the lists you two created, and she said something along the lines of wanting you to not be scared to live your life. I asked what that meant and she said that 'perfection stifles' . . ." He cleared his throat. "I couldn't stop thinking about it, so I wanted to ask you face-to-face."

I nodded. "I was curious because you've never asked me anything like that before." I gave him a hug. "Thank you and I love you."

"I love you, too."

I got in the car, and he closed my door for me. I started the engine, and with a wave, I backed out of the driveway. I knew in my heart that the next time I'd be back, Aunt Addy would be close to death. That thought made me sick.

*I need a distraction.*

Going to the sports network app on my phone, I selected the Monarchs' playlist of post-game press interviews. I listened to coaches' and players' breakdowns of the game. It was a good distraction while I drove. But when I heard Lamar Anderson's voice, I almost swerved off the road.

Collecting my composure, I turned the volume up and resisted the urge to pull over to watch the clip.

"They call you Hollywood," a reporter started. "Where did that come from? Is it because you're a star?"

Lamar chuckled. "My initials are *LA*, so since I played last week, they just started calling me Hollywood, and it stuck."

"This is your first league start, and you are already making a name for yourself due to your play. How exciting was it for you to get that sack to start the game?" a different reporter asked.

"Anytime I'm able to make a play to help the team reach our goal of winning, I'm excited," he answered.

"Okay, media training!" I exclaimed giddily, turning the volume up a little more.

The next eight minutes showcased his knowledge of the game, his ability on the field, and his overall intelligence. It was incredibly sexy, and I found myself wanting to squeal with excitement. Someone announced that the next question would be the last question, and I was disappointed because I could listen to him talk for five straight hours.

"And what would you tell others on the practice squad?" a reporter asked.

"I would tell them that it's your time when it's your time. The work you put in, the mindset you have, and the patience all work together. When it's your time, it's your time. So stay ready."

"Last question, last question!" a younger-sounding reporter shouted. "What motivated you to come into this game the way that you did? What was on your mind for your first career start?

"Someone special told me to play my game and to be excellent. Not perfect, but excellent. So I made it my mission to do that."

I gasped when I realized he was talking about me. "I said that!" I exclaimed giddily. "I'm the someone special!"

Fifteen minutes after I'd listened to his press conference, Lamar called. "Coach shouted me out specifically and gave me a game ball." His sexy tone and cool demeanor couldn't mask the excitement and pride in his voice.

"I'm so proud of you." I caught a glimpse of my smile in the rearview mirror, and my face flushed. "Aunt Addy actually grabbed my arm when you got that sack on the first play of the game. It was . . . you were incredible!" I gushed.

"She was impressed? I was trying to make a good impression."

I giggled. "Yeah, I think you did. She wouldn't have reacted if you didn't."

"And what about you? Were you impressed?"

"I am constantly impressed by you," I admitted.

"Good. That's all I wanted," he replied.

"So not to win, just to impress me?"

"Impressing you *is* the win."

I bit my bottom lip to keep from responding recklessly. *He doesn't have time for a relationship*, I reminded myself.

"Mm-hmm," I intoned.

"I'm serious. We're still on for Tuesday, right?"

"Yeah." I grinned. "Seven o'clock at Ember and Flame."

"Come to my place at six thirty. I'll drive us."

"I'm looking forward to it."

"Me, too. If you get here early, maybe we can— Oh shit, they're asking for me. Let me see what's going on and give you a call back. If it's after we land, I'll text you."

The call disconnected, and I sighed happily.

# 24

In preparation for the double date, Nina let me borrow a dress, and Aaliyah suggested the shoes. So, on Tuesday, immediately after work, I pulled on the dark burgundy dress with the flared hemline. It looked like a minidress on Nina, but since I was significantly shorter than her, the dress came to my knees. I looked good, but I wanted to look sexy. If it weren't for the sweetheart neckline subtly showing off my cleavage, the dress would look work appropriate.

I sent a picture of myself to the group chat.

**Jazmyn Payne:** This looked sexier on Nina. I look like I'm Teacher of the Year.

**Nina Ford:** More like the first lady of the church.

I laughed, but I was also freaking out. I had to leave in ten minutes to get to Lamar's place on time, and I was kicking myself for not trying the dress on sooner.

**Jazmyn Payne:** Omggggggggggggg! This isn't funny!

**Nina Ford:** I'm just playing! It looks just as sexy on you. It was just shorter on me. But turn around. What y'all couldn't see in my photo was the view from the back. It's the hips and ass that carry the outfit.

I read the text and then looked at myself in the mirror again. Turning around, I saw how my ass was almost emphasized by the hem.

*Ohhh, okay.* I nodded appreciatively. *I see the vision.*

**Aaliyah James:** You look so pretty! And you're going to Ember and Flame, not King of Diamonds! Why would you need your dress to be as short as Nina's was in that picture?!

**Nina Ford:** First of all Aaliyah, I have long legs. Second of all, you're not wrong.

**Aaliyah James:** I know your legs are long but long legs don't automatically mean your labia is gonna be on display.

**Jazmyn Payne:** Not labia!

My head fell back, and I laughed with my mouth wide open.

**Nina Ford:** On display is wild! You took Ahmad shopping and now you're the fashion police.

**Aaliyah James:** If I was the fashion police, I'd tell Jazz that the reason she doesn't feel sexy is because she doesn't have on the shoes yet. Once you put those shoes on, they're gonna take it to the next level.

**Jazmyn Payne:** Is the next level the upper room? Because I told you I would break my neck in those!

**Aaliyah James:** The upper room! I'm weak!

**Nina Ford:** I'm still on Aaliyah saying labia. I'm not ready to move on.

**Aaliyah James:** I didn't say it in a judgmental way! You know I would never judge you! I was saying it in a "I have eyes, and I can see your coochie" kind of way.

**Nina Ford:** Name one time you've seen my coochie this year!

**Aaliyah James:** This summer when we went to see India Davis at The Lyric Lounge, and you had that sexy little two-piece number on!

**Nina Ford:** Okay, name another time!

**Jazmyn Payne:** I'm so weak! What is wrong with y'all?

Cackling, I put on a pair of strappy sandals with a chunkier heel instead of the shoes Aaliyah had suggested, and I felt sexy. After changing into a sensible pair of flats for the drive to Baltimore, I grabbed my overnight bag and rushed to my car.

Traffic was fine at first but then got thick as I approached my destination. Fortunately, I was pulling up to Lamar's house right on time.

**Jazmyn Payne:** Hi! I'm outside! On time!

I switched my shoes and then grabbed my clutch. When I looked up, I saw him.

Wearing navy-blue pants and a blue-and-white button-up, Lamar was so handsome. The closer he came to me, the bigger the smile stretched across my face.

"Wow," he breathed, looking me up and down as he approached.

He reached for my hand and pulled me close.

"Wow to you, too," I complimented him back.

Tipping my chin with his free hand, he leaned down and kissed me softly. "I'm glad you're here."

"I'm glad to be here."

A bundle of nerves fluttered my belly as he escorted me to his SUV. Seeing him for the first time since I'd told him I wanted to be with him was slightly awkward. I didn't feel uncomfortable around him, but I felt exposed.

*I know I said to act like it never happened, but damn.*

Part of me wanted acknowledgement and the other part of me wanted to forget I said anything.

"What's on your mind?" he asked as he opened the passenger-side door for me.

"What's on yours?" I returned, unnerved by the way he seemed to read my thoughts.

His hand gripped my ass as he helped me into my seat. "You." Reaching over me, his fingers skated over the extra fat on my belly as he hooked my seat belt for me. "You in this dress." His hand gripped my hip. "You out of this dress." He leaned forward and pressed his lips against mine. "You look beautiful."

Before I could respond, he took a step back and closed my door. I settled into the buttery leather seats and waited for him to get in.

"Are you ready for the best wings you ever tasted?" he asked as he started the engine.

"You've been talking about these wings since we met. They better live up to the hype."

With a chuckle, he reached over and rested his hand on my thigh. "I'm glad you were able to come tonight. And I'm glad my friends get to meet you."

My stomach fluttered. "I'm glad I get to meet them, too."

We arrived at Ember and Flame seven minutes before our reservation. Lamar dropped me off in front of the restaurant, and then he went to park in the parking garage down the street. Waiting for him, I noticed a mural on the building next door.

*Oh wow.*

"Damn," Lamar said flirtatiously as he approached.

I spun around, grinning. "You like what you see?" I teased, allowing him to wrap his arms around me. "Before we go in, I want to get a picture of this." It was a huge colorful display of a phoenix rising from the ashes. "I love it." I pulled out my phone and snapped a picture.

"You want one with you in it?" Lamar asked.

I handed him my phone. "Yes, please."

I posed and smiled as he snapped one photo. When I realized he was done, I put my hand on my hip. "Did you take only one?" I laughed. "Take more, I need options!"

"Okay, okay, I got you," he said as he held the phone up and took more. When he handed me my phone, he smiled. "You're beautiful."

"Thank you." I rose up on my toes and puckered my lips. It took only half a second for him to lean down and kiss me. "Let's take one together," I murmured against his lips.

He got behind me, wrapping his arms around my waist, and I snapped a few selfies with the phoenix in the background.

"This is cute," I said of the picture.

He kissed my cheek. "Send it to me."

"Done."

He slid his arm around my shoulders, and we walked into the opulent restaurant. My eyes widened. From the marble flooring, to the chandeliers, and the mood lighting, the place was impressive. The place was filled with diners speaking quietly over white tablecloths.

"Welcome. Your name please?" a formally dressed man greeted us in a low tone. Lamar gave his name for the reservation, and then we were led to a table toward the front.

Lamar pulled my chair out for me, and then he took his seat. We were given our menus and then left on our own.

"You come to this place for wings?" I asked in a hushed tone across the candle in the middle of the table. Looking down at the menu, I didn't even see chicken wings. "I see frog legs but not wings."

He chuckled. "It's on the menu at the bar."

I followed his finger to the immaculate bar in the back. "Are we allowed to order them here?"

"Yeah. I wouldn't have picked this place if we couldn't get the wings. What do you have a taste for?"

"The filet mignon and thick-cut chargrilled vegetables," I answered, scanning the menu one more time. "What about you?"

"I'll get that, too. Medium."

"Ah yes." I nodded. "You like your protein alive and well."

He chuckled. "Medium is medium. You're acting like I'm ordering it rare!"

We were still snickering when a deep voice broke through the quiet atmosphere. "Sorry we're late."

"Yo!" Lamar rose to his feet and took a step away from the table.

A tall, brawny, light-skinned man with locs and a beautiful dark-skinned woman with a vibrant orange dress embraced Lamar. After greeting them, he took a step back and reached out for me. I put my hand in his, and he helped me to my feet.

"Jazz, this is Erickson and Tara," he started the introduction. "E, Tara, I'd like you to meet Jazmyn."

"Hi, it's nice to meet you," I said, extending my hand to shake.

"Nice to meet you, too," Erickson returned with a warm smile and an enthusiastic handshake. "I've heard a lot about you."

"It's so good to finally meet you," Tara squealed excitedly. Waving my hand away, she threw her arms around me. "I'm a hugger."

I gave her a squeeze. "It's so good to meet you, too."

Lamar pulled out my chair, so when the hug ended, I sat.

"You trying to make me look bad," Erickson joked as he rushed to pull out Tara's chair.

She looked at me. "He's not quite the gentleman Lamar is, but E has his moments."

Erickson sucked his teeth comically. "Lamar learned that shit from me!"

Tara pursed her lips and gave a side eye.

We all laughed.

The waiter came to take our drink orders, and then we fell into easy conversation.

"I'm going to order these wings Lamar keeps talking about," Erickson announced.

"And they better live up to the hype," Tara chimed in.

My smile grew. "I said the same thing!"

Lamar rubbed his hands together. "Y'all gonna eat those words."

The conversation flowed easily, stopping only when we placed our orders. It was beautiful to watch the dynamic between the two men. They were truly brothers, and it was evident in how they interacted.

"I'm so proud of you, bro," Erickson stated.

"We had a party and invited everybody over to watch your first game with us," Tara added. "We know you said not to say anything, so we just invited people over to watch."

"And then you showed up and showed out, and we couldn't stop bragging on you," Erickson chimed in.

Lamar grinned. "I appreciate that support."

Tara looked at me. "He's so modest!"

I nodded. "But also fully aware of his gifts." I glanced over at him, and our eyes locked. "Humble and talented and confident and . . ." I realized I sounded like I was gushing. "And the list goes on and on."

"Did he tell you how we met?" Erickson asked me.

I shook my head. "No. I just know you met in college, but I haven't heard the story."

"She doesn't want to hear your bullshit, E," Lamar injected with a laugh. "Especially not the first part."

Ignoring him and leaning forward, Erickson's smile grew. "Lamar and I met the summer before freshman year because we were both on the football team and we were working out and practicing before the fall semester started. So, it's the first day of workouts, and it's five thirty in the morning. Lamar comes in, trips over somebody's duffel bag, and falls right next to me. I'm not talking a little stumble; his big ass tumbles to the ground like a tree."

My jaw dropped, and I glanced over at Lamar. Looking like he was trying not to laugh, he hung his head in dismay. Realizing Erickson was, in fact, not bullshitting, I held in my amusement. "Oh no!"

"I helped him up since he's damn near on my shoe. Once we all knew he was good, everybody was laughing. I even saw the coaches laughing," Erickson continued the story. "Lamar dusted himself off and laughed, too. Some of the older players started calling him 'youngin' because he was just learning how to walk, saying he was too clumsy for the team. Just dumb shit. And Lamar just smiled. He turned to me and thanked me for helping him up, and then he got dressed out for drills. I started feeling bad for my man because he was catching it for a straight thirty or forty-five minutes. We went outside, and, I swear on everything, Lamar lit their asses up! I mean, he was trucking them. They stopped talking shit immediately when he showed them how good he was. That 'young clumsy' shit stopped that same morning it started. And I ain't never seen no shit like that before. Where we're from"—he gestured between him and Tara—"you talk your shit. When you're like that, you let it be known *you're like that*. I had never met somebody so good *and* so humble. I was like, 'I need to stick beside him.'" He leaned over and dapped Lamar up. "We've been locked in ever since."

The waiter came over and brought our food and refilled our drinks.

"We're going to taste the wings first," Lamar announced.

Each of us had one on our plate, and at the same time, we picked it up and took a bite.

*Oh!!*

"Mmm," I intoned as the crispy, seasoned bite flooded my mouth with flavor. "Okay." Nodding while I chewed, I gave my honest review. "It's good. You're right."

"Let me hear that again?" Lamar joked, cupping his hand around his ear and leaning my way.

"These are low-key in the top five wings I've ever had," Tara acknowledged, trying to daintily get all the meat off the bone.

Erickson shook his head. "I'm gonna be honest . . . I'm about to fuck these wings up."

"I'm trying to keep it cute so I make a good impression on Jazmyn, but there's something about this sauce." Tara pointed to the wing with her fork. "I'm about to put this whole thing in my mouth."

"Girl, please!" I exclaimed. "Do not let me stop you! You've already made a good impression on me, so handle that wing."

She winked at me. "Say less." Picking up the wing, she discreetly sucked the meat off the bone. After placing it on her plate, she demurely dabbed at her lips with a napkin.

"Me next," Erickson whispered to her.

All of us laughed.

He looked genuinely surprised. "Y'all heard that?"

"You ain't never been good at whispering," Lamar joked, before telling me a story about one of their many shenanigans. "The more alcohol in his system, the louder he becomes."

Tara lifted her finger in the air. "Can confirm." After our amusement died down, she looked at me and gave me a cunning smile. "So, I know you two met at a sports bar. But what's the story? What was your first impression of Lamar?"

I wiped my mouth after taking my last bite. "I'd had a rough day and just needed to clear my mind, so I was sitting at the bar, watching the game. And he sits down and just starts talking. He engaged me in conversation, and the more we talked, the better I felt. His energy is just so genuine and calming. As he talked, I saw how passionate and intelligent and funny he is. Obviously, he's handsome. But it was how he made me comfortable enough to open up to him in a way that I never have before that really drew me to him." I turned to face Lamar even though I was still talking to Tara. "He has felt like a safe space from the moment I met him."

Lamar reached over and stroked my cheek with the back of his fingers. Swallowing hard, he pulled his hand back and nodded. He didn't say anything with his words, but his eyes were speaking to me.

"Awwww," Tara squealed. "I love that!"

"Well, he called me the next day going on and on and on about you," Erickson informed me.

Ripping his eyes from mine, Lamar erupted into the biggest grin. "E, come on now."

Intrigued, I focused on his best friend. "Oh really?" I leaned forward a bit. "What did he say?"

Putting his glass to his lips, he finished his dark liquor. "Honestly, he said all the same stuff you just said about him. But what stuck out to me was that this man doesn't *ever* call me to tell me about a woman." He pointed at me. "But with you, it was different."

I glanced over at Lamar. "Really?"

"Really," Erickson answered for him. "And the way he talked about you in Dubai, I had no choice but to make sure you were added to the guest list."

Lamar looked at me, and a small smile played on his lips.

*He's inviting me to the wedding?!* I bit my bottom lip and nodded. *And I accept.*

"I think what Erickson is getting at is that I've been a big fan of yours from the beginning," Lamar said, reaching over to me. When I put my hand in his, he continued. "Still am."

"You got my boy's nose wide open," Erickson pointed out, almost giddily. "I love to see it!"

Lamar chuckled, but he didn't deny it. "So, did y'all ever figure out what you were doing with the house?" He turned to me. "They were renting out a house, and their renters had to be evicted."

"I'll let Erickson give you the update," Tara said, sliding her chair back. "I'm going to run to the ladies' room. Jazmyn, you want to come with?"

"Yeah," I answered, pushing away from the table.

Before I could even stand, Lamar was up with one hand on my chair and the other hand extended for me to take. I smiled as he helped me out of my seat.

"Thank you," I murmured, enjoying the closeness of Lamar as I eased by him.

Tara giggled as I joined her, and we made our way to the restroom.

"Erickson and Lamar are like brothers," Tara said as we turned the corner.

"I can tell. Lamar always speaks so highly of him. Of both of you really."

"I've known Lamar for years. He's also like a brother to me after all this time." She opened the door of the bathroom, and we both walked in. "He's such a good man. The type of man you want the love of your life to be best friends with because you know he's a good influence. So, as his big sister, I want him to be happy." Stopping at the sink, she pulled a lipstick out of her bag. "He's excelling in his dream career. He's doing well financially." She stared at me through the reflection in the mirror. "And for the first time ever, he's with someone who's good for him and he's good for."

"First time? What do you mean?" I asked carefully, not trying to jump to conclusions.

"Did he ever tell you about Milan?"

"The one who ended it when he didn't make the active roster?"

She nodded. "That was puppy love. When it ended, he said he wasn't getting into another relationship until he found exactly what he was looking for." She pointed at me. "You are exactly what he's looking for. He's always wanted someone he connects with deeply, and this is the first time I've ever heard of it happening. This is the first time I've ever seen him really in love."

My stomach flipped excitedly. "Oh," I murmured.

Her ruby-red-coated lips spread slowly. "This summer, sometime during training camp, he called Erickson and told him that you two only talked through editing his business plan. Erickson asked him why he's so pressed if you weren't calling or texting him back and you'd only hung out a few times. He said, 'She's different. This is different.' Erickson questioned him, and he said that you speak to his soul."

Looking down, I opened my clutch and pretended to look for something. "Well, we're not together, so . . ." Grabbing my lip gloss, I put it on.

Tara stared at me with a knowing expression. "All I know is that when we walked in and saw him looking at you, I saw all thirty-two of that man's teeth." She put her hand on my shoulder. "The way he talks about you, about the future, about life . . . I've never seen Lamar as happy as he's been lately. And a large part of that is you." She linked her arm with mine. "Let's get back to the boys."

We headed back to the table, and both men stood.

"What were y'all in there doing?" Erickson asked. "We know y'all were talking about us."

"And?" Tara replied.

I burst out laughing.

The waiter brought over our check, and we wrapped up the night. When we were standing outside on the sidewalk, we exchanged hugs and goodbyes.

"It was really nice to meet you," I told Tara, and I meant it.

"You, too," she replied. "And I look forward to seeing you again soon," Tara said as she climbed into the backseat of the rideshare.

I held up my phone and shook it. "And I just followed you back."

She grinned and scooted over to make room for her fiancé. I stepped back from the curb and happened to overhear Erickson whisper to Lamar, "You did good."

Smiling to myself, I pretended like I wasn't listening and looked down at my phone. Shifting from one foot to the other, I tried to reposition my pinky toe.

"Again, it was really good to meet you, Jazmyn," Erickson said, giving me a quick hug. "Take care of my boy. That's league greatness right there."

"A future Hall-of-Famer," I agreed, waving as he got into the car.

Lamar draped his arm around my shoulders and kissed the top of my head. "I'm sorry you were put on the spot."

I shook my head. "I wasn't."

"About E's wedding," he reminded me. "I asked them if I could add you to the guest list. I wanted it confirmed before I asked you to go with me. And then stuff kept happening, and I wasn't thinking about it. But I would love for you to be my date to the wedding."

I grabbed his sides, gently holding on to his shirt. "I'd love to. When is it?"

"It's after the season is over. I want to say April. The invitation is at the house."

"Give me the information when we get back to your place, and I can put it in my calendar. But, of course, I'll be your date."

His hands cradled my cheeks, and his head hovered a few inches above mine. In the pregnant pause that hung between us, I knew there was something else he wanted to say. It was clear there were thoughts he wanted to share from the look in his eyes, yet he just continued staring at me.

Emotion welled up inside me, and my eyes pricked with tears.

Leaning down, he moved his mouth over mine slowly, passionately. It wasn't a lust-fueled kiss. It was romantic, full of love and reverence. Our lips met repeatedly as if having a silent conversation that my heart understood but my ears couldn't translate. When he pulled away, the tortured look in his eyes caused my breathing to hitch.

"Are you leaving tonight or in the morning?" he wondered softly.

"I should leave tonight, but I want to leave in the morning. What do you think?"

"I want you to stay. I also don't want you to be late for work and regret staying. So whatever you want to do is what I want you to do." He pulled me into his body. "But I do want you to stay."

"Okay," I breathed, still feeling the effects of his kiss. "I want to stay, too."

# 25

With my back pressed against the front door and my eyes shut tight, I tried to say goodbye on Wednesday morning.

"I need more time with you," Lamar growled, before crashing his lips against mine.

Minutes passed, and it was clear we were both getting riled up. I placed my hand on his thick erection that stretched his boxer briefs enticingly.

He moaned into my mouth. "Don't start what you can't finish."

Pulling out of the kiss, I stared up at him. "If I didn't have to work, I'd stay longer. If you didn't have to work, I'd stay all day."

He gave me a soft kiss. "I was thinking . . . this weekend's game is in New York . . . But next weekend is a home game. You could come up on Friday"—he kissed one cheek—"and you could just stay here and chill until I get back from practice on Saturday, and then we could do whatever"—he kissed the other cheek—"and then you could come to the game on Sunday." He kissed my lips. "What do you think?"

"It gives me more time with you, and it marks another thing off my list," I said with a grin. "I think I like that plan very much."

We finally said goodbye, and he watched me until I drove away. I was downright giddy as I headed toward the highway. It was a fifty-eight-minute drive to Richland, and I probably smiled the whole way as I replayed the night in my head.

As happy as I was, it was still a long day.

But as soon as I left work, I called Aunt Addy.

"Addison, your favorite author is on the phone," Monica announced when she answered. "Jazmyn, your aunt and I were reading those chapters you sent all day yesterday. We're ready for that final chapter. We need to know who did it!"

"Thank you!" Grinning, I felt a mixture of pride and excitement as I turned onto the main road. "Hey, Aunt Addy!" I greeted her. "I'm going to be done with the book tomorrow. I didn't have time to work on it last night, but I'm almost finished."

"Addison is smiling," Monica reported. "We're on the edge of our seats!"

"I'm so glad you liked it." The tiredness that had plagued me all day temporarily evaporated as my pride and glee gave me a rush. "Now tell me about your day."

"Addison had some breakfast, took a nap, and now she's watching some game shows. She's pointing at the football, so I think she wants to know about your beau."

Snickering, I shook my head. Even though Monica was speaking, if my aunt could've said it, she would've. "He's not my beau! But Lamar and I did go out last night. It was a double date with his best friend. It was really nice."

"Met his family. Met his friends. Go on dates. Yep, sounds like 'just friends' to me," Monica teased.

"Haha," I mocked. "Aunt Addy, I just called to check on you, and Monica has jokes!"

"Addison shook her head because she agrees with me!" Monica laughed lightly. "But Addison has been doing well, is getting her rest, and she's got plans to see Rose tomorrow."

"I like what I'm hearing! I'm glad you're doing okay and feeling okay, Aunt Addy. I love you, and I'll call you tomorrow."

Saying goodbye, I sat in my sadness for a moment. It felt like I hadn't heard her voice in forever.

My heart ached.

And then I thought about her enjoying my story, and I smiled.

Even though I was tired, I went into my apartment, pulled out my laptop, and worked on that final chapter.

I had high hopes of finishing on Wednesday, but I was asleep by seven thirty. But I did finish Thursday night, and I sent it off to Aunt Addy's email account. And Friday after work, Monica called and told me that they loved it. I didn't realize how happy and fulfilled I felt hearing the praise.

I told Lamar when he called and got the same reaction.

"I'm proud of you," Lamar told me as I curled up in the bed. I had him on speakerphone, propped up on the pillow next to me. "You said this was something you've always wanted to do, and now look at you. That's what's up!"

"Thank you." I grinned, letting the warmth of his words coat me.

"Now, when are you going to send it to me?"

"I don't know . . ."

"You could send it to me, and I could read it on the flight."

"Let me get it edited and clean it up for you."

"I would love it just the way it is."

I put my hand over my chest and exhaled. *This man.*

"If you didn't have to wake up early, I would've asked you if you wanted some company tonight," I said sleepily.

"If the company is you, the answer will always be yes," he replied.

"You say that now, but you'd feel funny if I were waiting at your place when you got home." I giggled.

"I would love that shit."

The lack of amusement in his response sucked the laughter from my body. *What?*

There was thirty seconds of dead silence.

"You never told me what you were doing tomorrow," he pointed out, changing the subject.

"I have a hair appointment that I almost forgot about, and then I'm going to clean up and chill. Sunday will be church and then watching you kick ass."

He laughed. "I like that plan. Who does your hair?"

We talked for about an hour before his yawns got the best of him.

"You need to get your rest," I told him.

"Yeah," he agreed. "Send me a picture of you after you get your hair done."

"I will. I'll send you a few of them. Let me know when you land in New York."

"I'm letting you know when I get to the airport."

Grinning, I nodded. "Yes, please."

"Aight, I'll hit you up in the morning."

"Okay, have a good night."

"Good night, Jazz."

The grin on my face felt permanent.

Even my loctician made a comment as she dyed and then retwisted my hair the next day.

"You look happy," she noted as she turned me around in the chair.

And I was.

"What made you finally decide to try something other than the honey-blonde highlights?" she wondered, inspecting my midnight-blue locs. "A breakup or a new guy?"

"Neither, actually. My aunt and I made lists of things we had to do and dyeing our hair was one of them. So here I am." I smiled at my reflection in the mirror. "This is the eighth thing off my list."

"Is there some special meaning to dyeing your hair?" she wondered.

"Yeah," I said, looking down at my phone. Seeing the notification of a text from Lamar, I smiled. "This is me being bold and standing out. And it's a great fall/winter color."

"Mm-hmm," she said as if she'd caught me doing something I wasn't supposed to be doing. As soon as I looked up, she smirked. "Good to see you getting back out there."

I knew I looked goofy with how hard I was smiling, but I couldn't keep it together. "What?"

"New man," she concluded, answering her earlier question. "You have a glow."

So even though I didn't confirm or deny anything, she knew.

"My hair color is about my aunt, not about a man!" I argued.

"Maybe the hair color is about your aunt. But that glow . . . that's a man."

I couldn't do anything but laugh.

The highlight of my Saturday was getting my hair done. The highlight of my Sunday was watching Lamar kick ass.

"Well, hello, Mr. Playmaker of the Game," I greeted Lamar when he called me Sunday night.

He chuckled. "Hello to the beautiful Ms. Jazmyn Payne. Did you see that blitz?"

"Did I?" I reacted. "I screamed! I know my neighbors were concerned, but when you recovered the ball after Jones knocked it out, I was on my feet."

"When they called that play, you instantly popped into my mind. I try not to think about anything but football when I'm on the field. But I saw your face immediately, and I . . ." He paused. "I wanted to tell you that before we catch this flight."

I bit my bottom lip. "Well, I think about you constantly . . . just so you know. Like I said in my message to you this morning, you're really special. On the field and off the field."

"Those messages you send before the game put an extra battery in my back. So thank you."

"You're welcome, but you don't have to thank me for showing you love. I believe in giving people flowers while they're here and can smell them."

"If you're trying to convince me to come straight to your place when we land, it's working."

"I wish." I giggled. "I'd love to see you soon though."

"We're still on for Friday, right? You'll stay with me for the weekend? Go to the game on Sunday?"

"Oh absolutely." *I was just hoping sooner.* "I'm looking forward to it."

"Good. Because I need to see you."

My stomach fluttered. "I need to see you, too." I heard a commotion in the background. "I know you have a lot going on, but I'm glad you called. Text me when you land."

"Even though you're usually 'sleep, I always do."

I grinned. "You know me so well."

"I do."

We said good night, and I put my phone to my chest and exhaled. *This man.*

I got on social media to see if the Monarchs had posted any postgame interview clips yet. I wanted to see any and all interviews with Lamar. The first one that came up was a short one, a sideline interview that I hadn't seen when it aired live. He was so sexy and charismatic. I found myself smiling at my phone screen.

*I got it bad.*

Just as I was about to put my phone down, a familiar name popped up in the search results.

*Lemon Drop.*

The image was the group photo cropped to show just me and Lamar, which was a change from what had been happening before. I clicked on it tentatively and read the caption.

*After doing some digging, it would appear that Hollywood Anderson may not be single after all. An inside source has confirmed that the breakout defensive star was seen canoodling with the woman in this photo. Apparently at this event, an end of the summer birthday party, the two spent the whole night together. We don't know if it's a friendship, a one-night stand, a date, or a relationship, but we do know he's not married yet so he's still fair game. What do you think about this pairing?*

My stomach churned as the comments caught my eye.

*She doesn't look like an athlete's girl. She doesn't fit the aesthetic. Hollywood needs someone like me!*

*If she got him at that size, then why am I in the gym five days a week and single?*

*She's pretty and you can tell she has ass. Now that he's getting a contract, I bet he's going to get her a tummy tuck, breast implants, a nose job, and a wig so she'll look the part.*

*He's making that league money now. I hope she enjoyed the party. She's cute, but she won't be seeing him again!*

*Honestly, they look cute together but now that he's in the league, he's going to trade up. There's no way he's staying with her. She was fine when he was on the practice squad, but now that's he's Hollywood, he needs a baddie.*

Squeezing my eyes shut, I put my phone down, pulled the covers up, and went to sleep.

I woke up with a start a few hours later. My heart was racing, and there was sweat on my brow. I pushed myself into a seated position and tried to shake off the nightmare.

The problem was that it was easier to forget a nightmare than it was to forget a memory.

It had been mid-October of junior year of high school, and people were campaigning for homecoming king and queen. Someone hung flyers that featured a picture of me with the words *fat chance beating Olivia Chapman for homecoming queen* around the entire town.

It wasn't just embarrassing; it was humiliating. I was getting stared at, talked about, and laughed at during school. I received a bunch of sympathetic looks from random adults around town. For a full week, I had those flyers on my locker, at my desks, in my classrooms. After homecoming, all the flyers seemed to come down.

That was the incident that broke me.

I'd shied away from attention before then, but I'd gone out of the way to avoid the spotlight after that. The only thing that differed between real life and the dream was that the flyer had said, *Fat chance with Hollywood.*

I put my hand over my heart and tried to steady my heart rate and calm my breathing.

*It's not happening again.*

It took a while, but I finally got to sleep. So Monday was a long day.

While I felt like I played it cool, I was stressed all day at work and ready to get home.

Ben Riker appeared at my classroom door. "Hey, Ms. Payne . . . oh wow, you're in a rush!" he exclaimed as I came barreling toward him.

He moved out of the doorway just in time.

"Sorry, Mr. Riker, I have an appointment at four o'clock," I said as I passed by him. "If you're heading out, we can walk and talk, or you can just call me."

He jogged to catch up and then fell into step with me. "Jazmyn," he started, his voice low. "I was looking up info for my fantasy team, and I came across something." He dropped his voice to a whisper. "Is that you in that picture with Hollywood Anderson?"

We approached the door to exit the school. I glanced at him out of the corner of my eye. "It is."

"Holy shit," he mumbled as we made it outside. "Is that your—"

"Ben," I interrupted, pointing my key fob toward my car and starting the engine as we approached. "I can't say anything else, and I don't want my name out there. So, if you could keep it on the low, I would appreciate it."

"Yes, of course. But wow!" He walked me to my car and watched me throw my stuff in. "Tell him I said good work on Sunday. He's on my fantasy team."

I nodded. "Bye, Ben."

I hopped in the driver's seat and pulled off, shaking my head. I knew Ben was going to tell Alexa and his wife. Outside of that, I was confident he wouldn't tell anyone else or make videos on social media about it.

I pursed my lips as I sped home.

As soon as I got in my apartment, I called my best friends to talk about what I'd found out last night.

"'I think it's kinda cool that he likes a regular-looking woman who don't fit the beauty standards.'" I was reading the social media post to my best friends on a three-way call. "'She has a real body, a wide nose, locs, and looks kinda short. She looks regular. She's probably getting cheated on, but I know she cooks for him and treats him right. I'm rooting for this couple.'" I paused. "And this was a post *defending* me!"

I paced from one side of my living room to the other, trying to work off my annoyance.

"Wow, I'm so sorry." Aaliyah sighed. "You don't deserve this."

"That's some bullshit. But none of that is true, so I hope you didn't take any of it to heart," Nina responded.

"Apparently this has been going on for the last few days," I mentioned. "The topic—me and my worthiness to date a rising star—has gone viral. I saw it just last night, but there are so many videos and posts about it. There are so many people in the comments who are saying the meanest things about the way I look, and I just don't understand it. They are so pressed about Lamar's relationship status that they are dragging me and then projecting what *they* think he should be attracted to onto me. It's . . . dumb."

"It's fucked-up is what it is," Aaliyah corrected.

"You're right," I agreed, nodding. "It *is* fucked-up. But it's also dumb!"

"People say wild bullshit *unprovoked* on the internet because it's easy to talk shit behind a keyboard," Nina pointed out. "They feel like there's no consequences."

"I know you know." I sighed, thinking of all the online nonsense

Nina endured. "But it just brings me back to the reason why I left Chance, those bully ass bitches and all the people who let that shit slide. That was the last time I felt like I wasn't a person but an idea to be scrutinized. And it started in middle school with Olivia saying, 'How could that cool guy like her?' And now, it's like the world is saying, 'How could that cool guy like her?' All because I got some meat on my bones?"

"I signed up to be in the public eye, and I was still surprised by how horrible the comments could get," Nina admitted. "So I get it. But they don't know you or Lamar. They don't know shit. And honestly, they don't matter."

"Nina's right. They don't matter! What are Lamar's thoughts on this?" Aaliyah wondered.

"I don't know." I shrugged even though they couldn't see me. "I haven't talked to him about it because I just found out about all this last night before bed. I called the two of you as soon as I left work, so I don't know. He's still at practice." I hesitated. "But honestly, this is embarrassing."

"*They* should be embarrassed, not you," Nina argued.

"Yeah, they should," I agreed. "But if Lamar has seen this, has been sent this, that is embarrassing—"

"You should tell Lamar so he knows what's going on," Aaliyah suggested, interrupting what I was saying. "But I don't want you to feel embarrassed by this because you are not the embarrassment in this situation—"

"I love you both, but I want you to hear me," I interjected. "I'm not saying that *I'm* embarrassing or that any of the bullshit they are saying is true. I'm saying that this *situation* is embarrassing. Lamar is new to the active roster. He's living his dream. And because he was my date to the party, they are critiquing me instead of talking about how well he did on Sunday."

"Ahmad said he did really good in the game," Aaliyah mentioned.

I nodded. "He did. But listen to this . . ." I went to the screenshot I took of the popular comment. "DaPrize48237 said, 'I think we should all question Hollywood's ability to be a leader on the field when we see him making questionable choices off the field. The big-backed beauty may be an anchor to his career and until he frees himself from the deadweight, he won't be able to elevate his career. As soon as Channing got with the model Lourdes, he elevated and quickly. When they separated, he wasn't playing so hot last year. And their divorce finalized and that same week, he tears his meniscus. The moral of the story is that if Hollywood wants to see success on the field, he needs to see it off the field. For that reason, I can't vote for him for Defensive Player of the Month.' That has six thousand likes, almost double that in shares! That's bullshit for several reasons, but Lamar's level of play deserves to be rewarded and not hindered by this. And I don't deserve to be disrespected for no fucking reason!" I let out an angry shout.

"The fact that you seem more concerned about how it affects him than how it affects you tells me that you love him," Aaliyah said in a dreamy tone.

"It doesn't matter how I feel because a week and a half ago, I told him I wanted to be with him, and he . . . isn't interested in that. So—"

"Wait, what?!" Aaliyah screeched.

"Explain," Nina reacted.

I told them about the conversation. For them to understand the circumstances, I told them about him tying me up, and the conversation deviated for at least ten minutes because I had never had back-to-back orgasms like that before. But when I got them back on track, I told them verbatim what was said . . . and not said.

"You should talk to him about all this. He didn't *say* he didn't want to be with you," Aaliyah reasoned.

"He didn't *say* anything," Nina pointed out. "I mean, I believe he does. But I feel where you're coming from, Jazz."

I let my head fall back. "Either way, he told me from the beginning that he was too busy for a relationship, so I'm not mad at him. But now with him not saying anything and then the rumors that we're together and then the bullshit people are saying . . . that's a lot."

"He's a big boy," Aaliyah pointed out. "He can take it."

"Well, I don't know if *I* can," I replied. "With him being a public figure and me hating all these unnecessary eyes on me, I think it's for the best that he's too busy for a relationship. I'm not trying to put myself through that again unnecessarily."

"These people don't matter, Jazz," Nina reminded me. "And if they don't matter, they don't get to have any kind of power over you. Give it twenty-four more hours, and they'll have a new story in the news cycle."

"And I'm sorry," Aaliyah apologized. "You wouldn't even be in this bullshit if Mecca's nosy ass didn't post the picture online. I already told her about herself. But I feel like this is kinda on me. Mecca's bullshit put you both in some mess."

I shook my head. "It's not on you," I assured her. "And, Nina, I get what you're saying. But Chance scarred me. I don't ever want to go back to the version of myself that place created. And all day at work, I had to fight the feeling of being in a high school, being publicly ridiculed, and not knowing when it was going to end. I had students whispering, and granted, they're teenagers, and it could've been about anything. But it was the kids that I know watch football."

"I get that," Nina said gently. "You deserve better than this. And I would love to tell you that it won't ever happen again, but it might. Not to this degree. It's like this right now because it's new and because they're trying to figure out what's up with Lamar. Once he sets the record straight, the whole thing will be a nonissue."

"That's why you should talk to him as soon as possible," Aaliyah added. "In an ideal world, what would you want?"

"I would want none of this to have ever happened," I groaned, collapsing onto the couch.

"Meeting Lamar?" Aaliyah asked.

"No," I balked. "I'm talking about the internet stuff. I don't regret anything about meeting Lamar. I can't imagine how things would be if I didn't. But when we met, he was Lamar. And now he's *Hollywood*." I opened my mouth to continue when I got an incoming call. Pulling the phone away from my ear, I saw who it was, and my eyes widened. "Lamar is beeping in right now!"

"Answer it!" Nina demanded. "Russ just got here anyway. So I'm going to go, too."

"Answer it and call back and let us know what happens," Aaliyah added.

"I will. Thank you!" I said in a rush before answering the incoming call.

# 26

"Hello?" I sounded as nervous as I felt.

"What's up, Jazz?" Lamar greeted me.

"How are you? How was your day?"

"Typical Monday—we watch tape, we practice, we review. But one thing happened that was different: They had me break down what I saw on the first play of the game for me to get to the quarterback. That was a first."

My nerves melted away hearing his excitement. Grinning, I pulled my legs onto the couch. "That's so cool! How did it feel?"

"I'm not gonna lie, it felt good. It was nice having my hard work get recognized in front of my teammates and coaches like that. It's one thing in the game when we're all feeling it. It's another thing to be a spectator and watch it on the screen, break down the plays. And remember when you suggested a class on contract law for the rookies who opted to not have an agent? Well, I was introduced to a woman today who just so happened to be a retired contract lawyer."

"What?! That's amazing! That's the final piece. You have everything else you need if you can get her. Did you ask?"

"Nah, we were about to start practice. She was with someone in the front office. She was with the defensive coordinator's mom or something. I don't remember because once she said what she did, all I could think about was calling you."

I bit down on my bottom lip, giddy. "Well, I hope you at least got her name."

"And her email address."

"Okay, I see you!" I giggled.

"Now tell me how you're doing," he insisted.

"I'm . . ." My words faded out, and my cheeks flushed. "It's been a day."

"What's going on? Are you okay?"

The comments flashed in my mind, and anxiety washed over me.

The fact that people weren't voting for him because of me weighed on me. The risk of rejection, the public and private embarrassment, and the uncertainty of how our friendship would survive immobilized me.

"Jazz," he uttered. "Talk to me."

*Just say it.* I ordered myself to tell him about the social media shit-show. I opened my mouth, and no words would come out.

Swallowing my feelings, I changed the subject. "This school year is going to be a beast, and I'm overwhelmed with how much they expect us to do outside of actually teaching."

"Oh shit, already? School just started! What are they asking you to do?"

He listened as I went over the information that they'd shared in the newsletter that morning and how we were supposed to be meeting about it after work on Tuesday.

"When are you supposed to have time to do all that?" he wondered.

I threw my hand in the air. "That's what I'm saying!"

"They'd feel funny if you quit."

I laughed. "Quit and do what?"

"Something you're really passionate about. Writing books or something football related. Maybe running an organization designed to prepare athletes for professional ball."

"That would be the dream." I sighed. "Maybe one day."

"I'd like to see that."

I smiled. "Me too."

"Well, I was going to see what you were doing tomorrow so I could see you, but you'll be at the meeting."

"Unfortunately," I groaned. "But I really would like to see you. And soon."

"Friday?" he suggested. "I'll send a car for you or give you gas money—whatever I have to do to make it easier for you."

Grinning, I placed my hand over my heart. "Lamar, you don't have to do that. But I appreciate it. Thank you."

"I'm asking you to come see me, so I'm going to make it easier for you," he reiterated. "So, which would you prefer, getting driven up here or driving yourself?"

"I guess to get driven."

"Done."

My eyebrows flew up. "Really? That easy?"

"Come on, Jazmyn, you know that you can get anything you want from me."

Every time the words came out of his mouth, I melted a little more. "I love"—my heart seized as I realized what almost slipped out of my mouth—"when you say that."

He paused and my stomach plummeted.

*Did he hear that? Does he know?*

"You love . . . ?" His voice was deeper, and his words were slower and more deliberate. "You love when I say you can get anything you want from me?"

I swallowed hard. "Yes."

"And I mean it."

"That's why I love it," I explained softly.

"Jazz . . ." He let out a faint groan. "You have no idea."

We got off the phone a little while later, and I was still twisted up in knots about my Freudian slip.

I wasn't in denial about my feelings for Lamar. But I wasn't ready to share them. The last time I'd shared how I felt about us being together, he hadn't said anything. If I told him I loved him and he didn't say anything, it would be much worse.

I pursed my lips, determined not to get annoyed all over again.

*He really didn't say anything*, I thought, annoyed.

Later that night, I was in bed, under the covers, a few minutes from sleep, when my phone rang.

"Hey, Nina," I answered sleepily.

"Hey, so . . ."

Her serious tone forced my eyes all the way open and my mind to be alert. "What's wrong?"

"Umm, I just came across something . . . alarming and mostly confusing, and I'm just a little perplexed."

"About?"

"Did you create an anonymous social media page and announce yourself to be Hollywood Anderson's girlfriend?"

My entire face contorted as I tried to make sense of what she'd said. "Wait, wait, wait, wait, wait . . . what?"

"Hollywood Anderson's girlfriend," she repeated.

I rolled onto my back and stared at my ceiling in confusion. "Well, first of all, I don't call him 'Hollywood.' And second, you know I would never."

"I didn't think so, but I needed to confirm," she said in a teasing tone. "So, I'm about to text you something. This post popped up, and I just . . ."

My phone vibrated, and I pulled it away from my face to see it.

The image was a plus-sized woman in a skintight bodysuit. Her back was to the camera, so she was showing off her curves, namely her ass. Her honey-blonde-tinted locs were pulled into a ponytail. You couldn't see her face, but we were similarly shaped. I read the caption underneath the photo.

"'All this talk about me being Hollywood's girl, so why don't I just speak for myself,'" I read aloud. My eyes got wide. "What the fuck is this?"

"Someone trying to capitalize off the attention you've been getting the last few days. And this lady, who has already gotten thousands of followers and has 'Hollywood's girl' in her bio, is absolutely going to stir the pot. You need to do something."

"I don't know what I'm supposed to do."

"Lamar's the internet's flavor of the week right now. If he remains unclaimed, people will try to claim him. Case in point, the lady pretending to be you."

"So, I should do what? Tell him I want to make it official, let his decision to be with me ruin his career, and then watch him resent me for the rest of our lives?"

"Yes," Nina replied plainly. "You're not the problem here. So, if he resents you for anything, he's not who you think he is. And—Russell Long! Thank you!" Nina squealed out of the blue. "I'm on the phone with Jazz. Give me one minute, and then I can thank you properly. Jazz, Russ says hi."

"Tell Russ I said hi," I told her. "Spend time with him. It's past my bedtime anyway."

"Okay, I've reported the page as fraud but just wanted you to be aware. I'll call you tomorrow."

We said good night, and I lay awake for thirty minutes going over that woman's social media page. The first picture she posted was the cropped photo of me and Lamar. The second photo was the one of her from the back. The comments on the image of us ranged from complimentary to confused. The comments on the image of her were about her courageousness, but a surprising amount were downright derogatory. It was an odd sensation because even though they were speaking about her, they thought they were talking about me. So, the words were mean, but I almost felt disconnected.

*At least no one knows it's really me.*

I was about to put my phone down when I saw a name that made my blood boil.

*Olivia Chapman.*

I'd blocked her and every other person in her group back in high school. Unless she'd created an account under a different name, there was no reason I should be seeing her content. But since her video came up as a related topic, I couldn't resist clicking on the video.

"I went to high school with the woman in the photo. And I can guarantee you Lamar 'Hollywood' Anderson went to that event as a favor. He was doing charity work. He grew up in the town next to ours, and he's a nice guy. We hung out a little bit over the summer, and if you want to know his type, it's me."

"You have got to be kidding me," I muttered, rolling my eyes at her bold-faced lie.

I woke up late Tuesday morning, so I was rushing to work. I called to check on Aunt Addy as I was getting off the highway. Monica answered the phone on speakerphone.

"How are you, Aunt Addy?" I asked.

"She woke up and felt a little tired, but she checked her messages and had a smile on her face," Monica called out.

"Aunt Addy, did you read my text?" I wondered as I sped toward the school.

So, I've gone on dates—even had a whole thing with Lamar. I've written my book and explored a new city. I got my tattoo, my belly ring, and dyed my hair blue. I've learned how to swim and was a vegetarian for a month. That's eight things, Aunt Addy!"

Reflecting on what I'd accomplished and saying it out loud gave me an unexpected dopamine and serotonin boost. I felt proud.

"Your aunt is smiling," Monica reported. "What are your remaining things?"

"Go to a Monarchs game—which I plan to do this weekend. I haven't gotten tickets yet, but I'm supposed to be arranging that with Lamar."

There was a pang in my chest because it probably wouldn't be a good idea for me to go to the game this upcoming weekend.

"That's only nine," Monica pointed out.

I laughed as I backed into my parking spot. "The last one is pay off my student loan. Aunt Addy put that on there. At one point she said the book sales were going to take care of it." I shook my head, amused. "I wish!"

"I think Addison is right."

"The book is still being edited, so it's not on sale yet . . . or ever." My lips pulled into a smile. "But Aunt Addy always ends up being right somehow, so who knows. Now, how is she doing?" I asked.

"She's a little groggy, but she's comfortable," Monica answered. "I was just about to get her some breakfast, but I knew she wouldn't have wanted to miss your call."

"Well, I'm glad you answered." I pulled the key out of the ignition. "And I'm glad that you're comfortable, Aunt Addy. I have to run into work because I'm a little late, but I love you, and I hope you have a great day."

I ended the call, grabbed my stuff, and ran toward the building. I made it to my classroom and had a few students in there already. I had less than ten minutes before the first bell was going to ring. After a quick greeting, I rushed to get my laptop out of my bag and pulled out my files.

"Ms. Payne." Drea, a first-period student, came up to my desk with another student, Gianna, in tow. "We have a question."

"Yes?" I finished logging into the school website before I looked up at them and smiled. "How can I help you?"

"Are you really dating a football player?" Drea asked in a hushed tone.

I froze. "What?"

"There's this picture of this football player named Hollywood with a woman, and she looks like you," Drea explained carefully.

"And we think it's you," Gianna added.

"Some people at lunch yesterday said that it couldn't be you because you wouldn't be working here if your boyfriend was a famous football player," Drea continued.

Gianna flipped her phone toward me and showed me the picture. "But we have eyes and it's clearly you."

I stared at the image. "That does look like me," I said as evenly as possible.

"Because it *is* you," Gianna insisted, putting her hand on her hip. "Unless you have a twin sister, that is you."

I looked between them. "Even if it was me, do I ever discuss personal business with my students?" I asked, deflecting.

"No," they said in unison.

"So, instead of worrying about if someone looks like me or not, worry about if you read chapter four in your textbook." I quirked an eyebrow. "Did you?"

Drea turned on her heel and went back to her desk immediately, but Gianna remained.

"Ms. Payne." She lowered her voice. "I know it's you, and I just wanted to say that I think it's cool. The homecoming dance is in a few weeks, and I was hoping AJ was going to ask me." She glanced over at the boy in the corner of the room. "Drea said even though he likes me, he's not going to publicly claim me by taking me to the dance. She thinks because we're bigger than the other girls, popular guys like AJ aren't going to be out with us in public. And based on how things went down this summer at camp, I agreed with her. But after I saw that picture with you and Hollywood, I know if he wants to, he will."

The bell rang, and she immediately returned to her seat.

"Good morning, class," I greeted everyone, standing behind my desk. "Open your books to chapter four . . ."

When class was over, I watched AJ stare Gianna down as she was leaving class with Drea.

Gianna and Drea were on the heavier side and just as beautiful as any of their classmates. It made me sad to think they expected not to be taken out on dates publicly and not to be loved out loud. That mindset in childhood could stick with them and carry into their adulthood.

I couldn't shake that conversation. I planned to circle back with them to make sure they knew their worth. Also, I needed to find out what they'd meant by *people at lunch* and if the rumor was widespread yet.

A dark cloud was looming over Tuesday, so I tiptoed into Wednesday, waiting for the other shoe to drop.

As far as work was concerned, Wednesday was a good day. No one mentioned that photo, that rumor, or insinuated knowing something about me. I hadn't gone online because I wasn't trying to stress myself out. But I knew it was only a matter of time before the bullshit made its way to Lamar and he found out about it.

*And maybe that day is today*, I thought as I looked at the clock.

I hadn't heard from Lamar all day. I tried not to let any negative thoughts get to me. I reminded myself that Wednesdays and Thursdays were his long days. But as I climbed into bed, I thought about the woman I'd seen at my aunt's hair appointment. Like Decca, Lamar may not want to risk the social pitfalls of involving himself with me.

*Lamar's new to the active roster, and maybe he's realizing the extent of all this, and he decided that this is too much of a distraction—*

"Oh, thank God," I muttered aloud as my phone vibrated. I answered immediately. "Hey!"

"What's up, Jazz?" Lamar greeted me, sounding exhausted.

Just hearing his voice calmed the chaos within me. "Just got in bed. I'm glad you called."

I could hear his smile as he responded, "Is that right?"

"Yes." I exhaled. "I needed to hear your voice."

"I needed to hear yours, too."

There was something in his tone that was different. "What's wrong?"

"Just tired." He sighed. "It was a tough practice."

I rolled onto my side. "What happened?"

"I was off my game a little bit. Nothing too crazy."

"Did you get enough sleep?" I wondered.

"Yeah. I went to bed right after we said good night."

"Walk me through what happened that made you feel like you were off."

As he went into detail about what had happened, it occurred to me that he'd told me about only a couple of rough practices—one was during the preseason and one was during the first week. And the scenario sounded pretty similar, but he was taking it way harder this time.

"So it sounds like you're saying you missed the tackle. Am I understanding that correctly?" I clarified.

"Yeah."

He wasn't short with me, but I could hear his frown through the phone.

I smiled. "You missed *one* tackle. *One.*"

"I shouldn't have missed it. I should've anticipated what he was going to do. It wasn't the play. It wasn't that anybody did anything tricky. I just . . . blew it."

"You are extraordinarily talented, Lamar. You literally have all the qualities that make you a great defensive tackle. You can open-field tackle *and* rush the quarterback. Missing one tackle doesn't change that."

"This happened at the end of practice. My position isn't cemented, so blowing my coverage was the last thing coaches saw."

"I hear what you're saying completely, and I'm not invalidating that. But I want you to get out of your head. Don't overthink this because it was practice. It wasn't the game; it was just practice."

"I just don't want to do it in the game."

"It's unlikely you will. But even if you do, it's okay. That's what linebackers are for . . . they are backing the line."

He was quiet for a moment. "You're right," he murmured.

"And maybe you needed to miss a tackle today to remember that you are not meant to be perfect. You are meant to play *your* game. Because perfection doesn't exist, remember?" When he didn't say anything, I asked another question. "What do you think the difference is between today and when it happened at the beginning of the season?"

The silence was so absolute, I had to pull the phone away from my ear to make sure he hadn't hung up.

"I wasn't on the active roster when it happened before," he answered finally. "I don't want to fuck this up."

"When there's love and respect for what you're passionate about, you won't fuck it up. What's for you is for you. And it's been clear from the moment I met you that football is your passion. It's your first love. It's your gift. So I know you won't fuck it up."

I heard him breathing, quietly mulling over what I'd said.

He cleared his throat. "I'm glad you're in my life."

"I'm glad you're in mine."

# 27

**Nina Ford:** I know how you feel about the amount of attention being directed at you, but this video popped up and the love on that video was worth sharing and the comments passed the vibe check. Here's the link.

**Jazmyn Payne:** I've been trying to stay off social media but I'm glad to know someone is being kind. Thank you for the heads up. Lamar isn't on social media but it's only a matter of time before he hears about all of this bullshit.

**Nina Ford:** Well, let the love you see on this post remind you that the bullshit on the other posts is just that—bullshit.

I clicked on the link she sent and waited.

"I'm sure you've all seen the viral photo of the football sensation Hollywood Anderson out with a plus-sized baddie on his arm. It's causing a stir because so many people want to believe that if you have extra fat on your body, you can't get a good-looking, successful professional athlete. Hell, they act like you can't get a man, period! They want you to believe that your fat body can keep you from the love you seek. But truth be told, there are a lot of big women who are being loved out loud. There's a narrative that most 'quality' men don't want us, and even though we know that's not the truth, the media wants us to believe it is because it's a profitable narrative. This woman is beautiful! She looks happy! And the dress is fire!"

I clicked on the comments section, and it seemed like hundreds of people agreed.

I smiled slightly.

Nina was right. It was nice to hear that sentiment after receiving so much negativity. But I still hated that they were talking about me at all. I hated that my picture was floating around the internet, being dissected by people who didn't know me or Lamar.

*But maybe the tide is starting to turn.*

I was hopeful that the bright spot of positive commentary meant all the nonsense would die down. Once it died down, maybe people would stop caring and there wouldn't be any extra attention directed toward me.

*And then they can just focus on how great of an athlete Lamar is.*

I decided to hide out in my classroom for my lunch period. I wasn't hungry, and I could tell that the rumors were circulating by how often I was getting stares. I sat in the blind spot in the corner of my classroom, and usually, I tuned everything out. But boys talking in the hallway seemed louder than normal.

"You should go to the dance with Alexis," a boy said, seemingly from in front of my classroom door. "You'd be dumb as hell to pass up on that, AJ."

"I got somebody else in mind," AJ replied.

"Who?"

"Gianna."

"Gianna has a cute face. But, bruh, Alexis is a *cheerleader*!"

"Then *you* ask her to the dance. I'm asking Gianna."

"I tried, but I ain't got enough rizz to pull a senior cheerleader." He chuckled. "Gianna, huh? So, you're taking the Hollywood route?"

AJ snickered. "Whatever, bruh."

"But seriously man . . . you might want to reconsider. You know there's people talking about Hollywood's mindset because he like his girls big?"

"Nah, I ain't hear that."

"Yeah. So the girl you choose to pop out with matters, bruh." He paused. "You know everybody's saying it's Ms. Payne in that picture."

"I know. But what football player you know has a girl that teaches high school English? Maybe Ms. Payne has a sister," AJ speculated.

"Maybe. Because I ain't never seen Ms. Payne wear a dress like that. Have you?"

"Nah. She dresses like a teacher."

"You know, for an old lady, Ms. Payne is kinda bad. No cap! I mean she's big, but that's what happens when you hit middle age."

*Middle age? I'm thirty!*

I'd heard enough.

With my phone in one hand and my water bottle in the other, I got up from the chair.

"Aye yo, Ms. Payne could be back any minute," AJ warned with a laugh. "You're going to feel funny if she comes around that corner while you're talking shit."

"I'm not talking shit! I'm just saying she look good for her age. And—hey, Ms. Payne," the boy squeaked with wide eyes.

AJ spun around; his eyes were also wide. "I wanted to come talk to you about the test on Monday. Are you, um, were you in there the whole time?"

"Yes."

The other boy, Derrick, was a football player in the tenth grade. He was in Alexa's English class, so I didn't recognize his voice. He made a face. "Did you, um . . . did you hear us?"

"Hear what?" I asked, crossing my arms over my chest.

Derrick shook his head. "Nothing. I should get going." He turned and jogged away.

"Slow down!" I called after him. Shifting my attention to my actual student, I beckoned for him to follow me. "What did you need, AJ?"

"You know what? It can wait." He started backing away. Before he turned to jog after his friend, he cocked his head to the side. "Do you have a sister?"

I went back and forth for a second because I knew why he was asking. "No."

His smile grew. "Oh okay."

I made it through the rest of the workday with composure, but the minute I got into my car, I researched the Defensive Player of the Month controversy. There was a popular comment on a video that mentioned it, but I hadn't heard anyone else really talking about it. My eyes widened as I saw at least five videos claiming that Lamar wasn't worthy of a leadership award because he was making "bad decisions."

*How does dating me have any bearing on his performance on the field?*

I drove home and couldn't stop thinking about how they were essentially trying to punish him for dating me—and they didn't even know for sure that we were dating.

*Stressed* didn't even begin to describe how I felt. When I'd seen the comment before, I'd known it was an issue. But after going down the rabbit hole, five videos led me to ten more, I felt sick. Seeing people damn near campaigning to not vote for him because of me gave me anxiety.

"This is fucked-up," I muttered as I got home.

I knew I needed to talk to Lamar about it, but I was nervous. I thought it would come across better hearing it from me, but since the situation was so problematic, nothing could really make it better.

> **Jazmyn Payne:** Can we get together tomorrow and talk?
>
> **Lamar Anderson:** Yeah, of course. Everything cool? We're still on for this weekend, right? I'm sending the car for you.

With everything going on, I had forgotten about that.

> **Jazmyn Payne:** Yes. Call me when you get home from practice.

"Hello?" I answered later that night when Lamar called.

"You okay?" he asked.

"It's . . . I just need to talk to you in person."

I could hear him freeze. "What's wrong?"

Panic swept through me.

My face heated, the hair stood up on the back of my neck, and I instantly felt clammy. I sucked in a sharp breath and my throat tightened. I was having a visceral reaction.

I did not want to tell him.

It wasn't because I believed those things. It wasn't because I thought *he* believed those things. It was because of Chance. All I could think about was the way public opinion swayed at the popular girls' whim. How even those people who had been interested in getting to know me or who thought I'd be cool hadn't wanted to associate with me in public because of how it would impact them socially.

And if I were being honest with myself, I was scared to find out what Lamar would do under similar conditions with even more of that pressure.

"Jazz?" he called.

I wasn't sure how long I'd been silent.

"There's stuff being said on social media about us," I blurted. "But in particular, they are attacking me because they're infatuated with you."

"What? Who's attacking you?"

The rough edge in his tone tugged a small yet brief smile out of me.

"Have you not seen the posts and videos on social media?" I asked nervously. "Well, that's what it is. Just a lot of attention coming my way."

"No, I haven't seen anything. But I'm sorry about that. I know you don't like a lot of attention."

"Yeah." I paused. "I can't do it."

We were both quiet for a moment.

"I understand," he uttered.

There was so much I could feel he wasn't saying in his silence. But I didn't want to ask, because in turn, he would inquire about what I wasn't saying in mine.

"Is that what you wanted to talk to me about tomorrow?" he wondered.

"That's the overall theme."

He was quiet, waiting. "Jazz, talk to me. You know I got you, right? You know you can tell me anything."

I nodded, clutching the phone. "Yeah," I whispered.

A few seconds passed, and when I didn't elaborate, he sighed. "It was a long practice, and I need to get in the house and get me something to eat. Hit me up before you go to bed."

A heaviness blanketed me, and I couldn't shake it. "I'm going to bed now."

"Jazz . . ."

I knew he wanted to press me for answers, but I also knew he wouldn't.

"Tomorrow," I breathed.

"Okay. I'll see you tomorrow. Good night, Jazmyn."

"Good night."

I dropped my phone next to me and buried my head into my pillow. Letting out a muffled scream, I tried not to cry. I wanted to talk to Lamar before the internet could get to him. I hated that I was being dragged online and thrust into the center of attention against my will. But more than that, I hated that dating me was creating all this noise and overshadowing his accomplishments. I tried to think of different ways to salvage the situation. But by the end of the workday on Friday, it was apparent that the only logical way forward was for him to say we were just friends.

*Technically, that's what we are anyway.*

I'd already told him I wanted to be with him—that hadn't gone over well. I already told him that social media was shitting on me—and that was unbearably uncomfortable. We'd already talked about how I didn't like all this attention—and hundreds of thousands of people sharing, commenting, and posting about us was a lot of attention.

*I hate this.*

The entire situation made me so prickly, I felt sweaty. When I got home, I immediately took a shower. I didn't know when the car was coming to get me, but I wanted to be ready when it arrived. My body was oiled up and moisturized. My perfume was wafting through the air. All I needed to do was get dressed.

**Jazmyn Payne:** Hey! What time should I be ready?

**Lamar Anderson:** I'm pulling up now.

I stared at the phone for a second. "What?"

I had just stepped into my G-string when there was a knock. I pulled on a pastel pink T-shirt dress just to cover my body. My heart thumped in my chest as I headed toward the door. I took a deep breath before I opened it.

Just seeing him created a warmth inside me. "Hi."

"What's up, Jazz?" He leaned down and placed the sweetest, softest kiss against my lips. He handed me a gift bag. "It's good to see you."

"It's good to see you, too." I stepped back, opening the door wider. "Thank you. Come in. I thought you were sending a car."

Lamar walked in with gray sweatpants and a white T-shirt that stretched sexily over his chest. His cologne lingered in the air, and I inhaled deeply. The back of him was just as appealing with his strong shoulders, cute butt, and long limbs. He dropped his bag on the couch and then turned back to face me.

He remained standing. "I came straight from practice. I didn't want to wait to talk."

*I'm not necessarily prepared to talk right this second*, I thought nervously. My eyes danced over his body, momentarily distracting me from my nerves. I felt like I hadn't seen him in weeks, even though it had been only a few days. Just in case the conversation went poorly and it was the last time I was going to see him, I let myself appreciate the sight. From the defined waves on the top of his head to the defined outline of his package in those thin sweatpants, he knew exactly what he was doing.

*Touché.*

We were several feet apart.

"I, um . . ." I dragged my gaze from his dick. "You didn't have to get me anything." I peeked into the bag and then gasped, taking it out. "This is your jersey! In purple!"

"Yeah. Angel had some jerseys done up, and I wanted you to have one."

I held up the cropped purple jersey with the number ninety emblazoned on it. Clutching it to my chest, I smiled. "Even though I want one of your jerseys in Monarch green, I love this. Please thank her for me."

"I will." His eyes searched my face. "Now talk to me."

"Okay." I took a breath. "I don't like a lot of attention on me."

"I know. After you said something about social media and the comments, I went back to look at the post that was sent to me, and I saw some ignorant bullshit. But they don't matter—"

Hearing that he'd seen it made me wince, and I interrupted. "I can't do it . . ." My voice cracked, so I let the sentence trail off.

*I've come too far and healed from that period in my life. I will not let the general public drag me back there.*

His thick brows furrowed, and he stepped forward. "What are you trying to say?"

Holding my hand out, I took a step back. "Wait, let me get this out."

If he touched me, I wouldn't be able to speak.

He took two steps backward, and his brown eyes softened. "Okay."

"I don't know if I explained what it was like for me in Chance, but it was bad. I was the center of attention a lot, and it was never a good thing. It was a lot of mean-girl behavior and groupthink. And it started because a cute popular boy liked me, a cute fat girl. My parents believed that I should rise above it, continue to strive for perfection and I'd show them. Because that's what they did growing up. But it was a different time, and what I was going through was different than anything they had experienced. There were no allies. There were no support groups. I was being specifically singled out, targeted, and terrorized. For five years. And they would bully others out of a relationship with me." I chewed my bottom lip. "Reading those comments and watching the commentary surrounding you and me brought all that back up, and I don't want to go through that again."

"I'm sorry for what happened to you then." He ran his hand over his beard. "I'm sorry for what's happening to you now."

"I appreciate that," I murmured. "I really do. But I . . ."

"You what?"

"I can't do the negative attention, and I can't go back to how I felt in Chance."

"And you don't have to."

"I'm having nightmares. They're saying . . ." *I can't tell him I'm the reason he may not get Defensive Player of the Month.* "The focus should be on you and your career, not dragging me down. And the only way to avoid all this is to avoid the spotlight." My eyes started stinging. "And the only way to avoid the spotlight is to . . ."

"Is to what?"

I dropped my head and covered my face with my hands. "Is to not be in the spotlight."

"What does that mean?"

"It means that you should put it out there that we're not together." I let out a huff of air before lifting my head and looking at him. "If you told them that we're just friends, they'd leave me alone. They'd leave *us* alone."

His face was stoic and still. The tension in his body made him closed off and guarded. His eyes were different though.

He looked at me, and I couldn't tell if he was mad, hurt, disappointed, or confused. But he was clearly affected. The way his gaze burned into me felt hot. We were an arm's length apart, but I could feel the confliction radiating off him—and maybe he was feeling it from me, too.

Because on one hand, it was the truth—we weren't together. But on the other hand, I wanted us to be. I still wanted him in my life, even if we had to be just friends. I didn't want to lose him entirely, but I needed to protect my peace and my heart.

"And that's what you want?" he asked. "You want me to tell people we're not together?"

"Well, I mean, we—we're not," I stammered.

He took another step forward. "So, what are we then?" His voice was softer, deeper.

"I mean . . ." The rest of my sentence died on my lips. My heart was in my throat, so even if I wanted to speak, I couldn't.

He stared me down. "Say it."

My throat tightened around the words that were lodged there.

"I don't want to put you in an uncomfortable situation," he said. "I'll say whatever you want me to say, do whatever you want me to do. Publicly. But privately . . . I need you to answer my question. I need you to be real with me."

He was too close, too intoxicating, and I was too weak in such close proximity to him. I headed across the room, toward the hallway, so I could breathe.

He grabbed my arm and twisted me around so fast that I gasped.

Suddenly, Lamar had pinned me against the wall. His body was pressed against me, and his face was mere inches from mine. My eyes fell to his lips and lingered before traveling back to meet his gaze. He was so close. And despite wanting space, I burned in anticipation of his kiss.

"It hasn't even been two weeks since you said you wanted to be with me, and then you said forget it. And now you're saying you can't do this, and you want me to tell the world that we're not together." He dipped his head so that his lips were right up against my ear. "Which is it?"

Taking a deep breath, I exhaled audibly as his breath tickled my neck.

He brought his forehead to mine and waited. His intense eye contact, his cologne, his touch, and his voice all worked together to ignite a fire inside me.

"Which is it?" He repeated the question so sexily that I shuddered.

"Both." My voice was barely audible as I shook my head.

"You said you wanted to talk." He looked me up and down. "So talk to me." He reached for the hem of my dress and lifted it slowly. Seeing the tiny strips of fabric that barely covered my mound and didn't cover my ass at all, he let out a groan deep within his chest cavity. "Or did you wear this so I'd have no choice but to fuck it out of you?" He let go of my dress and met my gaze again.

My stomach fluttered and my heart raced. "Lamar," I murmured shakily.

Cupping my face with his hands, he parted my lips with his tongue. I wrapped my arms around him as he kissed me hard. When he attempted to pull away, I whimpered and pulled him back into me, holding him tighter. He groaned in response and kissed me deeper.

I slipped my hands under his shirt, and when they skated across his bare skin, he pushed himself firmly against me. I could feel how hard he was, and that only turned me on more.

He trailed kisses from my lips across my cheek and down my neck. "Talk to me, Jazzy." As he was nibbling on my collarbone, one of his hands worked its way under my dress.

"I want everything to be okay."

"Why wouldn't it be okay?" When I didn't respond quick enough, he ran his fingers against my thighs. "Do you trust me?"

Spreading my legs a little wider, I closed my eyes and nodded. "Mm-hmm."

He put one hand on my ass while the other skated along my inner thighs. "Look at me."

Opening my eyes and looking into his, I was overcome with desire.

He traced the panty line before sliding over the scant material. "Say it."

"I trust you."

"Now say how you feel."

My breathing changed as his fingers approached, but when they reached the apex of my thighs, I moaned his name.

"I love how your pussy gets so wet for me," Lamar whispered as he rubbed me through the damp material. Planting slow, teasing kisses against my lips, he made the sexiest noise from the back of his throat. "When I say you can get anything you want from me"—his mouth hovered over mine—"what do you think I mean?"

"That I can get whatever I want," I answered quietly.

"I mean that you can get *anything* you want from me," he said, just as he tore my G-string from my body.

I let out a noise that was part gasp and part moan as the thin strings of material briefly bit into my skin before ripping easily.

My knees were weak.

Angling me against the wall for leverage, he let his fingers make direct contact with me for the first time.

"Lamar," I moaned loudly.

He moved slightly to my left, and I could clearly feel how hard, how big, and how heavy he was as he pressed against my side. The pull deep inside me was unbearably good as his fingertips slid against me, slowly becoming more focused.

Groaning into my mouth, he allowed our tongues to caress before he pulled away. "I need you to tell me what you want so I can give it to you."

My breathing became labored as I gave in to his touch.

"Answer me," he growled, bringing his forehead to mine. His brown eyes flashed with the fire that existed in his touch.

There was no way I was going to be able to think, let alone speak while he touched me like that. My eyes fluttered shut, and I just wanted to succumb to the feeling.

But his fingers stilled. "You said you wanted me to tell people we're not together."

My eyes opened slowly, and he was watching me. My gaze dropped, following his tongue as he wet his lips.

"Did you mean that?" he asked again.

I didn't answer.

*I do think it'll solve the problem—*

"Mmmmmm," I moaned as his fingers resumed sliding across the most sensitive part of me.

"Did you mean it when you said you wanted to be with me?"

Holding his gaze and gripping his biceps, I didn't answer that question either.

Lamar nodded, hooking two fingers inside me and sliding them to his knuckles. I started to grind on his hand, but he held my hip in place, subduing me. I felt him starting to pull out, and I whimpered again.

"Do you want to be just friends, Jazzy?" he asked, before he pushed his fingers back in again.

"Oh God," I exhaled. Shutting my eyes made everything heightened.

I felt him staring at me. I felt the haggard bursts of air from his lungs. And I definitely felt his fingers inside me.

"I would do anything for you," he growled. His fingers expertly moved in and out of me as his mouth captured my own. "No bullshit on the internet changes that."

My arousal grew while we kissed with reckless abandon.

"Nothing changes that, you hear me?" Lamar whispered hoarsely against my lips.

"Yes," I moaned as he pulled his fingers out and played with my clit. "Right there." I felt myself approaching the cliff, and I was ready to fall. "Lamar, right there."

He pulled his fingers away.

I sucked in a sharp breath, missing his touch.

Pulling my dress up and over my head, he left me naked in front of him. His hands moved over my bare skin, leaving goose bumps in their wake.

"I'm not letting you come on my fingers," he whispered against my lips. Dropping to his knees, he threw my left leg over his shoulder and used his flattened tongue to drive me crazy. Once I started to shake, he sucked and flicked my clit until I came on his face.

When he rose to his feet, he crashed his lips into mine, kissing me feverishly. My hands roamed his chest before grabbing his T-shirt and deepening the kiss. And after a minute, I was pushing his sweatpants down and dropping to my knees.

"Jazz, you— fuck!"

As soon as I enveloped his dick in my mouth, he let out a groan so feral and needy, I felt compelled to take it to the back of my throat. I wanted him on the brink of exploding. Putting on the performance of a lifetime, I gave him head that was so sloppy, so nasty, so sexy that he'd never forget it. When I made eye contact with him as I was gagging on it, I could tell he was close.

"I want you inside me," I murmured as I rose to my feet.

Without warning, he lifted me, cupping my ass. I wrapped my legs around his hips, and he locked his arms in place. Sharing sloppy kisses, he carried me down the hallway with his fingers digging into my thick thighs as he handled my weight. When we stopped moving, he pulled out of the kiss, and when he slid me down his body, I could feel how ready he was for me.

He wrapped a hand around my throat and whispered, "Get in the middle of the bed."

I didn't know what was more intense: the throbbing in my chest or the throbbing between my thighs. My gut twisted, and my breathing hitched as I did as I'd been told.

Sitting on the edge of the bed, I kept my eyes on him as I scooted to the middle. He removed his shirt. And after pulling a condom from the pocket of his sweatpants, he removed those as well.

Heavy, hard, and with a slight curve to the right, his dick jutted prominently from his body, hanging from the weight of it.

I licked my lips hungrily. *Damn.*

As I watched him roll the latex over his thick erection, I ran my hands over my body.

Just the thought of him inside me, stretching me, fucking me was making me heady. I pinched my nipples and spread my legs wider.

Lamar wasted no time climbing on top of me and using his forearms to hold himself up and hover over me. The weight of him felt so good against me, pinning me against the bed.

We held each other's gaze for a few seconds before he parted my lips with his tongue.

Moaning, I closed my eyes and succumbed to his kiss. The way his mouth overpowered mine sent a chill through me. My body called out for him, but he just rested his dick against me, bumping up against my clit teasingly.

"Lamar," I breathed, excitement rippling through me.

He sat up, running his hands over my breasts and fondling me before he spread my thighs wide. Studying my face, he slid the tip of his dick along my slit. "Which is it?"

"Yes!" I cried out as he pushed the tip into me.

I rotated my hips, trying to get more of him inside.

His large hands pinned my hips, keeping me still. "No, not yet." The sexy grit in his tone gave me chills. "Which is it?"

"Lamar," I whined, trying to lift my hips.

"You trying to just be friends with me? You trying to distance yourself from me?" He pulled the tip out and rubbed my wetness against my clit. "Because I know you're not trying to end this."

I closed my eyes, inundated with feelings and unable to articulate myself.

"Open your eyes," he demanded roughly. "And answer me while I'm filling you up."

"Oh God," I moaned, my eyes fluttering when his words alone made me wetter.

My head tilted back as he applied pressure, stretching me to remind me of what I was missing.

"Talk to me. Don't hide from me." He uttered the commands with the same gentle restraint that I could feel in his touch. "And don't run away from me."

"Okay." I panted as I struggled to maintain eye contact.

"Which is it?" His voice was deep, rough, and full of want.

My heart rate increased with each passing moment. Panting, I confessed, "I don't want to end this."

"You still want me to tell people we're not together?"

Closing my eyes, I nodded.

"Nah, look at me. Use your words. Tell me what you want to do."

With our eyes locked, his skin on my skin, and his dick teasing me, it was hard not to be overwhelmed.

"You're going to make me fuck it out of you." His voice broke sexily as he inched his way in.

We moaned in unison.

With each inch, he filled me, stretching me out deliciously. When he pulled almost all the way out, he shuddered.

"Tell me how you feel," he uttered thickly, pushing himself all the way back in.

My eyes closed as I took all of him. "Lamar," I exhaled his name. "I don't want to lose you."

With each stroke, the yearning in my body mixed with the intensity of what was happening between us. My heart pounded in my chest, and knots coiled in my belly as he moved in and out of me.

"I love you." The words slipped out of my mouth mixed with a wanton moan.

He froze.

*Shit.*

I hadn't meant to say that.

I meant what I'd said, but I hadn't meant to *say* it.

After a few seconds, he started up again, and I peeked through my lashes.

As soon as our eyes met, I saw the emotion emanating from him.

"Say it again," he whispered.

Taking his right hand from my hip, he licked his thumb. In perfect timing with his strokes, he strummed my clit, causing a shock wave of heat to course through my veins.

"Say it again," he demanded roughly.

"I love you," I moaned, my orgasm building.

It was as if those words unlocked something within both of us because he fucked me like I'd never been fucked before.

"Yes, yes, yes, yes, yes," I cried out as I started bucking against him.

"That's it. That's it, Jazzy. Come on this dick."

"Oh, shit, yes, yes, yes, yes, yes." I breathed shakily.

My eyes fluttered closed as each moan grew louder than the one before it. I clawed at the bed while he slammed into me over and over again.

"Give it to me," he demanded as I worked my hips harder, meeting him thrust for thrust. "Yes, that's it! Let me feel it, Jazzy!"

"Please, Lamar . . . please don't stop . . . oh my God! Oh my—" I gasped, hitting the point of no return.

"Oh shit," he swore when my body started to shake.

Hearing his deep, guttural moans spurred me on. He fell forward, kissing me hard and desperately. His impending orgasm extended mine as we thrust into each other with reckless abandon. Feeling him lose control was it for me. The tension that had been building since he'd arrived released from deep in my core.

I came hard.

My mouth opened, yet no sound came out as the ultimate pleasure took over.

"Fuck," he groaned, his body becoming rigid.

All I could hear was our heavy satiated breathing as he collapsed beside me.

Lamar and I lay in sated silence. Exhaustion and satisfaction settled on me while butterflies and warmth settled within me.

"When I'm touching you . . . when I'm inside you, that's when you're the most vulnerable with me," he said in a low tone.

I opened my eyes, and when I turned to face him, I found him staring at me.

"I've told you from the beginning that you can get whatever you want from me." He placed his hand on my chest, and I knew he could feel my heart pounding. "And you're telling me you want me to say publicly that we're not together?"

Slowly, I nodded.

"Why?" he asked.

"Because we're not. And it's better if they just think we're friends."

"I don't care—"

"You should," I interrupted. "If you won't do it for you, do it for me."

He just stared at me.

A few seconds passed, and then, bringing his face down to mine, he kissed me softly, gingerly. My eyes pricked with tears behind my closed lids because the tenderness felt like something had broken.

# 28

Asking Lamar to tell the world that we were just friends had felt like the right thing to do in the moment. I did what I had to do to protect my peace. I also wanted to protect Lamar's peace. I wanted the think pieces and hate comments to stop. But the moment I'd said it out loud, there had been a hollowness in the pit of my stomach.

I didn't regret telling Lamar that I wanted to be with him even though it hadn't yielded the results I wanted. I also didn't regret being honest about my feelings. He hadn't verbally expressed it, but I could see the love, the care, the want, and the desire he felt for me.

And *that* was the problem.

That was always the problem.

Our connection was powerful, and our feelings were real, but from the beginning, there had never been a real path forward. He told me he didn't have time, and I wasn't trying to put myself in a position to be hurt. From the moment we met, I was scared for it to be more than what it was. And from the moment I realized my true feelings, I was scared for it to be less than what it is. And with the internet's commentary, it had been only a matter of time before history repeated itself.

Sitting on the side of the bed while Lamar was in the shower, I sent Aunt Addy a text. I knew she couldn't text me back, and I knew I probably wouldn't hear from her until the next day, but I couldn't go to bed without reaching out.

> **Jazmyn Payne:** I talked to Lamar and told him my feelings. Preserving his career and keeping our relationship intact was the most important thing. Just wanted to update you. Good night, love you!

And then I immediately sent a text to update my best friends in the group chat.

**Jazmyn Payne:** I talked to Lamar. He didn't know about the comments section, but he looked after I said something.

**Aaliyah James:** I'm glad you talked to him! Did you tell him how you felt about him?

**Jazmyn Payne:** I did but at the end of the day, the only way to make sure we're both okay is for him to deny we're together and go from there.

**Nina Ford:** Is that what you want?

**Jazmyn Payne:** I want to get on social media and not see people talking shit. I want people to stop saying they aren't going to give him his props for his on the field play because he's with me.

**Nina Ford:** Did you tell him that?

**Jazmyn Payne:** In so many words. I just think that if he says we're friends, his career won't be overshadowed by this.

**Aaliyah James:** So you self-sabotaged your connection with Lamar?

**Jazmyn Payne:** I protected it! I'd rather protect what we do have than risk it for what we could have.

**Nina Ford:** If you don't ask for what you want, how do you expect to get it?

**Aaliyah James:** Points are being made!

I put my phone down on the nightstand and stared at the ceiling. What my best friends were saying reminded me of something my aunt had said.

*Are you figuring out what you want, or do you know what you want and you're afraid to stand in it?*

I put my hand to my chest.

I knew what I wanted. But even if I weren't being dragged over social media and even if people weren't overshadowing his gameplay, I'd told him I wanted to be with him, and he'd said nothing. I'd *just* told him I loved him, and he'd said nothing.

Now that some time had passed since that last orgasm, I was able to think a little more clearly about what had happened.

*Because why wouldn't he say it back?*

I knew he felt it. I could see it in his eyes. But for him to allow me to be vulnerable and for him to not say anything again . . . I was bothered. So, when the shower stopped running, I was fully prepared to call him on it.

But then my phone rang.

Seeing who it was, I smirked. *Saved by the bell.*

"Hey, Aunt Addy!" I answered, knowing it was Monica who was likely making the call. "Just to clarify my text, everything is fine and"—I lowered my voice—"I'm still going to the game on Sunday. And you'll be happy to know that you were right when you said I loved him."

"Oooooooooooooh!" Monica exclaimed. "We love a good love story! Ain't that right, Addison?! She's smiling."

"I knew you'd appreciate that!" Amusement riddling my voice, I shook my head. "How are you?"

"Well . . . she's been resting a lot, but she hasn't had much of an appetite for the last forty-eight hours," Monica responded.

All the lightness I'd felt was gone. My stomach and my heart dropped.

Hearing about her loss of appetite set alarm bells off in my head.

I swallowed around the lump in my throat. "Do I . . . do I need to come down there and cook you something, Aunt Addy?" I wondered, trying to keep my voice steady.

"Well, you know Addison is always happy to see you, Jazmyn," Monica replied.

Tears pricked my eyes. "I can do that, Aunt Addy! What day are you thinking would be best for me to come and cook something?"

"I can't say for sure, and I know you have plans for the weekend—"

"That doesn't matter," I interrupted. "I'll figure that out. When?"

"Within the week."

My stomach dropped.

With my throat constricting, I asked, "Should I come tonight?"

"I don't think that's necessary, but . . . soon."

"Okay, sounds good. I have to go, but I'll see you tomorrow. Okay, Aunt Addy?"

"Her eyes are closed right now," Monica reported. "But she smiled when you updated her on your boyfriend." She laughed. "Now that got her eyes to open up!"

Putting my hand to my chest, I stared at Lamar as he pulled his boxer briefs on. "I'm glad that makes you happy, Aunt Addy. I love you. See you soon!"

As soon as I ended the call, I almost dropped my phone.

"Is everything okay?" Lamar asked, coming over to me.

I felt sick to my stomach. It was just an estimation, but I knew how Monica felt about Aunt Addison. If she was saying a week, that's what she truly believed.

I was shaking.

Dropping to his knees in front of me, he planted himself between my legs and forced me to look at him. "Jazz, what's wrong?"

"My, um . . ." Taking a deep breath, I responded. "Aunt Addy's nurse said that . . . it could happen soon."

His eyes widened. "Oh shit, I'm sorry, Jazz."

Nodding, I met his gaze and instantly looked away because I was about to cry. "I'm going to Chance first thing in the morning, so I won't be able to make it to the game. I know I said I would—"

"Don't worry about that," he interrupted, wrapping his arms around my waist and pulling me into him. "You need to be with your aunt. Is there anything you need from me? Is there anything I can do?"

I held him tight. "This."

He held me tighter. "I got you."

I tried to hold it in for as long as I could, but after being in his arms for a minute, the first sob rumbled out of me. For the next five minutes, he let me cry on his shoulder. When I was able to compose myself, I sat back and dried my face.

"I'm sorry," I apologized, looking at the large wet spot on his shoulder.

He cupped my face. "You don't have anything to be sorry about." He leaned forward and kissed my lips. "I'm glad I was here. I can stay as long as you need me to. As long as I'm at practice on time in the morning, I'm good."

"I'm glad you were here, too." I rested my forehead on his. "I don't want to keep you out too late. It's almost seven o'clock, and I know you have an early morning. And even though it's not an official bed time or curfew, I'm not going to do you like Quincy did Monica."

It took him a minute before he burst out laughing. "Yooooooooo." He rose to his feet and then pulled me to mine. "What is wrong with you?"

My lips curved into a small smile. "You know that was a psychological thriller." I buried my face in his chest as I felt another wave of sadness roll through my body. "I need to get packed and figure out if I'm going to leave tonight or in the morning."

I grabbed his hand, and we walked silently to the front door. When we reached it, he dropped kisses on the top of my head, the side of my face, and then lastly against my lips.

"If you get on the road tonight, call me, and I'll stay on the phone with you. If you wait until morning, call me and let me know. Either way, just let me know something. I'm here for you." He stared at me for so long, it felt like he was staring into me. "I . . . I'm always going to be here for you."

We kissed before saying goodbye.

Blinking back tears, I called my mom to ask her to go make Aunt Addy some yams as soon as possible because she needed to eat.

"They are in the oven right now," she informed me. "I'm staying the night with her, and that applesauce Monica was giving her earlier is fine, but we will not let Addison's final meals be trash."

My heart cracked, and my lips turned downward. "Monica thinks it may be sooner than later."

"I do, too. And I'm glad."

Horrified, I yanked the phone from my ear and then brought it back. "What? Why would you say that?"

"Because Addison hates this," Mom continued. "As much as I worried about her always doing what she wanted to do, being so vocal, moving and shaking and stirring things up, that was who she was. Not being able to speak or move, being in pain, sleeping her days away, not getting fresh air . . ." She paused. "She *hates* this. This isn't the life she wanted for herself, and when I sit with her and watch the tears roll down her cheeks, I know she's ready to go. So that's why I said it. And I'm sorry I didn't consider how you would interpret what I meant, but I know she's ready to go on to glory. Do you understand that?"

I was quiet, processing her words. "Yes," I murmured, wiping my tears. "It was just . . ."

"Hard to hear?" she guessed.

"Yeah." I nodded even though she couldn't see me. "I've been mentally preparing for this all summer, but it's still hard."

"It's hardest to let go of people you love. But know that I'm always here if you need me. I may not understand or like your choices, but I love you, and I want to see you happy. Always."

"Thanks, Mom," I whispered, my voice cracking with emotion. "I'll see all of you tomorrow. Have a good night."

"Good night, darling. I love you."

"I love you, too."

My mom's words stayed with me. I lay on my back, staring at the ceiling, pondering what she'd said.

*This is probably Aunt Addy's worst-case scenario.*

I hadn't thought about it like that. I'd watched the light in Aunt Addy dim, and everything I was holding on to, every reason I wasn't ready to let her go was rooted in *my* hurt, *my* pain, *my* selfishness. She'd told me from her own mouth that she was ready to go, and even though I'd heard her, I hadn't heard her. And it wasn't until my mom said it that it clicked for me the way it was supposed to.

I loved her so much that I wanted her to stay. But it was time for me to love her enough to let her go.

It was a sobering thought that rocked me.

I wasn't sure how much time had passed, but when I heard the knock at my door, I sat up abruptly and froze. Waiting and listening closely, I didn't move until I heard the knock again.

Grabbing my robe, I tiptoed my way to the door. I didn't see anything out of my peephole, but it was late and I wasn't just going to swing the door open. I waited another minute and then slowly cracked it open.

There was a large white box sitting outside my door. I saw my name emblazoned on the top, so I scooped it up and set it on the coffee table.

"What could this be?" I quietly wondered aloud, before I opened the box.

Three dozen white flowers—a mix of roses, hydrangeas, and peonies—a diamond crystal vase, and a note were located inside. I grabbed the note first.

*I know there's nothing I can do. But I'm here. You already know you can get anything you want from me. Just say the word. —Lamar*

My throat burned and my vision blurred.

I was in love with that man.

"Thank you for the flowers," I told Lamar as soon as he answered the phone.

"I'm glad you like them," he replied.

"I *love* them. How did you— When did you . . . ?"

"I wasn't able to have them delivered to you tonight because they were about to close, so I came back to drop them off before I got on the road."

"Thank you," I whispered.

I wasn't sure how he'd known those flowers were going to lift my spirits. But he always managed to anticipate my needs and make everything better.

*And I told him to say we aren't together.*

# 29

". . . and I told him to go on record and say we're friends, so I don't know why it bothers me," I told Aunt Addy late Saturday night.

Mom and Dad were sleeping in the guest room. Monica had gone home at noon and was slated to come back Sunday morning. It was the first time since I'd arrived that I was alone with Aunt Addy to update her. And while I'd planned on going to bed twenty minutes earlier, when I peeked in at Aunt Addy, she had her eyes open. So I sat in the chair next to her bed and started chatting.

Her frail form was shocking to me because I'd just seen her a couple of weeks ago. My fingers gently rubbed her bony hand. She was staring at me, and the sparkle had dimmed from her eyes. Her light had dimmed. As I talked to her about the latest with Lamar, I found myself missing her—the things she would've said, the jokes she would've made, and the advice she would've given.

"What do you think I should do?" I wondered aloud.

I stared at her, and she stared right back at me.

"Even if the entire internet weren't a dumpster fire, I told him I wanted to be with him, and he didn't say anything back. I told him I loved him, and he didn't say it back. And what's wild is that both times, I felt him feeling it, too. I know it sounds delusional, but I don't know how else to explain it. I could *feel* that he wants to be with me. I could *feel* that he's in love with me. Maybe he isn't trying to be in a relationship and he isn't ready to say the words yet, but I feel it." I paused. "As delusional as it sounds."

She blinked.

I looked around her room. "Enough about Lamar—look at all these flowers." I gestured around the room. "This is incredible! Those are my favorite." I pointed at a bright mix of blue, lavender, and pink flowers. "Oh wait, no, those . . ." I looked at the bouquet.

Standing, I crossed the room to the mix of white flowers in the same crystal vase that my flowers had come in. "Who got you these, Aunt Addy?" I plucked the card from the bouquet.

*Ms. Addison Payne, aka Aunt Addy, the two most important women in my life speak highly of you, so I just wanted to give you your flowers and let you know you're in my thoughts and prayers. —Lamar*

I put my hand on my heart as I read it again.

My head spun around before my body as I looked at Aunt Addy. A hint of a smile tugged at her lips before her eyes closed.

"Aunt Addy? Did you know about this?" I put my hands on my hips. "Aunt Addy?"

She was asleep.

"Good night. I love you," I whispered, before making my way to my room. I climbed into bed, still thinking about how I'd talked to Lamar before and after his practice, and he hadn't said he had sent flowers. And since it was one o'clock in the morning, I didn't want to call him and disrupt his sleep on game day. But I was tempted because those flowers and that note had touched my heart.

> **Jazmyn Payne:** Good morning! I know it's game day and you're in the zone. I just wanted to let you know that I saw the flowers you sent to my aunt. Thank you. I know they put a smile on her face. You are the most amazing man I've ever known, and I am thankful to have you in my life.

I almost put *I love you* in the text, but I didn't want him to feel pressured to say it back. I didn't want him to not be focused on what he needed to be focused on—which was the game.

> **Jazmyn Payne:** Your talent is yours. There is no one who can take that from you. Do what you know how to do. You are not just valuable. You are valued. That team needs you and you showed up at the right time. I need you and you showed up at the right time. You show up. That's who you are. So, show up today and handle your business. Play your game. Don't worry about anything else but playing your game. You got this!

Sitting at my aunt's bedside on Sunday afternoon, I watched her like a hawk until kickoff. My dad, my mom, and my aunt all watched the game in my aunt's bedroom. My mom didn't care for sports, but she wanted to be in the room with Aunt Addy. The four of us watched the Monarchs take the field on offense, and we rooted and cheered. Every time I looked at my aunt and she was awake, she had a smile on her face.

"Oh, my goodness gracious," my mom cried out as the Nighthawks kicked a field goal.

"That's it. That's the game," my dad concluded with a shake of his head.

I looked at Aunt Addy, and her eyes were closed.

"Addison, you didn't want to see that nonsense, did you?" my dad questioned, looking sadly at his sister. Turning to me, his eyes widened. "That was a nail-biter! But I guess the better team won."

I made a face. "I don't know about better . . ."

The game was close and had five lead changes, but the Monarchs lost to the Nighthawks by three points. Lamar played extremely well, and I had no doubt that they were celebrating him. I wanted to look for the team interviews and press conferences on social media. But I wasn't in the mood to come across any slander.

**Jazmyn Payne:** I see they had to try to double team you in order to keep you from sacking the quarterback. That is how you know you are a beast on the field and that your impact is felt. You are a difference maker. In the game and in life. So proud of you!

**Lamar Anderson:** I'm starting to think a pregame message from you is what gets me in the right headspace to play. And a postgame message from you is what gets me through a loss. Thank you. I needed that. And I'm glad Aunt Addy liked the flowers. I was able to set up next day delivery with hers so I just wanted to make sure she had something from me.

**Jazmyn Payne:** Well, that didn't just mean something to her. It meant something to me. You are incredibly thoughtful and sweet. And I promise to send you a pregame and a postgame message for as long as you want me to.

**Lamar Anderson:** For as long as I want? I'm going to hold you to that.

**Jazmyn Payne:** Please do.

**Lamar Anderson:** Is it limited to just for when I'm playing? Because I feel like I need a word from you before everything I do.

**Jazmyne Payne:** Consider it done. I send you messages before the game because I want you to feel the way you make me feel. And I'd do the same thing if you were going into work, running your business.

**Lamar Anderson:** And you said you'll do it for as long as I want?

**Jazmyn Payne:** As long as you want.

**Lamar Anderson:** What if I say I want it forever?

My eyes widened, and I read it three times. Even though my mind was sure he just meant he always wanted me in his life, my body interpreted his words as saying he wanted *me* forever.

*He has to know how that sounds.*

**Jazmyn Payne:** I'd say consider it done.

**Lamar Anderson:** Good to know. I'm about to talk to some reporters and then get out of here. But I'll call you when I get home.

**Jazmyn Payne:** Okay interviews! Do your thing! Win or lose, I'm so proud of you, Lamar. Talk soon!

Aunt Addy slept most of the rest of the day. I sat by her bed with a book in hand, but I didn't read it. I just stared at her.

Ever since my mom had put things into perspective, I'd thought about Aunt Addy's death differently. I was still extremely sad for me, but I wasn't sad for her to be released from her pain.

"You told me that I was deserving, and if I was inspired by anything you've ever done, I needed to be inspired by the way you lived your life," I murmured. "And I am. I've always been inspired by you and in awe of you. You always lived life on your terms. You always did things your way. You always made the most of every opportunity. You are fearless. Even now."

Around nine o'clock, I went to my bedroom. I was feeling a lot of different emotions, and I didn't want to unload on Lamar fresh on the heels of his loss. I didn't want to talk to Nina about it because she'd just reunited with her man after his business trip. I knew Aaliyah was preparing for a presentation she had to do for work in the morning.

*I'll talk to them tomorrow.*

As if he could sense my need, my phone rang.

"Hello?" I answered.

"Is everything okay?" Lamar asked.

Blinking rapidly, I put my hand over my heart. "I'm okay. Is everything okay with you?"

"Yeah. I'm about to crash, but I wanted to hear your voice. But you sound like something is wrong. Talk to me."

"I was just thinking about Aunt Addy."

"How's everything going? I mean, I know, but . . . how is she?"

"She's been sleeping a lot, so the meds are doing their job because she doesn't seem to be in any pain. I was talking to her earlier, and it got me to thinking about this summer." I swallowed around the lump in my throat. "I'm really glad I met you."

"I'm really glad I met you, too. I thank God for that wing craving every single day. And I'm here. For anything, anytime. I hope you know that."

My stomach fluttered. "I do."

He was quiet for a moment. "And the way you say I make you feel is how you make me feel. You know that, right?"

"Yes."

"You make sense. From the moment I met you, you've just made sense."

My cheeks heated. "Good. So do you."

We said good night, and his warmth coated me. His words were as powerful as any hug.

But I wanted to see him.

Searching for Lamar's postgame interview, I smiled when I saw a clip with Sports Athletes News Station.

"Lamar, you played a great game today," the interviewer started. "Even though things didn't go the Monarchs' way, you had eight tackles, two of those tackles for a loss. The defense keeps getting better and better each week. You keep getting better and better. What do you think about the offensive performance today?"

"We are a team. Offense, defense, special teams, we are all Monarchs, so if we lose, we all lose. I think we're going to go to practice tomorrow and make sure we handle business next week."

"Good answer," I murmured proudly.

"There are videos of people begging for more information about you," a different journalist asked. "For instance, they are really interested in your relationship status. What are your thoughts about that?"

"My only thought is for all of you to leave anyone you think I'm with alone."

"Does that confirm you are in a relationship with her?"

"It confirms that I want you to leave her alone. Some of the comments I've seen pissed me off to be honest."

"Because she's your girlfriend?"

"Because she doesn't deserve to be dragged like that just for standing next to me in a picture," he countered. "She's beautiful, smart, funny, passionate, tough . . . She's not any of the negative things that are being said about her. She's the person I most look forward to hearing from. She's the best person I know. And disrespecting her is disrespecting me."

My stomach flipped.

"So, she is your girlfriend?"

He hesitated. "She's . . . What if she was? What then? I'd be blessed to have someone like her in my life. And to imply otherwise would be some dumb shit."

"Do you think this negativity surrounding your . . . friend is fueling how you dominate the field?"

"No."

The next few questions focused solely on his gameplay. When the clip concluded, I replayed the part about me. I hadn't been expecting that, and it made my heart swell. To be defended so publicly did something to me. I put my hand over my heart and drifted to sleep.

A few hours later, Monica's soft, compassionate tone jarred me awake. "Jazmyn."

My eyes flew open, and my stomach plummeted. *Aunt Addy.*

I sat up quickly. "Monica?"

"You should come see your aunt."

The sadness in her tone told me everything I needed to know.

"Okay," I said shakily, getting out of the bed. "What's changed?"

"Her breathing. I don't know how much time she has."

I'd thought I had a week with her, but death didn't wait for anyone.

My mom was in the hallway with watery eyes and a teary smile. We hugged for a full minute, not saying a word but fully understanding. I walked down the hallway, and I saw my dad at his sister's side. His red-rimmed eyes and solemn expression tugged at my heart. When he saw me, he stood, wrapping his arms around me and squeezing me tight. I'd kept it together through those emotional embraces, but when I looked at Aunt Addy, I almost lost it.

"Aunt Addy," I whispered, hugging her lifeless body.

Her breathing was shallow, almost imperceptible, and strained. Her eyes were closed as if she were resting. Her cheekbones were more pronounced due to her weight loss and the way she was lying. More than anything, I wanted her to hug me back.

I shut my eyes tight, but the tears seeped through my lashes. "Thank you for everything." I spoke softly, as if I were scared to disturb her rest. "I'm sorry if I ever made you feel bad about dying. I was being selfish because I'm going to miss you. I wasn't thinking about you and what you're going through, what you've been going through for years. I'm so sorry about that. You're hurting. You're in pain. If it's time for you to go, I understand. Don't worry about me. I'll be okay. I am so thankful for how you took care of me, but now you have to take care of you. Thank you for this summer. Spending that time with you was everything. I'm sorry I didn't help you get your party. You deserved the party of your dreams. You deserve everything." A sob erupted out of me. "I would've died in this town if it weren't for you. It would've swallowed me up and suffocated me. Thank you for all the you that you poured into me. I love you."

I lifted my head and looked at her. I grabbed her hand and held it while I cried. She was relatively young, and her life ending at fifty-four was heartbreaking. Although she'd lived such a full, vibrant life, she still had so much she could've done and accomplished. So I cried for her—what she had done and what she had yet to do.

"Jazmyn?" Monica interrupted me twenty minutes later.

I looked up.

"I need to check her," she said softly.

I moved out of the way so she could do her job.

Monica called everyone in the room, and my dad said a prayer. We sat in silence for a few minutes while Monica used her stethoscope to search for a heartbeat. Shaking her head, she continued to monitor for respiratory effort. She lifted Aunt Addy's eyelids and confirmed her pupils were fixed and nonreactive to light.

"There are no signs of life present. Addison is gone," Monica announced softly, her voice breaking slightly.

It was a few minutes past eight o'clock in the morning.

There was a finality to the silence that filled the house after that announcement.

It felt like time froze and then I blinked, and it was nine o'clock and Rose had arrived.

My mom was in the kitchen cooking breakfast. My dad was in the living room making calls to family. Rose was in the office making calls to friends. Monica was on the other side of Aunt Addy's room completing paperwork. And I sat quietly, staring at my aunt's body.

"Addison left something for you," Monica said gently. From the nightstand drawer, she pulled out three sealed envelopes. Each had directions on the front that she read as she handed it to me. "This is for you to open now." She handed me the first one. "This is for you to open when you get back home." She handed me the second one. "And this is for you to open when you finish your list or on New Year's Eve." She handed me the third one.

"Thank you," I whispered, staring at my aunt's handwriting on the envelopes.

Monica made the call to arrange for the body to be transported and left me alone in the room.

I held up the envelope I couldn't open until after my list was complete. "Did you mean everything on my list except for the student loan repayment? I know you said I can do anything, but unless they forgive my loans, I need to remind you that I teach at a public school. I think we both knew that was unreasonable for me to complete by the end of the year." I let out a little giggle, and then my smile fell at remembering she was never going to laugh or smile back.

I took a deep breath and opened the first envelope.

*Jazmyn,*

*This was one of the best summers of my life and that is all because of you. I appreciate you being here for me more than you know. I enjoyed this time with you and I am thankful you chose to stay with me. I would've never asked you to do it because I know how you feel about Chance. You deserved so much more and so much better than this town ever gave you. Growing up here, I got to experience the magic of this place and the charm of the community. And I hate that you were denied the opportunity to experience that because of jealousy and hatefulness. I choose to believe you endured that in order to ensure you got out of here because so many people don't get out. So many people stay right here and settle. And the last thing I ever want you to do is settle—in any area of your life. I am so proud of the woman you are and the woman you will continue to evolve into. Now I forbid you to mope, mourn, and wallow. Intentional happiness means to be happy on purpose. Do things you love, be with the people you love, live a life you love—intentionally. So please, never stop fighting for yourself. Never stop fighting for what you want. Never stop fighting for what you deserve. And believe me, you deserve the world.*

*The lists we created, and all the things we did from the lists, are reminders of who we were and who we are, what we're capable of and what we can control.*

*For instance, I can't control death, but I can control how I go out. The last thing I have to do on my list is my party. This is my farewell party. So the reason I never talked to you about it is because my party is my memorial service. Because I don't want a stuffy, sad funeral. I want a celebration of life. I want a memorial. I want to go out with a bang.*

*I've planned everything, so you don't have to worry about a thing. Everyone can work together to execute it. The directions are on the second page, and I want everyone to come together to make this party happen. But under no circumstances are you to let Richard or Miranda choose the photos. I love them, but you saw the pictures they've chosen to put on social media for my birthday the last few years. The one from this year, I looked like I had been turned every which way but loose, and they posted it anyway. So photo selection duties are on you and you alone.*

*I love you.*

*Sincerely,*
*Your Aunt Addy*

*PS: Take a little bit of my ashes and spread them somewhere I'd get a kick out of.*

I called Lamar first, and he offered to leave practice so he could drive down to be with me. I told him not to because of the distance, but also because on the heels of a loss, leaving practice wouldn't be a good look. Next, I had a three-way call with Aaliyah and Nina, and they also offered to drive down. I told them not to since they said they were coming down for the service. And then I waited in the living room with my parents until the pastor came to pray and the funeral home came to collect her body.

"Aunt Addy wants . . ." My throat constricted and my eyes watered. I started over. "Aunt Addy wants to be cremated. She wants this to be a celebration of life and a farewell party. She left specific instructions for us to follow."

Keeping my page of the letter in the envelope, I passed the party directions to my mom, and she read them aloud.

Through tears, we smiled and shared light laughter at the over-the-top extravaganza. She knew the estimation of how much everything would cost and left cash for us to be able to take care of it all. Over the next three days, we were able to make Addison Payne's farewell party a reality. Everything she'd wanted, we got. Although we wanted to have the service on the following Saturday, the event space was available only on the following Friday—eleven days after her death. The décor, the caterer, the live entertainment, and the pastor were all scheduled. Everyone had their roles and responsibilities, and once I completed everything I needed to do for the party, I helped my parents pack up the house.

My parents and I stayed at Aunt Addy's house for the next three days while we got things together. It was the first time in a very long time that we'd spent that much time together. We talked, mostly about Aunt Addy, but also about how Aunt Addy had impacted us. There were a lot of tears shed and a lot of sweets consumed. But the entire experience of packing up the house and reconnecting with my parents was cathartic and healing.

Outside of a couple of texts to show proof of life, I hadn't spoken to anyone since calling the people closest to me on Monday to let them know what happened. It had been a few days, so I knew I needed to call Lamar, Aaliyah, Nina, and the principal at a minimum.

I'd planned to do that when I left Chance on Friday morning. But I chose a silent drive instead.

The anticipation of her dying, watching her die, *that* had been torture. That had broken me down. But her being gone left me empty. There was a hole in my heart, in my soul.

I got home, took a shower, and climbed into bed even though it wasn't even four o'clock yet. I wasn't necessarily tired, but I didn't know what else to do. I just wanted to disappear for a little while and start over the next day. I was all cried out. I was mentally exhausted, but my mind wouldn't stop running.

I woke up a few hours later and remembered Aunt Addy had given me an envelope to open when I returned home. I checked my voicemails as I headed over to the dresser. I picked up the envelope, pausing when the two messages from Lamar played. Just hearing his voice moved me.

*I should call him. Is it too late?* I glanced at the clock. *Eleven o'clock? He might be asleep. I'll see if he's awake after I read this.*

I opened my aunt's second letter.

*Jazmyn,*

*You are in love.*

*You just sent me a picture of you and Lamar on Sunday and you two look so good together. I couldn't stop smiling! I'm so glad I got the chance to witness you happy and in love. Look at the date. I don't know if I'm going to make it to the end of the month, so if you're reading this, that means I've already gone to glory and there's no sense in being mad at me or Lamar or Gwen. With that being said, I have a couple of confessions to make.*

*First things first, I sent that photo of you and Lamar to Gwen. And then we sat on the phone for thirty minutes talking about the two of you. She told me Lamar was going to be in Spring Hill on Tuesday for her grandbaby's birthday. So . . .*

*Second, I talked to Lamar on the phone. Gwen called me when he arrived and put him on. I told him I wanted to get to know him. I told him how extraordinary you are, but he already knew that. I asked him to take care of you because I could see that you two shared something real. He agreed and said he would. Based on the conversation, my assumption was right: he loves you. I asked him not to tell you about our conversation because I wanted to tell you myself.*

*I didn't tell you immediately because you're still in denial about your feelings and I'm still rolling my eyes every time you say he's your friend. I wanted to meet him and tell you how much I love him for you, so you'd never have to wonder what I would've thought about him. And I didn't tell you because you don't need my approval. You don't need anyone's approval.*

*I hope you realize it soon because life is short.*

*Now I need you to make some promises to me.*

*Stop being scary. Walk in your power because everything you've been through has made you stronger. Be honest with yourself and be exactly who you are because you are so amazing and deserving. Do not make yourself small or shrink yourself for anyone or anything. Stand loudly and proudly in who you are and whose you are.*

*Do not feel guilty about being happy. You deserve this.*

*I've wanted you to be happy and to thrive for so long, and it would be a disgrace to me if you tried to suppress or minimize or feel guilty about your love because I'm dead.*

*You can miss me, and you can be sad, but do not wait until you're not sad anymore to enjoy your love, your friends, your family, or your life. It doesn't have to be perfect to be right. Perfectionism is a flawed way to move through an imperfect world.*

*Speaking of . . . your perfectionist parents are imperfect. Tell Richard and Miranda about Lamar so they can stop worrying about the fact that you're divorced. Because you're in love and what you and Lamar have is the real thing.*

*Love always,*
*Your Aunt Addy*

I had tears in my eyes as I read. She'd written that at the beginning of September, and now it was October. In just a few short weeks, everything had changed.

Time was flying and life was fleeting.

I glanced at the clock and then hurried to call Lamar, hoping I would be able to catch him before he went to sleep.

"I'm sorry," I apologized, noting the grogginess in his voice when he answered. "I shouldn't have called this late."

"No, it's good to hear your voice. How are you?"

"I'm . . ." I looked at the letter in my hand. "I miss her, you know?"

"I know."

"But I was just calling to let you know that I'm back home. Thank you for your messages. I appreciate you and I miss you, too. So much."

"Can I come by after practice tomorrow?"

My aunt's written words swirled in my head.

She was right.

"Okay, I'll see you tomorrow," I whispered. "Good night."

"Good night."

I placed my phone on the nightstand and reread my aunt's letters. I felt so connected to her and loved by her. All of it was impactful and powerful, but I was overwhelmed.

I wasn't sure how long I sat on the edge of the bed, but all of a sudden, it felt *too* quiet.

Grabbing my remote, I turned on the TV and lowered the volume until it was just faint background noise. Just as I was turning my head, the sports network said a name I couldn't ignore. Whipping my head back toward the TV, I turned the volume back up to catch the tail end of what they were saying.

". . . not going to lie, I thought Anderson was a shoo-in to win. But we can't take away from the impact Lionel Timmons has had on his team to kick off the season. There's Sunday and Monday to consider with Bikowski still in the running, and he could have a big game, and Jenkins is playing on Monday . . ."

They flashed the names of who they thought the winners would be based on the votes right now, and they'd all picked Timmons as the predictive defensive winner.

Dread filled my belly with a lead-like heaviness, and tears streamed down my cheeks.

I turned off the TV.

# 30

Saturday, before ten o'clock in the morning, Aaliyah and Nina were sitting in my living room. I'd slept, but I didn't feel rested. I was tired, but I couldn't sleep. So my best friends and I snuggled on the couch, Nina on my left and Aaliyah on my right. None of us said a word while random images danced across the TV screen and music carried through the speakers.

"We can sit here as long as you need us to," Nina said, squeezing my arm. "But I'm going to order something to eat because your stomach is making beats."

Aaliyah giggled. "I wasn't going to say anything, but when was the last time you ate?"

Amused, I shook my head. "Before I left Chance."

"It's been twenty-four hours!" Aaliyah exclaimed.

Nina pointed at my stomach. "We have to get you something to eat because if it keeps going, I'm going to have to freestyle."

"You can't rap," Aaliyah argued. "And I won't be subjected to your nonsense."

Nina cocked her head to the side. "I know somebody else who can't rap, and a few months ago, you subjected yourself to *his* nonsense. In the kitchen if I'm not mistaken."

A laughed bubbled up from the depths of me at the mention of Matthew, Aaliyah's ex-situationship. It was the first deep laugh I'd had since Aunt Addy died. The sound echoed in all the hollow spaces inside me. The laugh turned into a cry as I hugged my best friends.

"I love you both so much," I cried.

"We love you, too," they said in unison.

I wiped my face with the bottom of my shirt and then grabbed their hands. Looking between them, I took a breath. "This summer was hard. It was the first time I had to confront that Aunt Addy wasn't getting better. I wanted to pretend like she wasn't dying, and I couldn't do that with either of you. You know me too well. So I didn't talk to you as much, and I'm sorry. I'm sorry I wasn't here for you"—I looked at Aaliyah—"while you were on your dating spree"—I looked at Nina—"and while you were taking the fashion world by storm."

I covered my face with my hands and dried my tears. "I'm so sorry. And it had nothing to do with anything you were doing except asking me if I'm okay. It had everything to do with the fact that I knew you could see through my bullshit, so I couldn't pretend or hide. If I told you everything was fine, you'd know it wasn't, and I wasn't ready to face that. You two were the first people to ever really get me outside of Aunt Addy. So I'm sorry for how I retreated this summer. It won't happen again."

"Jazz . . . it's okay," Nina assured me. "As long as you know you can talk to us, that's all that matters. Everyone processes things differently. And I'm sure it was even harder for you since you were there with Aunt Addy for her last days. You handled it the best way you saw fit."

"Yeah," Aaliyah agreed. "When my sister died, it was so sudden, I was in shock. I probably would've withdrawn from everyone for a minute, too, if I had to watch her die slowly. Losing the person who first saw you for you is hard."

I nodded, knowing she understood what that was like.

We spent the rest of the morning talking and eating and listening to music. They left around two o'clock, and before the door closed, I poked my head out of it.

"I'm happy for how this summer has changed your lives for the better," I called behind them.

"You, too," Nina replied.

"I know you're grieving now, but this summer definitely changed you for the better, too. It may not feel like it right now, but it's evident," Aaliyah acknowledged.

I waved goodbye to them.

Thirty minutes later, I received a call from Lamar.

"Hi," I answered.

"How are you?" he asked.

"I'm okay." And I really was. "Nina and Aaliyah came over this morning. They helped me pick out what I'm going to wear to the memorial service."

I caught him up on Aunt Addy's party and all the pertinent details.

"I wish I could be there with you," he said. "Depending on how the game goes tomorrow, I'm gonna ask Coach Rice if I can miss Saturday's practice so I can be there for you on Friday."

"I would like that, but I don't want you to jeopardize your standing on the team for the service," I told him. "Your mom and stepdad are going to be there, so they can represent you."

"Yeah, but I still want to be there. I know how much Aunt Addy means to you."

"Yeah," I sighed. "I just wish I could've finished my list for her . . ." I tried to swallow the swell of emotion that bubbled up. "I wish there were more time."

"You said she gave you until the end of the year."

"Yeah, but I wish she could've been here to see me do it," I choked out.

"What do you have left to do on your list?"

"Just . . . go to a game and pay off my student loans."

"I can . . . I got you covered. With both. With either. With whatever you need."

"No, I can't . . . I can't ask you to—"

"You're not asking. I'm offering."

My entire body quaked with unshed tears. "Thank you, but no. I have to do this . . . by myself."

"You're not by yourself. I'm here."

A few seconds passed, and there was a knock at the door. When I opened it and saw it was him, warmth coursed through my entire body. He didn't waste any time scooping me into his arms and hugging me. I felt his love, his protection, and his empathy. Overwhelmed, I clutched him just as tight as he clutched me.

When our eyes met, he didn't say anything. He leaned down and placed a gentle kiss against my lips, and then he searched my face.

"I got you," he whispered.

I felt so seen, so loved.

Just that acknowledgement sent my emotions into overdrive.

*Don't cry. Don't cry. Don't cry.*

I tried to blink the tears away, but that didn't work. I felt myself getting weepy, and I didn't want him to see it. I didn't want to explain that the tears were for my aunt recognizing I was in love before I had. I didn't want to explain that I was crying because I felt loved by him. I didn't want to say that his kiss was a bandage over the hole that pierced my heart and soul. So I tried to look away. But something about his stare had me locked in. I needed to put distance between us, but his hold on me had me securely in his grasp.

I was trapped.

I closed my eyes, and the tears streamed down my face. I didn't want to be out of his arms, but I also didn't want to break down in from of him. When I felt his forehead press against mine, I opened my eyes, and my heart skipped a beat.

Most people looked away when they saw someone else's pain . . . but not him. He stared at it and faced it with me.

We stood like that for at least ten minutes before I found my voice and broke the silence.

"You talked to Aunt Addy behind my back?"

Kissing me, he let out a light chuckle. "I was wondering when that was going to come up."

"Why didn't you tell me?"

"She said she would when it was time. She told me not to say anything until she did, and I respect my elders."

*At least I know he can keep a secret.*

I pulled him down to kiss him again. "Will you cuddle with me?"

He put his face squarely in front of mine. Looking deep in my eyes, he said, "Anything you want. You know that. You don't even have to ask."

He followed me to the bedroom, and we stripped off our clothes. We climbed into bed, and he spooned me. I was so tired. Kissing my shoulder, neck, and head as he held me, he whispered words of comfort against my bare skin.

With my back to his front, I cozied up to him as I started nodding off.

"I'm here for you, baby." The deep, soft tone of his voice lulled me to sleep. "Anything you need, I got you. I hate seeing you hurting. I'll do anything for you. I love you. I . . ."

*Did he just say . . . ?*

Sleep took me under before I could process what I thought I'd heard. Hours later, he roused me awake.

Cradling my face with his hands, Lamar hovered over me. "Jazz, I need to head home so I can make it before curfew."

Groggily, my lashes fluttered open. "Hmm?"

When we locked eyes, he searched my face. "You need anything?"

"Just you," I murmured, my voice still thick with sleep. "I'm tired."

"I know." His thumb caressed my cheek. "I didn't want to wake you, but I couldn't leave without saying goodbye."

"Leaving?" I managed to say before his lips covered mine.

The kiss woke my body up, and I gripped his shirt, pulling him onto me. If I hadn't been fully awake yet, I was after our tongues touched.

"Jazz," he whispered, pulling away fractionally.

I opened my eyes, and as soon as I met his gaze, my heart skipped a beat.

*He* did *say it.*

"I . . ." He swallowed hard. "Call me if you can't sleep."

"You have a game."

His lips brushed mine again. "I said to call me."

I nodded, a smile playing on my lips. "Okay."

He rose to his feet. "I'm going to lock the door behind me, but when you get up, put the dead bolt on."

"Thank you for coming," I told him. "I know—"

"Jazz, you don't have to thank me for being here," he interrupted. Leaning down so that his face was close to mine, he stared at me. "I wanted to be here. I *needed* to be here."

Tears pricked my eyes as I nodded. "I appreciate it."

He grabbed my face and planted the sweetest kiss on my lips. "I appreciate you."

He left my place a couple of minutes later and got home before curfew. Although I was worried about how he'd play, he proved there was no need. He played a great game, helping the team secure a week-five win. When he called Sunday night, he told me his coach had declined his request to take Saturday practice off. Even though he wasn't going to be at the memorial, he made a point to show up for me in every way he could.

He came over on Monday night and stayed with me. He held me, massaged me, and comforted me. I woke up Tuesday morning, looked over at him, and felt so thankful. Although I was somber, the school day went by faster knowing that Lamar was at my place waiting for me. But during the last class period, I heard some gasping, whispering, and overall gossiping.

". . . and this is why she was gone last week and looking sad this week," one of my students explained.

I looked up just in time to see the small group on the right side of the classroom staring at me.

"What's going on?" I asked, making my way toward them.

"Nothing!" they said in unison, flipping over the phone.

I put my hand out. "Hand it here."

"Ms. Payne," he complained.

"Phone, or you can go to the office."

One of the girls snatched the phone and handed it to me. "I'm not going to the office. I've already got my stuff for homecoming, and I can't get in trouble over something I didn't do."

I gave her a curt nod. "Thank you."

Opening the phone, I took a step and then froze.

I was staring at two pictures side by side—one of me and Lamar with a jagged red line between us and one with Lamar and another woman. Reading the caption, I immediately realized who it was.

*Milan.*

"What does this have to do with Maya Angelou?" I asked the students in the group.

"Nothing. It's just something from social media," the boy answered.

I nodded. "Get back to work," I ordered. "You can collect your phone after the bell."

Trying to keep my shit together, I went to my desk and looked at the image again. After taking note of the website, I counted the minutes until the bell so I could explore what the hell was going on. When I was alone, I picked up my phone, went to the site, and hit PLAY on the video.

"I keep getting tagged, so while I finish my makeup, I figure I should give you this story time," Milan started, flashing a bright smile. "Story Time: My Hollywood Love Story." She giggled. "Hollywood and I dated all throughout college. We met freshman year and became friends. He was serious about football, so he wasn't looking to get into a relationship. I was serious about my studies and then pledging my sorority, so I wasn't looking to get into a relationship either. But before sophomore year began, we had found ourselves in love with one another. We thought we would be together forever because we had the type of love that never truly goes away. He's not the type to say I love you if he doesn't mean it. It takes him a long time to utter those words, and once he locks in, it's forever. If he was ever going to be in a relationship while in the league, we talked about it being with me. We always said that when the time was right, we'd reconnect. Who knows . . . maybe the time is right now." She winked at the camera. "I don't know what his relationship status is or who the woman is he's pictured with, but I know him, and I know that his first love is football. And until I hear that he's in a relationship out of his own mouth, he's single . . ."

I hadn't been on social media since Aunt Addy died, so the Milan turn of events blindsided me. I immediately sent the video to the group chat. Unfortunately, in sharing the video, I opened the comments.

*Well, damn.*

The top comment said that Milan looked more like a professional athlete's woman and that she was more Lamar's type. I swiped off the video, and the next one happened to be someone talking about how it wasn't a coincidence that Lamar had played the best game of his life on the same day Milan posted her video.

I'd thought the comments were rude before, but the fact that Lamar's ex was my opposite—slim, light-skinned, straight hair, the "right" look—brought out the nastiest commentary.

*Seeing how he fumbled Milan, I can't even look at this man the same.*

*I can't vote for him this month. I need some time to get over this*, I read, rolling my eyes.

I hated the bullshit they were saying about me, because it wasn't true. But it killed me that they were detracting from Lamar's talent and plotting against him. His dreams had come to fruition, and they were using me to try to derail them.

My stomach lurched.

*This is not okay. I can't let this happen.*

Gianna and Drea from my first period walked in.

"Are you okay, Ms. Payne?" Gianna asked.

Drea gave me a sympathetic look. "Just in case it was you in that picture—"

Looking at Drea, Gianna pointed at me. "Do your eyes not work? You can see clear as day that it's her." Then she turned to me and frowned. "We're sorry about the breakup."

"It was really inspiring seeing you and Hollywood together," Drea noted. "I'm not feeling that Milan lady. I mean, she has some cute 'get ready with me' videos, but—"

Gianna put her hands on her hips. "Drea, read the room!"

"How can I read the room?" Drea snapped back. "My eyes don't work!"

Gianna's jaw dropped, and then they both giggled.

I stood up, grabbing my bags. "You're going to miss your bus," I told them.

"I drove," Drea countered. "But we really came in here to see if you were okay. Rumors are going around that you and Hollywood broke up and that's why you were gone last week."

"And his relationship with Milan is why you were looking sad this week," Gianna added.

I pursed my lips. "I'm fine," I told them as I ushered them out of my classroom. "And I don't know anything about any of that."

Gianna stared at me with a skeptical look. "I know it's you, Ms. Payne. And I'm sorry about this whole Milan situation. He looked better with you."

Drea nodded. "Sure did. And from the video, he knows it too."

I shook my head. "You two get home safely. I'll see you tomorrow."

Turning on my heel, I walked out of the building. As soon as I got in my car, I went to social media to find the video the girls were referencing.

"We really appreciate you taking the time to sit down with us to answer a few questions," the interviewer started.

"It's an honor to be invited. Thank you for having me," Lamar replied.

"How does it feel to be on the short list of defensive players up for September's Defensive Player of the Month?" the interviewer asked.

"It feels great," Lamar answered. "I've worked hard, but football is a team effort. I couldn't do what I do without the great defensive players around me. We work as a unit, so if I do get the honor, it's not just for me, it's for all of us."

"There are a lot of women who love the game and are passionate this season."

"Well, one of the most passionate football fans I know is a woman."

"How are you handling this newfound fame? You went from the practice squad to the spotlight. How are you navigating that transition?"

"I'm handling it. It's a change, but I'm handling it."

"There's a lot being said about your personal life. How do you deal with rumors?" the interviewer asked.

"I ignore them. I only want to deal with what's real."

"Some people are saying your personal life is overshadowing your playmaking on the field. They think you that you egged it on by not confirming your relationship with the mystery woman. What do you say to those individuals?"

"I didn't realize that was being said. But football is my career and that's your business. My relationship is my personal life, and that's my business."

"Is it okay if I ask you one more question about your personal life?"

"As long as it's not about the woman in the picture."

"I'm sorry, it is."

"I'm not answering questions about her. There's nothing to talk about."

"Well, just answer this . . . are you single?"

Lamar hesitated before finally saying, “Let’s move on.”

Hearing him confirm we were not in a relationship threw me for a loop. But the number of people who were in the comments laughing at the idea of Lamar breaking up with me was unsettling. They didn’t know anything about me, so their commentary was based solely on the amount of fat on my body. The fact that people were gleeful—saying it served me right and I needed to be humbled for thinking I deserved to be with an athlete—was chilling. It hadn’t taken long for people to start speculating that he’d rekindled with Milan.

*There’s something seriously wrong with these people*, I said as I made my way home. When I arrived, Lamar was sitting on the couch with his paperwork in front of him. *They have no idea.*

“I’ve been waiting for you to get home all day,” Lamar said as he walked toward the door.

Warmth crept up my neck when I saw the way his eyes lit up at the sight of me. Everything in the way he looked at me told me how he felt about me. But the comment about him not claiming me in public popped in my head when I remembered what had happened when I told him I wanted to be with him.

*He didn’t want to be with me let alone claim me when given the opportunity. But if he did claim me, how much further would I hurt his career?*

My smile faltered just as soon as the thoughts hit me.

Looking at that gorgeous man as he approached me, I knew I didn’t want to lose him, but I also knew I couldn’t be the reason his dreams got deferred. It hurt to even think of how his achievements were being overshadowed.

“What’s wrong?” he wondered as he wrapped his arms around me and pulled me close. He kissed the top of my head, my cheek, and then my lips. “How was your day?”

Letting his arms and his cologne temporarily distract me, I nuzzled him. “I missed you. Today was . . . tough.”

“What happened?’”

I hesitated for only a second. “Some kids saw your interview with *Flex Magazine*, and since you said you didn’t want to talk about me, they think I was out last week because we aren’t together anymore.

And it's become a whole thing at school because of the pictures, and you said you were single . . ."

He leaned back a little to see my face. "Like you wanted me to."

"I know, I know." I licked my lips. "I just . . . it's not just the students. When I was reading some of the comments, it made me feel . . ."

"Don't read the comments. Don't ever read the comments."

"It's not that . . ."

The comments were problematic and mean, but everyone saying he didn't want to be with me wouldn't bother me if he actually wanted to be with me.

He studied me. Taking his thumb, he caressed my cheek. "What's wrong?"

"I . . ." The words got lodged in my throat and I just exhaled.

"I'm sorry, Jazz," he apologized.

The care and tenderness in his tone were going to make me emotional. The way he looked at me and the way he treated me didn't make sense with his lack of a response about us being together. Swallowing my feelings down, I felt the weight of it in my belly.

*You told me what it was from the beginning.*

"You have nothing to be sorry about," I told him shakily.

"All I want to do is protect you."

"You can't protect me from everything."

"That doesn't mean I won't try." He took a half step back. "From the moment I met you, I've wanted to do everything in my power to make sure you're good, to protect you, to look out for you, to make you happy. But with those assholes online . . ." He shook his head. "You're getting all this attention that I know you hate because of me . . . and it fucking kills me. And yeah, fuck them because they don't matter, but *you matter.*"

"This isn't on you. It's on them. And that's not . . ." I closed my eyes and let my head fall back.

"Talk to me," he whispered. "I need you to tell me what it is you want from me."

My arms slowly slid from his shoulders as my heart raced. "No, I need you to tell *me* what it is you want from me."

"Everything. I want everything from you."

Confusion washed over me as I stared at the gorgeous man in front of me who was clearly playing in my face. But my brain didn't send the memo to my body because I still craved his body on mine.

"I told you what I wanted from you, and you said *nothing*." I put my hand on his chest. "Which told me *everything*."

"It wasn't like that." He grabbed my hand and brought my wrist to his face, kissing my tattoo. "You said it, a good twenty seconds passed, your phone rang, and then you left."

"Because if you wanted to be in a relationship with me, would you have hesitated?"

"I didn't hesitate. I was thinking."

My eyebrows flew up. "You needed to *think* about it?" I pulled my hand from him and raked my fingers through my locs. "That's not a good sign."

"Jazmyn."

"Lamar."

"One of the first things you told me was that you weren't interested in a relationship, and then the only time you've ever said anything about wanting to be locked in with me was after I made that pussy talk to me."

In my defense, I'd never come three times in a row like that before.

He tried to back away, but I grabbed his shirt and pulled him back close.

"No, if we're going to get into it, let's get into it," I argued softly. "Yes, I said I wasn't interested in a relationship *because I wasn't*. And then I got to know you, and I caught feelings. I'm not sure of the exact moment it happened, but I came to the realization *before* I actually said it." I let go of his shirt and reached up to touch his beard. "You told me you wanted me to feel all the ways in which you wanted me, and then you fucked me like you . . ."

*Love me.*

I swallowed hard before I continued. "Like you wanted to be with me. So I don't understand how me responding to that with 'I want to be with you' is inappropriate."

"It's not inappropriate. It's . . ." He turned his face into my hand and kissed my palm. "It's not."

"You can't make me feel like you have these feelings for me and then say nothing."

"I said nothing because I *do* have feelings for you! I fucking . . ."

His sentence trailed off, but I knew in my heart what he was going to say. I felt it in the passion of his words, his touch, his gaze.

My breathing hitched. "You fucking what?"

"You already know."

"Why can't you say it?"

"I don't want to fuck this up."

My hunched shoulders slumped. "Lamar . . ." I pulled his head down enough for me to kiss his lips. "Why do you think you're going to fuck this up?"

"Because of my schedule. Before you, if it got in the way of something, it didn't matter. But with you . . ." His lips brushed mine. "You mean too much to me."

"You don't think we could work with your schedule?"

"You told me time was the most valuable asset in a relationship, and I know I don't have much to give."

My brows furrowed. *I did?*

He must've seen the confusion on my face because he continued.

"The night we met, we were watching the game, and you said in football, in relationships, and in life, time was the most valuable asset to have and to give," he recalled.

I nodded, remembering. *I was talking about the game and thinking about Aunt Addy.*

"Okay, yeah," I acknowledged.

"That's why I tried not to touch you"—his eyes fell to my lips—"or kiss you . . . even though I wanted to. I told myself we could just get to know each other better because there was no way in hell I was going to leave that bar and never see or talk to you again. So I got your number. I spent time with you. And the more I talked to you, the more I got to know you, the more I wanted you. But I knew how my time looked. So, when things jumped off by the river, I tried to resist you. I tried to control myself. But it's you . . . and I've wanted you sexually since I laid eyes on you, and I've wanted to take care of you since our first conversation. As bad as I didn't want to fuck things up, the way you looked up at me and told me you wanted it . . ." He shook his head as if he were having a flashback. "I couldn't resist you. And I couldn't resist you because I was already about you. I've been about you since the day we met."

My heart thumped in my chest. "I wish you would've said that when I was at your place."

"Would it have made a difference? My time is still short. My schedule is still my schedule."

"But saying nothing made me feel like you didn't want to be with me."

He held my gaze. "Being with you is the only thing I want." Gripping my face between his hands, he brought his nose to mine. "You know I would do anything for you, right?"

Heat swept through my body. "I do."

"I don't want to fuck this up."

I nodded, brushing my lips against his. "When there's love and respect for what you're passionate about, you won't fuck it up." I paused. "Are you passionate about me?"

"Yeah."

"Do you respect me?" I whispered.

"Yes."

My stomach quivered before the question. "Do you love me?"

"You know I do."

"Then tell me."

I felt his body tremble.

"I love you," he murmured, searching my eyes before his mouth covered mine. "I love you so fucking much."

My stomach flipped hearing the words.

"I love you, too," I whimpered.

Still intertwined, we collapsed on the couch. My phone somehow ended up under me.

"My phone," I murmured into his mouth as my tongue met his again.

He tried to get it, but he couldn't without breaking the kiss. When he pulled it out, the screenshot of the comments I'd sent to the group chat was on the screen.

I could see the contrition in his face before he even opened his mouth.

"I'll fix this," he said gruffly.

I shook my head. "It's not on you."

"It is." With his body weighing me down and his face a few inches above me, he sighed. "There's gotta be something I can do. You don't deserve this. They are saying shit that don't even make any sense. You know it's bullshit, right?"

I reached up and stroked his beard. "I was surprised and triggered by how the internet did its thing. But what traumatized me wasn't what they were saying about me. I mean, I didn't like it. But I was worried that you would start seeing me differently because people en masse are saying you should."

His brows furrowed. "What?"

I nodded. "Also, I felt like all this bullshit was overshadowing your moment. You've worked so hard for this. The spotlight is on you, and they should be talking about how good you are and not why they think you should be with Milan instead of me." I hesitated, and then I told him all of it. "There were people saying that if you're with me, you make questionable decisions, and they"—I took a breath—"question your leadership."

I couldn't bring myself to say the real, tangible achievement he'd lose out on. My throat burned from even attempting to say the words.

"What? Get the fuck out of here!" He sat up and pulled me up, too. "Okay, first, I see you. From the day I sat at that bar beside you, I saw you and I wanted you. Inside and out, every inch of you is beautiful and sexy and mine. If we're just talking about the physical, if I were on that type of time, I would've tried to fuck you the same night we met."

A smile pulled at the corners of my mouth. "Lamar!" I groaned. "I'm being serious!"

"Me, too." He took my hand and put it on his erection. "You do it for me. Every single fucking time."

I licked my lips. "Good to know."

"Second, the right people are talking about what I'm doing on the field. Nobody else matters. Fuck them people."

"But this is your big moment and—"

"Fuck them people," he reiterated. "I don't want them talking shit about you because I want to protect you. But at the end of the day, your opinion matters to me. My family, my friends, my teammates, those opinions matter to me. I don't give a shit about what the people on the internet say. And they for damn sure aren't going to sway my thoughts about you or my decision to be with you." He got in my face. "You're it for me."

Throwing my arms around him, I climbed into his lap. "What does that mean?"

"It means I don't have much time right now." He brushed his lips against mine. "But the time I do have, I want to share it with you."

"Good," I murmured, before kissing him deep.

While the internet think pieces made it seem one way, Lamar and I were on my couch kissing, touching, and working through our relationship. I still thought it was best to keep a low profile until the internet chatter died down. He disagreed but was willing to go at my pace since I was the one being disrespected and dragged online.

"But I won't lie and say you're not mine if I'm asked," he whispered, running his hand over my thighs.

"Just for right now. Please," I pleaded. "We can figure everything out after Aunt Addy's funeral."

Instead of agreeing, he kissed me.

# 31

The rest of the week was a blur, and I did a good job of keeping my emotions in check. But when I arrived at the event space for Aunt Addy's memorial service on Friday, my eyes watered, and I literally gasped.

> **Jazmyn Payne:** Lamar! These flowers are beautiful! Thank you! You did not have to do this! Aunt Addy would've loved this!
>
> **Lamar Anderson:** You're welcome. Since the two of you had African violets on your wrists, I figured it had to be one of your favorite flowers. I'm glad you like it and that you think she would've liked it, too.
>
> **Jazmyn Payne:** She would've loved it! I love it! Thank you for being you. Not just for this. But this is just another example of how amazing you are. But I mean, in totality, thank you. I appreciate you.
>
> **Lamar Anderson:** You don't have to thank me. I just wish I could be there with you. Let me know if there's anything you need or anything I can do.

Aunt Addy had planned everything, so the flowers he'd had delivered perfectly accentuated the flowers that were already there. Even though it was October, the banquet hall had been transformed into some sort of spring garden party. There were flowers everywhere and twenty poster-sized photos of her that populated the space on easels. The program was a picture-packed booklet of her life and contributions both in and out of Chance.

One side of the room had a dance floor, round dinner tables, a band setup, and a dessert table. The other side of the room had rows of chairs facing an elevated platform. In front of that platform were African violets surrounding a unique jewel-encrusted urn that looked more like art than a place to store ashes.

As the memorial service began, I sat with my parents to my right and Nina and Aaliyah to my left. Relatives filled a few of the rows behind us. Every other chair was occupied with friends of Aunt Addy from Chance and all over the country. I didn't know most of the people, and the venue had standing room only when I looked back at the crowd. Seeing the impact my aunt had made and how loved she was restored something in me.

The pastor stepped on the platform, and a hush fell over the crowd.

"Good evening, everyone," he started. "I'm Reverend Brown . . ."

Five minutes into Rev. Brown's sermon, I became emotional. When the soloist performed and then the choir, my eyes watered. When people were invited to speak about their love for Aunt Addy, my throat burned. But when the final speaker was announced, I knew I wasn't going to be able to hold it together.

My parents and I had said we weren't going to speak. My aunt had written in her directions that she didn't want the pressure on us to speak and to let others take the lead. So I'd had no idea my dad had prepared any remarks, and from the look on my mom's face, she hadn't either.

"Hello, everyone," Dad started, looking around the crowded space. "I'm Richard Payne, and Addison Payne was my younger sister." He inhaled shakily, and that breath was caught on the microphone. His pain could be both heard and seen. "Our parents worked long, hard hours so that we'd have a better life than they had. Since they were working, I was the one tasked with taking care of Addison up until I was able to go to college. If you only knew her as an adult, she was the same way as a child. She was a handful, but she always had purpose. I didn't agree with her choices or the risks she'd take, but she always had a reason behind it. It was my job to protect her from the harm that could come her way. That's how I was taught to love." He frowned, looking down at the urn. "Taking care of Addison has always been what I was tasked to do." He paused, looking around. "But I couldn't take care of this. I couldn't protect her from this. And the only thing that gives me solace is knowing that she lived her life to the fullest. She had that spark in her. She didn't waste a minute. So, when you remember Addison, when you remember Addy, remember to not waste a minute of life. Remember to live it to the fullest. Thank you."

I wept hearing the emotion in my father, but also because I was moved by his words. I finally understood where his protectiveness, overbearingness, and quest for perfection came from. As he walked back to his seat, I felt like I knew him better.

After a prayer, the reverend stepped off the podium, and there was an announcement that dinner was about to be served. We sat down to eat, and then the band started to play. If it weren't for the urn in the middle of the room and the funeral programs littering the tables, it would look like a party and not a repast.

A smile tugged at my lips as I looked around. *Just the way she wanted it.*

"What are you thinking?" Nina asked.

"Aunt Addy would've loved this," I answered.

Aaliyah reached over and squeezed my hand. "Yes, she would've."

The event was a rousing success. There was so much joy, light, and love in the room that I could feel her with us. With a soft smile, I watched people take flowers with them as they said their final goodbyes to Addison Payne.

*This is the party of her dreams.*

After hugging my parents, Rose, Monica, and extended family members, I left with my best friends. We were staying at Aunt Addy's house overnight before heading back to Richland after brunch Saturday morning.

*The love we show at funerals should be shown on birthdays. We should make sure the love is heard and felt in life instead of hoarded until death.* I looked around, pleased. *Aunt Addy would've loved this.*

I was so glad to have my girls with me at Aunt Addy's because it was so quiet and still in there when we arrived. I would've never been able to be there by myself so soon after the memorial service. But being in the home of the only person who'd understood and accepted me in Chance with the first people who'd understood and accepted when I got to Hamilton University, I felt something within my soul sync up.

I was going to miss Aunt Addy forever, but as I fell asleep in my aunt's bedroom, peace blanketed me.

*Wake up.*

Saturday morning, my eyes opened, and it took me a few seconds to realize where I was. Pushing myself into a sitting position, I looked around.

*I miss her.*

I was up early, a few hours before my parents were coming with brunch, and I got ready for the day. I sat and reflected for a while before coming out of the bedroom. I heard the shower going and movement in the kitchen, so I knew my best friends were up as well.

"Good morning," I said to Nina, who was at the kitchen table, wide-eyed, staring at her phone. "I love that outfit."

The burnt-orange jumpsuit immediately caught my attention.

"Thank you. It's an RLF original," she said distractedly.

"Perks of the job or . . . ?" I noticed her frown. "Nina, what's wrong?"

"I'm just reporting pages and hopefully getting assholes banned from using social media."

"Why do people waste their time and energy sitting online, trash-talking people they don't know? It's dumb."

"It is," she agreed.

"What are they saying?"

She didn't respond immediately, and Nina never shied away from talking about the nonsense that was spewed about her online.

My stomach twisted.

"Nina," I said firmly. "Tell me."

"Oh, no, I'm not even looking at the comments anymore." She glanced up at me momentarily. "It's something else."

"What is it?"

"Your parents are going to be here any minute. I don't think—"

"Tell me," I demanded, interrupting her. Bracing myself, I took a deep breath. "What is it?"

"It's, um . . ." She cocked her head to the side.

Aaliyah walked in. "What's going on?"

"Nina is about to show us something," I told her, my eyes still focused on Nina.

Placing the phone on the table, her finger hovered over the play button. Milan, looking gorgeous, was frozen on the screen holding up a makeup brush. "This was posted." Nina took out her earbud and then started the video.

"So, I'm heading to Maryland to go to the Monarchs game tomorrow. Hopefully, I'll get a chance to talk to Hollywood," Milan said, wiggling her perfectly arched eyebrows. "Anyone who knows him knows he's never been big on social media. He obviously doesn't post much, but he also just isn't online like the rest of us. So I haven't been able to contact him there, and I'm sure he hasn't seen the sweet videos you've made about me. I don't want to reach out to his parents because that'll make it awkward—they loved me—so I'm just going to go to where I know he is and see if sparks still fly between us. Since we're both single at the same time, I really do have high hopes for this reconnection. And I'm not going to stop until I get him. So, fingers crossed! Wish me luck!"

The kitchen fell silent.

And then we all started talking at once.

"Oh, hell no."

"Absolutely not."

"What the fuck?"

"You're gonna have to shut this down, Jazz," Nina declared. "And I was going to wait until we weren't in Chance to say this, but Milan is a man-eater. And while I respect the game, anyone who is willing to fly *across the country* to try to run into her ex *at his job* in hopes that he *might* be interested in reconnecting is operating in delusion."

"Did Lamar say anything about her contacting him?" Aaliyah asked.

I shook my head. "No. But let him tell it, even if she did, he wouldn't be interested."

"I believe that," Nina stated. "But I think he's going to have to make it clear that he's not interested in Milan."

"I think he's going to have to make it clear he's not single," Aaliyah said.

I shook my head. "If he does that and then we come out as a couple, that's only going to make it worse for me. I think it'll be fine if he just makes it clear that Milan's not an option. Hopefully, that'll be enough for this whole thing to die down and—" The knock at the door interrupted my sentence. I looked at my friends. "To be continued."

Brunch with my parents and best friends was surprisingly great. The food was good, and the conversation was better. We filled Aunt Addy's house with good times and lots of love. My parents were even less overbearing than usual. When Dad stepped out the back door, I followed behind him a few minutes later.

"It's odd being here without Addison," my dad said softly, looking around the backyard. "Like something is off."

"Yeah." I nodded, eyeing the garden. "But I still feel her here."

He grunted, shoving his hands in his pockets.

We stood next to each other in silence.

"How are you holding up?" Dad asked.

"I'm sad, but I'm okay. I cried so much over the last few months that I thought I'd be all cried out at the service." I gave him a tight smile. "Turns out, there were still tears left."

He cleared his throat. "I'm glad you two had each other."

"Me, too."

"Did I tell you I had a dream about her Thursday night?" he wondered.

"No." My lashes fluttered open, and I looked at him. "What happened?"

"It was a funeral, a traditional funeral, but it was right here in her backyard. The casket was over there"—he pointed toward the shed—"and the chairs were lined up neatly between the flower beds. No one was here yet. I was just walking around, making sure everything was in place. And I got to the spot right back there—"

"Where the rosebush once was," I guessed.

He cut his eyes at me. "Don't start."

I giggled.

"I was standing in that spot, and I heard Addison say, 'She's been watered; watch her grow.' And I thought she was talking about the flowers I messed up, so I talked to your mother about it. We were already planning on planting some African violets in her honor. Now we're planting a rosebush, too."

I smiled. "She'd love that."

He turned and stared at me. "Watching how you handled everything—not just with the memorial service, but . . . everything—I just want you to know that your mother and I are very proud of you. I didn't tell Addison that enough, and I won't continue to make that same mistake with you. I'm proud of you. Even when you don't make the choices that I want you to make, I'm proud of you and the woman you've grown to be."

My eyes pricked with tears. "Thanks, Dad."

Without another word, he drew me in for a hug and squeezed me tight. The moment he released me, I heard the back door open. As he marched his way back into the house, my mom made her way to my side.

"We need to talk," my mom stated, placing her hand on my back. "Can you sit with me for a minute?"

I nodded. "Yeah."

We quietly made our way to the bench. Once we sat down, the afternoon sun gently baked my skin.

"I love you," she said, breaking the silence.

With furrowed brows, I looked over at her. "I love you, too, Mom." I paused. "Is everything okay?"

She looked straight ahead, seemingly holding back tears. "Did your dad tell you about the dream he had?"

I nodded. "Yeah. He just did."

She blinked rapidly before turning her head and meeting my gaze. "Outside of your father, everyone thought I resented how close you and Addison were. But I didn't. I was happy you had another person who loved you so much." She paused. "I held on too tight, and I loved that you had someone who could love you in a more relaxed way. She was able to see all the fun and life ahead of you when I was worried about the harm that could come your way and how to best set you up for success. So I wasn't jealous of the relationship you two had. I was grateful for it." She put her hand on top of mine and patted it. "I know you thought I wanted you to be perfect. But I just wanted you to be prepared."

"Prepared?"

"Prepared for this world. I just want you to have the best life. I've always just wanted you to have the best life. And at the end of August, maybe the Sunday after you left, I came out here to water the flowers. She was reading something, and she told me that I was going to overwater her flowers. It had been such a hot day, so I gave her flowers a little extra water. She sat right over there and fussed at me. She said I was going to drown it and that overwatering it was going to kill everything it was supposed to grow to be."

"Hmm," I intoned, hearing those words in my aunt's voice. I smiled. "I can absolutely hear her saying that."

My mom was quiet. "Later, over lunch, she said that I did those flowers like I did you," she said in a small voice.

My eyebrows flew up. I didn't know what to say.

"I brushed it off like I always did when she would tell me I was doing too much." She took a deep breath. "As I was sitting around, listening to you and your friends, it made me think about how much time I spend worrying about you and what will happen, what you need, what could improve your life. But while we were eating, you said something that sounded just like Addison, and then, out of nowhere, I heard Addison's voice."

I stared at her profile as she looked out into the garden. I wanted her to continue speaking, but I couldn't bring myself to break the silence. It felt like if I said anything, the moment would be gone. A full minute passed before she finished her thought.

She turned her head, looking at me with watery eyes. "'She's been watered; watch her grow.'"

I gasped.

She swiped at her eyes. "So I'm going to stop overwatering you."

My lip started to quiver.

"And I know I'm not your Aunt Addy, but I'm your mother and I love you and I'm here for you. Always," she choked out, barely opening her arms before I threw myself in them.

"I love you," I whispered, clutching her tight.

We got ourselves together, and then we returned to the house.

". . . he said he was fighting demons, whole time, he was fighting accountability," Aaliyah told my dad.

I laughed uncomfortably. "What?" I looked around. "What are we talking about?"

"Tyson," Nina, Aaliyah, and Dad all said in unison.

I groaned. "Why are we talking about the past?"

"He reached out to give his condolences," Dad explained. "And to ask for your phone number."

"Wait, wait, wait, wait, wait," I balked. "You talked to him?"

"No!" His frown deepened as he pulled out his cell phone. "He sent me an email."

Nina shook her head. "And spelled 'condolences' wrong. You dodged a bullet."

"He was a child left behind," I confirmed.

After a laugh, my dad continued. "I responded with a simple thank-you. If you wanted him to have your number, you would've given it to him."

"What do you think he wanted?" Mom mused.

*He probably saw the photo.*

"It doesn't even matter," I replied.

We talked for a few more minutes before we started to say our goodbyes. The girls and I ended up getting on the road at two o'clock, and our conversation was all over the place. I told them about my dad's dream, my mom's moving words, and the void I felt without Aunt Addy.

We spent the drive talking about life and death. With anyone else, it would've been a somber conversation. But with my girls, it was cathartic. It was healing. And it inevitably ended with some laughs.

We were making good time heading home. But Nina wanted to

stop in Richmond because of a boutique she'd heard about, and making that stop derailed the rest of the day. After shopping at three stores, we found a highly rated soul food restaurant, waited thirty minutes to be seated, and then devoured the most delicious cuisine I'd had in months.

"This is so good," I gushed halfway through my half rack of ribs and collard greens.

"Mm-hmm," Aaliyah acknowledged as she chewed the corn bread she'd just bitten.

Nina was chewing and pointing at her salad with her fork. After she swallowed, she said, "This chicken was so good, it's making this salad taste even better."

"Even with the little crumbles?" I wondered, knowing she'd requested no cheese.

"Fuck gorgonzola cheese, but today . . ." She stabbed the lettuce, followed it up with some chicken, and wiggled her shoulders. "Mmmmm."

I laughed.

"Speaking of fuck gorgonzola . . ." Aaliyah turned her head toward me. "What's the deal with Milan? What are we going to do?"

I coughed, choking on the barbeque sauce I'd just licked from my lip. "Where the hell did that come from?"

She pointed to Nina's salad. "Gorgonzola cheese originates from Italy. Right outside of Milan." She leaned forward. "Now, Milan is showing up to the game tomorrow. What are you doing?"

After pushing the collards around my plate, I scooped some into my mouth to buy me a minute to collect myself. Aaliyah and Nina knew what I was doing and sat silently and waited for me to swallow.

"It's funny how when she had macaroni and cheese in her mouth, she could crack that joke about your salad. But as soon as I ask a valid question, all of a sudden, she's chewing her food twenty-five times before swallowing," Aaliyah remarked in a stage whisper.

"I just want to know why she still has barbeque sauce on the side of her lip," Nina replied.

We all cackled.

After wiping my mouth with the napkin, I exhaled. "Milan was his college girlfriend, and she broke up with him because he was on the practice squad. He never talks bad about her. I mean, honestly, he never talks about her at all. All he really said was that she wasn't the woman for him and that he wasn't able or willing to give her what she was looking for."

"What was she looking for?"

"Celebrity status, WAG life . . ." I lifted my shoulders. "He said that they weren't compatible, and it became evident that she didn't want him for him when she accidentally sent a text to him that was meant to go to her friends."

"Oh, that's my worst nightmare," Nina mused.

"And with the types of texts you used to send to your roster, I could only imagine the fallout," Aaliyah replied.

"Now I'm only making dates with one man, so it's less of a risk." Lightly snickering, Nina shook her head. "I know she was sick when she realized he got that message."

"Oh, I know!" My eyes widened. "They were already broken up because they weren't on the same page, and she said he didn't have enough time for her—which he didn't. He admitted he didn't prioritize her. So that would've been that, but she sent that text, and he saw what type of time she was really on."

"So why does she think she can swoop back into his life?" Nina questioned, her lip curling in disgust.

"Because she looks like that and has probably always gotten her way," I answered honestly. "And if he's been single since they broke up, she may think he's pining away for her."

"Lamar is clearly in love with you," Aaliyah clarified. "Do you think he's going to be open or receptive to being friendly with her?"

"That I don't know. He's such a gentleman, so if she popped up on him, he'd probably speak." I shrugged. "Or maybe he's the 'forgive and forget' type. I really don't know. We never talked about it. But now I'm curious."

"Ask him," Nina advised. "Figure out what you are or aren't comfortable with, and then have the conversation with him. Because the way Milan was talking in the video, she's going to make a play for him."

Aaliyah nodded. "Yeah, she is. And she thinks he's single. You're going to have to figure out what you want to do about that, too."

I nodded solemnly. "I know. But I don't want to be the reason his career takes another hit."

*I wish I could ask Aunt Addy what she would do. She would know.*

On the way back to Richland, I tried to stay out of my head and enjoyed the company of my best friends. After dropping them off, I reached into my bag and grabbed the small vial of ashes. Squeezing it in the palm of my hand, I rode home in silence.

# 32

Between the sympathetic hugs and words of encouragement, the other teachers were offering support even though I insisted I was fine. It had been a week since Aunt Addy's memorial, and admittedly, I was quieter than normal. I was sad, but I was okay. So I wasn't completely surprised when I looked up before the final class of the day to find Alexa Rae staring at me with wide eyes and a pitiful expression.

"Why are you looking like that?" I wondered as she approached my desk.

"There was the breakup news one week," Alexa explained, keeping her voice down in my empty classroom. "Then the funeral last week. And with everything this week, I just . . . want to make sure you're okay."

*Everything this week?*

I cocked my head to the side. Something about the way she paused felt off. "Alexa, what's up?"

She looked behind her and then leaned across my desk. "I know you don't want to talk about it, but I saw a video about Hollywood and his ex-girlfriend reconnecting at the game on Sunday and being spotted together this week. With you losing your aunt and then you losing . . . the guy, I just . . ." She sighed, shaking her head. "Do you want to go out and get a drink this weekend?"

"I'm leaving town tonight."

"Oh! Okay, maybe next weekend."

"Maybe." I gave her a small smile. "Let's talk about it next week."

She came around my desk and gave me a hug. "I'm here for you," she said sweetly.

I hugged her back. "Thanks, Alexa."

Students started filing into the classroom as my final class of the day was about to start. The time moved quickly, and by the final bell, I didn't know who was more excited for the three-day weekend, me or the students. I packed up my belongings and was just walking out the door when Ben Riker popped up out of nowhere.

"Jazmyn," he called out from right behind me.

"Ben!" I yelped, jumping out of my skin. "Where the hell did you come from?"

He pointed down the sidewalk. "I had parking lot duty." He paused for only a second. "Just so you know, ever since that Milan bullshit popped up, I removed Hollywood from all three of my fantasy teams. No dude who does my friend dirty will get any playing time on my roster."

I furrowed my brows but kept walking toward my car. "He got one and a half sacks this past Sunday against a great offensive line, and the Monarchs are playing the Nightcrawlers on Sunday. The Nightcrawlers have one of the worst O-lines in the league right now. Was that smart?"

He gave me a look. "I was trying to be a good friend, but you know in that league with my college friends, the pot is a thousand dollars."

"Do what you need to do for the win. I'm not worried about what's being said about Hollywood and Milan. None of that has anything to do with me."

He looked skeptical as I unlocked my car. "Jazz, come on. It's me. You can tell me."

"There's nothing to tell."

"You know he didn't lose out on Defensive Player of the Month because of you, right?"

Feeling a chill down my spine, I climbed in my car. "I'll see you Tuesday, Ben."

"The way he played Sunday, he'll be up for it again in October." He waved and flashed a smile even though there was concern on his face. "See you Tuesday."

Even though Ben knew football and he saw the discourse online, his assertion that it hadn't been my fault was biased because of our friendship.

*Because it was my fault. Maybe not all my fault* . . . I made a face. *But I am the reason.*

I knew it wasn't *directly* my fault. But when they'd announced September's winner during the first week of October and Lamar didn't get crowned, I felt responsible. But with Aunt Addy's death and then her memorial service, it was the last thing on my mind. And he'd been so busy taking care of me, he'd never brought it up.

Neither of us was on social media a lot lately, so it was easy to forget—especially with how well he'd played. But Ben mentioning the monthly honor had reminded me that Lamar didn't know why he hadn't been rewarded. I honestly didn't think Lamar realized to what extent the backlash to us being together harmed his career.

There were people who'd voted for Lionel Timmons because he had been a league superstar for the last four years. What he did in the first week of the year with his sack, fumble recovery, and touchdown at the end of the game was exciting. He had a solid game every week, except for an uncharacteristically bad game two weeks ago, so him being in the running had made sense. But my unbiased opinion was that Lamar was better. Statistically, Lamar had more tackles, more yards for a loss, more fumble recoveries, and more sacks than Lionel.

But Lionel was married to a thin, racially ambiguous woman with blonde hair and a million followers on social media. I didn't keep up with her, but I knew who she was. And a couple of weeks ago, I'd seen at least two videos stating that Lionel's wife was the opposite of Lamar's alleged girlfriend, so they were voting for Lionel to get the honor.

And because Lionel was one of the GOATs in Lamar's eyes, it didn't even occur to him that the only reason he'd lost the title was because of his relationship with me.

So, while I appreciated Ben's positive outlook, I knew the truth.

And I felt sick about it.

My phone vibrated.

**Lamar Anderson:** Let me know when you're on your way. Just picked up your gift and about to head home. Let me know if you need anything.

**Jazmyn Payne:** I'm about to leave the school now and should be there at five o'clock. I hope you had a good practice, and I can't wait to see you!

We'd seen each other on Tuesday, but I was looking forward to being in his arms again.

> **Lamar Anderson:** Champs reached out to a couple of us to set up an interview. Just got to the store, I'll tell you more later. Drive safely.

"Oh wow," I breathed as I pulled out of the parking spot to head to Baltimore.

Champs reaching out to Lamar for an interview was a big deal. I was extremely excited for him and found myself grinning as I sped down the road.

Ben was right about one thing—Lamar would be up for Defensive Player of the Month again. I was scared about how that conversation would go, but I couldn't let his career keep taking hits.

Even if the conversation surrounding Lamar's relationship status would've died down like Nina initially predicted, Lamar's silence and Milan making multiple response videos had only made the social media speculation grow. And after Lamar played his ass off on Sunday, eyes on him intensified, so that only stoked the fire. I hadn't scrolled on social media in two weeks because I had enough to deal with, but from the looks I'd get at school and the comments the students would make, I knew things hadn't died down.

And while it felt like everyone was rooting for Lamar and Milan to rekindle their relationship, Lamar was making a case for us to go public with ours.

"I have something for you," Lamar told me after I arrived at his house an hour and a half later.

I sat on the barstool at the island and grinned at him. "What is it?"

"It could be a flight and a ticket to the game if you change your mind," he offered, leaning across the marble surface. "I'll book your flight and room right now if you just say yes."

I hesitated for only a moment.

I wanted to say yes. But the reality of the situation hit me.

"I don't think so," I answered, shifting uncomfortably in my seat. "I don't want to draw attention away from you."

He sighed dramatically. "I want you at a game." He walked around the island and pulled something out of his pocket. "But if I can't have you there yet, I like the idea of you being here." He placed the box in front of me and waited for me to open it.

My watery eyes widened as I lifted the top. "Lamar," I whispered hoarsely.

"I want— Are you about to cry?" he asked, pulling me off the stool and into him. Holding me tight, he rocked me from side to side as I buried my face in his chest. "It can be just for the weekend if you think it's too soon—"

"No, no, no," I interrupted, looking up at him. "You're giving me a key to your place. That's . . . I love it. I'm happy and excited, and I love it. I just . . ." I pushed up on my toes and pressed my lips against his. "I love it," I assured him. "I'm overwhelmed but in a good way."

He searched my eyes. "What's wrong?"

I didn't want to tell him less than forty-eight hours before a game. I'd rather tell him when he got back so he'd have more time to process and it wouldn't impact his performance.

Clutching the key to his house in my palm, I tried to smile. "You always manage to make everything better."

"Is it the bullshit online?" he wondered.

Ripping my eyes from his, I nodded. "Yeah."

*Just not what you think.*

He grabbed my head and forced me to look at him. "I don't give a fuck what anyone says about me. But I'm not willing to keep letting them slide when it comes to you. I'm tired of doing this your way, Jazz."

"If this is happening when it's just speculation, what will happen when it's confirmed? And once it's out there, it's out there. You know?" I explained.

"It's already out there. You said even the students at the school are asking you about it." His brows furrowed. "I don't know what you're trying to figure out."

"How to come out of this with the least amount of attention and damage possible," I answered, pleading with him to understand. "Each week something else happens that starts a whole new . . ." I closed my eyes and pinched the bridge of my nose. "I'm the one who's being dragged. The hate, the comparisons, the think pieces about how I'm ruining your career, that'll only intensify for me. Please, give me a little more time to figure something out."

His jaw clenched, and I could tell he wasn't happy.

"I'll do whatever you want, whatever you need me to do," he responded. "But I'm not lying, and I'm not going to let anyone disrespect you in my face. As much as I want to give you what you want, there's only so much I can let slide before I step in."

My stomach fluttered.

It was sexy as hell to hear *those* words out of *that* mouth from *that* man. The way he cared for me was exactly why I wanted to do what was best for him. The same way he wanted to protect me, I wanted to protect him. I couldn't allow his association with me to negatively impact his career, his dream, his legacy.

I knew if I said that to him, he'd say it didn't matter. He'd say anyone worth a damn would be focused on his on-the-field play. He'd say we'd figure it out.

But I knew how rare it was to get the type of opportunity he had at this moment. I knew what it meant to him, to his father. I knew how hard he worked and how much he sacrificed. And I knew how much being an active player meant to him and the ways in which it validated him deep down.

I couldn't be the person who derailed that dream or jeopardized his future—our relationship would never survive that.

"What you can do is go on social media and say you and Milan are not happening."

"Done," he said without hesitation.

My lips tugged upward sheepishly. "Thank you."

Resting his forehead against mine, he stared into my eyes. "You don't have to thank me for that." His lips just barely met mine. "I'd do anything to make sure you're good."

Sharing a soft, sweet kiss, we put the subject to rest.

We ate, watched most of a movie, and sucked and fucked our way into exhaustion. We fell asleep in each other's arms, and I had the best sleep I'd had all week.

I'd never felt more content in my life.

"I hate to have to leave you here," Lamar whispered against my ear. "But I can't wait to come back home to you."

"I love you," I murmured sleepily, barely awake.

"I love you, too," he replied softly. "I'll call you when we land."

He kissed my cheek and then my lips.

My mind, body, and soul roused when his mouth moved over mine with reverence. My arms wrapped around his neck as I brought him closer. He moaned and my nipples hardened.

"You sure you're going to be here when I get back?" he murmured.

"Yes."

"Good." He planted another kiss. "Text me when you wake up."

The whole thing felt like a dream until I heard the door close. I woke up with a start and had a hard time falling back to sleep.

I missed Lamar already.

Being in his home without him didn't feel as strange as I would've guessed. I rolled over and grabbed his pillow. Inhaling his scent eased me back to sleep.

I spent Saturday grading papers and catching up on the work that I'd fallen behind on while I was out. I managed to talk to Lamar when he made it to Nevada, but with the three-hour time difference, we didn't talk long.

I spent Sunday alternating between watching the games and cooking. Since the four-o'clock game that the Monarchs won ended around seven o'clock, Lamar didn't make it back home until well after three o'clock in the morning. But since school was closed on Monday, I happily woke up to greet him when he arrived.

"You were incredible," I whispered into his ear as he hugged me tight. "I'm so proud of you."

"I want you at a game."

"I want to be there."

"Good," he murmured, just as he kissed me.

We weren't up for very long.

We discussed the game and how he'd played as he prepared for bed. As he snuggled up next to me, he pulled my back to his front. I wiggled my ass against him as I got comfortable. He kissed my neck as he theorized that the two interceptions the Monarchs had thrown were the only reason they lost.

I nodded in agreement. "And even though the defense played well, there are some things that need to happen on offense to close out the game. The long drives resulting in field goals—or worse, no points—is not how you win games. Y'all shouldn't have lost this one."

"Facts."

"This is the best the defense has looked in a long time. Operating like a well-oiled machine."

"Right? And I know I've been getting a lot of attention because I'm the newest addition, but it's really all of us. We've been moving as a unit."

*You deserved Defensive Player of the Month*, I thought.

I wanted to say it, but I couldn't verbalize it. I'd said it via text when Lionel Timmons had been announced, but every time I tried to say it aloud, my eyes watered.

I swallowed hard.

"You get the attention because you deserve it," I told him. "The defense as a whole gets the attention because you all work well as a group. But when they are talking about you, it's not because you're the shiny new player on the field. Lamar, you are talented physically, but you're also incredibly smart. It's not just your athletic ability; it's your mind and the way you think."

He tightened his grip on me, but he was quiet.

After thirty seconds of silence, I turned my head and looked over my shoulder. When our eyes met, I started to ask if he was okay, but the words caught in my throat.

He twisted so his lips met mine. When he pulled away, he held my gaze. "I love the way you see me," he uttered, before resting his head back on the pillow and falling out of my line of sight.

"You're worth being seen," I returned.

I wasn't sure if he'd heard me before he fell asleep. But I meant it with everything in me.

Lamar was worth being seen.

He was worth being celebrated.

He was worth being Defensive Player of the Month.

I squeezed my eyes closed as the thought hit me. *I really am a social pariah.*

In his sleep, he drew me closer and let out a contented sigh. Instantly my eyes pricked with tears. I didn't want to lose him, and I didn't want him to lose opportunities. I was in love with him, and I wanted to do what was best for him. I hated that there was a small voice in the back of my head that felt like what was best for him was to not be with me.

*Nah, that can't be the answer*, I told myself, dismissing the thoughts.

I had to figure out a way to get out of the public's eye and shift the focus back on Lamar and his talent.

Not surprisingly, I woke up before Lamar. Instead of waking him up with head like I was tempted to do, I went downstairs and prepared everything for his steak-and-eggs breakfast. I was going to scramble the eggs once the steak was almost done. While I waited, I pulled out my phone to see the group chat was active.

**Aaliyah James:** Ahmad and I are heading to get breakfast. I'm so glad he took off to come here with me because they are saying it could take six or seven hours to winterize this yacht.

**Nina Ford:** I'm still stuck on the fact that you are paying five hundred dollars to winterize a yacht you've been on twice since it's become yours. I nominate your uncle to incur the expense.

**Jazmyn Payne:** You know good and damn well her uncle is going to use that as another reason to say women shouldn't own boats.

**Nina Ford:** He doesn't have sense, and he's worried about women having boats. He doesn't own a brain cell yet there he goes, thinking he knows best.

**Aaliyah James**: He happened to be coming to my parents' house as I was leaving on Sunday. He told me that I looked happy. Just as I was about to say thank you, he said to make sure I don't put on that happy weight and risk losing a good man. So, needless to say, I thought of a good comeback while we were driving to the dock this morning. I just wish I had thought of it in the moment.

**Nina Ford:** Not that you would've said it anyway. You're more respectful to people than they deserve.

**Jazmyn Payne:** It's sweet though, Aaliyah. Nina is reckless with her mouth and is disrespectful every chance she gets. I like both options.

**Nina Ford:** I know Cassius Clay ain't saying I'm reckless and disrespectful! Jazz, your mouth is just as disrespectful as mine. You just don't go back and forth.

**Jazmyn Payne:** I have one good comeback and then I'm done.

**Nina Ford:** Because then you're ready to fight, Money Mayweather! But I'm not mad at it because honestly, same.

**Aaliyah James:** Nina talking about "same" like she's really gonna throw hands. We can't fight, Nina!

**Nina Ford:** That's why the three of us go hand-in-hand. Aaliyah is going to overthink a situation and plan it out. I'm going to be the mouthpiece and possibly talk shit. And Jazz is going to either teach them a lesson or teach them a LESSON.

**Jazmyn Payne:** Not me being the muscle!

**Aaliyah James:** You and that big, strong man of yours can definitely be the muscle. I saw him knock somebody out yesterday and they had to get helped off the field.

**Nina Ford**: Two heavy hitters in love.

**Jazmyn Payne**: I cannot!

**Aaliyah James:** Speaking of love, how do you want to handle this Milan situation? It's getting out of control. The fact that she showed up to the game last week was over the top. But she's saying she's going to the upcoming Sunday night game, taking it too far.

**Nina Ford:** I will never understand how people are comfortable embarrassing themselves for engagement and likes. Because the way she has no shame being thirsty for a man who doesn't want her is wild.

**Jazmyn Payne:** Lamar said he was going to shut things down.

I glanced at the oven as it beeped to alert me that the steak was done. It didn't take long because he liked it undercooked. I finished off the steak and then scrambled the eggs while my mind raced.

It wasn't that I thought he wanted Milan. I knew he didn't. But the idea of her being at that Sunday-night game while I sat at home watching it on TV bothered me. I wanted to be able to go and support him without negatively impacting him.

*This is ridiculous—*

His footsteps and sexy grunts interrupted my thoughts as I finished cooking.

"Good morning, beautiful," Lamar greeted me as he entered the kitchen.

"Good morning," I replied without turning around. "How do you feel?"

"Good. I always sleep best next to you." He wrapped his arms around my waist and kissed the top of my head.

"I do, too." I turned my face and looked up to allow his mouth to cover mine. Pulling out of the kiss, I smiled. "Grab drinks, and I'll bring you your plate."

He got drinks while I plated our food. He was grinning as I walked across the room. "I could get used to this."

As I set his plate down in front of him, I kissed him in response.

Grabbing my face, he whispered, "I'm a lucky man."

Giddily, I sat next to him. "Tell me about this Champs interview you have tomorrow."

"Well, it's live. And it'll air on SANS."

Having anything air on the Sports Action News Station was a huge deal. My eyebrows shot up. "Oh my God! That's huge!"

He chuckled. "Yeah, I knew it was with Champs, but I didn't know it was going to be airing on SANS."

I screeched happily. "Lamar! Tell me everything!"

I listened to the joy and excitement in his voice as he told me about the segment. They choose different teams and different positions to spotlight, and while it was through random selection, they tended to pick standouts.

"I'm so proud of you," I told him dreamily.

"You know those messages you send me before the games are the reason I'm in the right headspace to do what I do on the field," he admitted.

I shook my head. "No, it's you." I poked him. "You, your talent, your abilities, your intelligence, your hard work. *You* are the reason you got here. I'm just thankful to be able to witness you achieve this."

After breakfast, he went to practice, and I drove home. Hours later, my phone dinged. I thought it was going to be Lamar letting me know he was on his way to my place; instead it was a link to the social media page of TJ Smith. With my brows furrowed, I pressed PLAY and waited.

"Ay yo, Hollywood," TJ Smith called out from behind the camera.

In the video posted on TJ's social media page while at practice on Monday, I watched Lamar get closer and into focus as he finished his last rep. His sweat-slicked body highlighted the muscles that defined his arms and his broad shoulders. The sleeveless T-shirt he was wearing clung to his firm chest and soft belly as he finished his last rep. His muscular arms tensed just before he dropped the weight.

"We're doing this now?" Lamar asked incredulously.

"You agreed to answer some questions for me, man."

Lamar shook his head, wiping his face with the towel he grabbed from his pile of stuff near the weight bench. "What's up?"

"There's this rumor going around about you and this chick named Milan. What's up with that?"

He shook his head. "I have no idea where that even came from. Milan is a woman I dated in the past, and that's it. My boy just showed me some of the talk happening on this app here. So I want to clear some stuff up—Milan and I are not together. We're not going to be together. We're not rekindling anything. There's no bad blood between us. To keep it a buck, there's nothing between us. I wish her nothing but the best though."

"And the woman with the social media page who says she's Hollywood's girl, who is that?"

"I don't know who that is," Lamar answered. "I know who it's not—my girl."

TJ burst out laughing. "Yoooo."

TJ Smith was the Monarchs' superstar wide receiver with millions of followers and lots of reach. It made sense for Lamar to make that announcement on TJ's account in order to get the word out as quickly as possible. With a satisfied smile, I slipped my phone into my pocket and felt confident that there was nothing else for people to run with.

# 33

*Once the focus of conversation shifts from who he's dating to how he's doing on the field, all will be well*, I assured myself on Tuesday as the school day started winding down.

"Ms. Payne," Gianna called right after lunch.

I looked up from my laptop to find her and Drea rushing to my desk.

"Yes?" I addressed them, looking back and forth. "Is everything okay?"

"Hollywood said you were his girlfriend."

"Your tea has been clocked, Ms. P!" Gianna cosigned.

I froze. "What?"

Gianna giggled. "There was a clip of Hollywood saying his dream girl was someone who quotes Malcolm X, and then he said, 'Education is the passport to the future, for tomorrow belongs to those who prepare for it today.' And Drea"—she flung her arm to the right and pointed to the poster on the wall—"what does that say?"

Drea tapped her chin. "It says 'Education is the passport—'"

"Do you know how famous that Malcolm X quote is?" I asked, interrupting the perceptive young ladies.

"You must not have seen the clip," Drea teased.

The warning bell went off, and I pointed to the intercom. "You two need to get to class because I'm not writing you a pass."

Giggling, they rushed out of the room.

As soon as they left, I pulled out my earbuds and immediately searched for the interview. My stomach was in knots as my thumb hovered above the screen before I hit PLAY on the first video to pop up.

"Describe your dream defense," the interviewer asked.

"And I know how this is going to sound, but I'm being real with you . . . The men I line up with every day is my dream defense," Lamar answered. "We have something special. The Monarchs are something special."

"How did you know the Monarchs had something special?"

"The work ethic from everyone from front office to the coaches to the players—the way everybody goes so hard is how I knew it was a special organization I was joining."

"Describe your dream woman," the interviewer asked.

"My dream woman is the woman who speaks to every part of me and compels me to want to do everything I can for her."

"And how will you know she's special?"

"A beautiful, smart, passionate woman who's knowledgeable about football and quotes Malcolm X is undeniable."

"Quotes Malcolm X? That's oddly specific."

Lamar's smile grew. "My dad drilled the words 'for tomorrow belongs to those who prepare for it today' in my head as a kid, and that became my motto. That's why I work so hard. So, to find a woman who randomly in conversation drops that quote . . ."

"It seemed like you were thinking about somebody in particular . . . which brings me to my next point. Some are saying that all the attention about your dating life is a distraction. Why do you think that is?" the interviewer asked.

"Because people are distracted by it," he answered, before clarifying. "People. Not me."

"Are you worried about how that distraction is going to impact your game?"

"I'm not distracted. And if someone else is distracted by trying to figure out who I choose to spend my life with, that doesn't have anything to do with me."

"Even if it isn't a distraction for you specifically, there's been evidence of how publicly speculated relationships distract from the game—look at what has happened in the past with girlfriends like Jessica, Kim, and Taylor and the negative impact the perception of their presence brought to the player and the game—unfairly, I may add. So have you considered the opportunities impacted from the spectacle of it all?"

"I don't see how or why that would be the case in this situation," Lamar answered. "But I stand by the fact that what's for me is for me."

"Did you know there were people who questioned your decision making?"

Before the interviewer could continue, Lamar shook his head irritably. "Yeah, I heard that."

"So, you knew about the campaign to not vote for you for Defensive Player of the Month because a group of people didn't like who they thought you were partnered with?"

Lamar couldn't disguise the confusion that crumpled his eyebrows. "What?"

"Unfortunately, some are saying you would've held the honor if it weren't for that collective effort."

He shifted uncomfortably as he stared into the camera in disbelief. "I . . . uh, I hadn't heard that."

"What are your thoughts on that?"

"I can't wrap my mind around something like that. My play on the field is my play on the field. My personal life shouldn't have anything to do with . . ." He shook his head and let his sentence trail off. "It is what it is," he concluded.

My heart ached as I watched a mixture of confusion and disappointment contort his face before he swiped it with his hand.

I felt sick.

The phrase *social pariah* kept swirling around in my head as the outcome I'd been trying to avoid bubbled to the surface.

"Do you think the attention you're getting and the expectations other people have for you and your partner will continue to take away from your career moving forward?"

Lamar seemed to tense for a moment as the question hit him. "Like I said, if someone else is getting distracted by my personal life, that's on them. So that's a question you'd have to ask them. But career wise, my only job is to perform at my highest level." He exhaled and leaned forward, closer to the camera. "Football has always been my first love. I've dedicated everything to getting to this point in my career. So no, I'm not distracted by anything that's being said about me."

"So what your teammates, your coaches, and your ex-girlfriend, who you confirmed will stay an ex via your conversation with TJ Smith, say about you is true: Football is your main priority and the love of your life."

A look crossed his face. He slid his hand over his jaw. "Football is my first love, but it's not the love of my life."

The interviewer seemed to pick up on the same thing I'd picked up on. "What, or who, is the love of your life?"

"My personal life has nothing to do with anybody but me and the woman I'm with."

"So, you are with someone?"

"Fuck it, yeah, I am," he answered in frustration.

It was apparent he was still thinking about what he'd just found out.

"Do you love her?" the interviewer wondered.

Without hesitation, he nodded. "Yes."

Students coming into the classroom forced me to hit PAUSE and slip the earbuds out of my ears. I put my phone away and got back to my job. But in the back of my mind, I couldn't stop seeing Lamar's expression when he'd learned that he'd lost only because of me. I thought about that look on his face for the rest of the day.

My stomach twisted into a knot.

I knew we had to have a hard conversation when I got off work.

> **Lamar Anderson:** Some stuff came up during that live interview and now I have a meeting with the defensive coaches at three o'clock and then a meeting with my manager. I'll tell you about it when you get off. But it doesn't look like I'll be in Richland tonight. Call me when you can.

My hand started to shake, and my eyes started to water.

Even if Lamar didn't care what the people on the internet thought, he absolutely cared what his coaches thought. And if they thought it was for the best, I wouldn't even be upset with him for doing what he needed to do. It was what I'd considered ever since I realized my presence in his life was distracting from his gameplay.

But the thought of his coaches calling him in on his day off to address what he'd said in his interview made it real.

I took a deep breath.

**Jazmyn Payne:** Is everything okay? I'm sad I won't see you, but I understand.

I started to type *I love you*, but I deleted it. Swallowing hard, I wrote a different message.

**Jazmyn Payne:** You prayed for and worked hard for this opportunity so, within reason, whatever you need to do to make sure your dream isn't deferred, I understand. Nothing and no one can dim how bright your star shines. You were crafted with divine purpose, and you were born to walk in your power.

When the final bell of the day rang, I rushed home. As soon as I arrived, I called Aaliyah and Nina. After filling them in on everything, I hoped something, *anything* my best friends said would make me feel better or, at the very least, prepare me for the conversation I needed to have.

"I thought you told him about the defensive-player thing," Aaliyah said as I paced across the room.

"I told him that people were questioning his leadership and on-the-field play because of me, but I couldn't bring myself to get specific," I informed them. "I didn't want him to equate me with the demise of his opportunities. But I told him there was stuff online, and I just assumed he'd check like he had before. But he looked so caught off guard . . ." I stopped walking and squeezed my eyes shut. "I don't know what's about to happen."

"Exactly," Nina said calmly. "So don't stress. Just breathe. Have you talked to him since the meeting?"

I looked at the time. "It's seven o'clock. His meetings should've *been* over, and I haven't heard from him." I felt the fire in my throat and the sting behind my eyes. "What if they bench him? Or worse . . ."

"If they bench him, that will hurt the team, so they wouldn't do that . . . right?" Aaliyah asked.

"If they feel like his personal life is a distraction, they could." I swallowed around the lump that was forming. "They'd put it under the guise of 'conduct detrimental to the team.'"

"But what is the detrimental conduct?" Nina questioned in frustration. "You know, it's funny how it's only *certain* players who get scrutinized and penalized."

"Exactly!" I damn near yelled. "And if he were to push back, then he's difficult and selfish, and they'll create the narrative that he's not that good, not worth the headache and not worth the money. Just like they did to that quarterback who took a knee for what he believed in and the kid in the draft because of his famous dad. They will work together as an organization to 'put him in his place' for not doing what they say. I don't want that to happen to him. But I *cannot* be the reason that happens to him."

"I know you like to consider the worst-case scenario," Aaliyah started gently. "But I think you should wait until you hear from him before jumping to the destruction of his career."

"Jazz has a point though, Liyah," Nina agreed. "It sounds like professional football is a lot like professional modeling in that way. As soon as you're labeled *difficult*, you're essentially blacklisted. It doesn't matter how pretty you are, how talented you are, or how perfect you'll be for a campaign. When the industry comes together to put one of us in our place, they weaponize everything they have so we feel the effects of the systems of power."

"I hear you both, and I completely understand what you're saying," Aaliyah argued. "But what *I'm* saying is to wait until he calls because it could be something else entirely."

I knew in my gut she was wrong, but I wanted to hold on to a glimmer of something resembling hope. "Okay," I relented, nodding slowly. "I get—"

My phone beeped.

I knew it was him before I even looked at it.

"It's Lamar," I exclaimed. "Love you guys. I'll call you back."

Without waiting for them to respond, I pressed the button to answer his call. "Hello?"

"Hey, what's up?" he greeted me in his deep, sexy voice.

"Just worried about what you had going on. Coaches never called you in on your day off before, so I was just wanting to make sure you were okay."

"I'm cool. I'm . . ." He was quiet for a moment. "The coaches wanted to talk to me about the performance metrics. The interview I did this morning brought up some stuff, and it got the coaching staff, my manager, and my agent involved."

He sounded like he was choosing his words carefully. I didn't know what he was going to say, but I held my breath as I waited.

"Statistically, my numbers were better than everyone nominated for Defensive Player of the Month," he told me. "The contract that I signed has different bonuses and incentives for hitting different benchmarks, and any type of weekly, monthly, or seasonal record or recognition holds weight in negotiations."

"Oh wow, so not getting Player of the Month . . . ?"

"I missed out on fifty thousand dollars."

*Fifty thousand dollars?!*

I hadn't known for sure, but I'd figured his stats were better. Hearing that he'd lost out on the honor *and also* lost money gutted me.

Blinking rapidly, I couldn't stop my eyes from filling with tears. "I'm so sorry."

"There's nothing for you to be sorry about."

My heart thumped in my chest.

I knew he knew I was the reason they'd campaigned against him.

"I just have to make some changes," he continued. "After meeting with the coaches, I met with my agent and manager. Because of how I played on Sunday, they want to ensure that I'm properly compensated if I'm eligible for October's Defensive Player of the Month."

"I understand if I'm the change you have to make," I choked out.

"What?"

"I'm sorry. I can't . . ." I whispered shakily, letting my head fall back.

*I can't do this to you. I can't do this to myself,* I finished my sentence silently.

"You can't do what?" he asked.

Lamar sounded so hurt, irritated, and confused—which only made things worse.

"I cost you fifty thousand dollars," I cried.

"You didn't—"

"Lamar!" I interrupted. "Can you honestly say that being with me didn't come up when you were in your meetings today?"

I heard the hesitation in the breath he took before he spoke. "Jazz."

Even though it stung, I knew the league was a business, and all press was good press until it wasn't. And because the manager and agent got a cut of whatever Lamar got, it would make sense that the fifty-thousand-dollar loss would make me seem like a liability.

"From the beginning, I wanted to help you because I believe in you. But I'm bad for your brand." I swallowed the sob that threatened to escape. "So, if helping you and supporting you means walking away, then I'll do what needs to be done."

"What the hell are you doing, Jazz? No. This isn't the answer."

"Tell me that they didn't say you should distance yourself from me. Tell me they didn't say it," I insisted, knowing he wouldn't lie to me.

"It doesn't matter what they said."

"Did it come up?"

"Yes."

Even though I'd known the answer, it still felt like a punch to the gut. "You always talk about how you want to protect me, and I love that. Now it's my turn to protect you. And I love you enough to protect you from losing everything you've built."

"Jazz—"

"I have to go now," I said, my voice cracking. "But I . . . I love you."

"I love you, too. So don't do this."

"Good night, Lamar."

He didn't say anything for a solid thirty seconds. "Good night, Jazmyn."

As soon as the call ended, I sobbed.

**Jazmyn Payne:** Please understand where I'm coming from. I'm doing this for you. I want us to figure this out, but not at the expense of your career.

**Lamar Anderson:** I've already figured it out. You call me when you do.

His words hit me in the dead center of my chest, and I thought about them for the next two days.

Wednesdays and Thursdays were always Lamar's longer practice days, but outside of a good morning and good night text, we didn't speak. I was devastated but I knew that Lamar's career would be better off. But on Friday, the anxiety I felt was almost debilitating. Just getting through the day was tough because everything reminded me of him.

"Are you going to be at the game tonight?" Drea asked me as she and Gianna strolled into my classroom toward the end of the day. "We got shirts made with our boyfriends' numbers on them, and we wanted to show you!"

"You're our inspiration," Gianna squealed.

"I'm really happy for the both of you," I told them, putting my phone away. "Make sure you're treating each other with respect."

They both nodded profusely. "Yes, ma'am."

Gianna looked around to make sure everyone had left. "If you want us to give you the name of the store that did our shirts, you can get one made for your boyfriend's game."

I almost broke into tears right then.

To disguise my heartache, I just shook my head. "You two won't quit, will you? Get to your next class!"

They laughed as they ran out of the room.

But I didn't feel like laughing.

Unfortunately, the day dragged, and when I finally made it home, all I wanted to do was climb into bed.

*With Lamar.*

I ate, took a shower, and was in bed before the sun set. Missing him felt heavy, and I couldn't stand it anymore. So, when I called him, the sound of his voice instantly soothed me.

"I hope this means you figured it out," he answered.

"I miss you," I admitted.

He paused, taking a breath before speaking. "I miss you, too."

"I need to see you. I want to talk in person. I want . . . to be next to you."

"I have a pre-workout cold-plunge appointment at six o'clock with a trainer, so I need to be here tonight. Why didn't you say anything earlier?"

"I didn't know if you'd want to see me," I answered honestly. "Things have been different the last few days."

"And why is that?" he replied in frustration.

I felt like I'd been punched in the gut. "You're right," I whispered.

He sighed. "I want to see you, too, but I can't leave tonight. You're more than welcome to come here. You have a key."

That last sentence rocked me.

"Do—um, do you want it back?" I stammered, scared of what his answer might be.

"Do you want it?" he countered, sounding as uncertain as I did.

"Yes," I whispered.

"It's yours. Come by the house tomorrow. Use your key. I know you have your hair appointment, but I'll be home after four."

I had forgotten all about that.

"It slipped my mind," I murmured, trying to open up my calendar.

"And I have a game on Sunday," he reminded me.

His statement hung between us.

I swallowed hard. "Well, can I see you on Monday after your practice?"

"Yeah. We can do that."

Since he had to be up so early, we said good night a few minutes later.

I started dozing off when I heard Aunt Addy's voice.

*Everything you've been through . . .*

It was faint, but it was unmistakably hers.

I tried opening my eyes, but I felt myself drifting faster and deeper to sleep.

My aunt's words rang in my ears as I woke up the next morning. Looking at the clock, I realized I'd slept in. I hadn't had a full eight hours in days, and hearing Lamar's voice had done the trick.

*Everything you've been through . . .*

Still thinking about what I'd heard in my dream, when I got out of the shower, I reread the letters from Aunt Addy. I was still pondering it when Nina and Aaliyah arrived.

They'd decided on Friday morning to come by to check on me because I'd been going through it.

Nina and Aaliyah arrived with lunch, and we sat around my living room ruminating over pasta.

"I'm literally just existing, and it's causing all these problems," I told them. "The fact that he lost fifty thousand dollars—"

"What?" Nina balked.

I pinched the bridge of my nose. "If he would've gotten Defensive Player of the Month for September, he would've gotten fifty thousand dollars. *That's* why I'm trying to end things with him. The internet bullies were maddening, and there was way too much attention on me. But the fact that simply being in a relationship with me caused him to lose an opportunity that impacts his finances, his standing with the Monarchs, potential points of negotiation for future teams, for great—"

"Fifty thousand dollars?!" Aaliyah shrieked.

"Okay, you feel me?!" I looked between the two of them. "They *think* we're together, and it robbed him of everything that comes along with the title *and* the money."

We were all quiet for a moment.

Nina put her plate down and leaned forward. "He found out the reason he didn't get it was because people were mad he was with you, and his response was 'Let's go public'?"

My stomach knotted as I heard the summary. "Well . . . yeah, kinda."

Aaliyah cocked her head to the side. "The first man you've ever truly fallen for knows what people are saying, and that doesn't faze him. He knows that some people are being idiotic right now, and yes, he lost a grip of money—*fifty thousand dollars* to be exact—but he's still in it."

"Yeah . . ." I said slowly.

Nina made a contemplative noise. "So the risks that you're worried about, he's aware of, and he's still willing to take the chance. Why aren't you?"

The question made my head spin.

Shifting my gaze to Aaliyah, I tried to change the subject. "Being in love has changed Nina."

"Yeah," Aaliyah agreed. "And it's changed you, too."

I exhaled loudly and was about to complain that they weren't helping when Aaliyah continued.

"To piggyback off what Nina said, are you scared it won't work out, or are you scared it will?"

*Whew.*

I shook my head. "Y'all are hitting me with the tough questions today." I took a bite of my food to buy time. Chewing slowly, I mulled over what they'd asked. I looked at Nina. "Because I'm scared," I answered her question. Shifting my gaze to Aaliyah, I answered hers: "I'm scared it'll work out at the expense of his career. But I'm also scared it won't work out because of all the external factors—the public scrutiny, his coaches, his management team. I'm scared the outside pressures will get to him and it'll blow up in my face—publicly. So I guess the answer is both."

*That's an excuse, not an answer.*

"So, the real question is would you rather lose him now or lose him later?" Nina asked.

"Whoa," I murmured, heart thumping in my chest. "I hadn't thought of it like that."

My conversation with my best friends lingered while I was at my hair appointment. I was so distracted by my thoughts, I almost missed when my loctician told me I didn't owe her anything for the appointment.

"Huh?" I replied, confused.

"Your man called and took care of it on Monday . . ." She went on about how romantic that was, but I didn't hear much of what she'd said. Emotion washed over me as I knew the only person it could've been was Lamar. I hadn't even remembered this appointment, and he had. And as I sat under the dryer, I replayed different moments between me and Lamar.

As my loctician finished my rope twists, I couldn't stop thinking about how Aaliyah and Nina's advice hit different today. But when I got home, I knew exactly why.

**Jazmyn Payne:** Your words today felt like they were coming straight from Aunt Addy. Thank you both.

**Aaliyah James:** That's the biggest compliment! Nina and I just want you to live your life to the fullest—just like Aunt Addy.

**Nina Ford:** And in football terms, you've been playing offense, now you need to play defense.

**Jazmyn Payne:** What does that even look like?

**Nina Ford:** The hell if I know! But if you're the coach and the other team has the ball and you need to make a stop, what are you going to do to shake shit up?! What's your favorite play?

**Jazmyn Payne:** A blitz.

**Aaliyah James:** I don't know what that means, but yes, blitz! Do that.

**Nina Ford:** Do *something*. Anything!

Snickering to myself, I shook my head. The metaphor she was going for had lost itself, and I was about to type that, but my aunt's advice to fight for what I wanted felt like it was embedded in my friends' words.

**Nina Ford:** What does blitzing look like in the game?

**Jazmyn Payne:** It's organized disruption. The ultimate go big or go home play outside of a Hail Mary.

**Aaliyah James:** Yes, blitz!

**Nina Ford:** Yes! Organized disruption. Go big and tell the world you're Lamar's girlfriend. And go home with him and throw that ass in a circle.

**Aaliyah James:** And doing it in a big way so it'll disrupt the weirdos like the lady who's pretending to be you, the ex-girlfriend who wants to take your spot, and all the other women who think they have a shot.

**Jazmyn Payne:** I was sitting under the dryer, thinking about what I'm sacrificing and giving up and I decided that as much as I don't want him to lose his career, I also don't want us to lose what we have. And if he's willing to try, then so am I.

My phone rang.

"Hello?" I answered.

"We're going to the Monarchs game tomorrow," Nina said in lieu of a greeting. "Hold on."

My eyebrows flew up.

"Hello?" Aaliyah answered as Nina merged the call.

"We can't just go to the game!" I exclaimed.

"We're going to a game?" Aaliyah wondered. "What game?"

I pulled out of the parking spot. "Nina thinks we should go to the game tomorrow so I can publicly stake my claim."

"*That's* how you blitz," Nina confirmed.

"I think that's a great idea!" Aaliyah agreed. "It's romantic. That's basically like sending him flowers to his job."

"Blitz! Blitz! Blitz!" Nina chanted, and then Aaliyah joined in.

"You don't even know what blitzing is," I complained as I tried not to laugh.

They cracked up.

I smiled. Addison Payne would've absolutely showed up at the game if she were me. It was the ultimate "go big or go home" gesture. And while I was worried my presence might be a distraction, I was tired of letting other people's bullshit control my social life.

*I'm not letting it happen again.*

"I'm down," I agreed. "Let's go to the game."

"Just snagged some tickets," Nina announced.

"Even if I come off just as thirsty as Milan," I half joked, as I was doing essentially the same thing that she had.

"You're a Monarchs fan going to a game. That's not thirsty," Aaliyah reasoned.

"Pretending like your ex still wants you is thirsty," Nina added. "Actually no, Milan isn't thirsty—that bitch is parched!"

"Dehydrated!" Aaliyah cackled.

# 34

"It's gaaaaaaaaame time!" Nina sang as soon as I answered the phone Sunday morning.

I was riding to the game with Nina and Russ. Aaliyah and Ahmad were driving separately, and the five of us were meeting at eleven o'clock.

With a laugh, I confirmed that I was ready, and I came out of my apartment in my jeans and T-shirt.

Nina was out of the passenger side of the car and meeting me on the sidewalk seconds after I stepped down. "No, ma'am," she said, shaking her head.

Confused, I stopped in my tracks. "Huh?"

We went back inside my place, and she put together something cute, much dressier than what I'd had on before. Once I'd changed my outfit, Nina and I made our way back to Russ's sleek car.

"And it's confirmed he's not a kingpin?" I asked as we approached.

Her head fell back as she laughed. "You know good and damn well he isn't!"

I lifted my hands, feigning confusion. "For a while there, we didn't know."

Snickering, we climbed in.

"Hey, Russ," I greeted him.

"What's up?" He looked back at me. "I see you changed."

"Nina said I looked like I was going to the game to sell concession snacks, but I didn't look like a WAG," I replied.

"What's a WAG?" he asked.

"Wives and girlfriends of athletes," Nina responded. "She looked cute before, but since this is the first game and she's ready to claim her man, she needed to come correct."

I looked down at my scoop-neck black jumpsuit and the cute green cardigan with the black *M* on the front and *Monarchs* on the back.

It was a much more pulled-together and sexy look than the skinny jeans and Monarchs T-shirt I'd had on before.

I lifted my shoulders. "I trust Nina."

Russ brushed Nina's cheek with the back of his hand. "Yeah, I trust her, too."

I grinned. "Y'all are cute."

Pulling out my phone, I sent two texts to Lamar.

> **Jazmyn Payne:** I'm so proud to have watched your dream elevate to this level. You are an inspiration to many, but I want to let you know how inspirational you are to me. You changed my life by coming in and making everything better. Just like you came into the starting position and made the D-line better. You are a game changer. With the Monarchs. And with me. Just by existing, you are already enough. Everything you do on that field is extra. And each week you show up and show out and remind them why they call you Hollywood.
>
> **Jazmyn Payne:** I look forward to watching you play today. We're going to be in Section 135, row 3, behind the Monarchs bench.

We arrived at the stadium, and Aaliyah and Ahmad were already there. We linked up, took some pictures, and then went inside. We had excellent seats. We were in the third row, slightly askew from the fifty-yard line.

"Nina, how much were these tickets?" I hissed.

"Huh?" she said, pretending not to hear me.

"Nina!"

"How are you going to do what you need to do if we're in the nosebleeds?"

"Thank you." I gave her a hug. "Let me know how much it is, and I'll pay you back."

"Ordinarily, I'd say no because you're a teacher and I know on a teacher's salary after rent, you have to forage for berries to afford food—"

I burst out laughing. "What the hell?"

"—but now that you have a professional-athlete boyfriend, I'll send you the amount to request from him."

"I cannot with her," Aaliyah commented through her laughter.

Since we were early, the stadium looked relatively empty. Most people were at the concession stands or in the parking lot tailgating. There were hardly any people in our section. I patted my regulation-size stadium-approved bag and gave my best friends the nod.

Nina and Aaliyah walked with me to the railing that overlooked the field. Looking around, I made sure security wasn't paying attention to me, and I said a silent prayer. Digging the vial out of my bag, I held it in the palm of my hands.

"You made it to a Monarchs game, Aunt Addy," I whispered as I took off the top. "You would get a kick out of this." Discreetly emptying the ashes onto the field below, I watched the wind sweep it up and float it toward the sideline. "I love you."

I stood for a minute, imagining what Aunt Addy would say about finally being back at the Monarchs' stadium. And when the sun heated my skin, I couldn't do anything but smile. Satisfied, I stuffed the empty container back into my bag, and we headed to our seats.

I was in the middle of the two couples, with Nina and Russ on my right and Aaliyah and Ahmad on my left. The five of us laughed, joked, and talked the entire pregame.

Prior to kickoff, I stared at the tunnel, waiting for Lamar to emerge, and when he did, I jumped to my feet.

The game was a good one, and the offense and defense on both sides of the ball were holding their own. But in the third quarter, Lamar got loose and sacked the Geckos' quarterback. The ball came out, and the Monarchs recovered. The five of us screamed like the game was over.

In addition to that sack, Lamar was instrumental on a number of tackles, and he spent the day rushing the passer. He did an exceptional job, and I was grinning from ear to ear.

People had started heading to the parking lot when there was one minute left on the clock. It was clear that the Monarchs were going to win, so Geckos fans were streaming out of Franklin Financial Field.

"So, how are we going to do this?" Aaliyah asked.

I shook my head. "I have no idea. If I go down there, would he even hear me?"

"If we all go down there and call his name, he'll hear us," Nina insisted. "But it's whatever you want to do."

Nerves swirled in my belly, but I nodded. "Let's go."

The five of us got up and headed down the steps to the railing. When the game clock hit zero, everyone was screaming, cheering, and exiting the stadium. The players flooded the field to congratulate the other team. A minute later, I saw number ninety walking around the bench and looking into the crowd.

"There he is!" I exclaimed, pointing him out. I cupped my hands around my mouth and screamed, "Lamar!"

"Lamar!" Nina and Aaliyah yelled.

It was so loud and there were people yelling "Hollywood," so I could understand how it would be difficult to find us. He located the section, and as he drew closer, I could see his thick brows furrowing as he scanned the crowd. We called out to him again, louder.

"Lamar!" the five of us bellowed in unison.

And then he saw me.

A smile spread across his handsome face as he approached.

"What's up, y'all?" he greeted all of us, even though his eyes kept returning to me.

"You did your thing out there," Ahmad told him.

"Yeah, you killed that shit," Russ agreed.

Aaliyah pumped her arms in the air. "Hollywood doing the damn thing!"

"I barely knew what was going on during the second half," Nina pointed out. "It felt like every time the Geckos got the ball, they had to give it back! You were all over their asses!"

"And that sack!" I put my hand to my chest. "So good!"

Aaliyah laughed. "Even if I don't know football like them, I know a good-ass play when I see it."

"Thank you, thank you. I appreciate that," Lamar said, reaching upward and dapping everyone up. When he got to me, he held my hand. "Jazz."

Electricity crackled between us. His thumb caressed my knuckles, and with each swipe, my stomach fluttered, and my chest heaved.

The combination of him looking deep into my eyes and caressing me while in his uniform was doing something to me. But I managed to speak. "Lamar."

"It's good to see you," he said. "I'm glad you're here."

"I'm glad to be here. Seeing you do your thing on the field was everything. *You* are everything."

"Come back to my place." He licked his lips. "Celebrate the win with me."

Excited, I nodded agreeably. "Okay."

His smile grew. Seeming to remember we weren't alone, he looked at my friends. "And y'all are more than welcome to come by my spot, too."

"This sounds like a celebration we shouldn't be watching," Nina joked.

Russ was weak. Aaliyah and Ahmad snickered. Lamar shook his head as he chuckled.

My face flushed. "I cannot." I bumped her with my hip. "You are a problem."

"We'd love to, but we have to get back before six," Aaliyah told us. "One of Ahmad's best friends is having a birthday dinner."

"It's not a birthday dinner." Ahmad chuckled. "We're linking for the Sunday-night game. It just happens to be Darius's birthday this week."

Aaliyah pursed her lips and then looked at us. "Birthday dinner."

As we laughed, some people jostled us to try to get Lamar's attention for pictures.

"Hollywood!" a man, someone from the coaching staff, yelled out. "Yo! Hollywood!"

Lamar looked behind him and noticed half the field had cleared out. "I need to head to the locker room, but"—he locked eyes with me—"go downstairs to the Chamber level. I don't have a pass on me to give to you, so I'll have to come out that way."

"I'll be there," I told him.

He dapped everyone up again, and then he got to me and lifted my hand to his lips. A tingly sensation raced from my hand up my arm. He attempted to let my hand go, but I continued holding on to his.

"Did you figure out what you want?" he asked when I didn't release him.

"I knew what I wanted the whole time. I was just afraid to stand in it," I admitted, leaning over the railing. "But I'm done."

As he rubbed his thumb across my knuckles, his eyes never left mine. "Done with what?"

I put my face within reach of his. "Hiding."

"If I do what I want to do"—his eyes dipped to my lips—"people are gonna talk. There's gonna be attention on you."

"Fuck them people."

Wrapping his hand around my throat, he brought me closer, and his soft lips moved against mine.

The stadium went silent.

Everyone disappeared.

"Chamber," he reminded me as he slowly backed out of the kiss.

I swallowed hard and nodded.

When he turned and jogged over to the D-line coach, that's when my mind registered all the other people around us. The kiss had lasted for three or four seconds, but I felt it for at least five minutes afterward.

"Oop!" Nina elbowed me before we walked up the steps. "Somebody is about to celebrate this win right."

I laughed. "I cannot believe you said that with all those people around."

Aaliyah made a face. "I can absolutely believe she said it."

The men chatted while the three of us cackled behind them.

"We need to get on the road," Aaliyah announced, checking the time. "But I'm so glad we did this. I'm proud of you."

"So proud," Nina echoed.

"Thank you both for doing this with me."

"We should do this more often," Nina proposed.

Aaliyah nodded. "Yes." She hugged us and then called Ahmad over.

When both men stepped over to us, all of us hugged and exchanged goodbyes. Aaliyah and Ahmad left to get to Darius's birthday dinner. I started to tell Nina and Russ goodbye as well, but Russ gave me a look.

"We're going with you down to link with Lamar," he stated, pressing the elevator button. "We're making sure you're good."

Nina smiled up at him, and I saw so much love and adoration in her eyes. "He's so protective."

I couldn't help but grin. *This man has changed her.*

"Well, I appreciate that," I said as the elevator arrived.

We found where we were supposed to be, and we were stopped by a security guard immediately.

Fortunately, Lamar was there.

"They're with me!" he bellowed, and everyone looked.

"They still need passes," the man grumbled as he waved us on.

Lamar jogged over to us. We were away from the cameras, the press, the majority of the people.

"Hi!" I greeted him excitedly.

Grabbing my face, Lamar crashed his lips into mine. Heat spread from the meeting of our lips through my entire body. When he pulled away, he smiled.

"I can't believe you're here," he uttered, staring at me. Tearing his eyes from me, he turned to Nina and Russ and dapped them up. "I haven't taken a shower yet, so I don't want to get too close."

After they exchanged pleasantries, he shifted his attention back to me. "I got your messages right before the game. Thank you."

"Anytime." I grinned.

He leaned down and brushed his lips against mine. "I finished with the press, but I need to shower and change. I'll find a pass and get it to him"—he pointed to the guard—"and then you can walk out the back with me."

My stomach fluttered. "Okay," I murmured.

He looked over at Nina and Russ, and while Russ was at least pretending not to listen, Nina was just staring at us and grinning.

I almost laughed out loud.

"Y'all coming by the house?" Lamar asked.

Nina flashed a cunning smile. "We're going to let you two"—she wiggled her eyebrows—"*celebrate* in private."

"But next time, we in there," Russ replied, dapping him up again.

Lamar nodded. "That's what's up." He gestured to Russ's shirt. "Is this you?"

A proud smile stretched across Russ's face. "Yeah, man. It's not out yet. Hits stores in a few weeks."

"I'm gonna have to cop one if you make them in big and tall."

"I got you."

Nina and I shared a pleased look as the two men shared a joke and a laugh. Russ traveled a lot and didn't have any local friends. And even though Lamar had teammates, his closest friends weren't local. Nina winked at me as a reminder of our plan to get Lamar, Russ, and Ahmad to become best friends.

Lamar returned to the locker room as I hugged Nina and Russ goodbye. Then I went to the guard and waited. Five minutes later, someone brought a pass for me.

Nervously, I made my way toward the crowd—a mix of press, photographers, Monarchs staff, players, and players' families. It was a bit overwhelming, and when a woman walked by in six-inch heels and a tiny Monarchs jersey dress, I hesitated for a moment.

*Now* she *is camera ready.*

Women all around were in varying states of dress. But the ones who were garnering the most attention looked like the woman who'd walked by—slim-thick, glam makeup, and an overtly sexy outfit. They looked fantastic. And even though I also looked good, I knew what the WAGs who were in the spotlight typically looked like and wore. People would assume Lamar was with someone like her before they would assume he was with me.

And that was their problem, not mine.

But as I saw the flurry of camera flashes and reporters, my stomach churned. Being with a public figure meant an influx of attention.

And I hated attention.

But I realized I didn't hate it more than I loved Lamar.

Twenty minutes after I had successfully faded into the throng of people, closer to the players than I've ever been before, my phone vibrated in my bag.

"Hello?" I answered.

"I promise I'm coming," Lamar responded. "You okay?"

"I'm okay." I put my hand to my stomach. "Hungry but I'm okay. Are you okay?"

"I'm going to feed you. Give me five minutes."

I grinned, thinking about all the ways I wanted to be fed. "Okay, five minutes," I confirmed.

We said goodbye and my stomach fluttered.

When he emerged from the locker room, he bypassed the people waiting around and came directly to me. I watched him approach in his green-and-black Monarchs sweatpants and a black shirt that hugged his biceps beautifully. I couldn't help but smile.

*The man is gorgeous . . .*

"You are so beautiful," he complimented as he wrapped his arms around me. "This outfit is sexy."

I squeezed him back. "And we match!"

Intertwining our fingers, we made our way out the door to a parking lot.

"You were excellent today," I gushed. "I know everyone is going to talk about your coverage during that first drive, because that was amazing. But your stop on fourth and one in the third quarter was a game changer. Truly. That shifted the momentum. That was the play that sucked the morale out of them."

"You have no idea how sexy it is to hear you talk like that."

"You like it when I talk football to you," I said flirtatiously, rolling my shoulders for added effect.

"You've known that since the moment I met you." Lamar's smile grew as we approached his car. He opened the door for me to get in. "But it's not just the way you say shit that's sexy. It's the way you pay attention to what I'm doing."

"It's very easy to pay attention to things I love," I said as he closed my door.

The grin that spread across his face made my stomach flutter.

He tossed his bag in the backseat and then climbed in on the driver's side. Grabbing my face, he kissed me hard. "I know I probably shouldn't have kissed you in the stadium. But I—"

"No, I leaned down specifically for you to kiss me," I interrupted.

"So when you said fuck them people, you didn't just mean the people around us . . . ?"

"I meant everybody. Are people going to take shots at me and talk shit for a while?" I made a face. "Unfortunately. But Aunt Addy came to me in a dream and reminded me that because I've been through this, I'm prepared for this."

"I hate that you've been through it at all."

"Me, too. But if growing up in Chance was to prepare me for a life with you . . ." I lifted my shoulders. "It's worth it."

"A life?" He started the engine and then gave me a look. "You want to spend a life with me?"

Grinning, I rolled my eyes. "Stop!"

"Nah, I like the sound of that. I like it way better than you saying you don't want to do this."

"I'm sorry about that," I apologized. "I just didn't want you to feel like you had to choose between me and football. I kept thinking about how affiliating with me was putting your job on the line. I knew there might be a couple of comments here and there. But when they were coming at me so hard, I worried it would make you want to distance yourself. But I never thought it would result in you losing money or opportunities. I never wanted that. And the fact that they did that because they *thought* you were involved with me . . . I just wanted to protect you." I squeezed my eyes shut. "I'm sorry. Fifty thousand dollars is a lot of money."

His hand gripped my thigh, and when I opened my eyes, a small smile tugged at his lips. "I appreciate you wanting to look out for me. But if I lose my position, if I get cut or get replaced, that's the nature of the game. I've been preparing for that. My business, which you helped me bring alive, is in motion, and when I'm done playing football, that's what I'll be doing." He took my hand. "But if I lose you, I don't have a plan for that. That's not something I'm prepared to do."

My heart slammed into my chest. "What?" I breathed.

"You've been mine in my head since we met. But I want you to be mine out loud. The only reason you came up in the meeting was because they figured if I hadn't come out and said we were together, it must not be real. And losing money over some shit that isn't real doesn't make sense. So I set them straight. And they were good with it, but it wouldn't have mattered if they weren't. And I'm about to set everyone else straight, too. Okay?"

My stomach flipped. "Yes, okay," I murmured.

"Good," he said as he kissed me slowly, sexily. "Even though it's nobody's business what I got going on in my personal life, I will be making it known that you're mine."

Heat crept up my neck, and I smiled against his mouth. "I like that."

*A lot.*

My entire body was on fire.

He pulled his phone out and flipped through the pictures of us he had saved. "You like this one?"

It was from the night of our double date.

I smiled. "I love it."

He opened one of his social media apps and uploaded the photo. Right before he hit SUBMIT, he looked at me. "Are you sure? You don't love attention . . ."

"But I do love you," I assured him softly.

With a grin, he posted the photo and then dropped his phone. "I love you, too. Come here," he uttered just before crashing his lips into mine.

# 35

"Lamar," I cried out, struggling against the wrist restraints.

"Say it again," he grunted.

"I'm yourssssssssssssss."

His face was still buried in my pussy as he groaned. "And?"

"I love you. I love you. I love—oh shit!"

My hips lifted from the bed, and an orgasm ripped through my body from his talented tongue. He flicked and sucked my clit in a methodical way that sent waves of pleasure through my body. My mind was blank, my heart was racing, and my body was on fire.

"Lamar," I managed to choke out as I finally unclenched my body and exhaled.

The blindfold was still covering my eyes, but I felt his breath on my thighs, so I knew where he was. For that reason alone, it shouldn't have been a surprise when he kissed the crease. But still, I inhaled sharply, and my entire body reacted.

"Mmmm . . . that was a good one," he whispered.

His bed dipped slightly as he moved, climbing upward. I shivered as his fingertips danced over my thighs.

"I love how good you taste," he continued. He grabbed my hips tightly, and he kissed my lower belly. "I love how good you look when you come for me. I love how soft you are." Moving his way up my body, he trailed kisses over the fleshiness of my belly and through the valley of my breasts. "And I love how you respond to me, Jazzy."

My skin tingled. "I love it when you call me that," I replied breathily.

"You like *Jazzy*?" He nuzzled my hardened nipples with his face before biting them.

"Yes," I moaned. "I want to hear it all the time."

"My Jazzy baby . . ." He sucked my left and then my right nipple. "I save it for when I can bury my tongue or my dick in you."

My lower body clenched, and my toes curled. My arms jerked against the cuffs. I wanted to touch him, to kiss him, to feel him.

"Lamar," I whined.

He kissed my neck.

The feeling of his lips on my skin caused a chill to run down my spine. I moaned softly as his mouth covered mine. He shifted his body so he could reach up and uncuff me. With that move, his dick, heavy and hard, pressed against my inner thigh. As soon as my hands were free, I wrapped my arms around him and pulled him closer.

The kiss deepened, and the head of his dick pressed against my wetness. A jolt of electricity shot through me, invigorating all my pleasure points.

I moaned loudly and wrapped my legs around his hips.

"Jazzy, baby . . ." He groaned, pulling out of the kiss fractionally. He pushed my blindfold onto my forehead and stared into my eyes. "I should get a condom."

I nodded slowly. "Yeah, you should."

He didn't move, and I didn't unwrap my legs from around him.

Lowering his lips to mine, he kissed me again, slower, sexier. Tasting myself on his tongue, I was reminded of all the ways that man knew how to please me, and I pulled him on top of me.

I gasped into his mouth as the head of his dick slid down my slit. "Yes."

His body was tight with restraint as he pushed himself up and held himself right over me. "Tell me what you want . . ."

I opened my eyes. I placed one hand on his cheek while the other held on to his bicep. "I want you to fill me up."

"Shit," he swore, shaking his head. "Don't look at me like that and say that."

"Why not— Oh!" I cried out as he pressed himself to my entrance.

He stopped moving. He was so still, it felt like he'd stopped breathing.

"If you let me inside you, I can't guarantee I'll be able to pull out," he whispered hoarsely.

Staring into the mixture of love and lust in his brown eyes, I lifted my head off the pillow so our lips touched. "Then don't."

"Fuck," he exhaled as he sank into me.

"Yesssssssssssssss," I hissed as I accommodated his size and let desire spread throughout my body.

Even though I was dripping wet, Lamar took his time stretching me out. I clenched around him as he worked his way into me. He paused, seeming to savor the feeling before forcing another couple of inches deeper.

I whimpered.

"Jazzy," he rasped.

The mixture of desire and restraint in his voice called to something deep inside me. I couldn't even speak.

"I love you," he continued as he reached the deepest part of me.

"I love you, too," I moaned.

He pulled almost all the way out and hesitated. "Are you sure? Because I know for a fact that if I go back in, I'm not coming out."

"Lie down," I demanded, pushing his shoulder until he rolled off me.

As soon as he was on his back, I straddled him. His hands immediately went to my breasts, tweaking my nipples.

"You're so fucking sexy," he breathed as his hands moved down my body and gripped my hips.

"I should blindfold you . . ."

"I want to watch you ride me." His eyes scanned my body. "But I'll do whatever you want me to do."

I bit my bottom lip as I ran my wet pussy against him. "Because you want it?" I asked teasingly.

"You know I do."

Rocking forward, I leaned down to kiss him. "How bad do you want it?" I whispered against his lips.

Without giving him a chance to answer, I sank down on his hard dick.

We moaned in unison.

Clenching tightly, I allowed the feeling of him filling me up to spread throughout my body. I lifted my hips and watched his face as I slowly rolled them.

"Shit," he grunted as I shifted from my knees to my feet.

Being in a deep squat, I was able to bounce on his dick with more strategic power. He gripped my hips, trying to take back control of the situation. But the look on his face and the low growl that rumbled from the depths of him made it clear that I had the control. Spurred on, I rode him insatiably, letting the sheer force of his thrusts to cause my insides to coil tightly. Letting my head fall back, I tried to keep it together long enough to make him come.

"Fuck," he swore.

When I lifted my head and our eyes locked, my heart skipped a beat.

As we stared into each other's eyes, the intensity between us grew. The look he gave me swept through my entire body, and I felt myself unraveling.

Dropping from my feet to my knees, I started grinding on him. Our movements weren't as frantic as they were when we were fighting for control. We were lost in the moment, in each other.

Our hands roamed each other's body, and I felt his touch everywhere.

"You feel so fucking good." He palmed my ass, forcing me forward. "I'm not going to last long with you looking like that and feeling this good."

Working my hips and popping my ass, I lifted myself up and down slowly. Relishing the way his dick, his hands, and his body felt, I felt myself becoming overwhelmed. He must've felt it, too, because he reached up, grabbed me by my neck, and pulled my face to his.

Our mouths collided with slow, decadent kisses as we moved in unison.

"Baby, I'm . . . almost . . . there," I moaned, gradually moving up and down his dick. "Oh God . . ."

"Come for me," he demanded as I tightened my grip on him. "You want to come all over this dick, don't you?"

"Yesssssssss," I answered, just as our tongues met again.

"Do it, baby. You can do whatever you want. It's your dick, Jazzy. It's all yours. I'm all yours."

I moaned in response.

As if I weren't wet enough, his words opened the floodgates.

With both hands gripping my ass, he guided me as I grinded on him. My clit was being stimulated each time I twisted my hips, so I was past the point of no return. The rapid bursts of air from my ragged breathing coupled with the soft, sexy grunts he let out only intensified the moment for me.

"I love the way you're gripping me . . ." His voice was low and full of want. "I love the way you sound when I'm inside you."

"Lamar . . ." My eyes shut tight as I quivered with want. "Shit . . ."

His words combined with his dick caused me to shudder. My walls clenched, and heat spread throughout my entire body.

"Fuck." His voice was hoarse and needy. "You feel so fucking good."

He sounded so sexy, and I felt myself tightening around his shaft.

"That's it . . . Give it to me, Jazzy," he groaned softly as our pace quickened. "Come on my dick."

"Lamar—ohmigod," I whimpered as my muscles clenched.

My mouth opened but no sound escaped.

*Oh . . . My . . . God!*

Quivering, I squeezed my eyes shut and rode the wave. My body jerked against his as I came all over his dick.

"You're gonna have to get up, baby," he said hoarsely. Gripping my ass, he forced my body to keep grinding on him as I came. "Jazz, if you don't get up, I'm going to nut all in your pussy."

I heard him. But I was still heady from the orgasm that had ripped through me, so I wasn't thinking clearly.

"Is that what you want, Jazzy?" he groaned as he held me tighter. "You want me to come in that pussy?"

"Yes," I panted, feeling almost feral. "Yes. Pleaseeeeeeeee."

"Fuuuuuuuuuuuuuuuuuuuuck," he exhaled as he rushed me toward a second orgasm. "Let me feel it, Jazzy. Let me—shit!"

The ache deep inside me exploded, and my eyes rolled into the back of my head. Pleasure ripped through my entire body, and his grip on me tightened. The guttural sounds that came out of him were intoxicating as his body jerked and shuddered beneath me. The minute I felt him pulsating inside me, filling me up, I lost it. I didn't recognize my own voice as I called out his name.

I came again.

Heart racing, I slumped against him, and our mouths instantly found each other. I trembled from complete and utter satisfaction.

"I love you," he murmured into my mouth. "I was not expecting that."

Seconds ticked by before I broke the kiss to reply. "I love you, too," I exhaled, still feeling tingly. After a few more kisses, I pulled up breathlessly.

Before I could dismount him, he grabbed my hips and held me in place. As soon as our eyes locked, his fingers dug into my flesh. "I love you," he repeated, slightly louder than before.

I swallowed hard, emotion welling up in my throat. "I love you."

His hands caressed my thighs as seconds passed between us. Rolling us on our side, he easily repositioned me to his left side. His fingertips danced over my skin. "As soon as my dick felt you . . ." He let out a long, heated breath. "I was done."

"It was reckless," I admitted.

"Do you regret it?" he wondered.

"Not at all. Do you?"

"Hell no." He turned his head so that our eyes met. "If you wanted me to put a baby in you, all you had to do was say the word."

I snickered. "Lamar! You know I have an IUD."

He pulled me in even closer. "I know, I'm just playing. But . . ."

My heart thumped. "But what?"

"Right now, I'm playing." He sighed. "But eventually . . ."

"You want a kid?"

"I want a kid *with you.*"

Our desire slowly leaked out of me at the same time as his whispered confession, and it shocked my system.

Staring at him, I was trying to process what he'd said. "You do?"

"I want the whole thing with you—the marriage, the kid, the life."

My mouth hung open, and his name fell out of my mouth breathlessly. "Lamar."

"Not today," he assured me. "But one day."

He fell asleep almost immediately after he'd said it, but I was wide awake. I thought about it until he woke up half an hour later.

Since we both had early mornings, I insisted on taking a rideshare car back to Richland early in the morning. I didn't want to be late to work, but it would be extremely difficult to leave Lamar. When my alarm went off, Lamar got up and said he was taking me anyway. We ordered coffee from a donut shop ten minutes away, and before we got on the road, that was our first stop.

I took a sip. "This is going to have me up for a week."

He chuckled. "They're going to try to test me for speed or some shit."

"What's in this? Cocaine? Why is it so strong? I can't teach while I'm high!"

"What the hell, Jazz?" He cracked up.

We stopped again so he could get me another caffeinated drink.

"You're so sweet," I said as he handed me the only soda I drink. "You do these little things that show me so much love, and I just . . ." I sighed dreamily. "When did you know you were in love with me?"

"Let Erickson tell it, it was in Dubai." I reached over and intertwined my hand with his. "And honestly, maybe it was. But when I knew for sure was when I realized how many choices I was making where the goal was simply to make sure you're good. I want you to be happy. I want to protect you. I want to make your life easier." He paused as if he were deciding if he was going to continue.

"Tell me," I encouraged softly, squeezing his hand.

"The day after our first date, I called Edwina's, the bookstore we went to, and bought that leather journal I saw you looking at. I knew this was different then."

My lips parted as I stared at him in awe. "You did?"

He nodded. "Yeah. I didn't want to do too much too soon, but I knew I was giving it to you one way or another. I saw the way you looked at it, and I knew it would make you happy. I've been on you since the beginning."

"I didn't even realize you noticed me looking at it."

"I noticed." He brought the back of my hand to his lips. "I notice everything about you."

"It had been six weeks since we were at Edwina's, so when I got the journal, it completely caught me by surprise." I bit my lip, thinking back to the moment. "I did feel loved . . . and seen."

"Good. Because you are—loved and seen."

"Do *you* feel loved and seen?"

"On our first date, when I let you read my business plan, I knew I had it bad. But when you got it and you added to it, I knew you saw me. So yeah." He paused. "Now that I think about it, I've been in love with you since then."

My heart thumped with his admission.

"Lamar." I placed my free hand on my chest and felt the steady rhythm. "You've been there for me in ways you'll never fully understand, and I've loved you for it," I told him, staring at his profile. "I needed to be seen as me and to get lost in feeling good, and you did that for me. I needed to work, and you allowed me to help you with your business plan. I needed to connect and feel safe, and you showed up in my life and did just that. I fell in love with you and didn't realize it because this summer was a lot. So thank you."

"You don't have to thank me, baby. I'd do anything for you. And you had a lot going on this summer. Even though I didn't know initially what was happening, I knew I didn't want to rush you. I knew I didn't want to lose you. And I knew we had something different."

I squeezed his hand, running my thumb over his skin. "I didn't want to lose you either. I wanted to be with you, but I was willing to be your friend since you didn't have time for more. And since I knew I was losing my aunt, I couldn't take the thought of losing you, too."

"I was never going anywhere. I've been locked in from jump."

"I felt it, but I didn't know for sure. And then, when I said I love you for the first time and you didn't—"

"I wasn't ready to say it out loud, and you weren't ready to hear it," he interrupted gently. "And even though I couldn't say it, I did everything I could to make sure you were good, to take care of you, to keep you happy, safe, and wanting for nothing. And that won't ever change."

"I love how you get me," I told him. "In my life, there have only been four people to instantly just get me: Aunt Addy, Aaliyah, Nina, and you." I bit my lip, not sure why that statement was about to bring me to tears. "You showed up exactly when I needed you, and I didn't even tell you why I needed you. That'll always mean everything to me."

"That was me showing you I love you. I knew you needed to keep what was happening with Aunt Addy to yourself for a minute. I didn't know why, but if I could give that to you, I would. So I did."

"I *did* need that," I murmured, feeling emotional when he glanced over at me.

"You never lied to me, but you sidestepped the hell out of questions," he joked.

"I don't want to ever keep anything from you again, but I appreciate you giving me that."

"I meant it when I said I'd give you anything you want or need."

Gazing at him, I considered calling out of work. *I love him.*

He cleared his throat. "But, uh . . . since we're not keeping things from each other . . ."

His long pause made me nervous.

"You're keeping something from me?" I asked with my eyebrow quirked.

He held my hand tighter. "When you said you didn't have a safe place in Chance, I paid for the library to finish the gazebo."

"Wait, wait, wait, wait, wait—what?" It took a minute for me to register what he'd said. My watery eyes bulged. "Lamar! That was you?!"

He nodded. "You said you didn't have your safe place, so I—"

Climbing over the middle console, I kissed him. My lips brushed against his firmly enough to stop myself from crying. "I can't believe you did that," I whispered, moving back to my seat to ensure he could see since we were still going sixty-five miles per hour.

"If I couldn't be there to protect you or to make you feel safe, I didn't mind paying to make sure you had a place go while back home." He paused. "That was me telling you I love you."

I stared at him in disbelief, no longer able to hold back the tears. I was at a loss for words.

He glanced over at me. "When you said you were worried about your rent—"

I gasped and then froze.

"—I paid it for the rest of the year, so it'd be easier on you. That was me telling you I love you."

Blinking rapidly, I inhaled shakily, fighting the sob that threatened to burst out of me. "Thank you. I just . . . you never said anything. You never took credit. I would've thanked you a long time ago!"

"I didn't need to be thanked. I just needed you to be taken care of. I needed you to be good. So, I know it took me a minute to say it out loud with my words, but I've been letting you know this whole time with my actions—the actions you knew about and the actions you didn't."

I felt emotionally overwhelmed in the best way.

To be seen, cared for, and considered was the ultimate show of love. For me, it wasn't about big, over-the-top grand gestures. It was being protected, being chosen, and being loved out loud despite what anyone had to say. His love wasn't loud. His love was genuine. He anticipated my needs and delivered—not because he needed me to know it was him but because he needed me to be taken care of. He didn't do it for credit. He did it for me.

With my throat constricted with unshed tears and stifled sobs, I whispered, "I love you."

He glanced at me before bringing my hand to his lips. "I love you, too, baby."

We arrived at my place and Lamar walked me to my door. I tried to convince him to sleep in Richland and then go to practice from my place. But the coffee had him wired, so he felt it was best to get on the road. We kissed, and as he said goodbye, he reminded me that he was coming back that night after practice.

I was on cloud nine.

I arrived at school early but not earlier than the photos of me and Lamar kissing at his game. From the first few students in my first period to Ben and Alexa alternating between texting me and showing up at my door, I didn't need to check social media to see what was going on. But come to find out, it was everywhere. The school buzzed with questions and excitement as the photo of me and Lamar floated around with his caption: *Mine.* Later that night, I created a whole new public social media account. I chose a different picture from our double-date night and posted that with a cute little caption and made sure the comments were turned off. And then I posted my first official statement:

Having so many people make negative comments about me and my relationship because they don't think I deserve to be with this man because of my size reminds me of those bullies from childhood. As a fat person, everything you do is perceived through a negative lens. Being fat is often equated to being lazy, ugly, unhealthy, and overall not good enough. And while that isn't true, I realized that there are so many people projecting because they hate to see a fat person happy or in love or successful or confident—especially if they believe those are prizes for thinness. If someone is thin and unhappy, unloved, or unsuccessful, they feel like they paid their dues (by being thin) and have earned happiness, love, success, and the right to be confident in a way that a fat person hasn't. If they aren't thin, and they are unhappy, unloved, or unsuccessful, they feel like the amount of fat on their body is what is stopping them. So when confronted with the image of Hollywood Anderson happily in love with someone like me, it shakes the foundation of what they believe to be true. But that isn't a me problem. If that's how you think, that's a you problem. And until you fix it, it'll always be a you problem. Be kind. And if you can't be kind, be quiet. And if you can't be quiet, be gone.

And for those asking if I can fight, I can.

Go Monarchs!

# epilogue

December 31

The announcement of our relationship had prompted some intense attention for two days, and then a cheating scandal rocked the Alabama Alligators, and everybody shifted gears and was on that. The last couple of months were a whirlwind of games, WAG events, commuting back and forth to Baltimore, and making the decision not to renew my teaching contract after the school year ended in June.

I went to every game except for the Monday-night one, and Nina and Russ made sure I looked good in my RLF attire. Aaliyah and Ahmad made sure I had blocks on my phone and computer so my algorithm didn't pick up any negativity. And Lamar made sure I was loved, taken care of, and supported every single day.

I was good. I was happy.

But I spent the last few days of the year thinking about how it would've been nice had I finished my list. Even though I knew that Aunt Addy had known that it was an impossible task, it was on my mind as the year was coming to an end. So, as I opened my final letter from her, I was a little disappointed in myself for not getting it done.

*Jazmyn,*

*It's the eve of a new year and I know a lot has changed for you. I'm congratulating you in advance because I know you've completed your list. I'm looking over your entries now and I can't help but think of all the ways in which you've reconnected with yourself. Learning to swim, getting your belly ring, and dyeing your hair for the little girl in you who has healed from being taught to shrink and hide herself. Trying vegetarianism to prove that you can do hard things, you can go without, you can change it up. Getting a tattoo to remind yourself that pain doesn't last. Exploring a new city had you embracing the unfamiliar and expanding your horizons. Writing your book and finally giving yourself permission to chase your dreams. Going to a Monarchs game to do something you love. Going on a date with Lamar and finding true love. And lastly, finally paying off your student loan so you can go into the new year free.*

*Paying off your student loan is the only entry on your list that you struggled with. From the moment I made you write it down, you were hesitant. And while I understand why, let me tell you why I wanted it on your list.*

*I want you to be fully free. And part of that freedom is financial freedom. Your student loan is your only debt. Once you are unburdened by debt, you are able to move in a different way. You are able to live life on your own terms. You are able to pursue your goals and dreams. You are able to buy instead of rent. More of your money is yours to live the way you want to live.*

*So here is the banking information for an account that I had Monica help me establish for you. In it you will find thirty thousand dollars to pay off your student loan. If you somehow already managed to pay it, use that money to publish your book and let this be the last school year you teach literature instead of being part of literature.*

*Because you deserve it.*

*Everything you went through in Chance, everything you went through in your marriage was not in vain. It was preparation for the life you're about to live. You are a woman who stands up for herself, whose worth isn't determined by bullies, who doesn't take shit, who doesn't crumble under pressure, who knows her worth, who isn't willing to compromise herself for a title or a position. Because of everything you've been through, you are a woman who doesn't settle. And I truly believe you survived the bad stuff early on so that you can appreciate and handle the blessings that are coming your way,*

*I want you to have the happiest, fullest, freest life, Jazmyn. I want your life to be adventurous, interesting, and full of the love that you have inside of you. I am so proud of the woman you are and the woman you will continue to evolve into. And it's been an absolute honor to call you my niece and love you like my daughter. So please, never stop fighting. Never stop fighting for what you want. Never stop fighting to be free. Never stop fighting for love. Never stop fighting for Jazmyn.*

*You deserve it all, sweetheart.*

*This upcoming year will be your best year yet. Happy New Year.*

*I love you, and never forget that everything I am, I poured into you.*

*Love always,*
*Your Aunt Addy*

"Good morning," Lamar groaned sexily as he stretched his arms out above his head. Seeming to notice my tearstained face, he jolted. "What's wrong?"

I looked down at the letter, careful not to get tears on the pages as I folded it and returned it to the envelope.

He pushed himself into a sitting position. "Is this about the tenth thing on your list? Because my offer still stands."

I lifted the letter. "It's from Aunt Addy."

His face fell and sadness creased his eyes. "Do you want to talk about it?"

"I do, but . . ." I shook my head and swiped the last tear from my eye. "It's not the letter. It's her. I miss her."

Wearing only his boxer briefs, he climbed out of bed and padded across the room to me. Wrapping me in his arms, he kissed the top of my head. Moving my locs, he kissed my forehead as well. "What do you need? What can I do?"

I hugged him tight, allowing myself to melt into him. "This."

I got a daily reminder of Aunt Addy every time I looked at my tattoo, and I missed her every single day. But reading that letter had been a reminder of what I was missing without her here on Earth with me: the advice, the encouragement, the support, the love. That letter allowed me to experience that type of love from her in a way that I would never be able to experience again.

"This was the last letter," I cried into Lamar's chest. "There's no more to look forward to. This is it."

"I'm sorry, baby," he whispered, hugging me tighter. Allowing me a few minutes to cry, he gently rocked me back and forth until I got myself together.

"I'm sorry," I murmured, pulling out of the hug. "Get back in bed. You should be resting. You shouldn't be standing."

"Don't worry about that. If you need a hug, I'm giving you a hug." He used his thumb to caress my cheek as my watery eyes allowed two fat tears to drop. "Anything you want, anything you need," he reminded me gently.

Pushing up on my toes, I pressed my lips against his. "I love you."

"I love you, too."

Taking a deep, shaky breath, I stepped back. "Get in bed and rest your ankle," I demanded.

Lamar had tweaked his ankle during Sunday's game. Because the upcoming week was the final game before the playoffs, he was allowed to rest New Year's Eve and New Year's Day. But he was back to practice on Friday.

Once he was laying down, I grabbed two throw pillows and elevated his foot. "What do you want for breakfast?"

With a wolfish grin, he looked me up and down.

Laughing, I rolled my eyes. "Lamar! I'm being serious."

"I'm good with eggs and bacon."

I knew he was going to say that. With a smile, I leaned down and kissed him. "Coming right up."

While on winter break, I'd been spending most of my time at his place. But we came back to mine because of the New Year's Eve party in Richland, and most importantly, because I needed to open Aunt Addy's final letter.

I'd loved being able to go to the back-to-back away games the last couple of weeks. I loved being able to cheer for him, be there for him, encourage him, and do it all from some of the best seats in the house. But when the Hawks offensive line realized they were no match for the Monarchs, a low block resulted in Lamar rolling his ankle. When he went down, I shot out of my seat. I gasped and didn't breathe again until he was back on his feet, hobbling off the field. Since it was toward the end of the game, they kept him out. Although it ended up being nothing serious, he was still supposed to be taking it easy.

"It's going to be breakfast in bed," I yelled when I heard him moving around.

He chuckled. "I'm just going to the bathroom, baby."

I logged into the account and paid the remaining balance on my debt. Then I shared the news with my best friends.

**Jazmyn Payne:** I paid off my student loan!

**Aaliyah James:** Did Lamar give you the money to pay it off?

**Nina Ford:** That's why she's been fucking him raw and doing those stretches.

**Jazmyn Payne:** I cannot stand the two of you!

**Aaliyah James:** They say it's not trickin' if you got it. But it is. And that's still okay.

**Nina Ford:** They need to mind their business because if you ain't got it, don't worry about who's tricking and who's treating. Okay!

I started coughing from laughing so hard at them.

**Aaliyah James:** Okay!

**Nina Ford:** Jazz fucked Lamar so good he gave her a new career and paid off her student loan. I know that's right!

**Aaliyah James:** I can't even imagine the nasty things she did to become Chief Operating Officer of the Anderson Way.

**Nina Ford:** I can, and I want details! There's a clothing company I have my eye on . . .

Laughing, I shook my head.

**Jazmyn Payne:** You know I can see these messages, right? And it wasn't Lamar. Aunt Addy put some money away for me to pay it off.

**Nina Ford:** I love that! Aunt Addy has always looked out for you, so I'm not surprised she had one last thing up her sleeve.

**Aaliyah James:** Aunt Addy has always been your guardian angel and clearly that hasn't changed.

**Jazmyn Payne:** I know, I got choked up just thinking about that. I love and I miss her. That's why I'm ready to go out tonight. She told me to live so I'm doing just that. What time should we be at Onyx? Lamar is going to need somewhere to sit to rest his ankle.

**Aaliyah James:** Ahmad reserved an area for us. So anytime between nine and nine-thirty is good.

**Nina Ford:** Not a triple date to ring in the new year. Remember last year? This is a far cry from that.

**Jazmyn Payne:** Yeah, because this year it's the three of us and our dates. Last year, it was the three of us and you brought three dates.

**Nina Ford:** In my defense, I only invited two of them, the third one just happened to show up.

**Aaliyah James**: In your defense, you liked the drama back then.

**Jazmyn Payne:** She's fucking the boss; she still likes drama.

**Nina Ford:** Not too much on me! Aaliyah is the one who likes drama; did she or did she not fuck her man while on a date with somebody else?

**Aaliyah James:** Wait a minute, that might be bad but Jazz doesn't get a pass! She likes the drama, too. She fucked a man she'd known for a week in the backwoods of Virginia!

**Jazmyn Payne:** Okay mine sounded like the beginning of a horror movie so I need to reflect on life.

**Nina Ford:** I'm so fucking weak!

**Aaliyah James:** Too funny!

**Jazmyn Payne:** But thank God it all worked out. For all of us.

**Nina Ford:** I'm so fucking weak!

**Aaliyah James:** Too funny!

**Jazmyn Payne:** But thank God it all worked out. For all of us.

# acknowledgments

First and foremost, I thank God for allowing me this beautiful opportunity to live out my dreams. For my first traditionally published series, I knew I wanted to write stories about fat Black women who are seen, who are heard, and who are loved. Aaliyah, Nina, and Jazmyn's stories are the amalgamation of my life and the lives of other beautiful, intelligent, funny, fun, intense, confident women who are also living in bigger bodies. *Curvy Girl Summer*, *Plus Size Player*, and *Big Girl Blitz* are centered on these women being fat, Black, and deserving—deserving of quality dating experiences (*CGS*), deserving of not having to settle (*PSP*), and deserving of being seen fully and loved wholly (*BGB*).

It means so much to me to have my first trad series feature women who look like me and who move through the world as I do. It isn't often that fat Black women get the opportunity to see ourselves in mainstream fiction (books, TV, movies, etc.) as the main character of our own love story. I want every big-bodied individual who has ever felt unworthy, unseen, unheard, and undervalued because of the amount of fat on your body, the melanin in your skin, the coarseness of your hair, or anything else society deems unappealing, to know that you are beautiful, you are worthy, you are seen, and you are heard. And for everyone who has sent me a message, an email, or spoken to me in person about how the Curve series has helped you feel more confident and beautiful, I am so happy to hear that and to have helped you see yourself with a clearer lens. Despite what the media tries to imply, we are beautiful, confident, desired, and loved. So, it is an honor to have my first traditionally published series highlight the full, lush lives that we live.

Second, I want to thank every reader, book blogger, content creator, librarian, author, industry professional, etc., who has supported this journey I'm on by buying my books, stocking my books, promoting my books, reading my books, platforming my books, loving my books, and getting something out of my books. It means everything to me, and I am forever thankful to have the readership, the support, and the love that you have given me. Thank you.

Finally, to my friends and family who have been on this journey with me from the beginning, thank you. Each of you individually knows how I feel about you and your role in my life. I am blessed to have some of the most thoughtful, fulfilling, meaningful, and loving relationships. My heart is constantly full because of you. I love you all to the moon and back.

And because *Big Girl Blitz* was written while the Philadelphia Eagles are the reigning Super Bowl champions, I would be remiss if I didn't add: GO BIRDS!

# about the author

Samia Minnicks Photography

DANIELLE ALLEN is a *USA Today* bestselling romance author, a professor, and a life coach. Living authentically has been the key to her living her best life. With a background in social sciences, helping people better understand themselves so they can become the best version of themselves is one of her passions. She aims to write contemporary romance novels that change the status quo of the genre.

authordanielleallen.com
Instagram: @authordanielleallen
Facebook: AuthorDanielleAllen
TikTok: @authordanielleallen

## Don't miss these jaw-droppingly hot romances by *USA Today* bestselling author

# DANIELLE ALLEN!

*Bridget Jones's Diary* meets *Survival of the Thickest* in Danielle Allen's *Curvy Girl Summer*, a smoking-hot, hilarious novel about the perils of online dating.

"Her wit is sharp, her writing crisp, and her spice—top-tier!"

**—KENNEDY RYAN**

Nina Ford is more than happy for her friend Aaliyah's relationship, but she's not about to put all her eggs in one basket. When her roster starts getting a little too serious, she'll have to decide how to play the game.

"Sweet, spicy, funny, clever—everything you want in a summer read! This book is a freakin' delight."

**—SARA RAASCH,**

bestselling author of *The Nightmare Before Kissmas*